THE FAERIE WAR

THE FAERIE WAR

CREEPY HOLLOW, BOOK THREE

RACHEL MORGAN

First Edition published in 2013
Second Edition published in 2015
This edition published in 2021

Copyright © 2013, 2015 Rachel Morgan

All rights reserved. No part of this book may be reproduced, stored in a retrieval
system, distributed, or transmitted, in any form or by any means, electronic,
mechanical, photocopying, recording or otherwise, without prior written
permission from the author, except in the case of brief quotations embodied in
critical articles and reviews. For more information
please contact the author.

This is a work of fiction. Names, places, characters, and incidents are either the
product of the author's imagination or, if real, used fictitiously.

ISBN 978-1-928510-37-6

www.rachel-morgan.com

For Andrew and Ruth.
Best brother and sister ever.

PART I

VIOLET

CHAPTER 1

THE FOREST IS DEAD. HEAVY SILENCE WEIGHTS THE AIR. No movement stirs beneath the blackened leaves and twigs that litter the ground. The trees left standing are naked. Even the sunlight filtering through skeletal branches is dull and weak.

I wish I could remember what it looked like before.

A month has passed since The Destruction, but Creepy Hollow forest shows no sign of healing itself. Everyone says it's because the fire wasn't natural. It was driven by magic. The kind of magic that knows nothing but devastation.

I take a step forward, my boot raising a small cloud of ash from the debris. I'm not here to lament the ruin of Creepy Hollow. I didn't even know the name of this place until someone told me. I'm here in the hopes that I'll see something to trigger a memory. Any memory. Anything that might tell me who I am or what happened to make me forget everything.

I continue moving forward, aware of the footsteps behind me. My companion won't let me wander far from his sight. In the distance, I see some sort of mound. A mound that looks like more than torn branches and crippled bushes. As I get closer, I realize what I'm looking at. This mound of splintered furniture and broken belongings was once a home. An entire home concealed inside a tree. Powerful magic kept it hidden—until a fire more powerful swept through and shattered the spells keeping the home intact.

A hand touches my arm. "This is as far as we go," my companion says.

I pull my arm away and turn to face the brooding young man at my side. Like all reptiscillas, Jamon's eyes are black, and his body is covered in fine blue-green scales that shimmer where the light touches them. His hair, dark as midnight, brushes his shoulders.

"But I haven't seen anything I remember yet. We haven't gone far enough."

"Doesn't matter," he says, revealing incisors like small knives. "I don't trust you. I'm not taking you any closer to the Guild."

Jamon was the first to try and kill me after I woke up Underground in Farah's home. He wasn't the last. Reptiscillas don't look too kindly upon guardians, and apparently that's what I am. It seems a little unfair to hate me for being something I don't remember, but Jamon didn't see it that way. Ten minutes after I woke up and realized I couldn't remember a thing about myself, he walked into the room, took one look at the strange markings on my wrists, and tried to crack my head open with a candlestick. Fortunately Farah stepped in before he could do any damage.

I fold my arms across my chest. "Don't you get it yet? I'm not some brainwashed faerie desperate to do Draven's bidding. I'm not about to run off and tell him everything I know about the local reptiscilla community."

Jamon tilts his head to the side and watches me closely. "Every other faerie who survived is brainwashed. Why should I believe you're any different?"

I step closer to him, making sure to get right in his face. "Do I look brainwashed, idiot?"

His eyes dart down. I follow his gaze and see purple sparks jump from my clenched fists and disappear into the air. I raise my eyes and meet his. He doesn't step away from me. "There's no need to lose your temper, Violet. You know I'm only looking out for the safety of my people."

"And why would Draven give an ogre's ass about finding you guys?"

"He won't stop until he has control over every race. That includes us."

"And I won't stop until I get my memories back." I glare at him until it becomes clear he won't back down. I take a deep breath and raise my eyes to the sky. I stare at wisps of grey cloud between the naked branches. Maybe if I'm honest about how lost and confused I feel, Jamon will lighten up a little. "You don't know what it's like," I say softly, "looking back at your life and seeing nothing but a gaping hole and a few pieces of random, unimportant information."

"No. I don't know what it's like. I also don't know what it's like to trust a guardian." He wraps his fingers around my upper arm. "Which is why we're leaving now."

Great. Attempting to open up to him was obviously a stupid idea. Back to the angry, argumentative Violet. I'm fine with that; hiding my true feelings seems to come more easily to me anyway.

Jamon attempts to direct me back the way we came, but instead of going with him, I grab onto a low branch with my free hand and refuse to move. "Stop it," I say. "Stop treating me like a criminal. I can walk without your assistance, so *stop pushing me around*."

He slowly releases his fingers. "Fine. But if you make a single move to—"

"I'm not going to—"

"Get down!" he hisses, pulling me to the ground before I have a chance to argue. "Something moved."

With our shoulders pressed together and our backs against the tree, we listen. After almost a minute of silence, I begin to wonder if Jamon lied. But then I hear something. Footsteps moving closer. More than one pair.

"The sensor was set off somewhere near here," a man's voice says.

"*Somewhere near here?*" a woman repeats, frustration evident in her voice. "Can you be a little more specific than that?"

"No. I can't remember exactly where the sensor is. Everything looks the same out here now."

I look down at the hand I wrapped around the tree branch. Black soot marks my palm. I rub my hand slowly against my pants, wiping it clean as I listen.

"We can't return with nothing," the woman says. "Only *un*marked fae set the alarm off. That means a potential threat to Lord Draven."

"I know," the man growls.

Jamon makes a similar sound. I can guess what he's thinking: something about it being my fault we're in danger. Of course, if he'd consider letting me out of his sight for a few seconds, we could easily escape this situation. He could use his reptiscillan magic to vanish in less time than it takes to snap a twig in half, and I could open a faerie path at my feet and drop into it. If only Jamon hadn't confiscated my stylus.

The footsteps grow louder as the man and woman approach the tree we're hiding behind. Jamon places his hand over mine and whispers, "Don't move." Without warning, my clothes begin to change color. My boots and pants blend in with the leaves and dirt. My sleeveless top takes on the color and texture of the rough tree bark I'm leaning against. The camouflage spreads up my body and along my arms. The same thing happens to Jamon.

By the time the uniformed man and woman come into view, we're practically transparent. Not exactly—I can see the outline of our bodies if I look carefully—but close enough. The two faeries wear dark blue uniforms with a shape I can't see properly stitched to the top of their right sleeves. They scan their surroundings as they walk, barely pausing when their eyes brush over the area we're sitting in. They look up, around, behind, but never back at us. We're invisible to them.

"Remain still," Jamon whispers. It seems to take an excruciatingly long time before Draven's guards are out of sight, heading toward where the Guild is supposed to be. When Jamon eventually lifts his hand off mine, the camouflage vanishes. "Let's get out of here quickly," he says. He pulls me to me feet, then releases my arm. At least he's learned he doesn't need to drag me along.

I run beside him. "Camouflage magic," I say as my arms pump back and forth. "That's pretty cool. Can all reptiscillas do that?"

"Yes." He throws a quick look over his shoulder, then faces forward and ignores me.

Fine. I can do the silence thing.

We run for at least half an hour. Jamon breathes as easily as if we were walking, but the sounds coming from my mouth start to sound more like gasps. My lack of fitness is a state I attribute to being cooped up below ground for a month. I've traveled around the tunnels with Farah, of course, but Jamon wouldn't let me above ground until today.

He slows suddenly, and I almost run right past him. I recognize this spot. It's where he took the blindfold off me earlier and I saw the sun for the first time in weeks. I felt so stupid stumbling around the Underground tunnels with that smelly cloth tied around my head. There were definitely people laughing at me before we managed to get above ground. With any luck, Jamon won't bother covering my eyes for the return trip.

"Time for your blindfold," he says.

No such luck. "Come on, seriously? This is ridiculous, Jamon. I'm *not* going to tell anyone where you live."

"Stop arguing with me." He pulls the offending rag from his pocket. He takes hold of my arm and tries to pull me forward—again—and that's when I finally lose my temper.

"I am so *sick* of this." I rip my arm out of his grasp. "*I'm* the one who's been wronged here. Someone stole my memories from me and left me out in the forest to die, and yet *every single day* I have to deal with you looking at me as though everything bad that's ever happened in your life is my fault."

"Violet, don't be so—"

"No!" My hands shoot forward and push hard against his chest. "I have *never* lied to you. Both you and your father have interrogated me, and I've never told you anything but the truth. If you hate me simply for being who I am, then let me leave. Otherwise start treating me with some kind of decency."

Red ripples flash across Jamon's scaled skin. "A guardian doesn't deserve decency," he snarls. "You think you're better than everyone else. You do whatever the hell you want. Well not anymore." He pushes me as hard as I pushed him, and I almost fall over. "Now you're under my watch, and I get to show you exactly what I think of—"

"Shut up!" Without pausing to think, almost as if it's instinct, I kick him as hard as I can. Before I can bring my leg back, he grabs it and pulls me down with him. I hit the ground, jab my elbow into his stomach, then roll over and spring up into a crouching position. It all happens so fluidly that I'm not entirely sure how I do it. I don't have time to wonder, though, because Jamon throws himself at me. I duck out of the way and tumble across the ground. Branches scratch my arms. The smell of ash fills my nostrils.

I jump to my feet just as Jamon slams me against a tree. With both hands, he pins my arms to my sides. "This is why you got me to come out here with you," he says. "So you could attack me."

"Ridiculous," I gasp as I bring my knee up to strike somewhere in the region of his stomach—possibly a little lower. He groans but doesn't let go of me, so I do it again. His grip loosens. I push him away, then bring my fist up to meet his chin. His head snaps back. I spin him around, lock one arm around his shoulders, and—I seem to be holding a knife to his neck. A knife I wasn't in possession of a moment ago. A knife that glitters and sparkles as if made of a thousand tiny gold stars.

In fright, I step back, open my fingers, and the knife vanishes. "I … I …" Jamon turns on me, and I raise my hands in surrender. "I'm sorry." I take another step back. "I didn't mean for all that to happen. I didn't even know I could fight like that. And where the freak did that knife come from?"

Jamon stares at me like I'm stupid. "Hello, you're a *guardian*. Where do you think it came from?"

I stare back at him, my mouth hanging open before I manage to say, "I don't know. Can … can all guardians do that?"

He shakes his head as he walks toward me. "You really are messed up."

I stand still as he places the blindfold over my eyes and ties it at the back of my head. A piece of hair catches in the knot as he tugs it tight, but I can't focus enough on the pain to be bothered by it. My brain seems to be stuck on repeat with the words *what just happened* playing over and over again.

"Are you going to attack me for touching your arm?" Jamon asks. "Because walking is going to be very difficult for you if I can't guide you."

I shake my head. He'd probably enjoy watching me stumble around, but I won't give him the pleasure. He grasps my upper arm and steers me forward. I can feel his scales against my skin; they're kind of slippery. It doesn't really creep me out, but I still wish I'd put my jacket on. I don't like him touching me. Invading my space.

"Mind the tree," he snaps. I move my hands through the air and feel the rough texture of bark beside me. Another step forward brings my knees up against something hard. I climb over the enormous root, thinking what a giant this tree must be.

"The entrance is in front of you."

I slide my foot forward, feeling for the edge of the hole. Based on my journey out of the tunnels earlier today, I know I'm about to head down a steep passage of narrow stairs cut into the earth. Not the easiest thing to negotiate while blindfolded.

"Stop right there!"

I hesitate. That wasn't Jamon's voice. In fact, it sounded like—

A hand strikes my back. I cry out as I tumble forward. I claw at the tunnel walls, but I'm moving too fast to stop my fall. I hit the ground on my side but can't stop the momentum from carrying me down the stairway, knocking air out of my lungs with every step I—

"Stop!" I yell, throwing a hand out and releasing magic. I slam into the invisible shield, which, fortunately, doesn't hurt the way slamming into the ground does. I tear the blindfold off my eyes and push myself up onto my feet. My pummeled body screams at me.

Somewhere above me, I hear shouting. Without hesitation, I dash up the steps. Tiny glow-bugs wiggling along the tunnel's walls light the way. Looking up, I see the entrance ahead of me: a circular shape of light.

I take the last few steps two at a time, slip just before I reach the top, and land on my knees and elbows. Digging my fingers into the dirt, I pull myself up the rest of the way and peek out the top of the tunnel. Over the tree's giant roots, I see orange sparks spinning and swerving and black leaves rushing into a swirl in the air. I climb out the tunnel and crouch behind a root so I can see what's going on.

One of Draven's guards, the male faerie we hid from earlier, tosses a handful of leaves at Jamon. The leaves turn into bats that screech and flap as they swarm around him. He ducks, drops to the ground, and strikes at the guard's legs with a fallen branch. The guard jumps out of the way as he sends more magic in Jamon's direction. A flame runs up Jamon's arm, and he cries out in pain. The guard advances on him.

I stand. Automatically, I lift my arms. Before I have time to consider what I'm doing, a bow and arrow as golden and sparkling as the vanishing knife appear in my hands. I jump onto the root I was hiding behind, aim at the guard, and let the arrow fly. It zooms through the air and pierces his chest where his heart is—exactly where I intended it to go.

Shocked, the guard looks up at me. Orange eyes, hot and furious like a raging fire, meet mine. For a second, I'm certain he's going to rip the arrow right out of his heart and kill me with it.

Instead, I see Jamon rising up behind the guard, a log grasped between his hands. He swings forward hard. The log connects with the guard's head with a loud *crack*.

The guard slumps to the ground.

Motionless.

CHAPTER 2

JAMON'S EYES MOVE FROM THE ARROW IN THE GUARD'S chest up to my face. "You ... you shot him."

I shot him.

I uncurl my fingers from the sparkling bow, and it disappears. "Of course," I say, sounding a lot calmer than I feel. "What was I supposed to do? Let him kill you?"

Jamon frowns. "I could have taken him out on my own."

"I doubt it. Before I shot him, it looked like *he* was about to take *you* out."

Jamon eyes the fallen faerie. "Is he dead? I know it's supposed to be difficult to kill your kind."

His words trouble me, but I try not to show it. "If you leave the arrow in, the magic will eventually fade from his body and he'll die. But if you remove it within the next hour or so, his magic will heal his heart and he'll be fine." *How do I know that?* I ask myself. I just do, it seems. It's general knowledge, like knowing the sky is blue and that faeries live for centuries.

Jamon narrows his eyes at me. "Did you mean to kill him?"

"Of course not. What do you think I am, a cold-blooded killer?"

Jamon raises an eyebrow. "Well ..."

"I'm not a killer." What I don't say is that I'm more than a little disturbed that I just shot someone in the heart. The only thing keeping me from freaking out is the knowledge that if we act quickly, the guard won't die. I walk over to him and lift his legs. "I'm also not stupid," I tell Jamon. "If we get the arrow out of this guy quickly, he'll survive. Then you'll have one of Draven's men as your prisoner and you can ask him whatever you want."

Jamon stares at me.

"What are you waiting for?" I ask. "Are you going to help me carry him, or should I push him down the stairs like you pushed me?"

* * *

At the bottom of the steep stairway, one of the reptiscillan guards takes over from me and helps Jamon carry Draven's faerie to wherever prisoners are kept. I'm left to wander through the tunnels back to Farah's home. The home that's been mine for the past month. Jamon doesn't mind letting me out of his sight down here; he knows the numerous guards on duty at the bottom of the stairway would never let me out. And if I continued along one of the tunnels in hopes of finding another exit, I'd probably run into some other guardian-hating creature before I found a way out from Underground.

Underground. It surprises me that there are things I remember about this place. I remember that it's a network of tunnels, dangerous because many of the fae who reside down here aren't the friendly type. There are various hidden entrances and many different communities. Some mix, while others keep to themselves. I also remember that I've been here before. My memories of exactly *what* I did down here are absent, but I do remember flashing, colored lights and hazy rooms of dancing fae.

Interesting. I can't imagine myself as the partying type, but maybe I am.

I walk along the edge of one of the wide tunnels, trailing my hand along the sandy wall. After almost winding up flattened like a faerie pancake, I learned that wagons and other transportation devices can travel down these tunnels at remarkable speeds. It's best to stay out of the way at all times. Fat glow-bugs of the bright white variety are stuck to the ceiling at regular intervals, ensuring that no matter where anyone chooses to wander, their path will always be lit. The smell of wet earth fills my nostrils, mingling with a hint of spices and incense.

I hear laughter behind me as three reptiscillan children run past: a boy dragging a toy cart behind him chased by another two boys. They disappear around a corner into one of the tunnels with homes along it. I look up as I pass the tunnel and read the sign hanging above the entrance. *Slippers Way*. I remember that one. Farah has a friend who lives down there. We visited her for tea one afternoon.

I pass several other people on my way to Farah's tunnel. They're all reptiscillas except for the dwarf carrying a lumpy bundle on his head. Most of them ignore me, but two or three glance warily in my direction before crossing to the other side of the tunnel. Only one person smiles as I pass: a girl about my own age with green ribbons tied in her black hair. Natesa, I think her name is. I've seen her with Jamon. It's the only time he ever smiles.

Farah's tunnel has a warmth to it that the main tunnel lacks, probably due to the orange glow-bugs on the ceiling and the tiny flecks of yellow light glinting inside the paving stones covering the tunnel floor. Baskets of flowers hang here and there between the doors. Flowers that never seem to wilt. There must be different people in charge of different tunnels because some are so pretty while others are completely bare.

I reach the door to Farah's home and push it open. "Hello?" I call. No response. She's obviously out. I shut the door behind me and cross the kitchen to the small bedroom that's been mine ever since I woke up in it a month ago. I light the lantern with a flick of my finger—Farah doesn't believe in using glow-bugs—before flopping onto the bed and staring at the ceiling. Like all the walls in this home, the ceiling is covered in a creamy-colored paint that Farah told me heats up in winter and cools down in summer. And like every other time I've stared at it, my heart starts racing with the impatient need to be *out there*, figuring out who I am and doing my part to bring Draven down. Every day that passes is more wasted time.

I sit up and run a hand through my hair. The note in my front pocket makes a crinkling sound as I cross my legs. I carefully slide it out. I don't want it to get too crumpled or I won't be able to read the words anymore. Not that it matters, I suppose. I've read it so many times I know every word by heart. I start to open it once more, carefully unfolding the softened edges of the paper, but I'm interrupted by the sound of Farah's front door opening.

"Grandma, are you here?"

"No, it's just me," I call out to Jamon, sliding the note back into my pocket. I climb off the bed and walk to the kitchen. "I don't know where she is. She wasn't here when I got back."

"Actually," Jamon says as he pushes his hands into his pockets and looks at the floor, "it's you I wanted to speak to."

"Oh." I lean against the small wooden table in the center of the kitchen and try to figure out why Jamon isn't giving me one of his death stares.

"Yeah, uh, I thought about it and figured that Draven's guard probably would have defeated me if you hadn't shot him, so … thanks."

"Oh," I say again. "That's … unexpected."

"Yeah, well, I know you think I'm an awful person because of the way I've treated you, but I'm not above thanking someone for saving my life. Even if I'm still not sure I should be trusting that someone."

I reach for the key around my neck and move it back and forth across its chain. "Um, okay, sure. You're welcome."

Jamon finally raises his eyes from the floor and looks at me. "Anyway, Draven's faerie is locked up now. The arrow has been removed from his chest. As soon as he wakes up, I'm sure my dad will want to interrogate him."

I'm sure he will, considering Jamon's father is the main leader of the reptiscillan community residing in Creepy Hollow. "Well, I hope he learns something useful."

"Yeah. Anyway, I need to go." Jamon turns toward the door, but before he can reach for the handle, the door swings open and Farah steps inside, a basket weighing her arm down.

"Jamon," she says in surprise. "Why aren't you at the meeting?"

"Meeting?"

"The leaders' meeting." Farah heaves her basket onto the kitchen table. Her eyes flick to me before returning to her grandson's. "The one about Violet."

The one about *me*? I feel suddenly sick, as though I'm whooshing through winding tunnels on one of the reptiscillas' high-speed transporters.

"What?" Jamon's eyebrows are drawn together, and his greenish-blue skin flashes lighter, then darker. "I thought the meeting was tomorrow."

Farah lifts her shoulders. "I suppose you got the days mixed up, dear boy."

"The days mixed—I couldn't—ugh!" He rushes out the door, slamming it shut behind him.

Farah chuckles and shakes her head while I reach across the table and pull the basket toward me. I start unpacking the food. "This is the meeting where they decide what to do with me, right?"

Farah nods, pulls a chair out, and sits down with a sigh. "But I'm sure you have nothing to worry about, Vi. You've been down here long enough for them to see that you aren't a real threat to anyone."

Right. I wish I could be as sure as Farah. "Does Jamon really need to be there? Didn't you say he isn't a leader yet?" I hope the meeting finishes before he gets there. He'd probably try to convince everyone to lock me up right next to the faerie I just helped him capture.

"He'll become a leader in a few months when he turns twenty," Farah says as she pushes her long grey hair off her shoulder. "But since The Destruction he's been attending all the meetings. He's desperate to do his part to protect us all from Draven. Since he's the son of the Leader Supreme, no one has objected to his presence at meetings."

"I see." *Please, please, please let the meeting end before he gets there.* I'm desperate to be set free. It would be a little scary above ground on my own, with most of my memories gone, but at least I could do more to find out who I am than simply chilling Underground. If I'm honest with myself, though, I'd probably be a little sad to leave here. The reptiscillas are the only people I know now, and they don't *all* dislike me. Farah's been very kind. She asks questions to try to jog my memory, and when it becomes clear that I don't know what she's talking about most of the time, she explains things to me. She told me about the guardians. She told me what Creepy Hollow was like before The Destruction.

"Violet?"

I blink and realize I'm staring at a pumpkin in my hands. "Yes?"

"It goes in the drawer next to the sink, remember?"

I smile. "Yeah, I know." I carry the pumpkin to the large drawer and add it to the collection of vegetables already there.

"Thank you, dear." Farah catches my hand as I walk past. "It's such a help to have you here. I'm always so tired after visiting the market that all I want to do is lie down." Her roughened hand squeezes mine before she stands and heads to her bedroom.

After packing away the food, I sit at the table and try to read one of Farah's books and *not* think about the leaders' meeting. I rub absently at the scar that encircles my right wrist like a bracelet. My right leg jumps up and down. One of my fingers taps against the table.

When the restlessness inside me threatens to explode, I stand up. I can't just *sit* here while a group of people decide my fate. I have to know what's going on.

I close the door quietly behind me so I don't wake Farah. Then I run. I run because I don't know how soon the meeting will be over, but I also run because it feels good. Not the desperate, Draven's-guards-might-catch-you kind of run Jamon and I did earlier, but a comfortable jog that gets my blood moving. I wish I could run more often, but everything feels too cramped down here. And Jamon might think I'm trying to escape if he saw me moving at any speed faster than a walk.

Fortunately, I know exactly where the leaders have their meetings. There's a large open area—and by 'open' I simply mean the ceiling is much higher there than anywhere else—known as the Circle where a number of tunnels meet, like a giant wheel with spokes coming off it. It's the area where the weekly market is set up and where the children's playground is. It also happens to have a 'spoke' that leads straight into a large hall. A hall where all important meetings and gatherings take place.

I slow down as I near the Circle; I don't want to draw attention to myself. As I walk into the Circle, though, I realize I needn't have worried. There are so many people bustling about doing their weekly shopping that I doubt anyone would notice a single running person. It's easy to slip unnoticed down the tunnel leading to the hall. I follow the tunnel as it winds around a corner, leading away from the Circle's noise toward a large wooden door.

I crouch down and press my ear to the oversized keyhole. "All right, at least we've decided that," an authoritative male voice says. Jamon's father, Asim. "But now that we have to keep her here, we need to determine whether she is our guest or our prisoner."

I close my eyes as my heart sinks. They're not letting me go free.

"If she's too dangerous to be allowed to leave," another voice says, "then surely she's too dangerous to be allowed to walk freely among us."

"I don't agree," a woman says. "*She* isn't dangerous; it's what she knows. We can't let her leave because she may give away our location to Draven or his followers, but she isn't a threat to us while she's living among us."

"But if she isn't on our side then she should be locked up."

Multiple voices chime in, arguing and muttering, and it becomes difficult to decipher what's being said.

"May I say something?" My heart jumps into my throat as I recognize the voice. It belongs to Jamon.

"Of course," his father says. "Go ahead."

"I think she *is* on our side. And I think we should do more than simply let her live freely here. I think we should ask for her help."

What?

Apparently I'm not the only one shocked by Jamon's words

because silence fills the room for several moments after he speaks.

"I thought you didn't trust her," Asim says eventually.

"Well, I've had a change of heart. I didn't want to say anything when I arrived at the meeting because you were already in the middle of discussions, but Violet saved my life earlier today."

More silence. I imagine raised eyebrows and doubtful expressions. Undeterred, Jamon goes on to describe our encounter with Draven's faerie. I shift my position so I can listen more comfortably. "We now have one of Draven's guards as our prisoner," Jamon finishes. "We can find out all the things we've wanted to know since The Destruction, and it's all thanks to Violet."

Mutterings fill the hall. "It's probably some kind of trap," someone says. "Violet probably plans to free this faerie."

Oh, for goodness sake. Why would I want to free someone I just shot?

"Then why didn't she shoot me instead of him when we were above ground?" Jamon counters.

Exactly!

After some more arguments and a whole lot of internal groaning on my part, Asim says, "All right, that's it. We can't afford to spend all day arguing about this. It's time to put the matter to a vote." I hear the sound of a chair scraping against stone tiles. "Everyone in favor of allowing Violet to live freely within our community please raise your hands."

I peer through the keyhole, but all I can see are chair legs and reptiscillan legs. Ugh, why is this stupid keyhole so low? I plant my backside on the ground again and take a deep breath as I wait. I tap my fingers against my arms. Man, he's taking a really long time to count. Perhaps there are more leaders than I thought there were.

Finally I hear the chair scraping again. "Okay. It's settled then."

What's settled? Why can't he just say it?

"Jamon, please fetch the guardian and bring her here."

Oh crap. Things are *not* going to end well for me if I don't move my butt right now. I scramble to my feet and dash down the tunnel as fast as if Draven himself were after me.

CHAPTER 3

I GET HALFWAY BACK TO FARAH'S, THEN STOP RUNNING, turn around, and start walking calmly back toward the Circle. If Jamon asks why I'm not at home, I'll say Farah sent me back to the market to get something she forgot.

When I'm still several minutes away from the Circle, Jamon finds me. He says nothing except that I've been summoned to the hall, even when I ask him what the leaders decided.

I enter the hall to find a circle of about twenty chairs and the eyes of each occupant on me.

"Miss Fairdale, please join us." Asim—an older version of Jamon with longer hair—sits in a chair larger than the others with cushioned armrests. He gestures to the center of the circle.

Okay, that's not going to be awkward at all.

But I can't disobey the Leader Supreme, so there's nothing to do but squeeze between two chairs and stand in the middle of the circle like a bug on display. I face Asim but keep my eyes down. It seems the most polite thing to do.

"Violet," he says, then stops himself. "Is it okay if I call you Violet?"

"O-of course." I can't remember him calling me anything during his interrogation of me in my first week here.

"May I see your wrists, Violet?"

He asks politely enough, but I know I don't really have a choice in the matter. "No" would not be an acceptable answer. I step forward with my arms out and my hands palm-up so he can see the curling patterns tattooed across each of my wrists. He's examined them before, of course, but perhaps he's learned more about guardians since then. Perhaps he knows something else about the markings.

"Do you know how old you are, Violet?"

"I'm eighteen." I don't know how I know this. I don't remember having birthdays. I just know that I'm eighteen, like I know that my name is Violet Fairdale, and I know that I'm a faerie.

He nods. "You must have only just graduated."

"Oh. So I haven't been a guardian for very long." I laugh in an attempt to lighten the mood. "Maybe I'm not even that good at it." In other words, *I am not a threat to you and your people.*

"Possibly," he says, "but this flourish here—" he points to part of the marking "—indicates otherwise."

Great. I'm a threat and I don't even know it. "Why? What does it mean?"

He lifts his gaze from my wrists and meets my eyes. "You graduated at the top of your class. You were the best guardian in your year."

Wow. I guess that would be cool if people weren't afraid of me because of it.

Asim leans back in his chair as I lower my arms. "Violet, we've taken a vote." He pauses. "We would like you to stay here with us. In fact, we'd like you to use your guardian skills to help us."

"But ... I don't remember anything about being a guardian."

Asim leans an elbow on the armrest of his chair and watches me. "Jamon says you can fight. Your mind doesn't remember being a guardian, but your body obviously does."

He's right, I realize. I don't remember ever seeing that bow and arrow before, but it *felt* familiar in my hands.

"Okay," I say. "How can I help you?"

"Draven has been busy these past weeks getting all the Guilds across the realm under his control. Now that that's done, he'll come after the rest of us. He knows about the Underground tunnels. It will be easy enough for him to find all the fae who reside down here. So we need to move. We need a new place to hide. It is an enormous undertaking, though, to move our entire community. We're not even sure yet how to do it. One thing is certain, though: we will need protection along the way. And although we have warriors, no one can fight like a guardian. I would like you to assist them."

"Okay," I say slowly. "So … you plan to go into hiding?"

He nods.

"But …" I pause, wondering if I'm allowed to speak my mind, or if I'm simply supposed to say 'Yes, sir' and keep quiet.

"What is it?" he asks. "Please speak your mind. Your input is valuable." There's a snort from someone sitting behind me. Asim looks past me and frowns.

When his gaze returns to me, I take a deep breath and use my politest voice. "I don't think you should be hiding. I mean, that won't work forever. Someone will eventually find you."

Asim's fist clenches slowly, but his face seems to remain calm. "And what would you propose we do?"

Apparently it's not as obvious to them as it is to me. "Well, you know … try to take Draven down."

From the chair on Asim's right, Jamon shakes his head. "You think we haven't considered that? Of course we want to take him down, but even if we allied with all the fae that

Draven doesn't yet have control over, we would still lose. Aside from the fact that he alone is more powerful than anyone else in the history of our realm, he also has the entire Unseelie Court on his side, as well as all the Guild members he's managed to brainwash. Not to mention everyone he's captured from the Seelie Court. That's some serious power he has on his side."

Crap. That certainly is a lot of power. "How did he get the entire Unseelie Court on his side? Surely the Unseelie Queen doesn't support him?"

"Perhaps they've also all been brainwashed," Jamon suggests.

"And the Seelie Queen?"

"She appears to have gone into hiding," Asim says, "and has so far done nothing to try and end Draven's reign."

Fantastic. "And this brainwashing you keep talking about. It's real?"

"It must be," the man on Asim's left says. "How else would Draven get everyone to follow him without question?"

I nod. Some kind of magical brainwashing does seem to make sense. I cross my arms because I still feel a little weird standing in the middle of this circle, and I'm not sure what to do with them. "Okay, well, you said I should speak my mind, and I have. I still think you should fight Draven. The only alternative is to go into hiding, and he *will* eventually find you. Then he'll brainwash all of you, and you'll have to serve him just like everyone else. But if you ally with every free fae community still out there, you at least have a small chance of defeating him bit by bit. And even if it takes years, it's better than losing your free will and basically becoming a slave."

"You make a good point," Asim says as he slowly rubs his chin. "We will need to fight him at some point, but I still believe our first priority is to get our people to safety. It may not be common knowledge exactly where we live, but it's no secret either. When Draven wants to know where we are, it will be easy enough for him to find out.

"So," he continues, and I step to the edge of the circle because I sort of feel like I've been dismissed, "as the rest of you in this room already know, we've found a suitable hiding place. I've also found several architect faeries who are not on Draven's side. They're already working on the hiding place to enlarge it and create suitable homes within it. We now need to figure out how to get everyone and their possessions there."

I feel my eyebrows knit together as I listen to Asim. I'm not quite sure why there's a problem here. Can't reptiscillas just do that thing where they vanish from one spot and reappear at another? I don't say anything, though, because there's obviously a reason why that wouldn't work.

"We'll be meeting at the same time tomorrow to discuss that problem. For now, I need to visit our faerie prisoner."

He stands, signaling the end of the meeting. The rest of the reptiscillan leaders rise, some chatting, others leaving the hall quickly, as though they have somewhere important to be. I want to thank Jamon for standing up for me during the meeting, but I know I can't do so without revealing my eavesdropping. He's busy talking to someone else anyway. "Okay, if you think it's a good idea," he says to a woman I can't see properly. He touches her arm. "I'll see you later, Mom."

Mom? I wasn't sure at first that Jamon still had a mother; he never mentioned her to me. But I've heard others speak of her since I arrived here weeks ago, always with the same respect they afford their Leader Supreme.

As Jamon steps away and heads for the door, I get my first good look at her. I'm startled to find she's already watching me, almost as if she were waiting for me. Ice shoots through my veins, drenching me in goose bumps.

I recognize her.

I recognize the shape of her face and her slender form. I recognize the hundreds of braids in her hair. Not from now, but from my previous life. The life I don't remember.

I walk slowly toward her. I open my mouth to say something, but she holds her hand up to silence me. I can only stare. My encounter with her in my previous life was brief, and the edges of the image appear fuzzy in my mind. But I remember *her* exactly the way she is now. Fire in her black eyes. Tight, dark clothing. Hair separated into many thin braids, each with a silver ribbon running through it.

When there is no one left in the hall but the two of us, she lowers her hand.

"I remember you," I say faintly.

"And I you."

"I fought you, didn't I? I ... almost stabbed you with an arrow. But you disappeared." I remember the slicing pain of her incisors when she bit my arm.

She nods. "I was trying to kill someone. You stopped me. In doing so you brought destruction upon all of us."

My eyes widen and my mouth drops open. "Excuse me? *You* were trying to kill someone, but *I'm* the one who brought destruction upon everyone?"

"The person I was trying to kill was Draven."

I didn't think it possible, but my mouth drops open even further. "But ... why would I stop you from killing Draven? And why was I anywhere near him?"

She sighs, then indicates that I should sit down. Good idea, since my legs are starting to feel like they aren't entirely attached to my body. "He wasn't Draven back then," she says. "He was just a boy who had no idea he had magic inside him. You were sent to his home by your Guild to protect him from me, and I was there because of the vision I'd seen. The vision in which he took on the power of the evil halfling Tharros and became evil himself. I decided to kill him before that could ever happen."

"But I stopped you," I whisper, feeling my back begin to bow beneath the enormous weight of responsibility.

"Yes. You were simply doing your job, and you did it well. I had to vanish or you would have killed me. When I returned a few hours later to finish off what I'd started, he was gone. When I returned again a few days after that, I found protective spells around his home. There was no way I could get to him."

I lower my head into my hands. "So … it's all my fault? The Destruction, everything? All because I saved his life when he should have died?"

"Yes," she says. "Or no. There are many answers to that question, depending on which part of his life you look at. You could blame his mother for bringing him into existence. You could blame anyone who may have saved his life after you did. You could blame me for knowing from the beginning that I would fail."

I raise my head. "What do you mean?"

She lowers her eyes. "In my vision, I saw myself attacking you first in the boy's garden, hoping to get you out of the way before I went for him. But you defeated me. So in reality, when I arrived in the garden and saw you there, I waited for you to go into his room. Then I went straight for him, hoping I could kill him quickly with one snap of his neck before you could even get involved. But, once again, you defeated me and saved him."

"As if he wasn't supposed to die," I say quietly.

She shrugs. "I don't know. I'll never know. It doesn't matter, though. The fact remains that he lived to take on Tharros' power."

I close my eyes and slump lower in my chair. "Why did I have to be *good* at being a guardian? Why couldn't I have messed up just that one time? Then none of these awful things would have happened."

"No one will ever know what might have been if I had managed to kill him," she says.

She. The reptiscilla whose name I don't even know. It seems silly to ask her now. Her name is completely insignificant next to the fact that I saved the life of the boy who turned into the most powerful and evil guy in our realm.

My brain taunts me with words I don't want to think: *My fault. My fault.* Even my heart seems to beat it out. *My. Fault. MY. FAULT.*

No wonder there are people down here who hate me so much. I open my eyes and ask, "Does everyone know about this?"

She shakes her head. "Not a soul. I was alone when I had the vision, and I certainly didn't want to tell anyone about it after I'd failed."

Oh. So people really do hate me simply for being a guardian. "Did you vote to have me locked up here as a prisoner?" I wouldn't blame her.

"Actually, I voted for you to stay here and help us."

I pull my head back in surprise. "Why?"

"It's quite simple," she says. "There is no one here who wants to defeat Draven more than you do now that you know you played a part in keeping him alive when he should have died. You will stop at nothing to rid the world of his evil because you have everything to make up for." She pauses, and her voice is quieter when she says, "As do I."

I sit up a little straighter and nod. "I'll do whatever I can. I'll try to help you form alliances with other fae. I'll fight beside you."

She reaches forward and touches my hand. "Good. We'll bring him down if it's the last thing we do."

* * *

After leaving the hall, I wander around the market for a while, thinking. It must be early evening by now because people are beginning to pack their stalls away. I head toward the playground. Farah's home is nice enough, but I'm tired of spending so much time there. Besides, Farah can talk as if it's her last hour on earth and she has to fill it with as many words as possible. That's great for someone like me who'd rather listen than talk, but right now all I want is to sit quietly somewhere and process the fact that I'm partly to blame for The Destruction and everything bad that's happened since. Because that is a BIG DEAL. The kind of big deal that makes me want to do something to fix it *right now*. Because if I don't, I might just shrivel up from all the shame and guilt eating at me.

I sit down on one of the swings and lean forward. Okay, so I let the bad guy live. Big mistake, obviously. But I didn't know what I was doing. I didn't know the world would just about fall apart because of it. So instead of berating myself, I should be thinking about how we can defeat him. Yes. That's what I'll think about. I'll try to be as—

"Violet?" I look up and see Jamon and the girl with green ribbons in her hair—Natesa?—strolling toward me. "Are you okay?" he asks.

I sit up straight. "Um, yeah. Why?"

The girl smiles. "You're staring at the ground as though it's done something terribly offensive."

Right. I make a conscious effort to smooth out my features as I say, "Uh, no, that's just my thinking face."

She laughs. "Well, anyway, I'm Natesa. We haven't actually met yet."

"Oh, yeah, hi." I should probably say something else, but I have no idea what. I think Natesa is the girl who left some clothes for me at Farah's house during my first week here, but I'm not certain. It would be weird if I thanked her and it turned out to be someone else. I wind a strand of hair around my finger and try to think up some appropriate words. Have I always been this awkward around people I don't know, or are social skills just something I forgot along with the rest of the details of my life?

"Okay, well, I need to get home." She rolls her eyes. "My mother's expecting me. She's been seriously overprotective ever since The Destruction."

"Oh, okay." I give her a little wave as she hurries away. When she's out of sight, I say, "I didn't scare her off, did I?"

"No, no, she was telling the truth about needing to get home." Jamon sits down on the swing beside me. "Natesa is one of the few people who *isn't* scared of you, actually. She's been telling me for weeks to get over myself and stop treating you like someone who's about to attack us all."

I scoot backward with my feet, then let myself swing forward. "I like Natesa."

"Yeah, everyone does. She's pretty awesome."

I swing back and forth, watching the dreamy look on his face each time I pass him. I want to tease him about her—I mean, it's *so* obvious he likes her—but I'm not sure we're at the point yet where I can do that. He might lose his temper and threaten to lock me up.

I bring the swing to a stop, then turn in the seat to face him. I want to know where we stand with each other, and there's only one way to find out. "Do you still hate me?" I ask.

He's silent for a moment, then shakes his head.

"So it's really that easy for you to change your mind about me? All I had to do was shoot our common enemy?"

He shrugs. "I suppose so. In my head, I've separated you from the rest of your kind. To me, you're not really one of them."

"So you still hate guardians in general?"

"Yes."

I wrap my hand around the swing's linked chain. "Why? I don't get it. Farah told me that guardians fight evil in order to protect people. Isn't that a *good* thing?"

He shakes his head slowly, but I can't tell if he means no or if he just means that I don't understand. "They protect humans. They protect themselves. Occasionally they protect other fae. Mostly, though, they seem to wind up killing or capturing fae creatures for crimes that I would hardly call evil. They dish out so-called *justice* to everyone else, but who judges them? Who do they have to answer to?" He raises his eyes to look at me. "I wonder how many you've killed."

His words startle me. *Killed?* There's a possibility I've *killed* someone? My hand slips down the chain, and I watch it, trying not to imagine it covered in blood. I have faint memories of fighting various creatures. Memories that dance at the edges of my mind, flitting away when I try to grasp at them. I suppose it's only logical that I ended up killing some of those creatures. "I don't know," I admit. "But I'm sure I wouldn't kill anyone unless they deserved it and they gave me no other choice."

"You're sure, huh?"

"Yes," I say with more certainty than I feel.

"Well, anyway, I have to get going." He stands up. "We're making preparations to move our entire community. It's going to be a major mission."

"Oh, I wanted to ask you about that. Your dad was saying you don't know *how* to get everyone to the new hiding place. Why can't you all just do your vanishing thing and end up there?"

"The children haven't learned how to do that yet. And what about all our belongings?" He looks at me like I'm stupid. "We may know some magic, Violet, but we can't do the things faeries do. We can't recreate everything from scratch with a snap of our fingers when we get there."

Right, like it's really that easy for faeries. "Am I missing something here?" I ask. "Why can't you take your stuff with you when you vanish?"

Now he's looking at me as though I have the intelligence level of a troll. "We can't *take things with us* when we vanish. We take ourselves and that's it. That's the way it works."

"Oh. So ... you've obviously tested that out?"

He rolls his eyes. "Obviously. Reptiscillas have known about this limitation for centuries, Violet. Anything bigger than, I don't know, a loaf of bread gets left behind when you vanish with it."

I stand up quickly, leaving the swing's chains rattling. "You know what? I think I can help you."

CHAPTER 4

TWO DAYS LATER, MORE THAN TWO THOUSAND REPTISCILLAS living Underground have packed up their belongings. They can't vanish with them, obviously, but that's where I come in. Being a faerie, I don't have the reptiscillas' limitations. I can take anything I want through the faerie paths with me, as long as I keep hold of it. So I told Asim that if everyone loaded their stuff onto carts, I could open a wide doorway to the faerie paths and pull the carts through with me.

I was excited about my idea, as were Asim and the other leaders, until I calculated that it would take me about *ten hours* of continuous work to get the hundreds of cartloads through the faerie paths. But I'm a guardian, so I can handle it, right? And doing this will prove to the remaining reptiscillan doubters that I can be trusted.

The only thing I can't help them with is moving their children. Reptiscillan children haven't learned how to vanish yet, and they can't travel through the faerie paths because it would kill them. So every child under the age of ten left on foot early yesterday morning for the new hideout, accompanied by their parents, several leaders, and a whole lot of warriors.

Things have been tense down here ever since.

"Okay, every family that owns a cart has finished loading up," Jamon says as he walks toward me. "You'll need to bring empty carts back for everyone else."

I nod. I'm standing in the middle of the Circle, and every tunnel I look down has carts lined up as far as I can see. Each cart is big enough to carry at least twenty people. Reptiscillas use magic to move their carts around, and I'm obviously going to have to do the same thing.

Asim shouts to me from the other side of the Circle. "All right, you're up, Violet. We're bringing the first cart."

I turn to Jamon. His eyes examine me, giving me a look that I think says, *We can trust you, right?* I nod. He reaches inside his jacket and pulls out a stylus. I was allowed to use it briefly this morning, but then he took it back. After a moment's hesitation, he hands it to me. I know this time he'll let me keep it. It's the same stylus that was hiding in my boot when Farah found me passed out in the forest. The same stylus Jamon confiscated from me about half an hour after I woke up.

I turn around and walk toward the largest piece of blank wall on the outer edge of the Circle. I chose this spot yesterday while everyone else was rushing around getting things packed. I raise my hand to the sandy wall and scratch the words to open a doorway into the dirt. Words that seem to come automatically to me, like breathing. Beneath my hand, the dirt melts away to reveal a black opening. I feel for the edge of the doorway and make a spreading motion with my hands, pushing the opening to extend it. I try not to think of all the people standing behind me watching me wave my hands around like a mad woman.

When the opening is wide enough, I turn around and see Asim standing nearby with the first cart. I slide one foot backward through the doorway to prevent it from closing, then motion to Asim to bring the cart closer.

"Ready?" he asks.

"Of course."

With his magic, he sends the cart rolling toward me. It slows and stops before bumping into me. I wrap my hand around a wooden piece sticking out at the front. With my free hand, I release some magic, send it flowing beneath the cart to the back, and push. Then I walk, the cart moving beside me, into the darkness. The light behind me diminishes. When it disappears completely, I know the doorway has closed.

I focus then on the new hiding place. It's inside a mountain. I don't know exactly where, but Asim gave me enough details for me to arrive at the correct place this morning. He met me there and showed me the room he wanted everything delivered to. As I picture the room in my head now, light forms in front of me. I push the cart forward through the rapidly expanding hole, and a group of young reptiscillan men waiting in the room jump up and whoop with excitement. I push the cart into the center of the room, then turn around and head back Underground.

It isn't hard work; it just gets boring after a while.

Open doorway, walk through, wait for doorway to open on the other side, push cart through, walk back.

Repeat.

People begin unloading the carts as soon as I push them through. After several deliveries, I'm able to start taking empty carts back with me. I lose track of time, but I must have been going for several hours when Asim makes me sit down to eat something. I assure him I'm feeling fine, but he insists.

I sit on a swing in the playground munching a sandwich he brought me, trying to ignore Jamon pacing around and around a set of climbing bars. Eventually I say, "Hey, Natesa's going to be fine. Stop worrying."

"What?" He stops and looks up at me. "What are you talking about?"

"I know that's what you're worrying about." Natesa's younger brother is nine years old, so he had to go on foot to the new location, along with his parents. Natesa refused to let her family go without her.

"Don't be silly," Jamon says. "I'm worrying about everyone out there."

I give him a knowing look before turning back to my sandwich. "Whatever you say."

I continue working late into the evening. After my third snack break, I'm sure there can't be that many cartloads left. With the end in sight, I try to speed up, opening doorways as quickly as I can. But just when I think I'm finally finished, Asim says, "Okay, once we get the transporters through we'll be done."

Transporters? "What? I can't drive those things."

He must notice the panic on my face because he laughs as he places a hand on my shoulder. "Don't worry, we don't expect you to drive them. We're busy loading the transporters onto the carts. These last few trips won't be any different from the other loads you've taken through."

I look over his shoulder and see a cart with an egg-shaped transporter balanced on top of it. Two men direct the cart carefully toward me. Just as I wrap my hand around the piece of wood at the front of the cart, I hear shouting coming from one of the tunnels. Most people have vanished by now, but I know there are still a few guards hanging around. And the guys who own the transporters, I guess. I peer around the side of the cart to see what's going on.

"They've found us!" yells the reptiscillan guard who comes running out of the tunnel. "Draven's faeries! They've—" He jerks to a halt, then falls forward onto the ground. Protruding from his back is a sparkling arrow exactly like the one I shot a few days ago. A moment later, faeries spill out of the tunnel into the Circle. They're wearing the same dark blue uniform I saw on the man and woman who came searching for us in the forest. Glittering arrows fly everywhere, missing their targets as reptiscillas start vanishing. Colored sparks dart and weave, and spears of ice shoot across the Circle. A knife sails toward me and lands with a *thwack* in the wooden cart just inches from my head. I duck down behind the cart.

"Get out of here!" Asim yells to me as he dives for cover behind another cart. He could have vanished by now, but as the Leader Supreme I suppose he thinks he should be the last one to leave.

I kneel down and drag my stylus through the dirt, writing words to open a doorway at my feet. Hands grab my arm, and something sharp slices the bare skin between my neck and shoulder. I roll onto my back and kick as hard as I can. The faerie stumbles backward just as a dark hole melts into existence beside me. I fall into it, feeling a hand grab for my jacket—and lose hold—as I disappear.

I drop out of the darkness of the faerie paths and land on my feet in the mountain room. Unloaded carts stand forgotten as chaos erupts like a crazed ogre on the loose.

"Where's my father?" Jamon demands, circling on the spot as his eyes search desperately between people. A moment later, Asim appears beside me, stumbling forward a few steps before coming to a halt, as though he was running when he vanished.

He pulls his son into a hug while asking me if I'm okay.

When I touch my neck, my fingers come away red. "I'll be fine. The wound doesn't feel that deep." I take a closer look at him. "But what about you? There's a long cut across your forehead."

"Also not deep. It'll be fine."

Jamon's mother rushes over to her husband and son. "What happened?"

"Draven's faeries arrived," Asim says. "A whole lot of them. I don't know if they found our entrance leading from above ground or if they simply opened faerie paths into our tunnels."

"Who did we lose?"

"One guard. Maybe more." He looks around. "I can't tell yet." He moves away through the crowd, his eyes searching over people's heads.

Jamon runs a hand through his hair, then lets out a long breath. "That was close. At least there weren't many of us left there."

"And we managed to get everyone's belongings moved before the faeries arrived," I add.

"Well, aside from the transporters, but that's hardly important."

"Hardly important?" A guy nearby grabs Jamon's arm. "Do you have any idea how expensive transporters are? I saved for *three years* before I could buy mine. It was the latest model! If you don't get it back, there are going to be some serious consequences for—"

"Hey, will you get over it?" I pull the man away from Jamon. "Just be thankful you're alive."

He turns on me. "You're the one who should be getting it back for me. This whole faerie paths thing was your brilliant idea. I should've just driven my transporter through the forest."

"So why didn't you? I certainly wasn't forcing you to put your stupid egg-shaped machine on a cart so that I would have even *more* work to do." I push him away from me. "If you want your transporter back, go get it yourself. Do your vanishing thing. I'm sure Draven's faeries will be more than happy to finish you off when you show up in the middle of their forces."

"Don't you dare tell me what to—"

"Enough!" Asim's voice rings above the clamor, commanding immediate silence. "We barely escaped with our lives, and you're fighting over *transporters*? It's not as though you'd even use them here. You no longer have endless tunnels to race along." He looks out over the crowd of people squashed into the room. "Your homes here will be tiny and cramped. Tempers will be short. You'll long for your old lives Underground. But this is a *war*. Sacrifices must be made. Be grateful you got out with your lives and get on with it."

I hear some grumbling, but people start moving toward the various doorways that lead off this room and down tunnels that are much narrower than the ones they're used to.

"Do you need my help with anything?" I ask Asim.

"No, you've done more than enough today, Violet. We're incredibly grateful. You can go and get yourself settled. Jamon—" he turns to his son "—we need to find out what's happening with the group traveling on foot. They should be arriving later tonight."

They disappear into the throng of people while I try to figure out which doorway I'm supposed to go through. The tunnel behind me leads outside the mountain, so I can rule that one out, but that still leaves me with five to choose from. I see a leader with a list in her hand, pointing people in various directions. I join the queue to ask her where Farah's new house is.

Farah will need help moving and unpacking her stuff, so it's a good thing I don't have many of my own belongings. Just a few clothes that Farah got hold of for me and—I pat my pocket and feel the paper there—the note from the guy I don't remember.

A gasp breaks through the chatter, and I look up to see someone pointing behind me. I swing around, my fingers already prickling with the instinct to fight. Protect. But I don't see Draven's faeries. I see a group of reptiscillas running, stumbling, crying. Many of them are children, the younger ones carried by adults, the older ones dragged along. I see blood and scratches and dirt.

A girl falls onto her knees and drags herself out of the way.

People start to gather around her, but not before I notice the colorful ribbons in her hair. I run toward her, skid to a halt, and drop onto my knees beside her. Natesa has a knife sticking out of her chest, just below her right shoulder. A knife that glitters like fiery golden stars.

Someone shouts for a healer.

Someone else screams that we're under attack.

"No," Natesa gasps. "They … they stopped. They saw the children and … they backed off."

"She's right," says a man clutching Natesa's hand. Her father? "They started attacking, but then they disappeared. We ran the final distance to get here, but no one followed." A woman beside him weeps as she clutches a young boy to her side.

I feel the crowd moving behind me. A second later Jamon is on his knees next to me. "We need a healer right now. Somebody find a healer!" He touches the knife but doesn't remove it.

"Can't you heal her yourself?" I say. "You know, with your magic."

"What? No. We can't do that. Natesa," he says to her, "everything's going to be okay." He touches her face, then pulls back and looks up. "Where's the healer?" he yells.

"Let me do it," I say. I place both my hands on her bare arm and get ready to release magic into her.

"What are you doing?" Jamon pushes my hands away.

"Giving her my magic. It'll help her body to—"

"You can't do that! Your magic isn't the same as ours. You don't know what it will—"

"Move aside." A woman with white ribbons twisted through her two thick braids steps through the rapidly parting crowd. Behind her is a man with strips of white fabric criss-crossing over his right arm. In his hands is a long, rectangular board. He sets the board on the ground, and he and the woman use their magic to move Natesa onto it. Swiftly, they lift the board and head down one of the corridors. Jamon and Natesa's family follow closely behind.

I look around and see more reptiscillas with white fabric or ribbons wrapped around parts of their bodies attending to various people in the room. No one seems to be as badly injured as Natesa, though. Guards run in and out of the room, and healers start sending patched-up people to find their new houses. I join the back of the queue again to find out where Farah's living while I try to wrap my mind around the most puzzling question of the day: Why did Draven's faeries back off instead of capturing every reptiscilla they could get their hands on?

CHAPTER 5

FARAH'S NEW HOUSE IN THE MOUNTAIN IS SO SMALL THE two of us have to share a bedroom. It's okay. I mean, it's not like she snores or anything. It's just a little weird lying awake at night and hearing someone else breathing from across the room.

The morning after we arrive, I tell her I'm going to spend a few hours familiarizing myself with the tunnel system. In reality, I need time alone to figure out some of my guardian skills.

I've been told what guardians can do—they have special weapons that only appear when they need them—but no one can tell me how it works. Weapons appeared for me when I fought Jamon and when I protected him, but I have no idea *how* that happened. My body just went ahead and did it without giving my brain time to figure it out.

I'm also told that guardians are fit and strong and fast and all these other things that I'm so *not* anymore after spending weeks cramped Underground with barely any exercise. But since I no longer have the status of Major Threat amongst the reptiscillas, no one should mind if I start some private training. The reptiscillan guards or warriors or whatever they call themselves probably have a special training area. No way am I going to embarrass myself in front of them, though.

The longest tunnel I can find is one that feels like it's taking me right into the heart of the mountain. I don't know where it ends, but I'll turn around before I arrive anywhere important. If this is an off-limits tunnel, I don't want to land myself in trouble.

After I've walked a good distance, I turn around and run back. Then I run it again. I repeat the process, trying to make each lap faster than the one before. When I'm gasping for air and can't possibly push my legs to move any faster, I slow down. I lean over and breathe deeply.

That felt good.

Without giving myself time to worry about how it will work, I straighten, shoot my hands out toward an imaginary foe, and— nothing. No sparkly weapon. I turn, sweeping my hand through the air as if slicing it with a sword—but still nothing. Great. Am I supposed to be *thinking* something specific? Is there a spell that goes along with these weapons?

I drop down to the ground and do some push-ups before trying the weapons again. After a while, I'm doing stupid things like snapping my fingers and shouting 'sword.' Not surprisingly, it doesn't help. I run a few more laps to work off my frustration, then head back to Farah's.

I suppose I should start thinking of it as *my* home too, not just Farah's. It's not like I have anywhere else to call home. I reach her tunnel, which isn't pretty like the one she lived in Underground, and push open her door. Jamon is in the kitchen frowning down at a piece of paper in his hand. The kitchen is a tiny room with barely any space around the table to pull the chairs out, which is probably why he's sitting on one of the stone counters.

"Hey, what are you doing here?" I ask.

He hurriedly folds the paper and shoves it into a pocket. "I thought you might want to know about everything we've learned from the prisoner you helped us capture."

"Oh, yes, definitely." I lean against the back of a chair and wipe sweat from my forehead. "I've been dying to ask, but I thought it was probably only leaders who got to know information like that."

"Well, usually, yes. But since you were instrumental in his capture, I thought you deserved to know what we've found out. And my father thinks you have the right to know everything that's happening with the Guilds now—since that used to be your life."

Right. It's probably a good thing I don't remember anything of that life anymore, or this would be a difficult conversation. "And everything the prisoner told you is the truth?"

"Of course. My dad can make a mean truth potion, you know."

"I didn't, actually, but thanks for the heads up. I'll be careful not to drink anything your dad gives me."

Jamon laughs, something I would have thought impossible less than a week ago when he was still perfecting his death stare on me. "Anyway, let's go outside and I'll tell you what we know. I feel like the walls in this place are about to squash me."

"I hear you on that one." I open the door as Jamon hops off the counter.

"Oh, and you might want to put a jacket on," he adds.

I lift an eyebrow. "Is there something I don't know?"

"Yeah. Winter's arrived."

"But ... summer's barely over. We haven't even had autumn yet."

He sighs. "Welcome to the reign of Lord Draven, supreme commander of uncomfortable weather conditions."

I groan, grab my jacket and one of Farah's jerseys from the hook behind the door, and head out after Jamon. He leads the way through the tunnels to the large room I delivered everyone's belongings to, then down the tunnel that ends up outside. An icy wind cuts through my clothes before we reach the opening. I hastily pull on Farah's jersey, followed by my jacket.

I expect to see more light at the entrance, but there's a boulder positioned on the mountainside in front of it, with just enough space on either side for a person to slip in or out. Guards line the walls of the tunnel, and Jamon tells me there are more guards scattered across the mountainside.

I stop and wait for Jamon to pull on some gloves and wrap a scarf around his neck. I guess he can't magically add warmth to his outfit like I can. "What do we do if Draven or his followers find this entrance?" I ask.

"The architect faeries who carved out the inside of this mountain are busy creating a tunnel that leads through to the other side of the mountain, goes around a lake, and ends up in a forest. We'll obviously have guards there too."

"And, of course, most of you can vanish from here if the mountain is ever under attack."

"Yes."

We slide past the boulder into a world whiter than I expected. A thin layer of snow covers the ground beneath my boots. "Snow?" I say to no one in particular. "Seriously? Oh, wait." I turn to Jamon. "If Draven's controlling the weather here, doesn't that mean he must be somewhere nearby?"

Jamon shakes his head as he looks down at Creepy Hollow forest. From the foot of the mountain, snow-dusted trees extend as far as I can see. "It seems like he can change the weather all across the fae realm."

My head snaps up. Is Jamon being serious? "All across the fae realm?" He nods, not looking at me. "The *whole realm*? That's not possible. That's ... that's ..." *Freaking mind-boggling.*

"That's who we're up against," Jamon says grimly. He turns

and peers up at the mountain looming above us. "Let's climb. I still feel like I need more space." We make our way up between the rocks and clumps of scraggly plants the sudden winter hasn't killed yet. "So," Jamon says as we climb, "the first thing we found out from our prisoner is that the brainwashing thing is true. He didn't call it that, though. He kept talking about marked and unmarked people."

"Marked?"

"Yes. Did you get a look at his right hand?"

A grunt escapes me as my fingers slip on wet rock. The spell heating my hands keeps melting the snow whenever I reach for a new handhold. I shift my fingers into a better grip and pull myself up. "No, I was too busy saving your life."

Jamon ignores my comment and continues. "He has an open circle tattooed on his right palm. It's actually a snake that's curled around so that its head almost meets its tail. It comes from a different symbol, one created by—"

"Tharros," I say, stopping my ascent as I remember suddenly. "He represented himself with the symbol of a griffin that has a snake instead of a tail, and the snake curls around the whole griffin." Why does my brain choose to remember *this* of all things?

Jamon looks down at me and nods. "Draven's using the same symbol, I guess because it's Tharros' power he's got inside him. It's the symbol stitched onto the blue uniforms all his faeries wear. But according to the prisoner, Draven's only using part of the symbol to mark his followers because he thought it was simpler and clearer."

Jamon turns and continues climbing. I follow. "Did someone have to tattoo every single one of his followers?" I try not to sound breathless when I speak. Damn, I really need to get my fitness level back up to guardian standard.

"No, he's using some kind of magic to brainwash everyone into supporting him. As soon as the spell touches someone, no matter what kind of fae they are, the mark shows up on their right palm. Oh, and he's got these invisible magical sensors all over the place to detect anyone who's unmarked."

"So that's what that faerie woman was talking about. The one we hid from when you took me above ground."

"Yeah. Just as we guessed, Draven wants to catch every single unmarked fae and force us to follow him."

"And then what? When he's got all of us under his control will he turn to the human realm?"

"The prisoner doesn't know. He wasn't part of Draven's closest circle of followers. He does know about the special army, though."

"Special army?"

Jamon stops on a wide ledge and stands there. "As well as having all the guardians fighting for him, Draven has an army of faeries with extra abilities. Magic that other faeries don't have. It's an army one of the Unseelie princes put together."

"Zell," I say. *Thanks, memory, for another random piece of information that doesn't fit with any of the other random pieces of information you've left me with.*

"You remember him?" Jamon asks. He steps out of the way as I climb up beside him onto the ledge.

"I remember his name and who he is. I remember hating him. Other than that it's all … hidden behind a fog."

"Okay, well, it was Zell who gathered these special faeries to form an army. It was Zell who found the chest with Tharros' power locked inside. He figured out how to open the chest, but then Draven killed him and took the power for himself."

"Wow. You've got to be really sure of yourself to take out Unseelie royalty." I place my hands on my hips and look out over the white-sprinkled world. I imagine Draven's influence spreading like the enchanted winter.

"Yes, but here's the real shocker," Jamon continues. "I'd heard rumors of this, but I didn't think it was true."

"What?"

"Draven is a Seelie prince."

"*What?*" My hands slip off my hips. "How did he wind up so evil then?"

"I don't know. We gather from the prisoner that no one knew much about him before he killed Zell and attacked the rest of the fae realm."

With a sigh, I turn my attention to the ledge beneath my feet. I send out a gust of magic from my hand. The snow vanishes, leaving the ledge dry. I sit down and wrap my arms around my knees. "So what's happening with the Guilds?"

Jamon takes a seat beside me. "The ones that were destroyed, like the Creepy Hollow Guild, are being rebuilt. The guardians still use the Guilds as their bases, but now they're working for Draven. He uses them to go out and find unmarked fae, who are either taken back to be marked or are killed if they put up too much of a fight."

I shake my head as I imagine guardians who might be my family and friends attacking the very people they used to protect. It makes hot anger burn deep inside me. I clench my fist and pound it against the cold surface of the ledge. "He can't be allowed to do these awful things. We have to *stop him*, Jamon."

"That's what we plan to try and do."

I put my head in my hands and moan. "And I'm supposed to help you, but I'm useless the way I am." I look up. "This prisoner of ours, is he a guardian?"

"No, he's from the Unseelie Court. He was one of Zell's personal guards."

"Oh."

"Why?"

I let out a long breath. "I really need to speak to a guardian. I need to know *how* to do what I'm supposed to be able to do. I mean, look at this." I point to my wrists. "This says that I'm *good* at being a guardian. I was the *best* in my year, and yet I can't even get the weapons to appear when I want them to."

"They appeared when you saved my life."

"Yeah, but they didn't appear when all those faeries invaded your Underground home yesterday. And they didn't appear earlier when I was practicing."

Jamon stands. "I think your self-preservation instincts need a good jolt." He smiles. "And I'm more than happy to be the one to jolt them."

"So you're going to attack me and scare the weapons into existence?"

"When you least expect it."

"And if it doesn't work every time?"

He shrugs. "I'll just have to keep scaring you until it does."

I get to my feet and peer down the side of the mountain. "Hmm. It looks a lot steeper going down than it did coming up."

"Good thing we've both got our own shortcut ways of getting back inside."

I cross my arms over my chest. "Are you backing down from a challenge, Jamon?"

He folds his arms to match mine. "Not if you really are challenging me."

One side of my mouth pulls up. "Then let's see who can get to the bottom first."

"You're on." He turns immediately and jumps off the ledge.

"And it doesn't count if you fall all the way down!" I shout as I jump after him.

* * *

I reach the boulder at the entrance to the mountain with nothing more than wet hands, a bruised ankle, and a scratch across my left palm. Unfortunately, Jamon reaches the boulder about two seconds before I do. No big deal. At least, that's what I tell him, because it's ridiculous how much of a sting I feel at losing this insignificant challenge.

I change the subject as we walk back through the tunnels, just to get the smirk off his face. "Natesa's still stuck in bed, isn't she?" His cocky smile transforms into something entirely different. He nods. "Okay, so let's go visit her. She's probably bored by now."

"Oh, uh, you go ahead. I've got other things to do."

Crap. That backfired. Now I'll have to visit her on my own. I imagine standing next to her bed not knowing what to talk about and making the situation super awkward.

"Do you know where she's staying?" Jamon asks as we enter the large central room.

"Uh, yes, Farah told me this morning in case I wanted to visit her."

"Great." He walks away, patting the pocket I saw him put the piece of paper into earlier. Out of habit, I touch my own pocket where I know the note from the guy I may never see again is hiding. I shake my head as I continue walking. Who cares if I never see him again? It's not like I remember anything about him.

Still. His note is the only link I have to my previous life.

Farah's directions are reliable, and I wind up at Natesa's new home without having to ask anyone where it is. After knocking, I hear her voice telling me to come in. I step inside. The carved-out home looks just like Farah's, except there are two bedrooms instead of one.

"In here," Natesa calls out.

I follow the sound of her voice to the bedroom on the right. There are two small beds inside, one of which is empty. I guess Natesa has to share with her little brother. I look across to the other bed and see her sitting up with several blankets pulled up to her chest and a book in her hand.

"Violet! How sweet of you to visit me." Aside from messy hair and skin a paler blue-green than usual, she looks fine.

"Um, yeah." I walk over to the chair beside her bed and sit down. I ask the obvious question: "How are you feeling?"

"Much better." She places the closed book on the bed. "I'm not in any pain because of all the potions they gave me, but they still insisted I stay in bed today. I felt so useless this morning with the rest of my family unpacking all of our things, but they would *not* let me get out of bed."

I chuckle. "Well, they want you to get better."

She rolls her eyes. "Yeah, I know, I know."

With no idea what to talk about, I reach for the only subject we have in common. "Has Jamon been to see you?"

Duh. Of course he has. Someone probably had to pry his body off this chair last night so Natesa could get some sleep.

"Yes." Her smile spreads wider as she traces her finger over the patterns of her blanket. "Twice today, actually."

Without thinking, I smile and say, "You like him, don't you?"

Well done, Violet. Act like you've known her for years instead of weeks. That'll really help the awkwardness in this room.

But instead of telling me to mind my own business, Natesa closes her eyes and lets her head fall back on her pillow. "Ugh, I know, I can't *ever* stop thinking about him. I mean, he's amazing. So kind and funny, always taking care of people, and gorgeous on top of everything else. Who wouldn't like him?" She stops suddenly, putting a hand over her mouth and giggling. "I'm sorry."

"For what?"

"I think I've startled you with my outburst. It's just ... I like him *so much* that even when there are far more important things to talk about, like the fact that we had to leave the home we've known for centuries or that we were attacked last night and could have all died, all I want to talk about is Jamon!"

I can't help laughing. This girl is so unguarded it's refreshing. "So why don't you just tell him? I mean, it's clear you're going to go crazy if you don't."

Her laughter mingles with mine but doesn't take long to disappear. Her sweet smile is sad as she says, "There wouldn't be any point in telling him. He's intended for someone else."

"Intended? Like … an arranged union?"

"Yes. His father is the Leader Supreme, after all; Jamon could never be with an ordinary girl like me. He's going to form a union with the daughter of a Leader Supreme from another community. I think it's supposed to happen about a year after he becomes a leader. Although," she adds, "who knows what will happen now that the whole world has turned upside down."

"Does Jamon know about this arranged union?"

"Of course. He's known his whole life."

"Oh."

"Why?"

"Well, it's just that it's obvious he'd rather be with you."

Pink ripples across her blue-green skin as she shakes her head. "No, that's silly. He's very kind to me, but we're just friends."

"Well, yes, you both *act* like you're friends." I lean forward and rest my elbows on my knees. "But I doubt I'm the only one who knows you both wish you could be more."

She shakes her head again but can't keep the smile from her face. "*Anyway*," she says, "what about you?"

I sit back. "What about me?"

"Do you remember having anyone who was special to you? You know, before The Destruction?"

My fingers itch to touch my pocket, but I resist. "No. I only seem to remember people who didn't mean much to me. Like this guy named Tank. I know he was a guard, but … I don't remember who or what he guarded." I laugh. "Isn't that silly?"

"Maybe he was *your* guard." She grins. "Was he hot?"

I shrug. "Sort of, I guess. But why would I need a guard?"

"Maybe you're, like, a princess. Or maybe your parents are super important and they have enemies, so their daughter needs to be protected."

"I'm a guardian. Shouldn't I be able to protect myself?"

"Hmm. Good point." She bites her lip, then starts rattling off another theory. I join in, feeling more relaxed than I have in weeks. By the time I leave—much later than I'd planned—I think I've spoken more words in one afternoon than I have in all the days I've been with the reptiscillas combined. I'm also feeling more determined than ever to find out who I really am and what happened to my memory during The Destruction. I don't want to spend the rest of my life making up stories about my past.

So, once again, I find a quiet corner of a tunnel and slide down onto the floor. I ease the note from my pocket, hoping that this time, *this time*, I'll recognize something I didn't recognize before. The shape of the letters, maybe. Or the tilt of the words. Or the nickname at the end.

I smooth the small page out over my knees and read the words again.

V,

I have to go somewhere. I can't tell you where or why or who sent me, but it's important that I leave now. Don't try to find me. It isn't safe for you to know where I'm going—someone might try to get the information out of you. I know I'm leaving you at a time of great uncertainty and danger, but I also know that you're more than capable of kicking any villain's ass without me. Just do me one favor: don't get yourself killed, okay? I'll see you soon, Sexy Pixie.

Ryn

PART II
RYN

CHAPTER 6

T<small>AKE THE FAERIE PATHS TO THE OTHER SIDE OF OUR REALM</small>
where the Dragon's Back mountain range is. Go to the foot of the
peak that looks like a dragon's tooth. Climb straight up for half a day.
Look for a grouping of three tall rocks like fingers in a row. The
entrance is at the base of the middle rock. It shouldn't be too difficult
to find.

Yeah. Right.

Eight days later and where am I? In the middle of flipping
nowhere. At the foot of a mountain range. Disheveled, hungry,
and frustrated. All because Kale, Violet's father, sent me off on
this mission. This highly important, highly secret, highly *unsuc-*
cessful mission.

I dump my pack at my feet and stare up at the mountain
peak I'm starting to hate the sight of. I think it's the right one. It
looks more like a dragon's tooth than any of the others. Unless …
dammit, they all look like dragon's teeth. And I've climbed up at
least five peaks in this mountain range. There's no grouping of
three tall rocks *anywhere*.

I close my eyes and rub my hand across my unshaven jaw.
What makes this situation even more infuriating is that I have no

communication devices with me. No amber, no mirror, nothing. Because what else did Kale say? *It isn't safe to use your amber. New magical technology allows people to track communication devices when you use them.*

Terrific.

The guy is clearly paranoid.

And I'm starting to think the Order of the Guard doesn't exist.

The Order of the Guard. A secret group of faeries guarding an ancient weapon that could destroy Tharros' enduring power. I'd like to believe this Order really exists, but I have to admit it seems unlikely. It was only the hint of a rumor that led Kale to begin searching for them in the first place. And it took him almost a year to gather enough information on where they might be hiding. Barely anyone knew what he was talking about. It's been so long since guardians destroyed Tharros all those centuries ago. Anyone who might have known about a secret weapon that could destroy the power he left behind is probably dead by now.

I sit on the nearest rock and weave a spell around myself to ward off the chill. It's worse here than back home in Creepy Hollow. The leaves have only just begun to turn autumn gold there.

I want to go home.

Yeah. As much as I hate the thought of failure, home is where I want to be. I want to get back to fighting bad guys, solving crimes, and having Violet try to sneak up on me in my bedroom. I want to sit at the top of the gargan tree whispering secrets in her ear and kissing her.

But I haven't forgotten the very last thing Kale said to me: *Do not return until you've found them. This is very important, Ryn. Tharros' power* will *be unleashed upon the world again, and this time, we need to destroy it.*

I asked him why he wasn't going on this mission himself, if it was so important. He said the Seelie Queen didn't want him disappearing on some weapon hunt she believed was futile.

Seems the Seelie Queen and I agree on something.

If Kale is certain Zell's going to unlock the chest of power soon, then shouldn't I be at home getting ready to defend the Guild with everyone else? Violet's contact at the Unseelie Palace may have already told her when Zell's planning to attack. The Guild might be preparing for battle right now. And where am I? Wandering the wilderness like a fool looking for something that doesn't exist.

But you have orders, a voice at the back of my mind says. *Orders from a senior guardian who reports directly to the Seelie Queen. That's not something you want to disobey.*

I'll give it two more days. That makes ten days. Surely that's enough? If there's no secret Order to be found out here, Kale can't expect me to search *forever*, can he?

I want to see Violet.

The desire strikes suddenly, sending an ache through my chest. The longing to see her hits at least once an hour. Sometimes I want to hold her so badly my arms ache. Part of me is surprised she hasn't shown up to demand why the hell I disappeared. I told her in the note not to find me, of course, but when did Violet Fairdale ever listen to me?

After running both hands through my messy hair, I stand. Two more days. Just two more days of silence and loneliness. Then I'll be back at her side.

* * *

I climb the peak again. The one that looks most like a dragon's tooth. After a few hours of steady climbing, I start walking in a wide zigzag. I don't want to miss these mysterious three rocks again. The chilly air makes the sweat on my brow sting like ice.

Tilting my head back, I see snow capping the peak. Thank goodness it doesn't snow further down at this time of year. That would make this pointless mission even worse.

I stop when I see a slim rock pointing toward the sky. Now *that* is what I imagine when I think 'tall rock shaped like a finger.' Too bad there's only one. Yup. One. Like this mountain is flipping me off. I start laughing, then stop when I realize how crazy the echoes sound.

I continue up. After several more hours of climbing, I figure I've gone too high. Seriously, those three rocks are *not here*. Maybe I need to get to the other side of this peak. Perhaps Kale left that part out of the instructions. *Climb straight up for half a day. WALK TO THE OTHER SIDE OF THE PEAK. Look for a grouping of three tall rocks like fingers in a row.*

Maybe. I'm doubtful ... but maybe. I'll have to try that tomorrow.

I head back down. The light fades quickly after the sun slips behind the mountains. I won't make it to the bottom before dark. Not a problem. I'm a faerie; I can make camping on a rocky, sloped surface into a comfortable experience.

I drop my pack onto the ground. Darkness creeps closer as I consider what spell to start with. Transform my pack into a sleeping bag? Enlarge the tiny bit of food I have left? Create a fire that won't die until I tell it to? Through the half-light, I see the finger-pointing rock I laughed at earlier. I find myself wondering if maybe, *just maybe*, there were once two other rocks beside this one. I stand up and head over to examine it, taking my pack with me.

I can't help the half-groan, half-laugh that escapes me when I reach the rock that's taller and narrower than I am. "Are you *kidding* me?" I say out loud. "This is what I've been combing the mountainside for?"

Here they are. The three fingers in a row. It's just that two of them must have been knocked down at some point, leaving nothing but a patch of jagged stone at ground level on either side of the pointing finger. I crouch down and examine the base of the middle rock. I brush away loose dirt with one hand while creating an orb of light with my other hand. The white glow illuminates an arrow carved into the stone. I run my finger along it as I consider using a simple doorway spell. It probably wouldn't work, but—

Light explodes from the rock. A second later, I'm hanging upside down in midair. Pain tears through my body. I try to grasp at my magic, but it slips away like water through my fingers. I writhe about, but I can't escape the pain and the invisible force holding me upside down. After willing myself to calm down, I notice the shape of a person silhouetted against a doorway of warm light.

"Who are you?" he asks. My first instinct is to try to read his emotions, but it doesn't seem possible to feel anything other than agony.

"From ... the Guild. I have ... the Seelie Queen's ... token." I squirm around and slap at my right back pocket for the ring Kale gave me. It's a one-of-a-kind piece, like all the Queen's jewelry. Her symbol is engraved in the metal beneath an oversized emerald. The ring falls to the ground. The man bends and picks it up.

"You're a guardian?" he asks.

"Aargh ... yes." I keep as still as possible so he can see the markings on my wrists.

He snaps his fingers. I hit the ground. The pain evaporates, but I'm left feeling like a troll ploughed through me. "I'd ... I'd like to speak to whoever's in charge," I say, "about the two missing rocks. Because it's taken almost nine days of searching to find this place."

"Nine days? You've done pretty well then," the man says, "considering the point is for us *not* to be found." I sense relief and a hint of excitement as he reaches for my arm and pulls me up. "Come inside. We're desperate to know what's going on, but we weren't sure if there was anyone left out there who still remembered us."

Feeling shaky, I reach for my pack and follow him through the rock's narrow doorway and into a large sitting room. It's like a faerie home, but concealed within a rock instead of a tree. "What are you talking about?" I ask.

He seals the doorway behind us, then turns to me. "The faerie paths. It's the only hint we've had that something's gone wrong. Well, that and the tremor."

I stare at the man, getting a good look at him for the first time. His anxious eyes are a very pale blue, like the strands that run through his blond hair. Like all adult faeries, he looks to be in his early twenties. But his eyes have that aged look I see on those who've been around longer than several decades. "I have no idea what you're talking about. I was sent here to find the Order of the Guard and the weapon they're hiding. I don't remember any tremor."

His confusion matches my own. "It happened about a week ago. If you've been searching this area for nine days, you would have felt it."

I think back to a night when I woke to find myself rolling out of my blankets and down a slope. The ground felt as though it was moving beneath me, but by the time I got to my feet, all was still and quiet. I'd put the incident down to bad dreams and restless sleep.

"Okay," I say slowly. "And what was that about the faerie paths?"

His frown deepens. "You haven't tried to use them?"

"No." Unease squirms around in my stomach. I wish this guy would get to the point. "What's happened to them?"

"After we felt the tremor, my brother walked down to the

foot of the mountain. He opened a doorway to the faerie paths and found a raging storm inside. He couldn't go through."

My eyebrows shoot up. "What? How's that possible?"

"We don't know. We started imagining the worst. A battle, maybe. A war going on somewhere."

A war going on somewhere.

Violet. My family. Calla.

I blink. I step back, my eyes searching the room for ... I don't know what. "I have to get back. I have to ..." I reach inside my jacket and pull out my stylus. I rush to the nearest wall, writing the words before my stylus even connects with the—

"No! Don't open it in—"

Crack!

I'm thrown back against an armchair as a fork of lightning shoots across the room and strikes a table, splitting it in half. Icy bullets of rain pummel my raised arms. Wind pins me down. I'm almost blinded by continuous flashes of lightning. The wind begins to diminish, then vanishes along with the rain and lightning. I lower my arms. The doorway has closed.

The faerie gets up from the floor, wiping rain from his face. "*That* was entirely unnecessary. Weren't you listening to me about the storm?"

I was, but ... "But my family!" I climb to my feet. "I have to get back to—"

"You can't. I'm sorry, but there's no way for you to get to them."

I push my hands through my wet hair. "I need ... I need your amber. Or a mirror. Something I can use to contact someone."

He shakes his head. "I'm afraid we don't have anything like that."

"You—what?"

"Communication with the outside world would make us vulnerable."

"But what if you need … I don't know, *something*?"

"We're completely self-sufficient here. We don't need anything."

This is un-flipping-believable. "Are you telling me you haven't left this mountain in centuries?"

"If we want to know what's happening out there, one of us will journey for a day from here, then take the faerie paths to a city or town. We can't take the chance that someone might follow us back through the paths to this hiding place."

"It's not *possible* for someone to follow you unless you're stupid enough to let them hang onto you!" I yell.

He remains calm as he says, "Do you know that for sure?"

I'm about to tell him that of course I know that for sure, but something Violet told me not too long ago echoes through my mind. *Did I tell you about the time Zell followed me through the faerie paths without having any contact with me?* And now I've opened a doorway inside the hiding place of the weapon that's been kept secret for centuries. The creator of that storm could be on his way here right now to destroy it.

Okay, stop freaking out and think about this. I lower myself into the armchair and cradle my forehead in my hands. I don't actually know what's happened. There may not have been any attack yet. This could be Zell's way of isolating everyone to make it difficult to coordinate a defense for when he does strike.

Emotions that aren't mine dig their fingers into my chest. Anxiety, irritation, curiosity. I hear footsteps, followed by another male voice. "What's going on in here? Who is this?"

"A guardian from one of the Guilds. He's been sent for the weapon."

I raise my eyes and meet the gaze of a man bearing a close resemblance to the faerie who let me in. He nods his head slowly and says, "After centuries of waiting, the time has finally come."

CHAPTER 7

EVEN THOUGH THE REST OF THE FAE WORLD IS PROBABLY consumed by storms and battles, the two guys standing in front of me seem happy to waste time on introductions. The faerie who let me in is Tryce, and the guy who just entered the room is his father, Yale. He's the one in charge here. After I've shown Yale my guardian markings, I try to get to the point. "One of the Queen's closest advisors heard rumors of the weapon you've been guarding ever since Tharros was defeated. The youngest Unseelie prince now has the chest containing Tharros' power. We know he's going to unlock it soon—if he hasn't done so already. We need the weapon that can destroy that power. That's why I was sent here."

Yale sighs, then motions for me to sit down. "The Queen's advisor obviously didn't hear the whole story."

Fantastic. Why is there always another obstacle? "What part did he miss?"

"The weapon will do you no good. There is only one person who can use it."

I throw my hands up. Why can't someone just give me the bottom line here? "And? Who is this person?"

"We don't know," Tryce says.

I stand up and start pacing. This whole mission has been a waste of time from the start. Now I'm stuck here with no way of getting home. Unless I start walking, which would take weeks. Or perhaps I could get hold of a pegasus … I stop pacing and cross my arms. "I know you've spent your whole lives guarding this thing, so forgive me for saying this: Your weapon sounds pretty useless."

"I understand your frustration," Yale says, "but that's the way it is. After Tharros was separated from his power and killed, the power was captured in a chest. The Order of the Guard was formed to protect the power until it could be destroyed. The head of the Order at the time, a man who had crafted weapons for centuries, received a prophecy one day while he was creating a sword."

My weary mind conjures up an image of a parcel arriving with a tag on it that says *Prophecy*. I press my lips together and try not to laugh.

"As the words came to him, he etched them onto the blade of the sword," Yale continues. "That is the sword we've been guarding for centuries. It's those words that say only one person can use it."

"So … can I see this sword?"

The two of them lead me through the house, past bedrooms, a large dining room, a library, and several closed doors. We come to a spiraling staircase, which takes us down to another level. I see a room that looks like a smaller version of the Guild's training center. Another room contains an enormous oval-shaped pool. At the end of a passage, Tryce and Yale stop in front of a blank wall. They each place a hand on it and wait for several seconds before the wall vanishes.

I follow them into a darkened room, bare except for a glass case in the center. The case is lit and appears to be sitting on air. Inside the case, resting on a cushion, is a sword. The hilt is inlaid with sapphires and engraved with ornate patterns. Etched into the shining silver blade are tiny words.

"Can I take a closer look?" I ask, stepping toward the case. I have a feeling that if I touch it, an alarm will go off or I'll lose a hand or find myself hanging upside down in midair again.

"Certainly," Yale says. He places three fingertips on one side of the glass. It glows briefly before vanishing. "You can pick it up."

With one hand beneath the blade and another beneath the hilt, I lift the sword carefully. "So this is what's supposed to save us all," I murmur. I bring the sword closer to my face and read the prophecy's words out loud. "'*Two halves in one have more power than a whole. The fae world will bow beneath his mark. Only the sword can stop him, and only one can wield the sword: the Star of the high land. She is hidden, but the finder will find her. She will break the whole in half. By the strike of the sword, and the death of innocence, evil will be laid to rest.*' Okay. Pretty cryptic."

"Do you understand now why we don't know who can use the sword?" Tryce asks. "We don't know anything about either the Star or the finder."

"Actually, the finder part makes some sense to me," I tell them as hope kindles a small flame within me. "I know someone who can find people. Anyone, anywhere. That is—" fear grips my heart and threatens to smother my hope "—if she's still alive."

"Really?" Tryce says. "You know the finder?"

"Well, I don't know if she's *the* finder the prophecy mentions, but she's the only one I know. I'd say that's a good start."

"That's more than a good start. I imagined us guarding this useless thing until the end of the world."

Yale sighs. "It's good to know you've always been wholeheartedly committed to our cause, son."

"Hey, I've never—"

"Right, so, I'm leaving as soon as possible," I interrupt loudly, hoping to dispel the mix of anger and annoyance I'm feeling from the two men. "On foot, since there's no other way. And obviously I'll take the weapon with me." I hope that isn't going to be a problem for these guys.

"We'll go with you," Tryce says immediately. His anger vanishes, quickly replaced by excitement.

Yale nods. "Yes, that way we can continue to guard the weapon."

"You don't trust me with it?" I ask.

"Trust has nothing to do with it," Yale says. "Our life no longer has meaning here if we have no weapon to guard. We may as well come with you and fight whatever new evil has been unleashed on our world."

"Right, okay." Makes sense, I suppose. "So ... you know how to fight?"

"It's not like we have much else to do here," Tryce says. He takes the sword from my hand and returns it to the cushion. The glass case appears around it once more. "I'll inform the others. We'll leave as soon as everyone's ready."

"Others?"

"Yes. The Order has eighteen members."

And here I was imagining only two guys protecting a weapon that could save the lives of thousands. "There are eighteen of you, but only one person came to see who was knocking at the door? What if I had overpowered you?"

Tryce laughs. "You obviously didn't see the other six who were out there watching you squirm upside down."

So I embarrassed myself in front of seven people instead of one. Fantastic. I cross my arms. "I have one more question, Tryce: If there are eighteen skilled fighters living here, how did a young guardian girl manage to sneak in and steal the chest containing Tharros' power?"

* * *

Angelica's theft of the chest is apparently an embarrassing story no one wants to talk about. After Tryce disappears to inform the Order members about what's going on, and after we wait for the six patrolling the mountainside to return, we finally get going.

Our group of nineteen moves quickly, navigating through the dark almost as easily as we would through daylight. The Order members don't say much. Normally I'd be fine with that, but right now I'd give anything to be distracted from the thoughts that keep tormenting me. Thoughts of the terrible things that could be happening right now to the people I love. I keep telling myself that Violet and my mother and father are entirely capable of protecting themselves. I just hope Dad managed to get Calla to safety before anything could happen to her.

I distract myself by focusing on individual Order members. I let their emotions wash over me. I welcome them, almost to the point of letting them overwhelm me. Excitement and enthusiasm are mixed in with a sprinkling of fear. I allow the excitement to invade me and take the place of the anxiety gnawing a hole in my insides. It works—sort of.

Grey light turns to pink, then orange, then yellow as the sun rises above the trees we're journeying through. We don't stop. We pass food around and wolf it down while walking. All too quickly, the sun travels across the sky and disappears behind the trees.

Another day gone.

Night wraps around us. Still, we keep moving. I'm not tired yet; whenever I think of what might be happening in Creepy Hollow, I'm energized. Several hours later, Yale stops us and asks someone to check the state of the faerie paths. After lightning burns a hole in the ground and half the Order winds up drenched and windswept, we manage to get the doorway closed. Yale decides we should rest for a few hours.

The mere thought of all the time we're wasting on this journey is enough to twist my insides into a knot. I think about continuing without the Order. After all, a single person is less conspicuous than a group of nineteen, and I won't stop to rest unless my body is crippled with exhaustion. But Yale convinces me that showing up in the middle of faerie civilization without a force of warriors—even a small one—isn't the best idea. Neither is dropping unconscious from exhaustion.

The next few days pass in the same way. Someone checks the faerie paths once a day. We then rest for two or three hours. I start to wonder if faerie paths are a thing of the past. Faeries have been using them for as long as anyone can remember, but what if they never function normally again?

On our fourth or fifth day—I'm starting to lose count—the leafy trees surrounding us give way to burned trees. Some stand with bare limbs pointing to the sky while others lie cracked and broken on the ground. I jog to the front of the group to speak to Yale.

"Where are we? Is this the middle of nowhere or somewhere specific?"

"I think we're in Black Rain Ridge."

"Does it always look like this?" I gesture to the blackened trees.

Yale shakes his head. "I think there's a Guild somewhere nearby. They must know what's going on in the rest of the world."

"If there's a Guild here, we won't find it," I tell him. "Guilds are hidden, just like faerie homes. Only those who are members here would know where the entrance is."

Yale exhales. "That's disappointing."

I clench my jaw. That's an *understatement*. I can't believe we're *this close* to a Guild but have no way of contacting them. Hopefully we'll come close enough to the Guild's entrance for their guards to see us. Or we'll pass someone walking through the trees. *Yes*, I realize with relief. No one here can use the faerie paths, so surely people will be walking.

"What's that over there?" Tryce, walking on the other side of his father, points toward a pile of something through the blackened trees. From here it looks like it could be a large mound of rubbish. We head toward it. My hand tingles, ready to reach for a weapon if I need it. As we get closer, I recognize some of the shapes on the mound. An upside down table, couch cushions, a bed's cracked headboard.

My blood runs cold as I realize what I'm looking at. I hear a sharp intake of breath from Tryce and a whispered "No" from Yale. Murmurings behind us indicate we're not the only ones who've figured out what's in front of us.

It's a faerie home. At least, it was.

Broken furniture and belongings are piled up amidst the splintered pieces of tree that once housed these belongings. The tree, which was meant to keep everything hidden and intact, must have split open.

"There's another one over there," someone behind us says.

"How is this possible?" Yale asks. "The spells concealing homes are supposed to be among the most powerful."

I don't answer him. The only thought passing through my mind is that this might be what my home looks like. This might be what the whole of Creepy Hollow looks like. *Oh, please, no. No no no.*

We wander through Black Rain Ridge, passing more and more destroyed homes. The only sound comes from the crunching of scorched twigs beneath our feet. There are no people. No animals or other fae. As the dim purple of twilight descends upon us, Yale suggests we try the faerie paths again.

I volunteer. I don't mind if I wind up drenched or covered in snow or hail. Anything to distract me from the possibility that the home I've always known is as bare and dead as the forest I now stand in. I pull out my stylus and start writing the words for a doorway in the air. I think of how jealous Violet used to be that this was the one thing I could easily do that she couldn't. I'm so consumed by how much I miss her that for a moment I don't see what's happening right in front of me: the storm's gone. There's only a black hole, inviting me to walk into it.

"It's working!" Tryce shouts.

It's working.

Hope. Relief. Determination. They're my emotions and everyone else's.

"I assume you'd like to lead the way?" A hand touches my shoulder. Yale's standing beside me.

Hell, yes. No one could hold me back now if they tried. I nod, then grasp his hand and walk into the blackness, trusting the others will form a chain behind me. I think of my home and hold fast to that image. My home is far enough away from the Guild that if something big is going on there, we won't arrive in the middle of it.

Light forms in front of me as a doorway opens. It's still afternoon here, several hours behind Black Rain Ridge. I freeze. Part of me wants to rush into the familiarity of Creepy Hollow, but part of me is terrified of what I'll find. I steel myself for the worst and walk out of the faerie paths.

Ruined.

My home is ruined. A pile of broken rubble. I thought I was prepared for the possibility, but the shock of seeing it is enough to suck the breath out of me. I crouch down and place my head in my hands, ignoring the footsteps of Order members walking past me. My home is gone. I have no idea where my mother is or if she's even alive.

"Was this your home?" Yale asks.

I nod. I'm not sure I trust myself to speak right now. I count to twenty, then stand as Tryce and another faerie jump off the mound of debris. "There's no one here," Tryce says quietly.

No bodies, he means. Because why would a living person stay with a pile of rubble?

"Do you want to look through your things?" Yale asks gently.

I shake my head. I don't want to remember my home like this.

"Well … we need to decide what to do now, Oryn. Should we go to your Guild?"

Oh, dear Seelie Queen, the Guild. Is it possible it looks just like this? Completely demolished? It can't be. The Guild is enormous. I can't imagine how much of the forest would be flattened if all the glamours and concealments of the Guild were shattered.

"Just … give me five minutes," I say. I turn away and write another doorway in the air. I walk through, thinking of Violet's home, wondering if by some small chance it escaped this destruction. But when I step out of the darkness, it's to see a scene almost exactly like the one I just left.

A moan of despair escapes past my lips. I don't often cry. I'm assaulted by countless emotions every day, including sorrow, but crying isn't something I generally do. Right now, though, tears seem like the only response. I've never felt so lost and helpless. I don't know how this happened or who did it. I don't know where anyone is. I don't know who's alive, who's captured, who's free. I don't know what I'm supposed to do.

I squeeze my eyes shut, forcing tears back before they come. I climb onto the heap, searching the clutter as I go. My heart speeds up with each piece of furniture I move aside; I'm terrified I'll find a body beneath one of them. I reach the top of the pile having found nothing. It's a relief, but I still feel lost. If Violet hasn't come looking for me it's because she can't. She's either captured or …

I don't want to consider the other possibility.

I look down at a drawer lying beside splinters of wood. Brightly colored ribbons catch my attention. The ribbons from Violet's grandmother. The ribbons I had Raven make into a bracelet. I crouch down and remove them from the drawer. I wind the ribbons around my fingers before pushing the multi-colored loop into one of my pockets. Then I take the tokehari ring Violet's father gave her and add it to the ribbons. I'll give these things to her when I find her. Because I *will* find her.

I stand and navigate back down the wreckage. I'm about to open a doorway to return to my home when I hear a whimper nearby. I swivel my head around, searching. When I hear the sound again, I step toward the tree I think it came from. A glowing knife tingles in my hand. Before I can take another step, a squirrel drops from one of the charred branches and lands on the ground. It stares up at me with large eyes before shifting into a white mink.

"Filigree?"

He squeaks and bounds toward me. He crawls all the way up my body and wraps himself around my neck. I pull him gently away and hold him in front of my face. "Do you know anything about Violet? Do you know where she is?"

He squeaks, reaching for my neck once more. I hold him closer, like a child hugging a toy, and listen to his pitiful whimpers.

I'll take that as a 'no.'

I let him wrap himself around my neck as I open a doorway and head back to my ruined home. I see a few raised eyebrows when people notice the shapeshifter pet clinging to me, but no one says anything.

"Okay, let's figure out what to do next," I say to the group.

"We need to check out the Guild, but we should definitely approach it carefully."

"That won't be happening." I jerk to the side and find the owner of the voice stepping in front of a tree. The two knives that appeared in my hands vanish when I see who it is.

"Dale." Relief washes over me at the sight of my friend, although it's hard to feel it amidst all the panic I'm receiving from everyone else in the group. "You're okay."

A strange smile curls on his lips. "Got you," he says, then raises his bow and arrow and shoots at me.

CHAPTER 8

FILIGREE LEAPS OFF MY NECK AS I HURL MYSELF OUT OF THE way. The arrow strikes a tree with a *thwip* as I reach into the air for my knives. "Dale, what the hell, man?"

Ten or so faeries, all dressed in the same dark blue uniform, spill through a doorway behind Dale. Male and female, some I recognize and others I've never seen before. Guardians and Unseelie faeries fighting together. I never thought it would happen.

"Try to take them alive," one shouts.

And the fighting begins. Arrows sail through the air along with sparks of all colors. Blades clang and clash. Bats and birds and shards of ice are thrown around. I dodge a small knife spinning end over end toward me and shoot an arrow at Dale before he can throw another blade. Bright green sparks singe my hair, but I drop to the ground before they can do more damage. I coax mist out of my hands and send it toward our enemies. It'll buy us a few moments to figure out what to do next.

How did they know exactly where to find us? And how are we supposed to get away? Will we have to kill them? I don't want that, but it's not like they're going to let us leave. I stand up and back out of the way as an Order member runs into the mist brandishing a sword and shouting some kind of battle cry.

Okay, nineteen of us and about twelve of them. We don't all need to be fighting …

I search our group, looking for the weak links. I grab the two Orders members who seem to be doing the worst job of holding off our enemies: the youngest faerie and one of the women. I grab Tryce as well because he clearly didn't answer my question correctly when I asked if he knew how to fight.

I pull them back. "Have you stunned anyone before?" I ask quickly.

"Yes," the woman says, "but that takes a lot of—" She shrieks as a bird with talons the size of dragon teeth soars toward us. It slams into my hurriedly thrown up shield and evaporates into a puff of smoke.

"A lot of power, yes." I hold my hand up, hoping the shield will remain there while I'm talking. "Stay back here where we can protect you and gather as much power as possible. Then stun whoever you can."

"But what if—"

"No buts. We'll never get away if we don't stun these guys."

I head back into the melee where the mist is clearing. I go for Dale first because I know I can beat him; I've always been faster and stronger. Before he can shoot another arrow or throw a blade my way, I barrel right into him. The sparkling bow vanishes from his grasp as we slam onto the ground. I'm about to pummel him when I get his knee in my chest. I struggle for breath.

"Don't fight this, Ryn," he says. "Draven is the master our world has always needed. You'll see that eventually."

Draven? Who the hell is he?

Dale pulls his hand back and closes it in a fist, but not before I see a circular shape inked in black on his palm. I grab the fist before it can reach my face and twist. I don't want to break his wrist—it makes me sick to hurt a friend, even a friend as annoying as Dale—but I will if I have to.

"Aargh!" Dale's fist slips from my grasp as an arrow pierces my shoulder. He forces me off him. A moment later I find myself on my back with a knee in my chest and a hand around my neck.

"Just give in now before I have to hurt you," he says. "You can't get away. The faerie paths are monitored now. Draven will find you no matter where you run."

The faerie paths are monitored?

"Not … happening," I gasp. Dale's observation skills clearly haven't improved since we were last together, because he hasn't noticed the knife I now have in one of my hands. I bring it straight down into his thigh, muttering "Sorry" at the same time, because even though he's trying to strangle me, he *is* still my friend.

While Dale yells and grips his bleeding leg, I scramble up, yank the arrow from my shoulder, and remember that one of the weapons in my invisible arsenal is a wooden beam. I haven't used it much, but now seems like a good time. I reach mentally for it, holding my hands out to grasp the large, glittering thing. I swing it across the legs of an advancing faerie. He falls forward and rolls across the blackened ground. I pull the beam back, then whack Dale over the head with it. He slumps to the ground without another sound.

I stand up, my bow and arrow already in my hands. I aim and let loose, but before the arrow can find its target, the guardian I was aiming at is thrown backward by an invisible force. He drops onto the ground and lies still. Stunned. Another two guardians drop down seconds later. That only leaves—I scan our attackers quickly for sparkling weapons—one other guardian. Easy. I can handle that.

I run to where four Order members are fighting one faerie. "You!" I pull one of them away. "Start gathering power to stun.

And you." I point to someone else leaning against a tree grasping his upper arm where blood gushes from a wound. "Same thing."

I crouch down, then jump. An extra spurt of magic helps shoot me into the air and onto a branch. Bow and arrow. Aim. Let go. *Thwip*—into the guardian's arm. *Thwip*—into his side.

With an angry shout, the guardian backs away from the three Order members fighting him—who I hope will be intelligent enough to preserve their magic now and try stunning someone. He makes eye contact with me, then throws his hand forward. Magic shoots out at a remarkable speed. I jump backward and somersault through the air before landing on my feet.

He's already running at me, the arrows I shot at him removed from his body. I plant my feet on the ground; no way is this guy going to knock me over. The second he reaches me, I turn, arms raised, to let my side take the full force of his blow. Then I strike. Hands and feet, kicking, jabbing, punching. We dance around each other. I spring forward with another punch, then hook my foot behind his knee. He stumbles backward. I spin and kick. My boot strikes his stomach, throwing him back against a tree.

The wooden beam is in my hands again. As he lurches forward, I swing it. The beam slams into his forehead, knocking him flat on his back. He groans, and I give him one final whack. He lies still.

I stare down at him, at the bleeding gash on his forehead. I hate that I did this to a guardian. Someone I recognize from my very own Guild. We're supposed to be on the same side. Why was he fighting me?

"Oryn!"

I spin and duck automatically, the beam vanishing from my hands as I spread my arms out for balance. A faerie—not a guardian—slashes at me with a black-bladed knife as she runs past. Ignoring the pain flaring across my cheek, I flick my wrist out. By the time I've finished the motion, a shining whip is in my hand, already curving through the air toward the faerie. The whip snaps around her ankle. I yank it back, pulling her onto the ground. She rolls over, raises the knife—and her arm drops to the ground. Eyes closed, her head rolls to the side.

I look up and see Yale, his arms outstretched and his face still screwed up with the effort it must have taken to stun the Unseelie faerie. He lowers his arms, looking around through the semi-darkness and seeing the same thing I see: all our assailants have been stunned or knocked out. "Let's get out of here," he pants, reaching for his stylus.

"Don't open a doorway!" I say. "The paths aren't safe. That's how they found us. We have to run." I grab the fallen faerie at my feet and toss her over my shoulder. We can question her later. A small, furry form drops onto my other shoulder and scurries down my arm into my jacket pocket. I pat the pocket.

Then I run.

* * *

We don't stop running for at least an hour. Well, running isn't quite the word; it's more like stumbling or hobbling as fast as the injured will allow us to go. The forest is in complete darkness now. Only the orbs produced by those of us who still have energy illuminate the ground ahead. When it becomes clear no one is following us, we slow down to check if any wounds need immediate attention. I'm a little concerned about the blood still dripping down one side of my face. The cut should have begun to heal by now.

I lower the unconscious Unseelie faerie onto the ground. I reach for a fallen branch and transform it into a long rope. After looping it around and between her ankles, I pull it tight. I repeat the process on her hands.

"Won't she be able to break out of those bonds?" Tryce asks from nearby.

"Not these ones." I wrap my hands around the ropes and reinforce them with magic. Then, dabbing at the blood on my face, I head over to where Yale is standing. "Is the sword safe?" I ask.

"Yes." After a moment's pause, he says quietly, "There were guardians in that group that attacked us."

I nod. "Yes, four of them. They must be under some kind of spell or influence. One was my friend."

I feel Yale's gaze on me. "I'm very sorry. Is she the one you brought with us?"

"No. I wanted someone we could question to find out what's going on. I'm pretty sure she's from the Unseelie Court. She probably knows more than the guardians." I wipe my hand clean on my pants—my clothes are already bloodied and dirty—and place it in my jacket pocket. Filigree is still there, curled up in mouse form.

"The ones who weren't guardians," Yale says. "Were they all Unseelie faeries?"

"I think so. Unseelie magic always feels different. Darker and colder. And I'm pretty sure this is all the Unseelie Prince's doing." I gesture to the ruined forest around us "Although, my friend did mention someone called Lord Draven. Do you know that name?"

"Oryn, we don't know anyone. We've been isolated for centuries. And I must apologize for something," he adds. "I said we could fight, but we weren't prepared for a surprise attack like that."

"No need to apologize," I tell him, even though it was clear some members of his group could do with more practice. "Imagine how that fight would have gone down if I'd been on my own."

"Yes, well, I'd say it's a good thing I convinced you to stay with us."

I nod. "Definitely."

"So, what next, Oryn? I know I'm technically the leader of this group, but you're the only guardian here. This is more your world than ours. What do you suggest?"

I take a deep breath and look around at our group. "I honestly don't know. If those guardians were fighting us, then I'm afraid the whole Guild may be ready to do the same thing." Oh, hell, what if my mother is under the same spell? Would she look me in the eye and try to shoot me, just like Dale did? I push the terrifying thought away. "I suppose the next logical step would be to look for others like us who aren't under this strange influence. But where would we even start looking?"

"Your guess is better than—"

"Shh." I hold a hand up and look around.

"Did you hear something?" Yale whispers. He slowly draws a knife from a sheath at his waist.

"Not exactly." I *felt* something, but Yale wouldn't understand that. I haven't shared my secret with him. I haven't told anyone since I told Violet.

I scan the exhausted group of Order members, but nothing seems to have changed. They look the same: defeated, lost, miserable, angry. But what I felt moments ago was a spark of hope. A flare of happiness. No one here looks close to feeling anything like that ... so who was it?

I raise my voice and say, "Whoever you are, show yourself."

Low rumblings of conversation cease as people look at me. Some grab weapons and jump quietly to their feet, their eyes searching. The silence stretches. I begin to wonder if I imagined the sudden spike of emotion. I try to locate the *something* that was out of place, but all I feel is wariness.

Finally, a voice from somewhere above us calls out, "Don't shoot, and I'll be happy to show myself."

I look up just as a figure drops through the air. He lands in a crouch and straightens immediately. "See," he says, raising his hands, palms facing us. "I'm unmarked. I won't harm you."

"Unmarked?" I take a step toward him. "That means nothing to us."

The faerie tilts his ginger head to the side. "You don't know about the mark? It's what Draven brands people with after he's brainwashed them. It's so he knows at a glance who his followers are."

I think of the circular outline I saw on Dale's hand. Was that the mark this ginger-haired faerie is talking about? I take another step toward him, my fingers ready—but not yet reaching—for a weapon. "You're a guardian," I say, noticing the intertwining lines on his wrists. "Normally that means I'd trust you without hesitation. Recent events, however—" I lift my hand and gesture to the gash on my cheek "—suggest guardians are fighting for the wrong side now."

"Not all of them," he says. "You'll be pleased to know that some of us got away."

"And I should trust you because … ?"

He shrugs. "Because you have no other choice. And because I heard you saying you plan to search for others like you who aren't brainwashed. Well, you need search no further. I can take you right to them."

He smiles, and it isn't the kind of smile that's just for show. It's the kind that reaches his yellow-gold eyes and lights up his whole face. The kind that's contagious. It makes me want to smile for the first time in days.

It also makes me highly suspicious.

I fold my arms and ask, "Who exactly are you?"

"I'm Oliver. And this is Em." He looks to his left as a woman steps out from behind a tree to join him. It's difficult to tell how old they are by the dim light of our orbs, but I think she's younger than him. Young enough for it not to have been too long since she graduated. She has a smile to match Oliver's and the same coloring as Violet's old mentor, Tora: green eyes the shade of spring grass and green streaking through her blonde hair.

"Hi, I'm Em. London Guild." She gives a little wave.

"Ryn," I answer hesitantly. "Creepy Hollow Guild."

Her smile spreads wider. "I always thought your Guild had such a funny name."

"Well, at least it's our own name and not one we pinched from humans."

She laughs. "I suppose I deserve that kind of comment. And the rest of you are … ?" She leans to the side and looks past me. I've forgotten there are eighteen people standing behind me. What have they been doing? Simply watching this whole exchange?

"We're not guardians," Yale says. "But we'd be honored to fight alongside you when the time comes. I have to ask, though, how you can laugh when surrounded by such destruction."

Em's smile dims somewhat, and she looks at Oliver before answering. "Well, it's either that or let myself be consumed by despair. What's the point in living if I can't find some joy in it? And right now, I'm overjoyed to find nineteen free men and women after five days of searching."

"Five days?" Yale asks.

"That's how far away our base is," Oliver answers. "It's where we'll take you now—if you've decided to trust us."

CHAPTER 9

SINCE, AS OLIVER SAYS, WE HAVE NO OTHER CHOICE, AND after searching their emotions and finding nothing but genuine delight, I decide to trust Oliver and Em. And since everyone in the Order seems to view me as some great guardian of awesomeness—they're obviously unaware I've only recently graduated—this means they also decide to trust Oliver and Em.

The two strangely cheerful guardians lead us to their base in Fireglass Vale, one of three safe locations the Guild Council built centuries ago in case the Guilds were ever attacked and compromised. I have a vague memory of learning about these safe locations in second or third year—not *where* they were, of course—and thinking they were unnecessary; how could the Guilds ever be compromised? Their protective charms were meant to be impenetrable.

I'm glad now the Council had the foresight to prepare for every eventuality.

At the end of the fifth day, as we journey across endless open fields, Oliver lets Em take the lead and drops behind to speak to me. "I thought I should warn you about something. You won't find many from your Guild here. The Creepy Hollow Guild was hit first and hardest. Council members from every Guild were there at the time, attending an urgent meeting. There was an explosion in the room where they were assembled. No one made it out alive. Almost everyone else who survived the explosion was captured and brainwashed."

"Damn." The good news just keeps coming. "If the Council is gone, what kind of leadership do we have now?"

"A handful of Council members, including me, weren't at the meeting that night. Once the attack was over and we knew for certain we couldn't return to the Guilds, two of us deactivated the spells that kept the safe locations locked. We began searching for anyone who hadn't been influenced by Draven. Anyone we found who was willing and able to fight was sent to Fireglass Vale. Everyone else was sent to either of the other two places. We're still finding survivors."

I look away and try to squash the ridiculous hope that Violet is safe and waiting for me at Fireglass Vale. I push away thoughts of my mother and father and my old mentor, Bran. *Don't hope and you won't be disappointed.* Instead, I listen as Oliver tells me how he wound up searching for survivors in Creepy Hollow. He tells me about the beautiful woman from the Creepy Hollow Guild he fell in love with a few months ago. The woman he's heard nothing from since our world fell apart. The woman named Tora.

At the mention of her name, my chest squeezes tight. Oliver must be talking about Violet's old mentor; I don't know any other Tora at the Guild. My stupid heart starts conjuring up ideas of Violet and Tora hiding out somewhere together. *Stop it. You know that's probably not true.* So I say nothing to Oliver except that I know Tora but haven't seen her.

Coral pink and burnt orange mingle in the sky as we descend into a valley. Long grass brushes the tops of our legs. Through trees with leaves turning golden brown, I see a river glittering with the sky's reflected colors. Draven's touch clearly hasn't extended this far.

We reach the river and walk along its edge toward a waterfall. Sheets of water pound the rocks at its base, the spray wetting our faces as we get closer. As Oliver takes his first step onto the slippery rocks, I realize the entrance to the base must be behind the waterfall. Oliver takes a few more careful steps before reaching forward and pushing his hand into the slamming water. Then he pulls it aside as easily as he would a curtain, revealing a gap large enough for us to climb through.

Above the roar of the water, he shouts, "Come on."

I expect to find myself in a cave behind the waterfall, but instead I walk into a large, high-ceilinged room that reminds me of the main foyer inside the Creepy Hollow Guild. Well, except for the domed ceiling of protective enchantments we had back there. The ceiling I look up at now is flat. Faeries hurry here and there, up and down the large stairway and along the corridors leading off the foyer. Oliver was right when he said I wouldn't find many people from my own Guild here. I don't see a single face I recognize—until my gaze alights on one that almost makes up for all the missing faces I long to see.

My father.

He's down the stairs so fast I barely have time to move. He wraps me in a tight embrace before pulling back and saying, "Ryn, you just *disappeared!* I've tried so many times to contact you. Are you okay? What happened to your face?"

I touch the square bandage that covers the gash on my cheek. "An Unseelie faerie and his knife. It won't heal."

Dad frowns. "Dark magic on the blade, maybe. Or a potion. I'm sure someone here can take care of it."

"Yeah, anyway, that's not important. Is Calla safe?"

"Yes, she's at one of the other bases with her mother."

I hesitate a second before asking, "And Mom?" I'm not sure I want to know.

Dad looks away with a slow shake of his head. "I don't know. No one has seen her."

I close my eyes and press the heels of my hands against them. "Just like Violet. She's also missing."

Dad places a hand on my shoulder and says, "If they're alive, we'll find them. We'll get them back."

"Yes," I murmur. "We'll get them back."

I don't open my eyes. I block everything else out. The chatter around me fades to silence as I stand there, holding fiercely to the promise my father just made. I will it to be true, hoping he means his words as much as I do. Because I *do* mean them. With all my heart. *I will find them.*

"Linden! Come on, let's go." The brittle cocoon of quiet I managed to wrap myself in shatters.

"I'm sorry, I have to go," Dad says. "Another search and rescue mission. I could be gone for a week or more, since we can't use the paths. We now have a herd of pegasi here at the base, but not nearly enough for all of us. The Council's still working on other means of transportation."

My brain joins the dots. "You're working as a guardian again? I thought you were finished with that life."

"Things change. Our side needs as many guardians as it can get." He squeezes my shoulder once more before letting go. "I'll see you soon."

And then he's gone, vanishing behind the curtain of water. The bustle of activity continues around me, but I feel as alone as if no one were here. I put my hand in my pocket and feel the warm, soft form of Filigree. As sad as it is to admit, the furry creature is the only thing giving me any kind of comfort right now.

CHAPTER 10

"DUDE, DID YOU KNOW IT'S *SNOWING* OUT THERE?" ONE GUY says. "About a day away from here."

I know I've lost track of the days since I started going on search and rescue missions, but it hasn't been *that* long since I arrived. Two weeks, maybe three. The last time I checked, we weren't even halfway through autumn.

"It's insane," his friend adds.

I'm sitting at a table in the base's massive dining room trying to turn the strawberry sauce on my pancakes into chocolate sauce. The two guys who've just returned from a mission and joined me at the table are both from the Creepy Hollow Guild. They graduated a few years ahead of me and left to find new and exciting jobs at other Guilds. I can't remember their names. We haven't exactly chatted much.

"It's probably Draven," I tell them, "messing around with the weather to make life difficult for us."

"Yeah, The Destruction obviously wasn't enough. He's probably going to subject us to an eternal winter or something."

The Destruction. That's what everyone seems to call what happened. It's a fitting name.

"Did you find anything more exciting than snow?" I ask. "Like, you know, survivors?"

"No," the taller, darker haired guy says. He shovels pieces of pancake into his mouth, chews, then adds, "Oh, we did come across a group of some other fae. The scaly-skinned ones."

"Reptiscillas," his freckled companion says.

"Yeah. We couldn't see properly through the trees, so we started shooting as soon as we realized someone was there. It was only when we got closer that we saw there were children in the group."

"You were shooting at *children*?" I say.

"We didn't know." Tall Guy looks offended. "We backed off as soon as we realized they were no threat."

"You should have tried to talk to them. We need as many fae on our side as we can get."

"They were terrified. We let them run. Besides, children can't fight. They're better off hiding out somewhere else."

"And they're most likely Undergrounders," Freckled Guy says. "You know we've never worked well with that lot."

I shake my head. "There's nothing wrong with Under-grounders. They treat us the way they do because they're afraid of us, and with good reason. We've never exactly been friendly toward them."

"Because they're a violent, unpredictable lot." Tall Guy looks like he's starting to wonder what's wrong with me.

What's wrong with me is that I've had enough of guardians and their ridiculous prejudices. I've had to deal with them for years at the Guild, and now, in the midst of impending war, I figure it's about time guardians got over themselves. "Yeah, about five percent of them are violent and unpredictable."

"And those are the only ones we ever interact with, so forgive me for painting the rest of them with the same brush." Waves of hostility start rolling off Tall Guy. I don't care.

"You've never *tried* to interact with any of the others," I say.

"And you have?" Freckled guy makes sure to get his two cents in.

"I'm willing to bet I've spent a whole lot more time Underground than most other guardians." I don't tell them why. I don't tell them where exactly. I don't explain that even though the Underground clubs are filled with far more people than I'd usually want to be around, the mix of numbness and euphoria are a whole lot easier to deal with than the many emotions spinning around the Guild. "This is going to turn into a war unlike anything our world has ever seen. You think we're going to win it on our own? We're not. We're going to have to play nice with all the fae we've thought of as inferior for so long. And people like you are going to have to suck it up and deal with it."

Okay, that last part was probably uncalled for.

Just as the situation is about to blow up in my face, Em and her cheery attitude appear at our table, complete with a tray of pancakes and rainbow colored milk. "Hey, guys, what's up? Can I join you?" If she could feel the enmity and aggression bouncing back and forth across this table, there's no way she'd want to sit here.

I stand up and say, "Enjoy the pancakes," before sending my tray through the air and into a slot in the wall. I turn and stride out.

My fists are balled as I walk along the brightly lit corridor. I hate living in a perpetual bad mood, but I can't seem to get out from under it. *Nothing* is happening. We haven't found anyone on the search and rescue missions I've been on, and I don't believe we're going to. Anyone who doesn't know how to hide has surely been captured by now, and those who *do* know how to hide aren't going to show themselves when we walk by.

As for the weapon that can supposedly put Draven's reign to an end … Well, it's hiding in a room somewhere because no one can use it. Council members spend hours poring over the prophecy trying to figure out who the 'finder' is, but I know it's all a waste of time. I'm almost certain the finder is Violet, and there's been no sign of her anywhere.

I slow my steps and put a hand against one of the wood-paneled walls. I feel weirdly disoriented. Sick. Dizzy. I lean over and stare at the shiny tiles beneath my boots. *What the hell is wrong with me?*

Then everything becomes black.

For a moment I'm weightless. Every one of my senses is blocked off. Even the air disappears. I feel like I'm being squeezed, tighter and tighter and tighter until—with a gasp I lurch toward the light growing in front of me.

Glittering knives form in my hands as I suck in air and take a few unsteady steps forward. I turn on the spot, ready to throw a knife at whoever did this to me. My eyes take in a small but opulently decorated sitting room. When I've almost turned a full revolution, I see the one who must have brought me here: Violet's father, Kale.

"Did you just *summon* me?" I demand. I'm not keen on the idea of my body moving from one place to another without my permission.

"Yes." He rises from a maroon couch covered in decorative cushions. "Difficult spell, but I eventually found someone who could do it."

Well, that's certainly worrying. "Aren't these—" my knives disappear as I point to the markings on my wrists "—supposed to protect me from things like summoning?" All the protective enchantments embedded in my trainee pendant were supposedly transferred to the markings when they were inked onto my skin during graduation.

"Yes." He comes toward me. "That's why it's taken me so long to succeed with the spell."

"If you succeeded, that means someone else could—"

"Ryn, that's not the point right now." He grasps my shoulders. "Did you find the Order? Did you get the weapon?"

If he's going to demand information, then so am I. "Where's Violet?"

His hands slip from my shoulders. He looks away.

"What? Tell me."

"I don't know," he says.

"You *don't know*? But you were *there* when all this happened. You weren't traipsing around a mountainside unaware of the devastation taking place everywhere."

"I wasn't in Creepy Hollow. I was with the Queen." He starts pacing. "The moment we knew the Guild was under attack, the Queen and her guards went to investigate. My first concern was for Violet, but the Queen ordered me to secure her hideout. Only when she arrived there hours later was I allowed to leave."

"So you chose your Queen over your daughter?"

"I couldn't abandon my duty, Ryn! I left as soon as I could. And I found …" He takes a deep breath. "Our home was destroyed. Vi wasn't there."

So I still know nothing.

"But I found someone else." My heart seems to freeze for a second, waiting for him to name the person. "It was Tora." He swallows. "I found her body near what remained of our home. She was crushed by a falling tree. Her injuries must have been too severe for her body's magic to heal them."

A wave of heat rolls over my body, followed by a chill of goose bumps. I didn't know Tora all that well, but Violet loved her as much as her own family. This news will devastate her.

"I looked everywhere for Vi," Kale continues. "I searched the wreckage of every home she might have been at. I hid near the ruins of the Guild and watched as Draven, this faerie—*halfling*— I've never seen before, weaved a spell over every guardian he'd forced to kneel before him. His army was small, but they must have possessed some power I don't know of because they controlled that crowd of guardians as if it was nothing to them. But I didn't see Violet there."

"Did you see my mother?" I whisper. A slow boil bubbles in my blood at the thought of her being forced to kneel in front of some lunatic halfling.

"No. But I saw others I remember working with." He stares at the floral patterned rug—or rather, he stares through it. Probably reliving a scene I'm glad I didn't have to witness.

"This Draven," I say between clenched teeth. "Who the hell is he? What do you know about him?"

Kale's eyes clear as he looks up at me. "He's half-faerie, half-human. He possesses more power than any single person should ever have. He created the storm inside the faerie paths. He's been changing the weather across the entire fae realm. And he killed the Unseelie Prince Zell."

"What?" And here I was thinking Zell might be hiding behind the scenes, using this *Lord Draven* as his puppet.

"Yes. He opened the chest that contained Tharros' power and allowed it to enter him. And there's only one thing that can destroy that power." He crosses the room to stand in front of me once more. "Which brings me back to the weapon I sent you to find. Please tell me you succeeded."

"I did, but it won't do you any good. The weapon can only be used by one person. And that person can only be found by the 'finder.' Who do you think that sounds like?"

Kale's gaze slides away from mine and comes to rest somewhere behind me. "Violet," he says quietly.

"That's what I thought."

"And no one knows where she is." He clenches his fist and presses it against his forehead. "Which means we're as helpless against Tharros' power as we've always been."

I nod.

"I need to take this information to the Queen."

"Great. Do you mind returning me to Fireglass Vale before you run off to do the Queen's bidding once more?"

He's quiet for a moment, watching me. He may not have my ability to sense emotions, but I'm pretty sure he knows I'm not happy with him. "It's not my fault that Violet is gone, Oryn," he says. "I'm as desperate to find her as you are, but I also have a duty to perform. I swore an oath the day I became a guardian, just like you did. That oath means something to me. Perhaps you should think about what it means to you."

And with that, he leaves the room. Moments later, a tall man with quiet steps and very little hair comes in. He holds something in his long fingers and begins chanting. His eyes never leave me as I feel the world begin to tilt again. It creeps me out. It doesn't feel right, this summoning thing—and I'm not just talking about the nausea and dizziness.

I stumble back into the corridor at the Fireglass Vale base, wrapping my arms around my aching chest and gasping for breath. I can't get Kale's words out of my mind. How can he think I'm not committed to my guardian duties? Being a guardian means protecting people. Keeping them safe. Rescuing them if they've been captured. So why would it be a betrayal of the oath I made if I put every ounce of effort into finding and rescuing Violet and my mother?

Because you're needed here.

My father said it himself. They need every guardian they can get if they're hoping to take down Draven. I can't go running off on my own little rescue missions.

Lord Draven. My arms drop to my sides as I remember what Kale said about him. *He created the storm inside the faerie paths. He's been changing the weather across the entire fae realm.* It almost sounds like ... But no. It can't be him. The boy who accidentally stumbled into the fae realm and was cowardly enough to hand Violet over to Zell to protect his own skin couldn't have caused complete destruction and overpowered thousands in a world he knew barely anything about.

"Ryn, there you are. I've been looking for you."

I turn and see Oliver walking toward me. *Oh, hell, I'm going to have to tell him about Tora.*

"I know you've been part of several search and rescue missions," he says, "but I'm putting together teams for a different purpose: gathering information. It'll be a lot more dangerous, as it'll most likely involve interaction with the enemy. If you agree to it, I'd like you to lead one of the younger teams."

Here's my chance to prove just how committed I am to the surviving guardians and their cause. "That … would be great. Thank you."

"Fantastic. Oh, and we're looking into alternate modes of transport, since the faerie paths are no longer an option. Come check this out." He waves for me to follow him. "I have a feeling you're going to love it."

PART III
VIOLET

CHAPTER 11

"I'VE ALWAYS BEEN JEALOUS OF FAERIES' HAIR," NATESA SAYS as she carefully separates three narrow strands of my hair and begins to braid them. "The vibrant colors are so beautiful. I imagine if there were lots of faeries in one room it would be an explosion of color."

"I guess it makes up for the fact that we wear black all the time," I say. "Well, guardians, I mean. Not all faeries."

"Black is boring," Natesa states. "All reptiscillas have black hair and black eyes. That's why I tie ribbons in mine, to add some color."

"I noticed," I say with a smile.

I'm sitting cross-legged on Natesa's bed in front of her. I came in a few minutes ago to pick up my new white cloak and told her, once again, how pretty her hair looks in braids and ribbons. She somehow manages to do it in a different style every day. The ribbons' colors keep changing, but green seems to be her favorite. Before handing over my cloak, she said it was time for me to get some braids in my own hair. That wasn't what I was aiming for *at all* when I complimented her, but since the idea seemed to excite her, I decided to go with it.

Braiding hair. Yeah. I don't know what I did with my free time in my old life, but I'm pretty sure it wasn't this.

After a few minutes of weaving strands of hair together, Natesa says, "I'm so glad Jamon decided to get over himself and stop hating you. I was certain he was going to hate all guardians forever after what happened to his friend, but it seems like he actually gets on quite well with you now."

"What do you mean? What happened to his friend?"

Natesa's fingers go still. "He didn't tell you?"

"Tell me what?"

"Oh dear." Her hands slide away from my hair. "I shouldn't have brought it up. I just assumed he would have told you."

"About what?" I know I shouldn't push her if this is some big secret of Jamon's, but I really want to know what she's talking about.

Natesa's fingers return to my hair. "Everyone else knows about it, so I suppose you may as well know too. It was about three years ago, I think. Jamon's best friend was having a hard time dealing with a difficult family situation, so he used to sneak out to go drinking at Underground clubs. Then he discovered that human alcohol has a much stronger effect on fae than our alcohol, so he started going into the human realm to hang out at their clubs. One night he got into a fight with a human teenager. A guardian showed up to intervene. Jamon's friend fought back, and ... well, he ended up being killed. Jamon was there, trying to convince his friend to come home. He saw the whole thing. He got his father to go and confront the Guild Council about what happened, but nothing ever came of it."

I close my eyes as I let out a long sigh. It now makes complete sense why Jamon hated me from the moment he first saw me. I think I'd hate guardians too if that happened to my best friend. I wish he'd told me about this sooner. It would have helped me understand him so much better.

"Thanks for explaining," I say quietly.

"Sure, but please don't say anything to him about it. Maybe he doesn't want to bring it up now that he's friendly with you."

"Yeah, okay."

Natesa works a little longer, then say, "Okay, I think I've done six braids. Go check it out." I stand and head to the small mirror hanging on her wall. I twist my head from side to side and see a few thin braids here and there, half hidden amongst my hair's dark brown and purple strands. It's actually quite pretty.

"And here's your cloak." Natesa goes to the large pile of white fabric in the corner of the room and removes the top bundle. I take it from her, let the cloak fall open, and pull it around my shoulders. It's now the perfect length for me. I'm still not sure if fighting in it would be a good idea, but camouflage is more important. *Don't let them see you, and you won't have to fight them.*

"It's perfect, thank you," I tell her.

"Oh, and your name's stitched into the hood," she adds. I remove the cloak and check inside the hood for my name. I burst out laughing when I see the small, purple-stitched words: *Property of Violet Fairdale, Most Kick-Butt Guardian of All Time.*

Natesa grins. "I thought you'd like that. It was Jamon's idea."

"Oh, and he would certainly know, wouldn't he. I keep kicking his butt every time he tries to scare me." I turn around and lay the cloak flat on Natesa's bed so I can fold it up. "I think he keeps hoping that one day he'll manage to—"

My vision goes black as something dark is yanked over my head. A string tightens abruptly, closing the fabric around my neck and almost choking me. I spin around with a kick and a jab. My strikes meet nothing but air.

Oh, he's getting good.

Something sweeps behind my legs and knocks my ankles. I fall back. I twist before I hit the ground, landing on my palms and toes instead of my butt. An exclamation of surprise tells me he's right behind me. I pull my knee forward, then kick backward, finally connecting with flesh. I hear his body hit the wall.

I grab at the material around my neck and pull it loose. I tug it off my head and slide out of the way as Jamon runs at me. I leap to my feet. He runs at me again. I jump and somersault right over his head. Land, spin, kick, throw him onto the ground, drop to one knee, press the other knee to his chest. I close my fist around open air, and by the time my fingers have tightened, there's a knife in my grip. A knife I'm now holding against his neck.

With a grin, I say, "I think this gets more entertaining every time."

He pushes my knee off his chest and sits up. "I think—" he coughs "—I can stop scaring you now. You seem to have the weapon thing under control."

I examine the knife in my hand. Its gold diamond-like surface sparkles and shines like sunlight reflecting off water. I let it go. "I had the weapon thing under control a week ago. I think you keep coming back for more because you like me wiping the floor with you."

"Well, the floor's clean now," Jamon says, "so I think my job is done."

"Thank goodness for that," Natesa says, stepping out from her safe spot in the corner of the room. "I was worried you were going to destroy my room."

"Oh, I'm sorry." Guilt spreads across Jamon's face. "I didn't even think—I mean, I—I guess I should have asked you—"

"Are we heading out again?" I ask, interrupting what was probably about to become another awkwardly overnice conversation between Jamon and Natesa. Honestly, someone should just put them out of their misery and make Jamon's arranged union go away.

"Uh, yeah, that's why I came to fetch my cloak." Jamon takes the white bundle from Natesa, who seems to have trouble looking him directly in the eye. "Thanks, Natesa. You've done an awesome job. We definitely won't be spotted in the snow wearing these."

"So, who are we making friends with this time?" I ask as Jamon and I head down a corridor. I step behind him to allow a woman and three rowdy children tugging at her arms to pass.

"Merpeople."

"Really?" I pick up the woman's scarf that slipped off her shoulder and hand it to her before running after Jamon. "Where?"

"Creepy Hollow, actually. I always thought they stuck to open rivers and oceans and things like that, but my dad says there's an Underground bar frequented by merpeople. We may as well go there instead of traveling to distant lands."

"Definitely. Especially since we have to go by foot." I found out the hard way that Draven's guards are using the faerie paths to track people. After being ambushed twice only minutes after using the paths, it wasn't difficult to make the connection. Fortunately only two faeries came after me each time—I guess they saw one person going through the paths and figured I'd be easy to catch—so getting away from them wasn't a huge challenge. I realized then that that's how Draven's men found the reptiscilla tunnels. They were obviously slower in getting themselves organized back then; now it only takes them minutes to show up, not hours.

"It'll be cool to see Creepy Hollow again," Jamon says. We reach his home, and I wait in the doorway for him as he fetches his bag and weapons.

"Yeah, it will." As farfetched as it is, I can't help the flicker of hope inside me that *this time* I'll remember something. Something that isn't just a fuzz or a person I don't care about. A memory that actually means something.

* * *

A thick blanket of snow covers the landscape. Jamon and I barely stand out against it in our clean, white cloaks. I'm able to lift myself slightly with magic so I can walk *on* the snow instead of trudging *through* it, but Jamon doesn't have the same luxury. Being stronger than me, though, he's able to plough his way through quite easily. We travel mainly in silence, but it's a companionable one rather than the hostile silence I received from him in my first few weeks with the reptiscillas.

Late at night, when it's time to rest, we find sleep difficult. When it's Jamon's turn to lie down, he starts shivering too much to get comfortable. When it's my turn, I keep jolting awake imagining sounds that aren't there. We're constantly on edge, expecting an attack from any side. It's almost impossible to relax, so our attempt at rest only lasts a few hours before we continue our journey.

We arrive at the appropriate Underground entrance late in the evening on our second day of traveling. None of Draven's forces have shown up to attack us, so we've obviously managed to avoid the sensors that detect unmarked fae. That's complete luck, since we have no clue where these invisible sensors are.

The Underground entrance is hidden beneath a bridge of interwoven tree roots that spread from one side of a quietly flowing river to the other. We climb carefully down the slippery bank and over a few ice-covered rocks in order to get beneath the bridge. I balance on one of the rocks while Jamon searches for the entrance and whispers, "Try not to get dragged underwater by any dangerous creatures."

I stare at the black water with suspicion, but I can't see anything beneath the rippling surface.

"Come on, here it is," Jamon says as he disappears into the shadows. I follow him and find a hole in the ground behind a rock. I wonder if this entrance floods when the river rises or if magic keeps the water out.

Once inside the tunnel, we remove our white cloaks and stuff them into our bags. Jamon leads the way. Torches held by fist-shaped brackets in the tunnel walls light our path, their flames flickering blue and green. A musty smell fills the air, and my boots crunch against wet earth. Perhaps I was right about the flooding thing.

We come to a fork, and Jamon takes a small piece of paper from his bag and examines it before heading down the left tunnel. It curves and zigzags and heads downward quite steeply until eventually we find ourselves at the edges of civilization. The tunnels are wider, with closed shop doors set into the walls and hundreds of footsteps pressed into the damp ground. Various fae walk past us: dwarves, pixies, and others I can't identify. Whoever they are, they have one thing in common: They all travel quickly, avoiding each other's eyes—and ours.

It's clear no one feels safe.

We continue onward—Jamon checks his directions once more—until we come to a tunnel with an aquamarine glow. "This is the one," Jamon says. I follow him down the tunnel toward a doorway where the glow becomes more intense. Slow, sultry music beckons us. We're about to step through the doorway when a large man appears, blocking our way. His hair is one color and doesn't match his eyes, so he can't be a faerie. Perhaps he's a halfling of some kind. Half an ogre maybe, judging by his size.

He speaks, and his voice is so deep I can almost feel it. "Show me your palms," he commands.

My fingers clench involuntarily. What's the ticket to get in here? Marked palms or unmarked? If it's marked, we'd better get ready to run. I look at Jamon, who nods. We raise our right hands at the same time, like some kind of salute.

The man steps aside and inclines his head ever so slightly. I let out the breath I was holding and walk forward. This Underground bar is nothing like I imagined it would be. The room is divided by a curvy counter that runs diagonally from one corner to the opposite corner. On one side of the divide is a pool with clear, turquoise water lapping a few inches below the level of the bar. The other side of the divide, the side we're standing on, looks a lot more like I expected: dry ground, regular bar stools, and some low tables and couches. In the center of each table is a bowl of luminous purple liquid with tiny white flowers floating on the surface.

There aren't many people here. A couple on a couch feed each other the white flowers before locking themselves into an inseparable embrace; someone with spiked hair hunches over the dry side of the bar; and two mermaids glide through the pool. Their heads break the surface of the water at the same moment. They rest their arms on the bar and smile at the spiky-haired guy.

"Is that who we're here to talk to?" I nod toward the two mermaids.

"I'm not sure if there's anyone in particular we're meant to talk to," Jamon says. "I don't know if my dad's message got here before we did."

We're about to walk forward when a girl wearing impossibly high silver heels sashays out of a side door and comes toward us. Her hips sway in time to the music. She tucks her flamingo pink hair behind one ear before saying, "Can I get you anything?"

When I don't answer, Jamon says, "Popular place, huh?"

"Oh. Yeah." The waitress rolls her eyes as she places one hand on her hip. "Everyone's hiding since The Destruction. It's totally boring here now, but since I'm the only one brave enough to come to work, my boss is paying me double not to leave. He figures people will start coming back eventually." She shrugs. "Hopefully he's right. Anyway, do you want a drink or what?"

"Um, have you got iced night?" Jamon asks.

"Yeah." She turns her uninterested gaze to me.

I don't know if I've ever ordered anything from a bar in my life. If I have, it must have been an important moment because my brain has chosen to forget it. "Uh, I'll have the same." I figure that's the safest option.

"Sure." She spins on her silver heel and heads back to the side room.

"Do you have any idea what you've ordered?" Jamon asks as we climb onto a pair of barstools.

"Nope. But if you can drink it, I can drink it."

I can't read his smile as he leans forward and waves the two mermaids over. "Hey, girls, I was hoping you could help me with something."

They slide beneath the water and resurface in front of us. Water drips from their turquoise hair and lips. Their ocean-colored eyes sparkle as they giggle. The one with the braid over her shoulder says, "I'm afraid you're not really our type."

Jamon chuckles. "That's a shame, but fortunately for you, that's not what I'm after."

"What can we help you with then?" The other mermaid crosses her forearms on the counter and rests her chin on them. She stares up at him from beneath her eyelashes. Considering Jamon isn't her type, she sure is doing a good job of flirting.

Jamon leans forward and lowers his voice. I know he's going to get straight to the point; he always does. "We're looking for allies in the fight against Draven and were wondering if the merpeople might be interested."

The mood changes as quickly as if ice cold water has been dumped on the counter. Both girls cast furtive glances around the nearly empty room. "You can't say his name here," the one with the braid whispers. "If someone from *their* side knew we were talking about him, we'd—"

"Two iced nights." Pink hair blocks my vision of the scared mermaids as the waitress leans around me and places two glasses on the bar in front of us. They're tall and narrow and flare out at the top like trumpets.

"Thanks," Jamon says, leaning back and placing a few silvers in the waitress's hand.

When the waitress is out of earshot, the braided-hair mermaid says, "Um, you should talk to our father. He's the owner of this bar. He'll know what to tell you." Before Jamon can respond, they sink beneath the water and glide away. They disappear through a dark, round hole in the wall.

I pick up my glass and examine the midnight blue liquid. Tiny sparkles float in it like stars in a night sky. "You don't think perhaps you should tread more carefully with a subject that clearly scares everyone?" I ask Jamon.

"It's all going to lead to the same question, so why waste time?"

I shrug before raising the glass to my lips and taking a sip. I swallow, then gasp as liquid colder than frozen metal burns all the way down my throat. I cough. "How can you ... drink this? It's *horrible*."

Jamon gives me one of his quirky smiles. "What was it you said? 'If you can drink it, I can drink it'?"

The dark liquid is so cold, I can't even figure out if it has a flavor. I slide the glass across the bar toward Jamon. "Here. It's all yours." I may be stubborn, but I'm not stupid. I'd rather not lose all feeling in my mouth and throat.

I watch the hole in the wall as a figure slips through it. Strong arms pull at the water, propelling him quickly from one side of the pool to the other. He surfaces in front of us, aqua-colored features dripping water and a frown already in place. He reaches for something below the bar, then slowly raises his arm and places a harpoon on the counter. His eyes examine the two us, then narrow in on me. With a sigh, I raise my palms to show him my unmarked status.

"A guardian and a reptiscilla," he says. "Interesting combination."

"Yes." Jamon ignores the harpoon and leans forward. "Did your daughters pass on my message?"

"They did. Sounds like you're looking to pick a fight with the biggest bully in the forest, and you need friends to help you do it."

"We're not the ones looking for a fight. Draven's going to come after us one day, and we'll have to fight back. It'll be better for everyone if we stick together and don't fight alone."

The merman nods slowly, his gaze sweeping the room behind us. "We have an agreement with the sirens. If Draven comes after us, they'll come to our aid, and vice versa."

"That's great. We've spoken to the elf and pixie populations that survived The Destruction, and they've agreed to fight with us. We were hoping—" Jamon lowers his voice further "—that if we gather enough fae willing to fight, then we won't have to wait for Draven to come after us. If we make the first move, maybe we can bring him down. Would merpeople and sirens be willing to join us?"

"I certainly hope so. I'm nowhere near in charge, though, but I can put you in contact with—"

"I said, GET OUT." The booming voice of the giant who blocked our way through the door echoes across the room. I swivel in my chair—and see them at the same moment Jamon grabs my wrist and pulls me onto the floor behind the nearest couch.

"Guardians," he whispers. "Marked guardians."

I nod. I saw the wrist and palm of the guy who was leaning casually in the doorway. I hold my breath, wondering how many friends he has with him and hoping they won't be interested enough in a dying bar to spend any time here. The dull thump of a heavy body hitting the floor kills that hope like a fist squashing a sprite. I peek around the edge of the couch and see the passed-out form of the giant.

Crap.

CHAPTER 12

I JERK MY HEAD BACK BEHIND THE COUCH. I DIDN'T SEE how many guardians there were, but they're definitely not leaving. I hear the sound of multiple pairs of footsteps entering the bar. They come to a stop, and I imagine the guardians looking around. They're probably trying to decide whether the few unmarked patrons in this bar are worth the effort. Or perhaps they're thinking how ridiculously easy this is going to be for them.

A single pair of footsteps moves toward the bar—toward the couch we're hiding behind. We creep around to the side, beneath the stuffed arm of the couch. I catch a glimpse of a male figure. Tall. Long, black coat. Dark hair with blue-black streaks. I duck down and watch through the legs of a low table. He takes slow, purposeful strides toward the bar. His black boots are heavy against the ground, filling the room with an ominous *thud*. *Thud*. *Thud*. Chunky metal buckles reflect the room's turquoise glow, and when he comes to a halt, I can see a twisting pattern of thorns engraved into the metal.

He stops in front of the bar. Everyone in the room must surely be holding their breath. The couple on a couch somewhere, the spiky-haired dude, the merman who owns this place, the pink-haired waitress.

"We don't want any trouble," the merman says.

"We're not looking for any." The guardian's voice is low and non-threatening. Which somehow seems a whole lot more threatening than if he'd shouted. "We're off duty. We heard about a place down here. A place where … *our kind* like to hang out. Have some fun. Relax when we're not busy marking people." He lets out a low chuckle. "You know what place I'm talking about?"

A pause. And then, "You must mean Titan's Tavern," the merman says. "Go left out of here, make another left, and go past the crystal stream."

Silence again. I'm still holding my breath, waiting to see if this guardian is about to laugh his ass off and then attack. And that harpoon would be as useful as a toothpick against him, which means I'd have to jump out and get involved. And while I might be a match for him if it were only the two of us, I know I could never take down a whole group of guardians.

"Thanks," the guardian says. His boots scrape the floor as he turns and strides away. Other footsteps join his, growing quieter as the group leaves the bar.

I feel Jamon relax beside me. "That was close. I didn't think we were going to make it out of here unmarked."

A couple of hours later, Jamon and I slip quietly back through the tunnels. We walk as fast as we can without breaking into a run, which would no doubt be suspicious to any passersby. We make it back to the river without incident. Before venturing out into the winter world above ground, we retrieve our cloaks and pull them back on.

"That didn't go too badly," I say as we climb up the river bank and into the snowy forest. Puffs of condensation form in front of my mouth when I speak.

"Yeah, a meeting with the merpeople's leaders is exactly what I was hoping for, but I didn't know if we'd get it. My dad will be pleased."

"Do you want to send him a message now? Let him know?"

"Hmm." Jamon pats his pocket. "I didn't bring my amber. I could send him a message the other way, though. I guess he'll want to know now, even though the meeting's only next week." Jamon opens his hand and starts writing words onto his palm with his finger. Some reptiscillas use amber like faeries do—although they write with their fingers instead of a stylus—but most do what Jamon is doing now. When he finishes writing, he brings his hand up to his face. He blows gently across his open palm, and black shapes that look like smoky words rise from it. They twist and curl and disappear into the air.

"You still need to teach me how to do that," I say.

He winks. "Reptiscillan secret." He flips his cloak's hood up over his head. "Oh, can you do that spell where you cover my footsteps? I don't want anyone to track us."

I raise an eyebrow. He rolls his eyes. "Fine, I'll teach you the messaging spell when we get back."

I give him my sweetest smile. "In that case, I'd be happy to cover your tracks." Being able to lift myself and walk on top of the snow means I leave barely a hint of brushed snow behind me. Jamon's great big footprints, however, are a glaring giveaway. I crouch down and spread my hands over the indentations in the snow. With whispered words, I coax the surrounding snow to start refilling the holes. I move my hands away and stand. The holes keep filling slowly. "That should do it," I say. If I keep part of my mind focused while we walk, the footprints will keep filling themselves.

"Thanks." Jamon sets off, and I walk beside him. I tuck my

hands under my arms to keep them warm. Magic could do the job, but I don't want to lose the strands of power I'm already holding onto. Multitasking has its limits.

Silence is our companion once again, which gives my mind space to wander over the stark beauty of the forest. The white frosting on blackened trees glitters beneath the moon's soft blue glow.

A shadow swoops over us, and a nighttime creature chirps.

What the …

"Stop," I say quietly, touching Jamon's arm. "Did you see that?"

He nods, looking up at the bare branches around us. "And did you hear that noise?"

"Yes. But I thought everything was dead here. No creatures, nothing."

"So did I," he says, turning slowly on the spot.

My fingers prickle. I tense, waiting for someone or something to jump out at us. Perhaps we passed beneath a sensor and Draven's guards have come for us. Perhaps we—

"Stop where you are!"

I drop immediately to the ground and scoot behind the nearest tree. I look back and see Jamon frozen, camouflage magic spreading rapidly across his body until he looks like nothing more than air, snow, and shadows.

With my back against the tree, I hear someone chuckle and say, "I can see you. Well, I can see your outline. It's a good disguise, but not good enough."

I twist my neck and lean slowly to the side until I can just see past the tree. Four guardians in dark blue uniforms stand with arrows and blades pointed at Jamon. The one in front is the dark-haired guy who spoke with the merman owner of the Underground bar. The other three must be the companions I couldn't see while hiding behind the couch.

"Look, we're not interested in hurting anyone," the dark-haired guy says, "so why don't we put away our weapons, you drop the transparency act, and we all have a civilized conversation."

A civilized conversation, my butt. They'll probably mark Jamon as soon as they get hold of him. I pull my white cloak tighter, making sure the hood covers my head, then creep away in a wide circle.

"Okay, look, I'll put my weapon away first," the guardian says. Through the spindly trees, I see the bow and arrow's glow disappear. I continue sneaking around them, my feet barely touching the snow as I keep myself elevated. Finally, as the front guardian holds both hands up and urges Jamon to show himself, I stop directly behind them.

"We've all put our weapons away," the girl in the group says. But I can see a knife strapped to her thigh, so I don't trust her.

The guardian in front lowers his hands and takes a few steps toward Jamon.

I raise my hands and find my favorite weapon blazing in my grasp. "Stop right there!" They spin around so quickly I almost miss the movement itself. One second their backs are facing me, and the next thing I know I've got four sets of glowing weapons pointed at me. "I know you're lying," I say, "and there's no way you're taking either of us without a fight."

The dark-haired guy pushes past his companions, his weapon vanishing in an instant. He stares intently at me, as though trying to see past the shadow of my hood. He comes closer, slowly, step by step. I can see his blue eyes and the shock on his face.

"I said *stop!*" I yell. What is wrong with this guy? Does he want an arrow through his neck? My fingers twitch, split seconds away from releasing the—

"Violet," he whispers, and my hand jerks in surprise. The arrow sails past his ear, but only because he flinches out of the way. "*Flipping* … You just shot at me!" He looks horrified, but he doesn't back away. "Violet. It's you, isn't it?"

A shiver electrifies my skin. He knows my name. He *knows* me. But he's marked. He's on the other side now. As much as I want to ask him a zillion questions, it isn't worth it to end up as Draven's slave.

So I stand firm and say, "Stay back or I'll shoot you again." He's getting way too close. He could reach out and touch my hand if he wanted to.

"Shoot him and we'll shoot you," the girl behind him says.

"And then *I* will shoot *you*," Jamon says, walking out the shadows and taking his position beside me. "Or stab you." From the corner of my eye I see light glinting off a blade.

"No!" The guardian in front of me raises his arms as if to hold his companions back. "There won't be any shooting or stabbing." He leans forward, distress plain on his face. "V, do you honestly not recognize me? Are … are you marked?"

"No. But you are."

"I'm not—"

"Show me your palms," I snap.

He slowly turns his hands so that his palms face forward. I can clearly see the black circle marking his skin. "It isn't real," he says. "It's our disguise so we can go unnoticed among Draven's followers."

"Oh really? Well, isn't that convenient?"

He slowly moves his left hand in front of his face and blows into it.

"What are you doing?" I demand. "Stop that!"

He lowers his cupped hand, and I see water glistening in it. He lets the water trickle onto his right palm, then takes his thumb and rubs across the mark. Black ink smudges his skin.

"See? It isn't real." His blue gaze moves across my face. "Come on, it's me. Ryn. Please tell me you remember me."

Ryn. The mention of his name sends another shiver across my skin. "What … what did you say your name is?"

I see a flicker of hope in his eyes. "Ryn. Oryn."

It can't be. This is the guy who wrote the note I've been carrying around with me? The guy I must have cared about in my previous life? But … *nothing* about him seems even remotely familiar. I slowly loosen my grip on my bow. It disappears. "I … I'm sorry. I don't know who you are."

He doesn't respond. He doesn't even move until one of the other two guys says, "Ryn? You okay, man?"

He blinks, then steps back, looking around at his companions. "Yeah. Lose the weapons, okay? V, you're coming with us. You're welcome to bring your friend."

"Excuse me? I'm not going anywhere with you." Sure, I have a lot of questions to ask him, but he doesn't get to push me around just because he used to know me.

He frowns. "Where exactly do you plan to go?"

"With my friend. There are a whole lot of us in hiding, and I don't plan to abandon them. Why don't *you* come with *us*?"

Ryn's eyes move to Jamon. "There are more of you? I mean, more *free* reptiscillas?"

"Yes. Are there more of you?"

The girl behind Ryn laughs and walks forward. "There are a *lot* of us. And we have a massive hidden base where everyone who's willing to fight Draven is gathering."

Jamon turns to me, lowers his voice, and says, "I think we should go with them."

I start nodding as I process this new information. A whole base of guardians. I probably know some of them. Maybe I have family members there. They can help me remember the life I've lost. But Jamon … "Are you sure?" I ask him. "You hate guardians."

"Yeah, I know, but they can't all be that bad. I mean, you

turned out to be a decent person. And besides, I don't have to *like* them. The point is that we need allies, and they're just as willing to fight Draven as we are."

"Okay. You can send a message to your father once we're there." I turn back to the group of guardians. Ryn is facing the darkness, his arms crossed and hands clenched into fists. From the way his shoulders rise and fall, I can tell his breathing is faster than it should be.

I push my hood back and say, "Okay, we'll come with you."

"Cool," the girl says.

"Um, am I supposed to remember any of you?" I can imagine myself asking this question many times if I'm about to meet a whole lot of guardians.

"No." She laughs and sticks her hand out. "I'm Em."

I reach forward and grasp her hand. "Violet."

"Violet, huh?" Her eyes skim over my hair. "Looks like your parents had the same idea mine had." She points to her head—blonde with green streaks—and adds, "My full name's Emerald. *Emerald*, for crying in a magic well. *No one* calls me that."

"Not if they want to live to see another day," one of the two guys says. He's the shorter and broader of the two, with curly black-and-blonde hair. He smiles as he steps forward to introduce himself. "I'm Max. I'm from the London Guild, like Em."

The other guy, who doesn't seem as friendly as Max, introduces himself as Fin, from the Estra Guild. He's so pale he's almost transparent. White skin, white hair, white eyes. He looks like he's never met the sun.

"So, this base of yours," Jamon says as Ryn leads the way through the trees without another glance at me. "Is it far from here?"

"Yes, but we have transport," Em says with a wink. "Some teams still travel by foot, but we're lucky."

"Or stupid," Fin mutters.

"You guys are a team?" Jamon asks.

"Yup," Em answers. "We're Team Troll's Butt."

I find myself choking on unexpected laughter while Fin gives Em a look that says, *What is wrong with you?*

"What?" she asks. "I'm not going to apologize for myself. Every team needs some comic relief, and I feel it's my duty to provide that for this team."

Fin shakes his head while Max tries to smother a laugh. Ryn is ahead of us, so I can't see his reaction.

"Come on, Fin," Em says. "What happened to your sense of humor? People tell me you used to have one."

With a dead straight face, Fin says, "I guess it disappeared along with The Destruction."

I wonder if Fin lost people he loves or if he's just taking life seriously now because nothing since The Destruction seems to be worth joking about. I'm pretty sure I agree with him, but Em continues as if nothing's wrong. "Nonsense. I saw you laughing your ass off when Max got too close to the backside of a pegasus and found himself kicked clear across the room."

"So?"

"So I guess The Destruction spat your sense of humor right back at you after you tried to ditch it and get all serious."

"Um, where did the team name come from?" I ask, hoping to dispel a possible argument.

Max grins and says, "When Ryn told Oliver, 'I don't give a troll's butt what anyone else thinks about magic carpets. We're using one.'"

"Magic carpets?" I ask.

"Yes." Ryn stops and turns to face us. "We travel by magic carpet." He looks up at the sky and makes a chirping sound. The same chirp I heard earlier when a shadow flew over us. Moments later something dark and flat swoops down from the sky, spins around a tree, and comes to rest in front of us, hovering a few inches above the ground.

A carpet. Big enough for at least ten people to sit on.

"Wow," Jamon says. "I thought magic carpets didn't exist. Just one of those spells no one could ever get right."

"Yeah, that's what everyone thought," Em says as she climbs on, "which is why we were the only team happy to use it."

"And it's safe?" Jamon asks.

"Of course." Ryn sounds a little annoyed. "We made some adjustments. Put a domed shield over the top so we can travel at high speeds without anyone falling off."

I climb onto the slowly rippling fabric and sit down before anything embarrassing can happen. "Cool. I've never ridden on one before."

Ryn coughs and gives me a pained look.

"What?"

He shakes his head. "Nothing. Let's just get out of here."

CHAPTER 13

I THOUGHT THE EGG-SHAPED REPTISCILLAN TRANSPORTERS were fast, but they were nothing compared to the speed Ryn manages to make the magic carpet fly at. If he hadn't put a shield over it, the wind would have swept us away long ago. Ryn sits up front, neither looking back nor speaking to anyone. The other three members of his team chat quietly to each other, and Jamon —biggest guardian-hater of all time—joins in, telling them about the mountain we've taken refuge in.

Not long after the sun rises, we're zooming high above grassy fields and shooting toward a valley in the distance. We slow down as we reach it. Just as we sail over the rim, a bright orange light flashes and fizzles around us, then disappears.

"What was that?" I ask in alarm, getting onto my knees and looking over the edge of the carpet. "Is someone attacking us?"

"No, no, don't worry," Max says. "There's a giant dome of protection over the entire valley. It only lets unmarked people through."

"Oh. Cool." I sit back down.

The magic carpet zips between trees and rocks on its descent into the valley. Then, before I have time to gasp, shout, or even point, the carpet dives straight into the river. For a second, I expect to find myself submerged in foaming bubbles, but then I remember the shield covering the carpet. I breathe normally and watch water, stones, plants and underwater life shoot past us. Up ahead, the water foams white. Bubbles surround the carpet and its dome, gurgling and churning. Seconds later, we shoot out into a high-ceilinged room long enough and wide enough to be a landing strip. Closed doors line the empty strip.

Ryn brings the carpet to a halt, and a popping sound indicates the shield is gone. We climb off. Em stretches her arms out above her head while Max and Fin roll the carpet up with a flick of their hands in the air. Ryn opens one of the doors leading off the landing strip, and the other two guys send the carpet flying into it.

Ryn closes the door and turns to Jamon. "Hey, um, would it be okay if Max, Fin and Em show you around? I need to talk to Vi."

After a glance at me, Jamon shrugs and says, "Yeah, okay. I just need to send a message to my father to let him know we're here."

"Sure," Em says.

A space between two doors houses a wide flight of stairs. I follow Ryn up them. Then up another flight of stairs, and another and another. When I've lost count, he turns right and heads along a corridor. He walks so quickly I can't get a good look at where I am. He reaches a door, pushes it open, and steps back to allow me in. It's a bedroom, and I assume it belongs to Ryn. Other than the basics—bed, table and chair against a wall, small chest of drawers beside the bed, armchair in one corner—it's quite bare. The only personal touch is a stack of books and a small wooden box on the table.

Ryn closes the door behind him, leans against it, and lets out a long sigh. I imagine he's been holding that sigh in the entire journey back here. He raises his eyes and looks at me. It makes me uncomfortable, being watched like that by someone I barely know. I don't look away, though. Maybe if I stare long enough I'll remember something about him. The silence stretches between us, making the room feel bigger than it is. I don't know what to say. It's ridiculous, actually. There are so many things I want to ask about who I am, but words seem to flee as I try to take in everything about him. The deep blue in his hair that matches his eyes. The shape of his face. The way he leans against the door. The ring of pale skin around his wrist that—shockingly—seems to match the scar on my own wrist.

And still I remember nothing.

"I don't get it," he says eventually, shaking his head in small motions. "You just *vanished*. What happened to you, V? Why can't you remember anything?"

Something in the way he's looking at me, his eyebrows pinched together, puts me on the defensive. "Are you *blaming* me for this?" I demand, my tongue suddenly finding the words that have escaped me until now. "I have *no idea* what happened. I woke up Underground with the reptiscillas, and I've been with them ever since. I don't remember Creepy Hollow. I don't remember guardians. I don't remember The Destruction. And I don't remember *you*."

The look on his face tells me I may as well have slapped him. "Not at all?" he whispers. "Nothing? Not even from when you hated me?"

That part throws me. "Hated you? But ... well, I got the impression that you and I were, you know, more than friends."

"We are. Were." He steps away from the door, shaking his head. "I don't—"

"Then why did I hate you?"

He starts pacing. "It was a misunderstanding. About my brother. I—he died. A long time ago. And I blamed you because

I was stupid and hurting. And …" He stops and runs both hands through his hair. "None of this matters now. I just … I don't understand what happened. What *do* you remember?"

It's my turn to look away. "Random, fuzzy things. Nothing important. No one who means anything to me."

He stares at me. His mouth is slightly open but no words come out.

I take a deep breath and ask the question I'm almost afraid to know the answer to. "Do I have any family here? Or were they …" I don't want to say it. *Brainwashed. Killed.*

He sits on the edge of the bed and stares at his feet. He seems resigned, as though he's starting to accept my lack of memory. "No. You don't have any family here. You have no siblings. Your mother died on a Guild assignment when you were three. Your father … well, he was also a guardian. Everyone thought he was killed a number of years ago, but you and I discovered recently that he's alive. His faked death was part of a major undercover assignment."

"So I have a father?"

"Yes, but he isn't here. He works for the Seelie Queen."

I take a step back and lean against the table. *So I really am alone.* Well, except for the guy across the room from me. "Um, you wrote me a letter before you left Creepy Hollow."

"Yes." He sits up a little straighter. "You got it?"

I nod. "I found it in my pocket after I woke up." I'm quiet for a while, but he doesn't say anything else. He waits for me to ask my questions. "Where did you go? What was so important that you couldn't tell me anything about it?"

"I …" He hesitates, and I can see him trying to figure out if he should tell me. "Your father sent me to find a weapon that can destroy Draven's power."

"Oh." I'm not sure what I expected him to say, but it wasn't that. "That's a big deal. A *really* big deal. Did you find it?"

He nods. His eyes catch hold of mine and don't let go. "But only one person in the world can use it, and we don't know where that person is." He shakes his head once more. "I wish I'd never gone, V. I wish I'd been there to protect you from whatever happened that night."

I want to look away, but I can't. I want to ask him if I loved him, but that would be awkward. I want to ask him if *he* loves *me*, but that would be even more awkward.

A desperate squealing sound interrupts the silence. I jerk away from the table in fright. Ryn turns to the source of the sound, which seems to be coming from one of his pillows. The pillow shuffles, and out from beneath it comes a mouse. The mouse scurries across the bed faster than any mouse should be able to move and leaps off. By the time it hits the ground, the mouse is gone, leaving a grey cat in its place. The cat streaks toward me, changes into a squirrel, starts clawing its way up my pants, and becomes a bird. I swat at the black shape with blue wings as it flaps around my neck.

"What is—why is this—"

It swoops beneath my hand, lands on my shoulder, and becomes a mouse once more. A mouse that seems to be nuzzling its tiny, cold nose into my neck.

"Ryn, what the freak is going on?" I yell, trying to get the animal off me.

The mouse freezes, then scurries down my clothes. It reaches Ryn's leg in monkey form, wraps an arm around his ankle, and stares up at me with an expression of uncertainty and confusion. I know it's just a shapeshifting animal, but I swear I can see hurt in its eyes.

"Hey, it's okay," Ryn says, reaching down to pat the monkey's head. "She just doesn't remember you, that's all. Once she gets her memory back, everything will be fine."

Wait, I'm supposed to remember this creature? "What—who —is that?"

Ryn bends to pick up the shapeshifter, which transforms into a purple-haired bunny. "This is Filigree. You've had him since your mom died. Your dad didn't want you to be lonely while he was at work."

For some inexplicable reason, I suddenly feel like crying. I blink a few times and say, "And … he can understand what we're saying?"

Ryn shrugs. "Mostly, I think. He's definitely smarter than the average animal."

I step closer to Ryn and run my finger over Filigree's soft, purple fur, from his ears all the way down his back. "I—I'm sorry. I don't hate you. I just got a fright with all the … flapping and stuff." Large black eyes stare up at me. The only response I get is a blink.

Ryn places Filigree on the bed, then walks to the door. "We need to fix you. Now."

Once again I find myself following him along corridors. The floors are tiled and the walls are wood-paneled; it's a whole lot smarter than the reptiscillan hideout. We turn a corner into another corridor, and Ryn almost walks into a ginger-haired faerie reading something on a piece of amber.

"Oh, Ryn, you're back. How was the—oh, is this someone new?" A smile spreads across his face when he sees me, lighting up his gingery eyes. "Did you find more survivors?"

Ryn seems reluctant to stop and chat, but he answers the man's question. "Uh, yes. Oliver, this is Violet. I was going to come and tell you we found her, but I—"

"Violet?" The smile slowly slips from Oliver's face, and he leans closer to the two of us. "*Violet?* The finder?"

Ryn nods.

My gaze swings back and forth between the two of them as I try to figure out what I've missed here. "Finder? Finder of what?"

Ryn shakes his head. "It's … not something …" Then he grabs Oliver's arm and pulls him to the side of the corridor. "Look, she doesn't remember anything." His voice is low, but it's not like they're standing far away; I can hear everything he's saying. "I still have to explain a lot of things to her. I mean, like, everything. Her whole life."

"What?" Oliver looks over his shoulder at me, then back at Ryn. "She doesn't remember *anything*? Not even about Tora? I mean, it happened right there by her home. I was hoping—"

"I really don't think now is a good time to—"

"Tora?" I ask, because I'm not about to pretend I can't hear them. "Who's she?"

Ryn tips his head back and lets out a sigh before looking at me. "Just … someone you knew. Look, Oliver, I'm taking her to Uri to see if he can help. Can I talk to you later?"

"Yes, certainly, of course. But this is great news, Ryn." He clasps Ryn's shoulder and his smile returns. "You *found her*!" He squeezes my arm as he passes, which is pretty weird since he doesn't know me. Or maybe he does. He certainly seems to know *about* me.

We continue down the corridor. "Who's Uri?"

"He's actually a friend of yours. Well, sort of. I mean, you know him a lot better than I do. At least, you did. He was the potion maker at the Creepy Hollow Guild. He makes all kinds of potions, so I thought he might possibly have something that can help you."

"Are there a lot of people here from the Creepy Hollow Guild?"

"No. Uri probably managed to escape because he's small and ugly and people in general like to stay away from him."

I frown. "That sounds rather harsh."

"Well, it's the truth. He's an urisk. They're just not that attractive. You'll probably get a bit of a shock when you first see him. Actually—" Ryn stops walking "—you stay here. I'll go talk to him first." And he heads off once more before I can answer.

I lean against the corridor wall and run my fingers along one of the tiny braids Natesa put in my hair. Then I push away from the wall and follow Ryn. He's been keeping his thoughts locked up since he first realized in the forest that I don't know him. There are things he isn't telling me, but perhaps he's going to say them to this Uri guy.

I peek around a corner and see a pole reaching from the floor to the ceiling in the middle of the corridor. Ryn wraps himself around the pole. When a hole appears in the floor beneath his feet, he slides down and out of sight. *Cool, that looks like fun.* I hurry after him and peer down the hole just in time to see Ryn stop two floors below me. Then the floor seals up and my view of him is gone. I step closer to the pole, but the floor remains intact. I wrap my arms and legs around the cold metal, and that's when the surface beneath my feet vanishes. I slide swiftly down, a lot faster than I was expecting. I tighten my grip on the pole and jerk to a halt at the floor Ryn got off at. Tiles reform beneath my feet. With a shaky laugh, I detach myself from the pole. Another corridor stretches out ahead of me, with doors here and there. I walk forward, keeping my footsteps quiet. A strange smell hangs in the air, pungent and unpleasant. As I near an open door, I hear Ryn's voice.

"… and I really, *really* need you to fix something."

A gravelly voice that sounds much older than Ryn's responds with, "You people are always walking in here with demands."

"I guess we are, but you'll want to listen to this one." There's a pause before Ryn says, "We found her."

Silence. I hear a shuffling walk, and then Uri says, "You found Violet?"

"Yes."

"Oh, thank goodness. Is she okay? Where is she now? Will anyone mind if I visit—"

"Uri, wait. There's something else. She … she doesn't remember anything. She doesn't remember *me*. *At all.*" Ryn's footsteps move across the floor. He's probably pacing again. "I can't tell you how I felt when I first saw her. I swear, my relief and joy were so intense they almost knocked me over. My brain was screaming, *She's safe! You found her!* All I wanted to do was wrap my arms around her and never let go—and then she tried to shoot me straight through the neck."

"Hmm. That can't be the first time that's happened."

"No, but at least she used to know who she was trying to hurt. This time there wasn't the slightest glimmer of recognition in her eyes. And … Uri, I'm going to go flipping insane! I finally have her back. Everything in me aches to touch her and kiss her and hold her, but she'll *completely* freak out if I do because I'm nothing but a stranger to her. A stranger, dammit!"

Okay, maybe I should have stayed up there where Ryn told me to. I wanted to know what he was thinking, but this is a little too much. I turn around and tiptoe back to the pole. *Great, how am I supposed to get back up?* There must be stairs somewhere. I hear footsteps behind me. *Too late.*

"V?" Ryn says. "What are you—I told you to wait up there."

I swivel around. "Well, perhaps I don't like you telling me what to do."

He rolls his eyes. "Same old Violet," he mutters, "even if you don't remember anything."

I follow Ryn back down the corridor. "Can Uri help me?" I feel a twinge in the region of my stomach at the possibility that I might just be about to get my memories back. It's what I want, of course, but it scares me at the same time.

"He doesn't know. He wants to ask you some questions."

The unpleasant smell gets stronger as we enter a laboratory with several parallel workbenches. Glass beakers and cylinders of all shapes and sizes cover the benches. Most of them are filled with liquid of varying colors. Sparks jump from a giant pot in a corner, and puffs of smoke rise here and there, joining the haze that hangs near the ceiling. The whole room looks like a disorganized mess to me, but perhaps Uri enjoys working in chaos.

"Violet!"

I jump as I see the short creature coming around a workbench toward me. His head is completely bald and weirdly misshapen. Wrinkled skin hangs from his scrawny body, and the hair that's missing from his head seems to have found a home in random patches on his arms and legs. My body wants to shudder at the sight of him, so I focus on the broad smile stretching across his face. It works. I find myself smiling back, caught up in the radiance of this ugly creature's joy.

"Violet, my dear, dear girl." He takes my hands in both of his. His skin feels worn and leathery, and I see a few scars and burns across his knuckles. Potions work can be dangerous, I guess. "I'm so relieved you're not in the clutches of our enemy," he says.

"Yeah, me too. So, Ryn thinks you might be able to help me."

"Possibly, possibly." He lets go of my hands and hoists himself up onto a high stool. "Is it true that you don't remember anything before The Destruction?"

"Well, I remember a few things, but they aren't very clear. And none of them seem that important."

"Okay. Why don't you sit here—" he pats the stool next to him "—and tell me everything you remember."

CHAPTER 14

WE TALK FOR A LONG TIME. URI ASKS RYN IF HE NEEDS TO be somewhere else, but Ryn clearly isn't interested in going anywhere. In fact, it seems like he plans to run through every person I've ever known and every incident that's ever happened to me. *Do you remember Raven? Do you remember Flint? Do you remember Nate? Do you remember Amon?*

Most of my answers are 'no,' as I knew they would be. *No, no, no, and ...* "Amon? I can picture a guy called Amon surrounded by loads of books. Is that right?"

With a nod, Ryn says, "Yeah. He was the head librarian at our Guild. We haven't seen him since The Destruction."

And so it continues. Until Ryn has exhausted his supply of questions, and I'm starting to feel the need to scream. Uri sits quietly on his stool, tapping his chin with a skinny finger and murmuring, "Interesting."

I lean my elbows on the bench, slide my hands into my hair, and stare at two beakers stirring themselves with glass spoons. Apparently patience isn't a virtue of mine, because the words *what's so freaking interesting* are threatening to tear themselves free of my lips.

"It's fortunate for you that I'm here," Uri says eventually, "because I'm almost certain I'm the only one who knows what happened to you."

My hands fall away from my head, and I sit up straight. "You are? What happened?"

"I don't think it's an answer you're expecting."

"Whatever it is, just tell me."

He nods slowly. "Okay. No one did this to you, Vi. I believe you did it to yourself."

"What?" I grip the edges of my stool tightly. "Why would I do that?"

"*Why?*" He raises his hands. "I have no idea. I think I can help you with the *how,* though. Several months ago, you came to me with an unusual request. Someone had broken your heart, and you were so angry and upset that you wanted to forget you ever cared for him. I created a potion for you, but I didn't trust it, so I recommended you didn't take it."

"But you think I did," I whisper.

"I think something happened during The Destruction that made you decide to take it. And it didn't make you forget only that specific person you wanted to forget. It made you forget everyone and everything you've ever cared about. So you remember the librarian and the man who guarded the entrance because you weren't close to them. You remember basic spells and magic, but nothing that has to do with being a guardian—because you loved that life."

Ryn's fist thumps down onto the workbench, causing Uri, me, and a number of glass objects to jump. "Why did you give her the potion if you didn't trust it?"

Uri shakes his head and raises his skinny shoulders. "I suppose I didn't think it had the potential to go *that* wrong. And Violet's always been a sensible person. I didn't think she'd actually take it."

Ryn closes his eyes and mutters, "I don't think The Destruction left any of us in a sensible frame of mind."

* * *

We leave Uri's lab after he promises to try and come up with a potion to counteract the effects of the one I took. I'm not exactly hopeful, though; the last potion he gave me certainly didn't work the way he planned.

After finding one of the many unused bedrooms for me to sleep in—I guess the guardians who built this place ages ago were expecting a lot more people to use it—Ryn leaves me alone with little more than a short "Get some rest." It's difficult to read him, but I'm pretty sure he's angry with me. I don't blame him. *I'm* angry with myself. I know The Destruction was a terrible, horrible thing to live through—I've heard too many stories not to know that—but it was a selfish and cowardly thing to make myself forget everything. And having spent the past several weeks blaming it on some non-existent person makes it even worse.

I curl up on the bed, trying to push away the blanket of shame that wants to wrap itself around me. I won't go there. I won't wallow. I'll rest, as it's been a while since I slept, and perhaps when I wake up Uri will have something that can fix the mess I've made of myself.

* * *

The loud knock startles me from an underwater dream of mermaids and turquoise hair and deep blue eyes that watch me with sadness. I sit up and push my hair back. "Come in." My voice is croaky. I clear my throat and watch the person whose eyes are still swimming in my mind enter the room.

"Sorry, I know you've only been asleep a few hours," Ryn says, "but there are important things we need to talk about."

"That's okay. I don't need much sleep." I push the covers away and try to erase the image of Ryn floating in water just out of reach.

"Um, there's a bathing room at the end of this corridor, if you want to use it," Ryn says. "Do you know how to get to my room from here?" I nod. "Okay, meet me there when you're done." He leaves, closing the door behind him. I wanted to ask him where Jamon is, but that'll have to wait a few more minutes.

After washing myself in a pool of magenta colored water with matching bubbles—that popped and vanished along with the water when I got out—I walk down one flight of stairs and find Ryn's bedroom. There's no reply when I knock, so I let myself in. Another armchair has been added to the room, probably so that one of us doesn't have to sit on the bed. I wander over to the table against the wall and pick up one of the books. It's a collection of poetry by someone I don't recognize. Did Ryn rescue these books from his home in Creepy Hollow, or did he get them here? Perhaps the base has a library.

I turn my attention to the wooden box resting beside the books—and my heart tumbles over itself when I see my own name engraved on the lid. I run my finger over the grooves of the letters. I place both hands on the sides of the box and try to lift the lid. Nothing happens. It must be—

The door behind me creaks open. I swivel around quickly. Cold guilt rushes over me, even though the box I was trying to open must surely belong to me. Ryn frowns, his hand still on the door handle. "What did you do?"

"Um ..."

His eyes slide to the table behind me. "Oh, the box. It's yours, V. You don't need to feel guilty about looking at it." He closes the door while I turn back to the box. I pick it up and carry it with me to one of the armchairs.

"So what's the story? Why do you have it?"

Ryn sits in the armchair opposite mine and leans forward, elbows on his knees. A sad smile stretches his lips before he says, "I wish you knew how badly you wanted that box. Your mother left it for you, but … it got lost. You've never even seen it before."

I rest the box on my knees and touch the hole where a key should fit. "Where did you find it?"

"Underground. I have contacts there who were keeping an eye out for it. On one of my recent visits I checked in with one of them. Turned out he'd found the box. I just had to … *retrieve* it from its latest owner."

I raise an eyebrow at the word 'retrieve.' "Does that, by any chance, mean *steal*?"

"It's not stealing if it originally belonged to you, is it?" He nods toward the box. "Go ahead. Open it."

"But it's locked."

"Well, isn't it convenient, then, that you have a key."

"What—" I stop and reach for the gold chain around my neck. My fingers find the tiny gold key with its outspread wings. The key that's been hanging around my neck since the day I woke up. Is this the key he's talking about? As if he can hear my thoughts, Ryn nods.

"There's probably nothing inside," I say, more to myself than to Ryn. "I mean, if it's been lost Underground for so long, it's probably been forced open already and its contents removed."

"Protective enchantments," Ryn says as he leans back in his chair, watching me. "Only the key can open it."

I unfasten the chain's clasp and hold the key between my fingers. I insert it into the hole on the front side of the box, turn it, and hear a small click. I lift the lid and tilt it all the way back so it rests on its hinges. Inside is a folded piece of paper. I expect it to look aged and discolored—after all, it must have been written fifteen years ago or more—but it looks new. Perhaps the enchantments protected it against aging as well.

I remove the page and unfold it. A curling script marks the paper in dark ink. I start reading, the hairs on my arms rising and my heart thumping as though trying to break free of my chest.

My darling child,

You have not even been born and already a burden has been laid upon your shoulders. I met an elf woman today. It wasn't a meeting that was supposed to happen, but now that I think about it, all the events of the day conspired perfectly so that I would be in that room with her at that precise moment. Alone.

She came up to me, having never spoken a word to me before, and said, "You will have a daughter. She will play a role in bringing great evil into our world. But she will also be the one to undo that evil."

I was afraid, thinking the woman must be crazy. But then she told me things about myself. Things that only I should know. I started to believe her—and that made me even more afraid. Afraid for you, my precious child, and afraid for our world. I asked her what great evil she was talking about. She said one word that sent shivers scurrying all over me.

Tharros.

It was his power that I'd spent so many years trying to find. His power that I'd finally realized was pure evil and could never be used for good the way I'd always wanted to use it. Is this my punishment for seeking out that power? Will you have to pay the price for the delusions that consumed me for so long? If so, I can never apologize enough.

"Your daughter will save a halfling boy from death," the elf woman said, "and that boy will one day choose to take Tharros' power into himself. Your daughter will be responsible for that

choice. She will also be the one to send his power to its final resting place."

I wanted her to explain further, but she was gone before I could ask anything else.

I'm still not sure I should be writing this down. If it falls into the wrong hands, someone might try to hurt you before any of this can happen. But I'm also afraid that I might not be around to tell you this, and when the time comes, you won't know what to do.

Whatever happens, I love you with all my heart, my dear child. Your mother

I lower the page and stare at the rug on the floor. I didn't notice it before. It's dark green with a grey pattern of squares.

"Well, what does it say?" Ryn asks.

Without a word, I hand the page to him. His eyes scan quickly across the words, his frown growing as he gets closer to the bottom of the page. When he reaches the end of the letter, he stands abruptly. His eyes stare through the page at something far beyond it as he says, "It is him. I suspected, but I never thought he could actually … But he did." Ryn is quiet for a moment before he blinks and looks up at me, as though realizing suddenly that I have no idea what he's talking about. "I know who Draven is."

Still partly stunned from what I've just read, I whisper, "Who is he?"

"His real name is Nate. He's the same person you wanted to forget. He's the reason Uri made that potion for you. He was supposed to be nothing more than an assignment to you, but …" Ryn looks down at the letter. "Well, it's a long story, but he became more to you than that. You cared about him. And he betrayed you to Zell, the Unseelie Prince. When he came to find you in Creepy Hollow to apologize and explain his actions and ask your forgiveness, you told him you never wanted to see him again." Ryn walks back to the armchair and sits on the edge of the cushion. "If he was angry and heartbroken, he would have been in the perfect position to kill Zell and take Tharros' power for himself."

Ryn's words are like a story about someone else's life. "He … he can't be much older than us then," I say. "Considering how powerful he is, I was imagining someone far more experienced."

"I think we were all imagining that."

I take the letter from Ryn and read it again. Then I drop my head into my hands and let the paper float to the floor. "I'm responsible for everything that's happened," I moan. "That's what the letter says. I mean, I already knew about the assignment where I saved Draven from death—there was a reptiscillan woman who told me about that—but the fact that I'm responsible for his decision to take Tharros' power? And then to use it to destroy everything? That makes me, like, *doubly* responsible. I should never have been born, Ryn. That's what the letter is basically telling me. None of this would ever have happened if I didn't exist."

"Yes, it would have." Ryn pulls my hands away from my face, and I find him crouching on the floor in front of me, his eyes fierce. "If it hadn't been Draven, it would have been someone else. It probably would have been Zell who took Tharros' power. And maybe he wouldn't have been as powerful as Draven, but he still would have needed to be destroyed. And the part of the letter you seem to be ignoring is the part that says *you* will help put an end to Tharros' power. So stop feeling sorry for yourself and let's figure out how we're going to do that."

I stare at him, my gaze moving across his face. I nod, pull my arms gently from his grasp, and say, "Okay. Tell me what I need to do and I'll do it."

He returns to his chair. "Okay. Here it is: We have a weapon that can supposedly destroy Tharros' power. It's a sword, and only one person can use it. But no one knows who or where that person is. You—" he points at me "—are the only one who can find that person."

"I am? That's how I'm going to put an end to Tharros' power?"

"Yes. We have no way of finding the Star—that's what the words on the sword call this person—without you. That's why Oliver was referring to you as the 'finder' earlier."

"Right." I have a feeling I'm about to disappoint Ryn once again. "And ... *how* exactly am I going to find this person?"

Ryn leans his head back against the armchair and sighs. "This would be so much easier if you hadn't swallowed that damn potion."

"Yeah. I know. But I did. So can you please just tell me what magic trick I'm supposed to perform to find this Star?"

"You hold something that belongs to a person and your mind will tell you where that person is. Anywhere in the world. That's your magic trick."

I narrow my eyes at him, waiting for a laugh or a punch line. Because that has to be a joke, right? There's no spell that can find a person that easily.

He doesn't even crack a smile.

"Are you joking?" I ask. "Because I was joking when I said 'magic trick.'"

"No joke. You, Violet Fairdale, can do something that no one else can do: You can find people."

"By holding something that belongs to them?"

"Yes. Holding one of their belongings creates a connection to them. If you already know the person, then the connection's already there."

"But I don't know the Star."

"No."

"And nobody else knows the Star, so you obviously don't have something that belongs to him or her."

"Her. And no."

Is he being intentionally dense? "So," I say slowly, "don't we have a problem then?"

"Well, just think about it." He leans forward. "The sword can *only* be used by the Star. Doesn't that mean it technically *belongs* to her?"

I wind a piece of hair around my finger. "I guess. Maybe."

"Well, it's the only idea I've got, so it'd better work."

"And what if I don't know how to do it anymore? Find people, I mean."

He raises an eyebrow. "V, you may not know this about yourself, but you have never backed down from a challenge. If you don't remember how to find people, you won't stop trying until you figure it out."

I suppose that sounds right. When I couldn't get my guardian weapons to appear, I let Jamon scare me over and over until I was confident I could reach for them every single time.

"Why don't you try it now?" Ryn says.

Now? I feel immediately self-conscious. I'd far rather try out this finding thing in private. But Ryn is waiting expectantly, and I'm not supposed to back down from a challenge, right? I stand up and walk over to one of the corners. If I'm about to embarrass myself, I'd rather not do it *right* in front of him. "Um, who should I find? And don't I need to hold something that belongs to that person?"

"Not if you already have a connection to him or her. So it needs to be someone you have a relationship with. I imagine there aren't too many people who fall into that category right now." There's a hint of bitterness in his voice, which I choose not to dwell on.

"So, like, Jamon?"

"Yes." Ryn stands and walks around to the back of his armchair. He leans on the back rest and stares at his hands. "I imagine you have a connection with the reptiscilla."

Something in the way he says those last few words makes me ask, "Do you have something against reptiscillas?"

He shakes his head slowly. "Not in general, no. In fact, I'm probably one of the most open-minded guardians you'll come across."

"So ... you have something against Jamon?"

"Look, it's not important, V. We just need to know whether you can find him or not. So close your eyes and—"

"Wait, are you *jealous*?"

"Violet!" Ryn's hands are clenched around the back of the chair. "You have no idea what I've been through since The Destruction. You have no idea how much you mean to me. You don't know how my mind has tortured me with all the terrible things that could have happened to you. And when I finally find you—alive and safe—you don't have a flipping clue who I am, and you're traveling around with another guy. Of course I'm jealous of him!" He pushes the chair out of his way and comes toward me. "You know him a whole lot better than you know me, yet I've been part of your life since *the day you were born*."

I back into the corner as Ryn gets closer, realizing I have no idea whether or not he has a tendency to get violent when he's angry. "It isn't my fault I don't remember you, Ryn."

"Isn't it? You're the one who took the stupid potion, V. You don't have anyone to blame but yourself."

He's right. I know he is. And I hate it. "Fine. I'm sorry I acted like a coward. Is that what you want to hear?"

"No! I want to hear you talk to me like you actually know me. And why do you keep backing away from me? Do you think I'm going to *hit* you? What kind of monster do you think I am?"

"I don't know, do I? You're certainly angry enough to be a monster."

"I'm angry because you're so ridiculously stubborn that you won't just accept responsibility for what you did and apologize like you actually mean it."

I push away from the wall, closing the distance between us. "And I don't see why I should be apologizing to you!"

His face is so close I can feel his breath on my skin. His voice is quiet when he says, "You wanted to forget everything, Violet. And you know what that says to me? You wanted to forget me too."

CHAPTER 15

RYN LEAVES ME ALONE IN THE ROOM WITH NOTHING BUT the echo of a slammed door and Filigree's twitching squirrel face peeping from the half-open top drawer beside the bed. I flop down into the armchair with a groan. "This is such a mess, Filigree. I need to fix it." A *meow* makes me look up. Cat-formed Filigree, black with one white paw, sits in the middle of the bed and watches me. "Are you also angry with me?" I ask. He blinks and flicks an ear. "Well, I'm not quite sure what that means, but I'll take it as a 'yes.' And I'm sorry, Filigree. I really am. I didn't mean to desert you."

I tilt my head back and close my eyes. I should go after Ryn and apologize. Perhaps I should give him a little more time, though. I don't want him to end up shouting at me again. My thoughts turn to Jamon. I realize I haven't seen him since we got here. Hopefully he's catching up on sleep instead of getting stressed out by the fact that he's surrounded by guardians.

My eyes pop open as something occurs to me. If I can find Jamon using this ability I supposedly have, then I won't have to guess what he's doing. I take a breath and let my eyelids slide shut again. I think of Jamon and try to picture the base around me.

I've only seen a little bit of it, so most of the picture is imaginary. I relax, try not to feel completely stupid, and let my mind wander. It travels along corridors, brushing against people. It begins to soar, gaining speed as it rushes past more and more people and shoots out through a waterfall and over a river. On and on, streaking so fast I can't make out the land below me. The next instant, I feel like I'm hanging in midair. I start to drop.

I open my eyes with a gasp. I'm still safe in my armchair in Ryn's room, my fingers clutching at the armrests. "That can't be right," I mutter. I should be seeing Jamon somewhere in this base. I guess I did something wrong and my imagination took over to fill in the gap.

I push myself up and head to the door, waving goodbye to Filigree before I leave. I don't have a clue where Ryn might be, so I ask the first person I come across if she's seen him. After two negatives, the third person I pass says he saw Ryn in the dining room. I follow his directions down one level and into a large hall humming with chatter. Rows of tables and benches line the floor. People carry trays of food to and from a serving area. Above the hatch on a white patch of wall, words form as though painted by an invisible hand:

Make sure your amber has the latest anti-tracking spell embedded in it before contacting anyone. Visit the second floor below ground for anti-tracking updates.

The words vanish only to be replaced by another message:

DO NOT use mirrors for communication with the outside world. If you have no other option, visit the second floor below ground for supervised mirror use.

I start walking around the edge of the hall, searching for Ryn. The words on the wall change again.

Lunch will be over in 10 minutes.

The ten starts ticking down, but moments later the announcement is replaced by yet another message. Something about flying trays being dangerous. I ignore it and continue searching. A shock of white hair catches my attention amongst the colorful heads. Fin. I look further down the same table and see Ryn along with the rest of Team Troll's Butt. I smile to myself as I head toward them; I can't even *think* the name without wanting to laugh.

I reach the table and notice that Jamon isn't there. He must be sleeping like I thought. Ryn stands when he sees me. "Um, can I talk to you?" I ask. I feel awkward now that everyone at the table is looking at me.

He nods and heads to the edge of the room. I follow close behind. He leans against the wall and pushes both hands into his pockets. "Sorry about slamming the door on you," he says. "That wasn't my most mature moment. I ... well, I kept telling myself I wasn't blaming you for this, but when all those words flew out of my mouth, I realized I was."

"And you were right. There isn't anyone to blame except me." I twist my hands together. "I'm sorry, Ryn. And I mean it this time. I don't know what I was thinking when I took that potion, but I'm pretty sure I didn't do it to forget you."

He looks down at the floor as he nods. "Yeah. I know."

"So ... can we put an end the shouting?"

"You know what's funny?" Ryn says without answering me. "When we were fighting in my room, that felt more like the real us than any conversation we've had since I found you."

"Really?" I feel my eyebrows pinch together. "So … we used to argue a lot?"

"'A lot' would be an understatement."

I nod as I try to figure out what kind of relationship Ryn and I had. I find my nod turning into a shake. "That doesn't really sound … healthy. Or enjoyable."

"There was a lot of kissing too," he adds with a grin. "And, once we got together, the arguing was generally of the good-natured kind."

I smile, but I feel hollowness forming inside me. Is that all I had with this guy? "Arguing and kissing," I say slowly. "Was our relationship about anything more than that?"

"Of course," he says with a laugh. "Way more." I watch his face grow serious. Maybe he can tell I don't really believe him. He comes closer and gently takes my face in both his hands. His eyes won't let me look away. "It was about growing up together. It was about knowing your fears and dreams. It was about forgiveness. It was about making you laugh and being there when you cried. It was about knowing that even if we lived for centuries, I'd never get tired of having you at my side."

I don't know how to respond. I'm terrified he wants me to feel the same way. I carefully remove his hands from my face. "Look, I don't know what to tell you," I say gently. "I know we were together before The Destruction, but I don't know you anymore. You can't expect me to feel the same way you do. It isn't possible."

He steps away, releasing me—finally—from his magnetic gaze. When he looks up at me again, it's with a smile that almost makes me wish I *did* still feel the same way. "Are you telling me I have to win your heart all over again?"

I'm pretty sure that's not what I was telling him, but when he smiles at me like that I think it might not be such a bad idea. So I shrug and say, "I guess."

The smile curls higher, making his eyes sparkle. "Challenge accepted."

"What? No, that wasn't a—"

"Hey, Ryn, I just got us a new mission." Ryn looks over my shoulder. I turn and see Em standing there. "A mission of epic importance," she adds.

"Great, what is it?"

"Uri finished the latest version of his cure for the mark, and guess what?" She leans over and does a drum roll on the nearest table. "It worked! That prisoner we brought back last week is a fully functioning guardian once again. But Oliver wants a team to go out and find other marked people to test the cure on."

"And he wants to send us?"

"Well, not exactly." Em pulls a face. "He was busy telling someone else how he wanted to send a team of older, more experienced guardians, but they're all out on missions. I happened to be eavesdropping at the time, so I volunteered Team Troll's Butt."

"Thanks, Em. You're awesome."

She lifts a shoulder and grins. "What can I say? It's my default setting." She spins around, then looks back over her shoulder. "Oh, and Oliver said Vi can join our team. He figured she'd want to."

"I do. But wait, Ryn." I grab his arm before he can follow Em back to the table. "Don't we need to find this Star person? Isn't that the most important thing at the moment?"

"Well, it's not like we're about to face Draven *right now*. Let's check out this cure first, then we can find the Star." He weaves his way through people carrying empty trays to a hole in the wall beside the serving area.

And let's hope Draven doesn't spring a surprise attack on us tomorrow.

I reach the table as Ryn says to his team, "So, where are we heading to test this cure? The closest marked guardians we know of are in Creepy Hollow, right?"

"I feel another magic carpet ride coming on," Max says with a grin. He stands and starts piling empty trays together.

"Yes, I think Creepy Hollow is the best option," Oliver says, appearing at our table. He has a rectangle of amber the size of a book balanced on one arm and a stylus in his other hand. "Two guys coming off a lookout shift said they saw a man hiding in the trees about a day from here. But if he's on Draven's side, he'll be able to use the faerie paths. He's probably gone already."

"What's someone doing so close to our base?" Ryn asks. "Shouldn't we be concerned about that?"

"It's probably a coincidence. And it was only one person."

"So he could be a survivor," Em says.

"Could be. I'll send someone to check that out." Oliver writes a note on his amber. "And your team is off to Creepy Hollow." He makes a flicking motion across the amber's screen with his stylus, then writes another few words. "Remember to collect a set of cures from Uri before you leave."

"Oliver," I say as something occurs to me. "If Draven has brainwashed guardians on his side, doesn't that mean he knows exactly where we are? Any one of them could tell him about this place."

Oliver shakes his head. "Guild regulations state that only one Council member from each Guild should know where the safe locations are. Two of us survived and are now here. Every other person who had access to that information was at the Creepy Hollow Guild meeting the night of The Destruction. None of them made it out alive."

I swallow. It's devastating to hear about so many deaths, but it's also a relief to know that we're safe here.

"Right, off you go then, Team … what was it, Em? Troll's Butt?"

"Yes, sir." Em salutes Oliver as a horrified look crosses Fin's face.

"I cannot believe you told him that," he murmurs.

"Oh, lighten up, Fin," Oliver says, clapping Fin's shoulder. "You're far too young to be taking life so seriously." And with that he heads off into the bustle of the dining room.

"Well, forgive me for thinking The Destruction and everything that's happened since is something that should be taken seriously," Fin mutters.

Em touches his arm. "We do take it seriously, Fin. It's just that for people like Oliver and me, if we didn't laugh we'd probably cry. That's just the way we roll." She stands on tiptoe and gives Fin a quick kiss on the cheek. "You should try a smile once in a while. It would look good on you." She pats his arm, then picks up the empty lunch trays and carries them away.

"Okay, everyone get ready. We'll meet down on the transportation level," Ryn says. He nods for me to follow him out of the dining room.

"Hey, I should probably tell you something," I say once we reach the corridor and head toward the stairs. "I tried the finding thing earlier, and it didn't work. I looked for Jamon and my imagination conjured up an image of somewhere in the air way above the ground."

"Oh, yeah, that makes sense. Jamon's on a pegasus right now."

"What?" I stop walking.

"Yeah, sorry." Ryn closes his eyes for a moment and shakes his head. "I was supposed to tell you. He left earlier for the reptiscilla hideout with one of our Council members. They're going to discuss the possibility of bringing all their warriors here to the base."

"He left without saying goodbye to me?" I know we're not

that close, but I wouldn't have expected him to leave without saying anything.

"You were sleeping. He didn't want to wake you." Ryn climbs the stairs, and after a moment's pause, I follow him.

"*You* didn't seem to have a problem with waking me."

"Well, the things I needed to talk to you about were actually important." We reach Ryn's level and he heads to the left.

I roll my eyes and start climbing the next set of stairs. "Whatever. I'll see you down by the magic carpet."

"Bring extra weapons if you've got any," he calls after me. "You never know when they might be useful."

* * *

The magic carpet ride is just as much fun the second time around —well, except for the beginning. Ryn takes off so fast the rest of us shoot backward and land in a heap, pressed up against the dome-like shield covering the carpet. After Max and Fin attack Ryn and the carpet almost steers itself into the river bank, we settle down for a comfortable ride.

We've got several hours to kill, so Max, Em, and Fin fill me in on their stories. Em's parents, like mine, were killed on assignment before she graduated. Instead of scaring her off, it made her even more determined to be a guardian. Oliver is the only family she has left—he's her father's uncle or something like that—and she's been with him ever since The Destruction.

Max picks at the laces of his boots as he tells me what happened that night. He had to watch Draven's army carry away his parents and girlfriend, and there wasn't a thing he could do about it unless he wanted to wind up with the same fate. He hasn't seen them since he joined up with Oliver and Em, but he still believes they're alive. They were excellent guardians, he says. Draven would want them on his side.

Fin doesn't want to talk, but he nods when Em asks if she can tell me what happened. He lost everyone he cared about. He was the only guardian in his family. His parents, older brother, girlfriend, and her family were crushed inside their homes when Draven's enchanted inferno swept through the Estra forest and destroyed everything. He wanted to end his own life, but decided ending Draven's would be more satisfying.

We sit in silence after that, each of us lost in our own thoughts.

Late into the night, with snow falling thickly around us, we arrive at Creepy Hollow forest. We glide above the trees until Ryn judges we're close to where the Guild was before The Destruction. We descend slowly, everyone looking out for possible threats. We pull our jackets, coats, and hoods on—which I notice with a smile are all white now, just like the cloak Natesa made for me—and climb off the carpet. An icy breeze permeates my clothes immediately. I blow into my hands to start the charm that will heat me up while Ryn sends the carpet into the air above the trees to wait for us.

"Are we marking our hands?" Max asks.

Ryn shakes his head. "Not necessary this time. We're not trying to gain anyone's trust to get information. We just want to knock someone out and give him or her the cure. Let's go this way." He indicates for us to follow him. I pull my hood further forward to keep the snow from falling into my eyes. "And don't worry about elevating yourselves this time," he adds. "The falling snow will fill our tracks."

The gathering breeze turns into a wind that sounds like distant screams. Draven must be in a bad mood tonight. I wrap my arms around myself and hug my magically heated clothes.

"Everyone got their extra weapons, just in case?" Ryn asks above the wind.

"Yes," I say, along with the rest of the team. I've got a dagger in each boot and a knife strapped to the top of my right leg.

"Okay, I don't know exactly what we're heading toward. It could be a massive ruin, or it could be a brand new, completely hidden Guild. I don't know if Draven's people have finished rebuilding. So let's split up here. Em, Max, Fin—go that way." He points left. "V and I will go this way. Em, you've got those cures I gave you before we left?"

"Yes."

"If you see someone alone, make them take the cure. Otherwise, stay hidden. Keep me updated on my amber. You've all got the voice-activated messaging spell, right?"

More nods.

"Okay. Let's go."

I follow Ryn. After several minutes of barely being able to see, the snow ceases to fall and the screaming wind disappears. I brush white flakes off my arms as we walk. "Out of curiosity," I say, "what exactly do you mean by 'just in case'? Shouldn't we always be able to use our guardian weapons?"

"We should, but Zell had this method of blocking people's magic. I'd be surprised if Draven isn't doing the same thing to faeries. It's—Whoa. I think we've found what we're looking for." He stops and points ahead.

Through the trees I see a clearing. There are shapes that could be broken walls and piles of rubble. Piles a lot higher than the destroyed faerie homes I saw with Jamon. We head toward the clearing, navigating our way over fallen trees. When we can't go any further without climbing onto the ruins, we stop.

Silence presses against my ears. The snow has returned, but it drifts down in tiny flakes instead of swirling around us in a blizzard. If I let my imagination go, I can almost smell the burning forest the way it must have been that night. The falling snow becomes ash in my mind, covering the landscape in black and grey. But the ash couldn't bury this much wreckage, and neither can the snow. It's still here, like a memorial reminding us of what we've lost.

"So this is what our Guild looks like now," Ryn murmurs.

"This is the first time you've seen it?"

He nods. "I've been Underground a number of times since The Destruction, but I haven't been here to the Guild."

I think about how much worse this moment is for him than it is for me. He knows exactly what's been lost. I can only imagine it. "I wonder how far the damage extends," I say. It's not like we can see much past the large amounts of debris in front of us.

Ryn reaches for the nearest branch and pulls himself up into the tree. "If we get high enough, we can see." I follow his lead and hoist myself up. I could propel myself all the way to the top with magic, but I enjoy the climbing. It feels like something my body's missed. I advance from branch to snowy branch, following Ryn until we can't climb any higher.

"Look at it," he says quietly.

The snow-dusted ruins spread out before us as far as I can see. Silent. Unmoving. "I can't imagine how this was all hidden inside a tree once."

"And beneath the ground," Ryn adds. "Really powerful magic, obviously." He looks around. "I wonder where they're building the new one."

"We'll have to keep searching." I start climbing back down.

"Wait, look. Someone's out there."

I look up to see where he's pointing and follow his hand to where three figures are climbing onto the ruins. "It's the rest of your team, silly," I tell him. "See Fin's white hair when he moves past something dark?"

"We should tell them to stay in the trees." Ryn opens his

jacket and reaches inside, probably for his amber. "If we can see them, someone else might be able to—*Oof!*"

A dark figure slams into Ryn, and he goes crashing through the branches—along with the mysterious figure—toward the ground.

"What the …" I get ready to jump down.

"You're about to join him," a voice behind me says. With a gasp, I turn toward the voice. I catch a glimpse of a woman with dark curly hair before her foot connects with my stomach and shoves me out of the tree.

I slow my fall seconds before I hit the ground, which means I have at least some air left in my lungs when I jump to my feet brandishing my bow and arrow. Ryn struggles with his assailant and manages to flip him over his shoulder. The man scrambles on the ground for a few seconds before jumping up. Ryn backs away and slashes a sword through the air just as the woman lands beside her accomplice.

The four of us freeze, weapons ready, each trying to anticipate the next move.

Without warning, Ryn's sword fizzles and disappears. "Mom?" he says.

CHAPTER 16

"Oryn?" The woman lowers her bow and arrow but doesn't let go. I don't move mine an inch. "Ryn, it's really you!" With a smile, she steps forward. "Where have you—"

"Stop." A knife appears in each of Ryn's hands. "Show me your palm."

She hesitates. Her smile slips. "Ryn, honey, I'm so relieved you weren't hurt. We need to talk about—"

"Show me your palm."

Her bow and arrow disappear, but she doesn't raise her hand. "It isn't what you think, Ryn. It isn't what any of you think. Draven isn't this evil overlord everyone is making him out to be. He wants the best for our world. He wants everyone to be united, both Seelie and Unseelie."

"You're marked, aren't you?" Ryn says, his voice hitching slightly.

"I'm loyal to Draven, if that's what you mean." She raises her right hand so we can see the open circle inked into her skin.

Ryn sucks in a deep breath, and I hear it shake slightly as he lets it out. Guilt washes over me. Why didn't I think to ask Ryn about his family? I've been thinking of no one but myself.

"We have a cure you can take, Mom. You don't have to serve Draven."

She frowns. "But I want to. And you should too. You and Violet can come back with me and—"

"No." Ryn shakes his head. "We're not going anywhere with you. We're going to cure you of the delusion Draven has placed on you. Then you'll know the truth." I see his hand move slowly toward his pocket.

Ryn's mother looks over at her companion, a large man holding a sword in one hand and a sparkling metal disc in the other. Shadows make it difficult to see his face. The bow and arrow return to Ryn's mother's hands as she looks back at Ryn and says, "I don't want to hurt you, but if that's what it takes for you to come back with me, I'll do it. I won't lose my son again."

Ryn shakes his head again. "Don't make me fight you, Mom."

"I'm sorry ..." She raises the bow—then jerks forward and slumps to the ground. Unconscious. Em stands behind her, arms outstretched. The man in dark blue spins around and flicks his wrist. The metal disc sails toward Em, but it strikes an invisible barrier and disappears.

Max and Fin step out from behind the trees and move slowly toward the man, their hands raised as though pushing something through the air. "We've got a shield bubble around him," Fin says. "Give your mom the cure."

"You *stunned* my *mother?*" Ryn shouts as he dashes to the fallen woman's side.

"Yeah." Em rolls her eyes as she reaches inside her jacket. "Never mind the fact that she was about to *shoot* you, Ryn. And it was barely a stun. We didn't have time to gather enough power for that. She'll be awake in a few minutes. Here, give her the cure." Em opens the pouch in her hand and removes a small glass vial.

"Hey, Vi, we could use your help here," Max says. The man is throwing himself at the invisible barrier surrounding him. When he starts shooting sparks of magic at it, Max groans. "He's really strong. I don't know how much longer we can contain him."

I run over and add my own shield around the struggling man. I look over my shoulder at Ryn and his mother. He holds her head up with one hand and pours the vial's liquid into her mouth. "Come on. Wake up and drink it," he urges. Moments later, she coughs and splutters and pushes him away from her. She rolls onto her hands and knees and crawls a few feet away. A shiver passes through her body, and she takes a gasping breath.

Please work, please work, I chant silently. I stumble back as the man batters against my shield. I plant my feet firmly in the snow and strengthen the magic pouring out of me.

Ryn's mother climbs slowly to her feet and looks around at us.

"Did it work?" Max asks. His face is twisted with the effort of keeping his shield intact. "Is she cured?"

She doesn't respond. Her breathing is heavy as she watches the snow at her feet, her eyes flicking across it. Then she clenches her right hand into a fist and says in a dangerously low voice, "That was very stupid of you."

I guess that's a 'no.'

Before I can think of what to do next, I find myself thrown backward onto the ground. I sink into the snow as I throw up a shield once again—to protect myself this time. Sparks shower down and bounce uselessly off the barrier between me and the man in dark blue. I jump to my feet, along with Fin and Max.

Ryn sends a flock of flapping birds at his mother. As she backs away, he drags Em behind him and gets his own shield in place.

"Are we going to do this all night?" His mother shouts from the other side of the shield. The flapping birds have vanished.

"Should we try to stun them and take them back with us?" Em asks. "Five against two. We should be able to do it."

"I don't know. Just let me—"

"Look there!" Max points past our two assailants to the old Guild ruins. Guardians are pouring out of a doorway in one of the broken-down walls.

"Oh … crap," Em whispers.

Crap indeed. We can't fight that many faeries. Our best chance is to—

"Run!" Ryn yells.

I turn and make a dash for it. I keep my shield up behind me as long as I can, but the magic hammering against it soon becomes overwhelming. I let go. Sparks, shards of ice, and grains of sand that sting shoot past us. I duck and dodge and continue running. As far as I can tell, everyone else on the team is still running too. I don't know how close our pursuers are, but I'm not about to waste time looking over my shoulder. I hear a chirping sound from Ryn, and moments later the magic carpet swoops down through the trees. It zooms ahead of us, swerving to avoid the trees.

"Jump on!" Ryn shouts to the rest of us.

The carpet slows, but doesn't stop moving. Ryn reaches it first and jumps. He moves out of the way as Max and Fin leap through the air and land on the carpet. I reach it at the same time as Em. We jump—and Em screams as something tugs her back. I roll across the carpet and look up to see Em hanging onto the tasseled edge with Ryn's mother's hands grasping at her jacket. I lunge across the carpet and grab Em's arms. I pull as hard as I can, and Em tumbles over me as Ryn's mother loses her grip. The dome-like shield goes up around the carpet, and we shoot up through the trees and away from our pursuers.

"Are you hurt?" Ryn shouts back as he steers.

"No," Em says, rubbing her arms. Her breath comes out in gasps. "She got the bag of cures I was carrying, but I'm fine."

"Man, I haven't run that fast in a while," Max says, his breathing matching Em's. "It was quite exhilarating, actually."

I know what he means. I can feel the adrenaline high pumping through my body. Ryn says nothing as we gain speed and the forest slides beneath us faster and faster. I want to say something about his mother, something reassuring or comforting, but I don't know what.

"Wait, what was that?" Em is at the edge of the carpet looking down. "Slow down, Ryn. I saw someone back there."

"We're trying to get *away* from them, Em," Max says.

"No, it was a person in the top of a tree. He wasn't wearing dark blue like Draven's people. It could be a survivor."

"Hiding in a tree?" Max sounds doubtful.

"Yes, and if you were still out there hiding from Draven, you'd want to be rescued too. Ryn, can we go back?"

"Em, it's probably a trap," Ryn says, but I feel the carpet slowing anyway. Ryn twists around and catches my eye. He raises his eyebrows. Is he asking me what I think?

"We should probably go back," I say quietly. "I know if I were alone out there trying to stay hidden, I'd want to be rescued. And if he or she starts attacking us as we get closer, we can always fly away."

Ryn nods and turns the carpet around.

Em leans over and whispers, "Remind me to get *you* to ask him for stuff in the future."

"Em, you're supposed to be looking out for this person," Ryn says.

Em moves to the edge of the carpet again. "There." She points. "See that green shape?"

Ryn nods. "Okay, I'm going to get closer slowly. I don't want to alarm whoever it is."

We glide through the air toward the green shape. It soon becomes clear that it's a man. A man huddled near the top of a tree with his arms wrapped tightly around the trunk. He's looking down at something.

"Hey, I think I know him," Ryn says, steering the carpet around so we can see the man's face beneath his hood. "You know him too, V. At least, you did know him. He was the head librarian at our Guild."

Amon. That's what Ryn said when he was questioning me in Uri's lab, right?

Amon looks up and almost falls out of the tree. His face turns the color of the snow on the branch beside him, and he grips the tree even tighter.

Ryn drops the carpet's shield and calls out, "Amon. It's me, Ryn. Are you okay? I'm not marked." He holds up his hand as proof.

Amon closes his eyes and shudders. He holds up a shaking hand, free of Draven's mark. "I'm s-so glad you found me."

"Here, take my hand," I say. Snowflakes drift onto my arm as I lean over the edge of the carpet and reach out toward Amon. He looks up at me, his moss green eyes filled with fear.

"Violet. You're okay too." He detaches one arm from the trunk and wraps his hand around mine. "I was starting to think I'd die out here." With a clumsy jump, he lands on the carpet beside me. He's a skinny man, lacking the athletic build I'm used to seeing on faeries who are guardians. "You should go quickly," he says. "There are guardians down there. Traitor guardians."

The shield reappears, and Ryn turns the carpet around. Seconds later, we shoot away through the sky. Em, Max, and Fin introduce themselves as Amon pulls off the damp, green cloak he was wearing. It probably doesn't belong to him, considering how short it is.

"So you escaped from the Guild, Amon?" Max asks. "Where've you been hiding since The Destruction?"

"Underground, with the dwarves. There was a massive explosion at our Guild. I got out of there as fast as I could. The messenger dwarves were running too, so I ran with them. I think most guardians who survived stuck around to find out what was going on and to fight whoever was attacking us, but I ..." Guilt twists his features. "I mean, I-I ... I'm just a librarian. I don't know how to fight."

"Hey, no one blames you for running," Em says. "You probably would've ended up brainwashed if you'd stayed there, and that wouldn't have done you or anyone else any good."

"And guess what?" Max adds. "The base we're heading back to has a library. It's small, I think, but it's still a library. You'll feel right at home."

"Oh, that's wonderful." Something resembling a smile finds its way onto Amon's face but doesn't stay there long. The poor man seems traumatized.

"What were you doing in that tree?" I ask.

"Draven's men invaded the dwarves' portion of the tunnels. We ran, and I somehow ended up separated from them. I knew I couldn't use the faerie paths, and I certainly couldn't outrun trained guardians or anyone else from Draven's army, so I climbed. Haven't done that in ..." he shrugs and shakes his head "... well, centuries, I suppose. I wasn't sure I'd be able to do it. I guess fear gave me the strength I needed."

"Fear can do that," Fin says quietly.

Max and Em nod in agreement. I look at Ryn to see if he's nodding too, but he's facing the front of the carpet. Both of his hands are flat on the carpet's surface as he directs its journey through the sky. He's probably thinking of his marked mother, not listening to us.

"And then the five of you suddenly appeared," Amon continues, "and I honestly thought it was them. I thought that was the end for me."

"Well, you can relax now," Em says, patting his shoulder. "We're a lot better hidden than the dwarves."

"That's good. I'm starting to think we might have to hide for the rest of our lives."

"That's not going to happen," Max says. "We have a weapon that's capable of destroying Draven. We just need to figure out how to use it."

Ryn twists around and frowns at Max with a shake of his head.

"We're not supposed to know about that, remember?" Em mutters between clenched teeth.

"You … have a weapon?" Amon asks as his eyes flit between Max, Ryn, and Em. "Is that the one I've read about in old texts? Guarded by a secret Order?"

Ryn turns fully, surprise on his face. I feel the carpet begin to slow as he says, "You know about it?"

"Well, I've been around a lot longer than you may think. Lots of time to read. Study. Learn things. Find out about Tharros and his history."

Ryn slowly swivels back to face the front. The carpet speeds up as soon as he places his palms down. "You know what, Amon?" he says. "I'm really glad we found you. I have a feeling you're going to be a valuable addition to our base."

* * *

"I don't understand why it didn't work," Oliver says. He dumps Ryn's bag of useless cures onto Uri's desk and drops into one of the chairs. "It worked on the prisoner we had. The mark is gone from her hand, and she's horrified at the things she believed and did. Why didn't it work on your mother?"

"No idea," Ryn says. He paces to one side of the cramped office attached to Uri's lab and leans against the wall with his arms crossed. He hasn't said much since we arrived back.

"Perhaps it was specific to the prisoner," I say. Since it's only Oliver, Ryn, Uri, and me in the room, I don't mind making a suggestion that might be way off. There aren't many people to embarrass myself in front of. "Perhaps ... perhaps you have to make a new cure for each person."

I sincerely hope I'm way off.

Uri shifts in his chair on the other side of the desk. "As disheartening as that sounds, it's a possibility. I did use the prisoner's mark as a basis for creating the cure."

"Well, that's hardly practical, having to make a new cure for each person," Oliver says. He places his hands on Uri's desk and pushes himself to his feet. "So, capturing masses of marked fae in order to cure them isn't a plan that's going to work out."

"For more reasons than just a faulty cure," Ryn mutters.

Oliver walks over to him and places a hand on his shoulder. "I know you're upset about your mother, but you can't let that distract you from your determination to fight Draven's rule. In fact, it should strengthen your resolve to see his reign ended. You're an excellent guardian, Ryn. I don't want to see this bring you down."

I feel an ache in my heart for Ryn. He just found out his mother is fighting for the other side. He may never get her back, in which case she's as good as dead to him now, and Oliver won't even allow him a few hours to mourn her. Having seen a little of his temper, I expect Ryn to respond with anger. Instead, he straightens somewhat and uncrosses his arms.

"Yes, sir," he says quietly, his eyes never leaving the floor.

"Good. Now, you can still catch a few hours of sleep before breakfast. After that, we'll be meeting to put a plan in place to find this Star person." His gaze lingers on me, and the fear that I won't be able to find the Star settles on me once more. "The sooner we find her, the sooner we can make our move against Draven."

Oliver leaves through the laboratory. Uri climbs out of his chair and comes around his desk to stand beside me. His head barely reaches my shoulder. "You should probably rest while you can," he says. "You never know when you'll have another chance."

Ryn nods. Without a word, he heads out to the lab. I follow him.

"Oh, and Vi," Uri adds. I turn back to where he's standing in the doorway between the lab and his office. "I'm working on a potion for you, but ..." With a frown, he picks up a round object from a counter attached to the wall. "This wasn't here earlier," he mutters. "I'm not sure what this ..." He shakes his head and replaces the object. "Anyway. Uh, yes, I'm not happy with the potion yet. I'll keep you informed."

"Thanks." I hurry out of the lab after Ryn, wondering if I can really trust a scatterbrained potion maker who made me a dodgy potion once before.

"Ryn," I call out as he turns a corner at the end of the corridor. He stops and waits for me. "Um, are you okay? About your mother. I mean, I know you're obviously not *okay* with it, but ... I guess what I'm asking is ... how are you doing?"

Stop. Blabbering.

Ryn gives me a small smile. "I'm ... a whole lot of things. Angry, upset, worried, determined. I knew there was a possibility of my mom being marked, but it was still a shock to find out for sure. Oliver's right, though. I ..." He runs a hand through his hair and looks away from me. "I have a tendency to act without thinking when it comes to the people I love. But I can't let that happen anymore. I need to be sensible. We need to plan properly. That's the only way we can bring Draven down."

I nod. I can't help wondering if I'm one of the people he loves.

"Well, I'll see you at breakfast in a few hours," he says. He leans toward me—to kiss me? Hug me?—then blinks and takes a step back, as though suddenly remembering that this is the new me and not the old me.

With a sigh, he heads upstairs. I follow after a moment.

Up in my room, I lie on the bed without bothering to change my clothes. I roll onto my stomach and think about sending a message to Jamon. Or Farah or Natesa. I miss them. I have no amber to send a message from, though. I'll have to visit the second floor below ground to see if they can help me out. I also need to ask someone about my father. I know he's working for the Seelie Queen, so he can't just leave to come and visit me, but does he even know that I'm here? Would he *want* to come and visit me if he did?

I haven't asked Ryn anything about him, mainly because I'm afraid of what the answers might be. The kind of father who would fake his death and abandon his daughter might not be the kind of father I want to know about.

After turning over several more times, I eventually fall into a light sleep. I drift below the surface of reality. My dreams become bumpy, rocking me over a sea of trees and snow. An explosion erupts somewhere in the forest ahead of me. I feel myself falling —and I sit up with a start.

People are shouting. The ground shudders.

The explosion was real.

CHAPTER 17

I jump off the bed and rush to my door. I throw it open—and almost collide with Ryn.

"What the hell is—"

"I don't know." He grabs my hand and drags me through the throng of people rushing around in the corridor. "I'm guessing we're under attack. We need to get out of here."

"What?" I pull my hand out of his grip and stop running. "No, if the base is under attack, we have to help defend—"

"You're our only hope of finding the Star, Violet." He grips my shoulders and bends to look me in the eye. "I'm not going to let you die here fighting brainwashed warriors when our real fight is against Draven."

"But we can't leave everyone to—"

"Oliver!" Ryn reaches out and grabs Oliver's arm as he hurries by. "Do I have permission to get Violet out of here?"

"Yes! Go!" Oliver makes a shooing motion with his hands. He turns to leave, but Ryn won't let go of his arm.

"Where's the sword?" he asks.

Oliver hesitates, then leans closer to Ryn. "My room. Break open the wooden paneling behind my bed and you'll find it."

Then he hurries away, shouting at the top of his voice, "You all know where you should be right now!"

"I'm taking Arthur!" Ryn yells after him before catching my hand once again. He pulls me through the crowd, against the flow of people still tugging on shoes and items of clothing as they run. I realize we're by my door again when he says, "Get your jacket and shoes. I'll get the sword. Meet me down at transportation."

My brain kicks into action and sends me dashing into my room. I shove my arms into the thick, padded jacket Farah gave me. I roll up my few belongings, including the not-so-white-anymore cloak, and stuff them into my bag. I pull my boots on; they lace themselves up to my knees as I run out the door, my bag bouncing on my back.

I make my way to the corridor with the pole. When I get there, though, I see a hole in the floor and no pole. The tiles around the hole are cracked and broken.

I turn around and try to remember the way to the nearest staircase. There's no one to ask. The base has become eerily silent. I start running, knowing I'll come across stairs soon enough. I round another corner and see the main stairway. I dash toward it, but as I reach the top step, another explosion shatters the silence. The ground shudders beneath my feet, and I slip and tumble down several stairs before I'm able to stop myself.

"Vi!" Ryn jumps down the stairs and pulls me to my feet. He has a sword and a bag slung over his back. "You okay?"

"Yeah."

The tremor is gone, but I keep my hand on the banister anyway as we run down. Just in case. Dust hangs in the air, and by the time we reach the next level down, we can barely see through the greyish haze. Instead of smooth tiles, I feel rubble crumbling beneath my boots. I stop running and look around. "This is where it happened," I whisper. My eyes search for movement, but I see none. Whoever did this is either hiding or has moved on to attack another level.

"Come on," Ryn says, his foot already on the next step leading down.

"Wait, isn't this the level with Uri's lab?"

"Yes. Lab, training center, spare weapons."

"Shouldn't we—"

"No." He takes my hand and pulls me after him. "As selfish as it sounds, you have to think of yourself right now, not Uri. That's the only way we can end this."

We keep running down. Ryn doesn't let go of my hand. We reach the transport level, but instead of turning left toward the room where the magic carpet is, Ryn sprints across the landing strip to a door almost as wide as the entire dining room upstairs. Two massive levers attached to the door sit in a horizontal position. Ryn goes to the one on the left and points to the other. "Lift that, would you?"

I get beneath the lever and push up—with the help of a little magic—until the lever is vertical.

"Okay," Ryn says as he grasps a handle at the bottom of the door. "Don't freak out." In one swift motion, he slides the door all the way up.

"Why would I—Oh my *freak*." I jump back as an enormous clawed foot slams down on the ground beside me. Scales the color of a burning sun cover a face that rises toward the ceiling high above us. The roar that follows almost deafens me, and the flames that curl from its mouth sear the air.

"A *dragon*?" I say. "We're riding a *dragon*?"

"Yup. This is Arthur."

"That. Is. So. Cool."

Ryn looks at me with new appreciation. "I didn't know you were a dragon fan."

I didn't either, but I'm almost certain that rushing through the air on a magic carpet is *nothing* compared to the thrill of soaring the skies on a dragon's back. "I guess you never asked."

We enter the enclosure, which, although enchanted to look like a forest clearing, isn't exactly big. I imagine Arthur can barely spread his wings in here. Ryn lays a hand on one of Arthur's forelegs, and the dragon bends down so we can climb onto the harness on his back. His scales are smooth and cooler than I expected.

"Is he friendly?" I ask as I settle behind Ryn onto Aruthur's back.

"Sure. Toward people he knows." Ryn pats the dragon's neck. "And yes, he knows me."

Arthur stands up. His body rolls and sways as he heads out of the enclosure, and I almost slide off his back. I grab onto Ryn's jacket.

"Here, put this around your waist." Ryn reaches down for a strap attached to one side of the harness. "Wrap it around yourself once, then clip it in on the other side. Okay, can we speed things up a little, Arthur? We're kind of in a hurry."

Arthur lurches forward, and I grab onto Ryn once more. The strap around my waist doesn't feel like nearly enough to hold me in place. Arthur raises his wings, then brings them down again. Again and again, faster each time. Wind gusts around us, and soon we're in the air, swooping toward the end of the strip. Instead of hitting the wall, it vanishes the moment we reach it. I remember the river at the last second and take a deep breath of air, tensing in preparation for the ice cold water. It never hits me, though.

"Good thing one of us remembered to put a shield up," Ryn says. I open my eyes and see a bubble of air separating us from the dark water. It disappears a moment later as Arthur breaks the river's surface. His powerful wings lift us from the water, splashing us with ice-cold droplets as they sweep through the air.

I half expect to see the valley overrun with Draven's warriors, but there's no one out here. I twist my head around and look back at the waterfall hiding the base and the intruders that managed to find their way in. I feel like a coward, flying away from a fight that people we care about will probably die in.

"Stop it," Ryn says. "It's your responsibility to find the Star. It would've been *ir*responsible of you to stay and fight, so stop feeling guilty that you left."

I duck my head down behind his back—finding a space somewhere between the sword and bag—to shield my face from the wind's chill. I raise my voice and say, "And what about you? Don't you feel guilty at all?"

He hesitates before saying, "Of course I do. The rest of my team's back there. My father's there. But it was more important to get you out safely, and you weren't going to do it on your own."

I know he's right.

We soar up and out of the valley. The bright light that flashes around us as we pass through the protective dome causes Arthur to roar and twist around. He blasts the now-invisible dome with fire before Ryn manages to calm him down. He snorts, sending a puff of smoke into the air, before gliding away from the valley across land that becomes more densely covered in white the further we go.

Now that I don't feel like I'm about to fall off, I shift away from Ryn slightly and release my hold on him. I bet he was enjoying having my arms wrapped around his chest, but I don't want him to get the wrong idea. I raise my arms at my sides and tilt my head back. The wind whips at my hair and pushes at my arms. My fingers grow numb from the cold, but I don't mind, because when I close my eyes, I feel like I'm flying.

Exhilaration.

"Having a *Titanic* moment back there?" Ryn asks.

I open my eyes and lower my arms. "What?"

"Never mind." I can hear the smile in his voice. "You never did get any of my movie references."

I look over Ryn's shoulder to see where we're heading. On the horizon, a faint orange haze means dawn's about to break. Ryn leans forward along Arthur's neck and says something I don't recognize. Perhaps there's a special dragon language I don't know about. I open my mouth to ask, but Arthur makes a sudden drop toward the earth, leaving my stomach hanging somewhere up in the air above. A shriek escapes me, and I catch hold of Ryn.

Plummeting.

Air rushing.

The ground growing closer.

Aaand … suddenly we're gliding again, Arthur's wings spreading wide to catch the currents in the air. He banks and swoops past a clump of bushes before landing.

I push away from Ryn and slide down Arthur's leg. "You did that on purpose."

"What, you didn't enjoy that?" Ryn climbs down with an innocent expression. "I thought you were looking forward to the rush of riding a dragon."

"The rush of riding a dragon, yes. The rush of plummeting to my death? No."

"Don't be silly," he says, which somehow annoys me even more than the fact that he just tried to scare me. "You're a faerie. You would've caught yourself long before you hit the ground." He reaches over his shoulder and removes the sword and bag from his back. Then he pulls out a cloak, speaks words to enlarge it, and lays it on the frozen ground. He sits down on it and places the sword in front of him. "Let's figure out where the Star is."

Anxiety zings through me, replacing my irritation. I sit down on the cloak opposite Ryn and cross my legs.

"Hey, there's really no need to be anxious about this." Ryn

leans forward and touches my hand. "This is what you do, V. It's going to work. You managed to find Jamon, remember?"

Yeah, apparently I did. "So I hold this sword and then …"

"Uh, search with your mind. Something like that. If this sword really does belong to the Star, you should see where she is."

"Okay." Ryn removes the sword from its sheath. I wrap my fingers around the hilt, then jump as Arthur blasts a spindly bush nearby with a spurt of flame, turning the brittle branches to a burned crisp. He proceeds to uproot the blackened bush with one bite. He crunches, swallows, and licks his lips with a forked tongue.

"That's … weird," I say.

"Yeah, he doesn't just eat meat. Anyway, the sword?"

I turn back to the weapon in my hand. I hold it up and see tiny words engraved along the blade's edge. "This is the prophecy you were telling me about," I murmur. My eyes scan the words.

Two halves in one have more power than a whole. The fae world will bow beneath his mark. Only the sword can stop him, and only one can wield the sword: the Star of the high land. She is hidden, but the finder will find her. She will break the whole in half. By the strike of the sword, and the death of innocence, evil will be laid to rest.

"Well, I sure hope I'm the finder this prophecy is talking about." I close my eyes, try to ignore the fact that Ryn is watching me, and let my mind relax. I slide my fingers across the cold metal ridges of the sword's hilt and imagine someone else holding this weapon. Someone who can use it against Draven. My mind soars, and I feel like I'm flying. Faster than Arthur. Faster than the magic carpet. Fast enough to cover great distances in only seconds. Everything I see is a blur, until I finally slow down. Even then, I can't really see anything clearly. I brush past hundreds of other minds, but none of them are the one I'm searching for.

And then I stop. Somewhere far away. Somewhere near the ocean where a pink sun hangs above a horizon of water.

I open my eyes and find Ryn leaning toward me. "It worked, didn't it?"

I nod. "It did, but not exactly. I got a sense of the general region." I sit up and turn in the direction of the pull I can still feel. A soft but undeniable tug within me. "It's that way, but I don't know how far away."

"If you didn't get an exact answer, then it must be quite far. That's how it usually works for you. As you get closer, you'll be able to determine her location with greater accuracy."

"Okay, so, that means we've got a long journey ahead of us." I look over to where Arthur is munching on another toasted bush. "And as cool as it is to fly on a dragon, we can't make him fly nearly as fast as the magic carpet."

"No, but I'm not that concerned about speed this time." Ryn slides the sword back into its sheath and stands. "I have a different plan."

"Which is?"

"The faerie paths."

I laugh as I stand. "Are you insane?"

"Possibly. Sometimes. But not right now. We have a *dragon*, V." He slips the sword strap over his head so that it lies diagonally across his chest. "We can open a doorway in the air and fly right through it and beyond. We don't have to hang around on the other side. By the time Draven's guards arrive, we'll be long gone."

"Unless they're also riding dragons now," I point out, "in which case it wouldn't take them long to catch up."

Ryn thinks about that for a moment. "That wouldn't be cool,

but I don't think it's going to happen. We've never seen them on dragons before."

"Okay. Well, if it happens, I'll try not to say 'I told you so.'"

A smile turns Ryn's mouth up into that expression that seems to do something odd to my insides. "You won't try at all. You'd love to be able to say—oh, hang on." He reaches into a pocket and pulls out his amber, which reminds me that I still haven't sent a message to Jamon. "It's from Oliver." Ryn's brow furrows as his eyes scan the words on the amber's surface. Then he closes his eyes and breathes out a sigh. "There was no attack," he says, looking at me. "They've searched every level and can't find any intruders."

Relief floods my body. "So the explosion ..."

"They're saying it came from Uri's lab. It destroyed the whole laboratory, as well as the spare weapons room and part of the training center. No one was seriously injured, though."

I remember the clutter in Uri's lab. Couple that with his scatterbrained nature, and it seems entirely possible that the explosion originated there. "Poor Uri. He must feel awful knowing he's responsible."

"Yeah. Anyway, Oliver says we should just go on and find the Star. They're all busy there fixing up the damage." Ryn removes his stylus from an inside pocket of his jacket and flicks it across the amber's screen. "There's also a message from Em." He laughs, then shakes his head and writes a quick reply. "She says the most ridiculous things." He slips the amber and stylus back inside his jacket while something strangely resembling jealousy stirs in my stomach. I push away thoughts of Em and Ryn before they can take hold in my mind.

After an odd look in my direction, Ryn says, "Okay, you open a doorway, and I'll bring Arthur over here. Once we're inside, you're directing the way."

I dig inside my bag and find the stylus I haven't used in a

while. I half expect Draven's guards to show up the moment I start writing the words on the ground, but no one appears. I drag a large doorway open like I did when I helped the reptiscillas move their belongings.

"Okay, jump on," Ryn says. He reaches down for my hand and swings me up as Arthur lumbers to the edge of the dark hole. He spreads his wings, takes a step forward, and dives down into the darkness. I expect air to rush past us, but the faerie paths don't do things like that. We could be speeding faster than light, or we could be suspended in the blackness of nothing. "You're directing us, V," Ryn reminds me.

I hold the image of the ocean and the pink sun in my mind, feeling that tug within me that wants to pull in a certain direction. Warm light brushes my closed eyelids. I open them to find us flying above an ocean reflecting the pink-orange sky. The sun is a little lower now than when I saw it in my head. I guess we've left a rising sun for a setting one.

"Which way?" Ryn asks.

"Uh, that way." I point a little to the right.

Ryn twists around and looks behind us. "You mean away from shore?"

I turn and see a strip of land behind us. "Yeah, I guess so."

Arthur swoops low and drags his back feet through the water, spraying us with foam. I laugh and wipe the wetness from my face. The water is cold, but not as icy as the air we just left behind.

"Do you have any idea what we're heading toward?" Ryn asks.

"No, but I'm hoping it'll become clear soon."

"Well, if not, you'll need to use the sword to try and find her again."

"Yeah, okay." I look over my shoulder to watch the land disappearing behind us. It definitely seems further away now, but what catches my attention are the two small shapes that rise into the air and start to grow bigger. I frown, trying to figure out what I'm looking at. After several more moments, my eyes make out wings attached to the two shapes.

Wings. Which means flying creatures. Coming toward us.

"Uh, Ryn? I think we have company."

CHAPTER 18

"Crap." Ryn urges Arthur forward, but the flying creatures are gaining on us.

"Would now be a good time to say 'I told you so'?" I ask. Ryn was so certain Draven's guards wouldn't show up on dragons, and yet here they are. Flying toward us.

"Probably not. How about later?" Ryn twists around to get another look at our pursuers. "Although … I'm not entirely sure those are dragons."

Arthur roars and swerves to the right as sparks strike his left wing. I clutch Ryn's waist to keep from being thrown off while Ryn wraps an arm around Arthur's neck. Moments later, a spear glances off Arthur's thick hide. "They're not guardians," Ryn says, watching the ordinary spear plunge into the ocean. Arthur twists his long neck around and sends a burst of flames behind us. He flaps his wings fiercely and spins in the air to face his attackers.

"Flip, those are *manticores*," Ryn says.

Now that they're only a dragon's length away from us, I can see the lion bodies, human faces, and scorpion tales of our pursuers' steeds. The riders look like faeries, and the sparks of magic they're sending our way certainly suggest they're faeries, but their shaved, tattoo-covered heads aren't something I remember seeing before.

Arthur sends another blaze of flames curling and licking through the air. The manticores scream in fury, baring their several rows of teeth. Their riders throw spears and knives and sparks that turn into sharp pieces of bone. We deflect everything with shields, then strike back with our own magic.

The air is soon filled with curses, smoke, and bursts of light as the three creatures whirl around each other. Arthur is much larger than the manticores, but they're faster and more agile. They claw at his sides and strike with their stingers. I slash at them with a sword whenever they come close enough, and Ryn tries to dismount the riders with a few snaps of his whip. Nothing seems to do any good, though. Even arrows are useless with so much movement going on.

I'm starting to tire—both from magic use and the effort of staying on Arthur's back—when a ball of white flame comes speeding toward us. I throw my hand out and stop it with a shield, but it bounces off at a weird angle and strikes Arthur's neck. He rears up and lets out a roaring shriek, throwing Ryn and me backward in the process. The flimsy strap around my waist snaps.

I'm falling.

Falling, falling, falli—*splash*. The slap of the water stings my body as I plunge into an ocean of bubbles. I float, weightless. Then I pull at the water with long strokes, reaching for the surface. The bag on my back isn't heavy, but I still feel like it's dragging me down. Finally, my head breaks through. I suck in air as I tread water, looking around for Ryn.

"V!" I hear the shout behind me and swing around. Ryn swims toward me, the sword sliding back and forth across his shoulders. "You okay?" he asks, pushing wet hair out of his eyes.

"Yeah. You?"

He nods and looks up. I follow his gaze and watch Arthur flying away. One of the manticore riders sends a few sparks after him. The other rider throws something mesh-like through the air to his partner, but keeps hold of one end. It hangs in the air between them. The moment they snap it tight and dive toward us, I realize what it is.

A net.

"Get down!" I shout. I take a great gulp of air and drop beneath the rolling waves. But it's too late. The net is weighted and sinks easily through the water and over us. I try to swim down and out the bottom, but the weighted ends move toward each other like magnets and stick together, leaving us trapped inside. I stick my fingers through the lattice and get a good grip on the net, meaning to tear the thing apart with as much magical strength as I can muster. But a burning starts in my palms the moment the mesh comes into contact with my skin.

Burning, burning, *burning*—I snatch my hands away, no longer able to stand the pain. I turn in the water and see Ryn about to do the same thing. My 'no' comes out as a distorted rush of bubbles. Before he can reach the edge of the net, it rushes toward us, tugging us up and out of the water in a dripping heap. The net touches my neck, my face, the back of my right hand. I jerk away from the burning, managing to get into a position where only my clothes and boots touch the enchanted mesh.

I find a snarling manticore and its tattooed rider hovering in the air in front of me. The other one is to the side, facing Ryn. The net floats between them, held up by some invisible force they're no doubt controlling.

My back is pressed against Ryn's, so I hear rather than see the sparks he shoots at the rider. A second later, pain zings across my shoulder as the sparks tear through the edge of my jacket and dissipate in front of me. I recoil as Ryn says, "Flip, what the—"

"You shouldn't do that," the rider facing Ryn says. "The net will contain any magic or weapons you try to throw at us."

"I'm sorry," Ryn mutters to me. "I didn't know it would—"

"Hey, you're not marked!" I blurt out as I catch a glimpse of the rider's right palm.

"No." His lips twist into a smile that doesn't reach his eyes. "We're not. Lucky, aren't we?"

His manticore swipes a claw at the net, causing it to lurch to the side. I fall against the net. My skin burns. Ear, chin, hands. I push away from the net with my elbow. "Wait, stop! We're not marked either."

The rider swings his manticore around so that his own sneering face is now inches from mine. "That's the point, sweetheart." He looks across at his partner and gives him a small nod. I twist to see the other rider. He raises both hands and—

* * *

My thoughts are slow and heavy. I struggle to get them turning. It's like swimming through thick syrup. A voice keeps saying my name, but I can't muster enough strength to break through the syrupy layer and answer him.

So I wait.

As my mind dips in and out of darkness, the heaviness slowly dissipates, until finally, *finally*, I can force my eyelids apart. The first thing I notice is the pain. The heaviness masked it, but now I'm fully aware of the burning on my face, hands, and lower back. I blink a few times, but things seem to be taking a while to come into focus.

"Stunner spell," I mumble.

"Yeah," Ryn says, his voice sounding close. "Always love waking up feeling like I've been drugged."

I realize I'm lying on my side. I push myself up carefully,

trying to use the heel of my hand instead of my palm. I'm on a hard, cold surface inside what looks like a dingy prison cell. Metal bars block off one side of the room, and dim light comes from a passageway on the other side of those bars. If I listen carefully, I can hear the quiet, continual slosh of water against a shore. I guess we're not far from the ocean.

"You okay?" Ryn asks.

Seems like kind of a dumb question. "Aside from being burned, stunned, and locked up? Sure. I'm just peachy." I blink again and see a crisscross pattern of red marks on one side of his face. "Ooh, ouch. Is that what my face looks like?"

"Yeah, and your back. Your jacket must have gotten pulled up after we were stunned."

I twist around and lift the back of my jacket, but I can't see much. I shake my head and try to ignore the hot pain. "I don't get it. If these guys aren't marked, and we're not marked, shouldn't we be on the same side?"

"I don't know. It seemed like the reason they caught us was *because* we're not marked."

"I wonder if—Wait, where's the sword?" I suddenly remember we had more with us when we fell from the sky.

"Where do you think?" Ryn asks, gesturing vaguely toward the bars. "It's not like I dropped it in the ocean, so they must have it."

"Crap. We have to get it back, Ryn."

He rolls his eyes. "Thanks, V. Tell me something I don't already know."

"Hey, why are you getting mad at me? It's not my fault we ended up in this situation. In fact, I think it was you who suggested we go through the—"

"Yeah, it was," he interrupts, pushing himself up off the floor and walking to the bars. He presses his forehead against them. "It's not *you* I'm mad at," he says quietly.

So he's mad at himself. I stand up, noticing for the first time that my clothes are still a little damp. I stand next to him and look out at the passage. It's as bare as the cell we're locked in. "I guess we could say it's your fault, but it's not like that's going to help, is it? So instead I'll say this: We *will* get out of here because we're guardians and we kick ass, and no manticore-riding, bald guys are going to stand a chance against us."

Ryn looks down at me with a smile. "There's that overconfidence I've missed so much." His eyes slide down my face to my shoulder, and his smile fades. "I'm sorry about the sparks that hit you. I really didn't mean to hurt you."

It's my turn to roll my eyes. "Of course you didn't. Besides, it barely grazed my skin. It's probably already healed." I slide my fingers beneath the layers of my clothing and feel my shoulder. "Yup. Perfectly healed. Nothing to worry about."

His smile is small. "That's good." He turns back to the bars. "I'm guessing this cell keeps magic contained the same way the net did."

"Probably." I gently rub my still-burning palms together until a mist begins to pour from them. I blow it toward the bars. It curls through the air, but instead of passing between the bars, it meets an invisible barrier. "Yeah. Same as the net."

When I look back at him, Ryn is watching me with an expression I can't quite define. Sadness and longing? More than that? Just when I start to feel a little weird, he looks away. He leans against the bars and examines his hands. "At least we can still use magic, even if it's only in here."

I frown. "Why wouldn't we be able to use magic?"

Instead of answering me, he pushes back the sleeve of his right arm. Then he reaches forward and takes my right hand. He gently pushes my sleeve up until I can see my guardian markings and the scar that rings my wrist. The scar that matches his. "I started telling you about it before," he says, "but I was interrupted. Zell discovered a metal that blocks magic. He fashioned the metal into strips that could wrap around a person's wrist and stick there, blocking the use of magic. I've worn one. You've worn two." He touches my wrist, sending a shiver up my arm. "The metal is incredibly painful to remove from your skin, and when the procedure is finished, it leaves a scar."

"Unlike any of our other wounds," I murmur.

"Yes. Anyway." He folds his arms across his chest and walks to the other side of the cell. He leans against the wall and says, "We need to be smart about this. There's no point in trying to attack them when they're on the other side of the bars. But they'll have to come inside eventually, to move us out, if nothing else—"

"And that's when we'll strike."

"Yes. We'll need to gather power so that if the opportunity comes to stun them, we can take it."

"But we won't know when they're coming, and once they do, there won't be enough time to gather all that power."

"There might be, if we keep them talking before they come in."

I sit down on the floor and cross my legs. I nod. "We can try that." I look up. "Do we fight well together? I mean, not *against* each other, but as a team?"

He joins me on the floor, but on the opposite side of the room. "We do. At least, we did before you forgot me."

Right. So the fact that I took that stupid potion is once again ruining everything. But I don't want to go back to talking about that because there's really no point. I don't know what else to talk about, though. There are so many questions I want to ask about my past, but how can I when they don't seem nearly as important as our present? When the silence between us begins to feel awkward, I say, "I assume they took your amber and stylus?"

Ryn nods. "I checked as soon as I woke up." He taps one finger against his knee, then says, "You know, silence used to feel natural between us. We were friends for a long time before we hated each other. And then we were friends again before we were … more. The point is, I don't want you to feel weird around me. Yes, I miss the way things were, but I'm certainly not going to force myself on you. If the only thing we can be is friends, then I'll take that. So …" He gives me the smile I was probably madly in love with in my previous life. "No weird silences?"

I return the smile. "Okay. No weird silences. But just so you know, if you *did* try anything, I'd—"

My words are cut off by the echo of heavy boots in the passage outside our cell. Ryn and I jump to our feet immediately. Any remaining sluggishness from the stunner spell vanishes from my system. I mentally reach into the core of my being and start gathering power. I hope Ryn is doing the same.

A bald, tattooed manticore rider slows to a lazy swagger as he comes into view. "Well, well, look who's awake." He grasps the bars and leans forward, obviously confident we won't be able to hurt him from in here. "Did you have a good night?" he asks with a smirk.

"Look, I think there might be a mistake here," Ryn says carefully. "We're not marked; you're not marked. Surely we should be on the same side?"

The rider faerie laughs. "We're on no one's side but our own."

I make sure I'm still gathering power before I say, "So why lock us up? Why not just let us get on with our own business?"

"Because that would be bad for *our* business."

"Which is what exactly?" Ryn asks, not quite as politely as before.

Tattooed Guy scratches his chin before saying, "I guess you could call it bounty hunting."

What? "And we're the bounty?"

"You got that right, sweetheart."

Ryn moves a little closer to me. "Why? What did we do?"

"Oh, nothing, nothing." Tattooed Guy waves a dismissive hand. "No need to blame yourself. It's all about *who* you are, not what you've done. You see, we have a deal with some of Draven's men. They steer clear of our territory, and we bring them unmarked fae. For a fee, of course. And guardians are worth the most." He rubs his hands together, probably in anticipation of his payout. "So, you'll be visiting the Unseelie Court. Not yet, of course. We like to collect at least ten fae before making the trip. Until then, and as long as we have another free cell, we should probably separate the two of you."

Ryn takes another step toward me, so that his body is partially blocking mine. "I don't think that's necessary."

"Oh, I think it is." Tattooed Guy looks to the side as another pair of footsteps makes its way toward our cell. The second rider who aided in our capture saunters into view with a large cylinder held over his shoulder. He watches us with a smug expression, and I know he wants us to ask, so I do.

I nod my head toward the cylinder and say, "What is that?"

The smug smile stretches wider. "I know you guardians have your pretty weapons, but this is something that'll blow the underpants off anything you've got."

"I doubt it," Ryn mutters.

"Do you now, young master guardian? Well, I've always been a collector of shiny things, and right here—" he pats the cylinder "—is where I keep my lightning collection."

My eyebrows climb higher.

"Yup, I've been fortunate lately with all the storms Draven's been throwing around. Plenty of opportunity for collecting lightning." He takes a step closer to the bars and watches me with unblinking eyes. "Ever been fried by lightning, missy?"

I don't actually know, but I'm guessing probably not. Before I can say anything, his partner pulls out a key from his pocket, holds it up, and says, "So. You two just behave yourselves, and no one will get hurt."

I return my attention to the power I'm gathering. I've definitely got enough to stun one of them. I look over at Ryn, but he's watching the rider insert the key into the lock. The key twists, and the loud click tells us the door is open. He steps inside and beckons to me. "Come quietly, little guardian, and I won't have to hurt your friend."

I don't move.

With a sigh, he walks toward me. I'm about to send all my stunning power straight at him, but Ryn gets there first. He throws his arms out faster than I can blink. But instead of seeing the rider fall, I see bright, crackling light flash past me. I recoil as I hear it strike the wall.

After blinking my temporary blindness away, I find the three of us inside the cell still standing, along with a small crater in the wall. The second rider is standing in the doorway with his lightning cylinder pointed at Ryn. The smug smile is gone.

"Next time, it'll be your face, pretty boy," he warns.

He must have shot lightning at Ryn's power to keep it from striking the rider inside the cell. There's no time now for Ryn to gather more power, which means it's down to me. If I can stun the lightning guy before the cell is locked, hopefully Ryn can take down the guy who now has his hands on me.

I put up a fight as he drags me from the cell, but only for show. I *want* to get out so I can get to the other guy. Ryn grabs my arm as I pass him, but the lightning cylinder swings to point at me instead, and Ryn backs off at once. Lightning Guy steps back from the doorway to allow my captor and me to leave. The moment I pass the bars, I tear one arm free and shove it toward Lightning Guy, releasing all my pent up power. He knocks my arm to the side with his cylinder, sending all my power straight into the passage wall instead. The wall shudders, and a crack appears.

Dammit!

I jab my elbow backwards into my captor's stomach and slam my boot down onto his foot. His hold on me loosens enough for me to pull away from him and aim a punch at Lightning Guy. Before I can swing my arm forward, the cylinder flies at my head.

I hear Ryn's shout, but I can't see anything for a few moments. When my vision clears, I find myself lying on the passage floor with a throbbing ache threatening to split my head in half. I see Ryn struggling with the first guy. Then I see the flash of crackling light that strikes Ryn in the chest and throws him back into his cell.

"*No!*" I scramble up onto my knees, but Lightning Guy grabs a fistful of my jacket and drags me across the floor to the next cell. I kick him as hard as I can, and he kicks me right back. The impact of his foot in my stomach sends me across the threshold and into the cell.

The door slams shut.

CHAPTER 19

As soon as I'm able to breathe again, I start calling out for him. "Ryn? Ryn, are you okay? Are you there?" I pat against the wall, then start banging with my fists. I stick my arm between the bars at the edge of my cell and stretch as far as I can to the side. I can't reach the next cell, but I slap my hand against the wall and call for him some more.

Nothing I do gets any response from him.

Please, please, please be okay. I realize my face is wet with tears. I don't know why I'm crying. I only just met this guy. We're barely even friends. But I know what he's *supposed* to mean to me, and maybe I was starting to feel just a hint of that. I figured that with time, maybe I'd come to realize why the old me cared so much for him, and maybe I'd care for him too. But what if that time is up? What if he's gone and I didn't even get a chance to know him again?

No. He can't be dead. I clutch my aching head in my hands and start pacing the cell. Like Jamon said, it's really difficult to kill faeries. The only way Ryn could die is if his injuries are so bad that his body's magic can't heal them before it runs out. His injuries would have to be really severe. Does lightning count as really severe?

Of course it does, the horribly logical part of my brain screams at me. It's *lightning*, for crap's sake. If lightning collected from an enchanted storm could gouge a crater into a solid brick wall, what could it do to a faerie's body? I don't want to imagine it. I don't want to think about the state he's in right now. I don't want to know if the burning flesh smell lingering in the air is real or imagined.

I continue pacing the floor of my cell because there's nothing else to do. I can't bear to sit still. Every few minutes I start calling Ryn's name again. He never calls back. I have no idea what time of day or night it is because this cell has no window either, and the dim light in the passage never changes.

Eventually—has it been hours yet?—I take off my jacket and transform it into a mattress big enough for me to curl up on. I lie next to the bars so that I'll be the first to hear it if Ryn makes a noise. I don't think it'll be possible for me to fall asleep—and I don't think I *should* sleep, what with Ryn close to death next door—but the next thing I know, I'm opening my eyes to the sound of disappearing footsteps, realizing I didn't hear them approaching in the first place.

I guess I fell asleep, but whether it was for two minutes or two hours or more, I have no way of telling. "Ryn?" I tap on a metal bar with my knuckle, then call his name again.

Still nothing.

I notice a different smell in the air. Something like food. I sit up and find a bowl of soup at my feet. Vegetable chunks float in a pool of brownish liquid. It doesn't look particularly appetizing, but the smell draws me closer. I guess it's not in the bounty hunters' best interests to starve their prisoners. I'm sure strong, healthy faeries fetch a better price than malnourished ones.

The last thing I want to do is accept food from these people, and the thought of Ryn lying seriously injured—or worse—next door turns my stomach. But I also know it's not in *my* best interest either to starve myself. When the time comes to take that trip to the Unseelie Court, we *will* fight our way out of here. So I take the bowl of soup in my hands and start eating.

When one of the tattooed faeries returns to take my bowl, I jump up. "The guy next door," I say. "Is he okay? Is he ... is he still alive?"

The faerie smirks at me, bends to take the bowl from beneath the gate, and leaves without saying a word.

"Wait!" I shout after him. "Just answer me, dammit!"

I sink back onto my mattress. Maybe I should have asked nicely. Begged or used the word 'please,' at least. As disgusting as it would make me feel, I could try begging next time he comes by. This is about Ryn, after all, and he's more important than my pride.

I realize my headache has passed. I examine my hands and see that the crisscross of red burns has healed, which explains why my back doesn't hurt anymore. Maybe I was asleep for quite a long time. Which means ...

Why hasn't Ryn woken up yet?

I resume my pacing and my silent begging. *Please, please, please be okay.* I shake the bars and bang on the walls a few more times to release some frustration. It doesn't really work, but it does reveal to me that there's a tiny hole in the wall that divides Ryn's cell from mine. It's at the level of my hip and can't be bigger than a pinhead. *The crater*, I remember suddenly. It must have broken almost right through the wall.

I kneel down and press my eye to the hole, but of course I can't see anything. I drag my mattress over and sit next to the hole. This will be better than shouting into the passage when Ryn wakes up.

Because he will wake up.

I lean against the wall and tilt my head back. I lift my hand and blow air gently over it until a bubble forms. It floats off my hand and into the air. I create more bubbles, trying to fashion each one into a different shape. It passes the time and helps to relax me. Instead of thinking about Ryn never waking up, I think about telling him all the complex shapes I was able to create when he *does* wake up.

I've just blown a bubble that looks like a rabbit when I hear a dull thud through the wall behind me. I freeze with my hand in the air.

"V? You there?"

Relief explodes within me like warm, golden rays of sunlight. I scramble around and speak into the hole. "Ryn! You're alive!"

"Of course I'm alive," he croaks. "No manticore-riding, bald guys stand a chance against me, right?"

My words sound so weak repeated back to me now, but I'm so happy he's alive that I laugh anyway.

"Are you okay?" he asks me.

"Am *I* okay? Ryn, you got hit by lightning. Are *you* okay?"

"Yeah. What's the word? Peachy. I'm totally peachy."

I shake my head, but I can't help smiling. When I said it, I made sure to put as much sarcasm behind the word as possible, but the way Ryn says it tells me he's *not* peachy but doesn't want me to know. I place both hands against the wall. "You can't possibly be peachy, Ryn. Tell me how you really are."

"Well, there might have been a hole in my chest at some point, but it seems to be healing. I don't think the lightning that hit me was as powerful as the one that hit the wall."

A hole in his chest? And he survived that?

"Anyway, you didn't answer me," he continues. "Are you okay?"

"Yes. Bored and frustrated—" *and terrified you were dead* "— but otherwise fine."

"Good. Uh, there's a bowl of cold soup on my floor. Do you know if it's safe?"

"Well, I ate mine a few hours ago, and I'm still alive."

I wait for him to fetch his bowl. When a shadow moves past the hole, I assume that means he's returned to the wall. I remember my promise about no awkward silences and decide to fill the quiet before it becomes awkward. "I was thinking about what that guy said about taking us to the Unseelie Court. That must mean Draven is based there."

"Probably. Although it sounded like we'll be handed over to Draven's men, not directly to the *lord*. The prisoner we had at our base for a while—the one who's now been cured—told us Draven was probably using the Unseelie Court as his base, but she didn't know for sure."

"Well, as much as I want to see Draven up close and put an end to all this, we can't do that until we find the Star."

"No. We need to get away long before we reach the Unseelie Court." He goes quiet, probably eating his cold soup. After a minute or so he says, "I hope Arthur's okay. Oliver certainly isn't going to be happy with me when he finds out I lost his dragon."

"Well, he can comfort himself with the fact that Arthur will be happier in the wild than locked up in a cramped enclosure."

"Arthur is a shrinking dragon, V. Space was never a problem as long as he was in his shrunken form."

"Oh. A shrinking dragon? That sounds vaguely familiar. Did we learn about them at school?"

"Yeah. Junior school. And one of our early group assignments involved a shrinking dragon."

"Oh." I lean sideways against the wall and twist a piece of hair around my finger. If I have to find something positive in this situation, it's that I can learn more about my past.

"You know, I was thinking about something before that explosion at the base." Ryn's voice sounds a little further away, as if he's lying down now. "Why can't you remember any of your assignments? It's not like you loved the creatures you had to fight."

Good point, but I stopped trying to figure out my memory problems a while ago. "Um, I do remember brief flashes of fighting various creatures," I say, "so I haven't forgotten them entirely."

"I suppose the potion got confused," he says. "You didn't love those creatures, so you shouldn't forget them. But you were performing a guardian duty in fighting them, and you've always loved the life of a guardian."

"I must have really loved it if I've forgotten so much about my life," I say quietly. Did I love it *too* much? Was I obsessed?

"You did, but only because you had nothing else. And I think the reason you've forgotten so much is because nothing in life is isolated. Everything is interlinked somehow. The things we care about are always mixed up with things we don't care about."

I close my eyes. "Getting all philosophical on that side of the wall, are you?" I tease.

"Well, there isn't much else to do on this side. You telling me your side's more exciting?"

"Totally. I've got loads of entertainment here. A pink troll riding a unicycle and juggling fire sprites."

"Hmm. Sounds like you need some sleep, V."

"Now that you mention it, I could do with another nap. Turns out worrying about people is more exhausting than I thought."

"Oh? And why were you worrying about me?"

My eyelids spring apart. *Oops.* He wasn't supposed to know just how scared I was that he hadn't survived that lightning strike. "Come on, Ryn," I say quietly. "You got blown across the room by *lightning*. What do you think I was worried about?"

Instead of answering me, he goes quiet. I start to feel uncomfortable. Dammit, what happened to there being no more awkward silences?

"V?" he says. "I need to tell you something."

"Uh, okay." I shift a little closer to the hole.

"And it would be great if you didn't get mad."

"Why would I get mad?"

"The last time I told you this, you kicked me out of your house."

"Well, I can't exactly do that this time, so you've got nothing to worry about."

"I'm more concerned about the part where you might get upset and stop talking to me. I imagine it could get quite lonely in this cell with no one to talk to."

I pause, then say, "Is what you have to tell me really that bad?"

"Not exactly. I just ... should have told you a lot sooner last time. I don't want to make the same mistake this time around. I didn't want to freak you out with too much info when you first got to the base, but I really don't want to keep it from you any longer."

"Okaaay," I say.

"So ... you know how you have extra magic that helps you find people?"

"Yes."

"I have extra magic too. And my extra magic makes me feel whatever people around me are feeling."

I open my mouth, but I honestly can't think of a single thing to say to that. My first thought is to try to figure out what I'm currently feeling and whether it's telling him anything embarrassing about me. *Oh, crap.* Each time he's given me that smile that's made my stomach flip over weirdly, did he *know* that? Did he feel it because I was feeling it? I try to remember how many times it's happened, but I seem to be freaking out a little too much to come up with an answer.

"Yeah, I know, most people would freak out and feel like I'm invading their privacy," Ryn says, "which seems to be what you're feeling now. That's why I don't generally tell people. But I had to tell *you* because you knew everything else about me before, and I couldn't keep it from you any longer. And now I'm telling you again because I don't ever want you to feel like I've lied to you."

I still don't know what to say. Even though there's a wall between us, I feel as exposed as if Ryn were looking into my soul. But it can't be *that* bad, right? I mean, how much can he really know just from a person's feelings? It's not as though he can hear thoughts. That would be highly embarrassing.

"Aaand now would be a good time for you to say something."

"Um …" I stare up at the ceiling. "Well, I'm not mad."

"Yeah, I know."

Right. Of course he does. "And I'm not going to kick you out of your cell or stop talking to you."

"Wow." He sounds impressed. "You know what? I think the new you might be less inclined to overreact than the old you."

"Then aren't you lucky you're locked up with the new me instead of the old me?"

"I'd be lucky either way."

I roll my eyes and mutter, "Such a suck-up."

"I learned from the best," he says, and I can imagine his smirk.

I ignore the jibe and say, "So tell me something no one else knows about me."

"Finally," he says. "We've reached the part of the conversation where I get to share embarrassing stories about you."

"You know that's not what I meant."

"And you know it's going to happen anyway."

We launch into a discussion that feels something like a weird first date, where I ask questions for both of us, and he answers for both of us. Our favorite foods. Our best and worst assignments. The best tricks we ever played on each other. Our secret fears when we were little.

Hours later, when my head is slipping to the side and I'm starting to fall asleep, I force my eyes open and ask the question I've been avoiding since our conversation began. "Ryn? Does my father know about me? Does he know that you found me and took me back to the base?"

"No. I didn't know how to contact him. He's with the Seelie Queen, and no one knows where she is."

So it isn't that he didn't care enough about me to come and see me at the base. He just didn't know I was there.

Obviously picking up on my relief, Ryn adds, "He cares about you, V. A lot. It broke his heart to leave you when he had to fake his death and go undercover. But he did it to protect you. It's a long story, but ... just know that he did it because your life was in danger and it was the only way he knew how to keep you safe."

I definitely want to know more about *that* story, but maybe another time. Ryn needs to rest to keep healing, and for some strange reason, I seem to be sleepy too. It could be from all my worrying about him earlier, but my last thought before I slide away from the wall and onto my mattress is that the bounty hunters might have spiked our soup with something.

Something to relax us ...

Something to keep us from getting too violent ...

Something ...

CHAPTER 20

"HOW ARE YOU FEELING TODAY?" I ASK RYN AFTER HE TAPS on the wall to let me know he's awake. "Less like you had a hole in your chest?"

"Yeah." He makes a noise that suggests he's stretching. "I'm not in so much pain anymore."

Guilt attacks me at the realization that he was in pain the whole of yesterday and didn't say a word about it. And I didn't think to ask.

"Stop it, V," he says. "It's not like you can do anything about my pain, so guilt is pointless."

I really need to keep in mind that he can feel what I'm feeling. It keeps catching me off guard.

Footsteps sound in the passage. I tell Ryn to keep quiet before pulling my mattress to the other side of the cell and sitting on it. I don't want to be moved further away from him just because we've been talking. I'm not sure if they have more than two cells here, but I don't want to take the chance. The footsteps stop next to Ryn's cell. A few moments later, they move to mine. The same tattooed faerie who delivered the soup slides a bowl of lumpy white stuff—porridge of some sort, I'm guessing—under the gate before heading back down the passage.

I wait for his footsteps to disappear before scooping up the bowl and resuming my position beneath the tiny hole in the wall. I dip the spoon into the bowl and try a mouthful. Just like the soup, it tastes better than it looks.

"At least they're feeding us," Ryn says from the other side of the hole.

"Yeah, so that Draven can have strong, healthy guardians on his side."

"That's not going to happen. The last thing I'll do is fight for him. I'd rather be dead."

"Ryn," I say quietly. It feels a little too soon for him to be saying things like that when he *was* almost dead yesterday.

"I'm serious, V. Think of all the awful things he could make us do if we were brainwashed. He could make us hurt people we care about, just because he can. I'd never forgive myself if I somehow got out from under his brainwashing influence and realized what I'd done."

"So …" I push my bowl of porridge aside, no longer hungry. "Are you saying you'd rather your mother was dead than working for Draven?"

My tentative question is met by silence. I hear the scrape of his bowl as he pushes it across the floor. The seconds tick by as I wait. I start to regret my question. Eventually I hear Ryn's quiet voice. "I don't know. Of course I don't want her dead, but I don't want her to have to do things so terrible that if she ever gets through this she won't be able to live with herself."

I nod, even though I know he can't see me. And because I seem to be incapable of coming up with any words that are actually comforting, I say, "I'm really sorry she was captured."

More silence, and then Ryn says, "Okay, this is far too

depressing, V. You're supposed to be entertaining me, not trying to get me to cry."

"What? I'm not trying to—"

"Tell me a joke."

"I …" *haven't the first clue how to tell a joke.*

"Don't worry, I was kidding. You're not really the joke-telling kind."

I frown. "Why not? Did I take life too seriously?"

"Yes. Definitely."

That sounds rather depressing.

"And then we stopped hating each other, and life became a whole lot more fun for you."

"Of course it did." I roll my eyes. "Fine. If I can't entertain you with a joke, then let's play a game." Which means I now have to think of a game that can be played inside a prison cell with the participants separated by a wall. "Uh … you tell me three things about yourself, two of which are true, and one of which is a lie. I have to guess the lie."

He laughs. "I have to say, V, that doesn't sound like the most thrilling game ever."

"If you want something thrilling, you'll have to come up with it yourself. I'm the *serious* one, remember? So it's either two truths and a lie or you tell me more trivial details about my life."

"Hey, the details I tell you don't have to be trivial," he says. "I mean, I could tell you about the first time you realized you were in love with me. I just thought that might make you a little uncomfortable."

I freeze with my mouth half open. *Yeah. Definitely uncomfortable.*

"Sorry," he says, sounding serious now. "That wasn't fair. I said I didn't want you to feel awkward, and I meant it. So … just ignore that. The two truths and a lie game, the trivial information game, whatever. I really don't mind."

"No, wait," I say, hoping I'm not going to regret going down this path. "I … I loved you?"

After a pause he says, "Yes."

I place my hand on the wall that separates us. I'm glad we're not in the same room right now. "Did I tell you that?"

A longer pause this time. "No. You were too scared."

"I'm sorry," I say softly. I don't know why, but I feel the need to apologize for my younger self who was silly enough not to say the words she should have said when she had the chance.

"It's okay. I knew what you really felt."

I squeeze my eyes shut and wish with a sudden, fierce intensity that none of this had happened. That Tharros' power was still locked away, never to be found by anyone, and that no one had to die. I wish that instead of being locked inside a prison and unable to do a damn thing to fix our broken world, Ryn and the Violet I used to be could have had their happily ever after instead.

But wishing is so pointless and useless that it makes me want to cry. And the tears wouldn't be tears of sadness. They would be hot tears burning with the rage boiling up inside me. Anger at myself for the selfish choices I made that led us all up to this point, and intense frustration at being able to do *absolutely nothing* about it right now.

"Hey, are you okay over there?" Ryn asks. "What happened? You're hurting my chest with all that anger."

I suck in a deep breath and let it out slowly. "Nothing. Nothing happened. I was just … thinking about stuff."

"Okay." His voice moves away from the hole. "Things are obviously getting far too serious on your side of the wall, so I propose a competition."

"Okay." I sniff back the tears that never fell. "I like the sound of that."

"I knew you would. And since you're a fitness freak, you'll like it even more when you hear the details."

"I'm a fitness freak?"

"You are. You've spent a gazillion more hours in the training center than anyone else who's ever set foot in our Guild."

I cross my arms. "That sounds like a bit of an exaggeration."

"I don't think it is. So. Competition number one is this: most push-ups in two minutes wins."

"Ryn, you had a hole in your chest yesterday. Push-ups probably aren't the best idea."

"That's exactly why you might stand a chance of winning. If I were fit and healthy, I'd leave you so far behind you'd be choking on my dust."

I raise an eyebrow and lean closer to the hole. "And you expect me to believe *I'm* the fitness freak?"

"Come on, V." I hear something that sounds like his hands rubbing together. "Are you going to forfeit before we even begin?"

My competitive spirit jumps up. "No way. Bring it on."

By the time our fifth day—I'm guessing it's our fifth day—in captivity rolls around, I find that push-ups and other exercises are a great way to blow of the steam rising from my frustration at *still* being locked up. We've discussed everything under the sun, ranging from things I never would have guessed about Ryn—like the fact that he can recite poetry—to crazily insane plans for how to escape our tattooed captors. But we can't just talk every minute of the day, so that's where the games come in.

Ryn beats me at most of the fitness competitions we come up with, which sucks but makes sense considering he's a whole lot stronger than I am. When he beats me at riddles and guessing games, though, that's when I start to get really annoyed.

Yes. Riddles and guessing games. That's how bored we've become.

"Uh … six," Ryn says.

"No. Wrong again. That's another ten sit ups for you." Every guessing game has a different penalty for an incorrect answer. Five push-ups, ten sit ups, fifteen star jumps. Whatever the questioner feels like. At this rate, Ryn is going to have killer abs by the time he reaches the correct answer for this question.

I wander around my cell and try not to imagine the muscles hiding beneath Ryn's T-shirt while he carries out his penalty. "Really?" he says when he's finished. "More than six reptiscillas tried to kill you after you woke up there?"

"Threatened," I remind him as I return to the hole and lean against the wall. "They *threatened* to kill me. Only a few of them actually tried it. So, what's your next guess?"

"Give me a clue," he says.

"If I give you a clue, will you tell me the answer to Guessing Game Number Twenty-Four?"

"Nope."

Guessing Game Number Twenty-Four is the only guessing game I haven't found the answer for yet. *What item of yours did I lose and then find eight years later?* I did eleven backflips off the cell bars last night before giving up.

"How about this?" I say. "I'll give you a clue if you give me a clue."

"Hmm. No. I've decided I'd rather wait until you remember Number Twenty-Four's answer for yourself."

"And if I never remember?"

He goes quiet. This is one of the few things we haven't spoken about. What if I never regain my memory? What if there's always this big void between us where all of our past shared experiences have disappeared? Although, after all the things we've talked about in the past four or five days, I have to admit the void feels a whole lot smaller.

Ryn is spared from answering me by the thud of boots in the passage. I quickly pull my mattress to the back of my cell and lie down. I figure if I pretend to be sleeping, I'll seem like less of a threat. I've just curled up with my face to the back wall when I hear the clang of something hard against Ryn's cell bars. I sit up immediately, all pretense of sleep gone. If they're about to hurt Ryn, I'll do whatever I can to stop them.

The clanging moves to my cell, and I see Lightning Guy— without his cylinder this time—dragging a piece of metal across the bars. "Time to get going," he says.

I stand up. "What? But you haven't caught ten fae yet. You haven't caught *anyone* since you locked us up." And Ryn and I haven't decided which escape plan to go with.

He shrugs. "Times are tough. There aren't many unmarked fae left out there, and we need to get paid."

"O-okay." I should be glad we're finally getting out of here. I just hope Ryn and I can coordinate our attack without actually talking about it. I start gathering power so I'll have enough when it comes time to stun someone. I won't miss this time. I'll be the passive, easy prisoner until the right moment comes.

"So." Lightning Guy produces the key to my cell and inserts it into the lock. "We won't be having any trouble this time, will we, sweetheart?"

The way he says 'sweetheart,' with a disgusting leer on his face, makes me want to spit on him. But I clench my teeth together and shake my head.

"That's right." He pushes my gate open. "And I won't be taking any chances." He lifts his hand as if holding an invisible ball above it.

Oh no.

I jump to the side and try to divert my magic into a shield as he throws his power at me. For a split second I think it's worked, and then—

CHAPTER 21

STUNNED. AGAIN. I GUESS I SHOULD HAVE SEEN THAT coming.

The cold is the first thing I feel. The pathways in my brain are still as sluggish as if someone blocked them with cotton wool, but I can definitely make out the cold. It seeps through my clothes and starts a shivering deep within me. I wonder what happened to my jacket, and then I remember transforming it into a mattress.

The second thing I notice is the song. Distant, eerie, and beautiful, it conjures up images of travelers being lured through mists to their demise. It's too far away for me to make out the words, but the hypnotic melody has woven its way into my mind in a way that makes it difficult for me to think about anything else.

With a great effort, like lifting a slab of stone with only my hands, I finally force my eyelids apart. I'm lying inside a cage. My back aches from being pressed against the cold, hard pieces of metal, but I feel something softer against my right arm. I turn my head to the side and see Ryn's face near mine. He's still knocked out. I move my hand slowly—I don't want to catch anyone else's attention—until I find his. I squeeze it, but he doesn't respond.

I look up through the cage's squares of space and see frost-covered branches moving against an inky blue sky and twinkling stars. I think perhaps the cage is floating because the movement feels far too smooth for it to be riding over the ground. I twist my head to the other side and see a forest dressed in winter. I catch glimpses of statues and fountains with moonlight glistening from icicles. The ground is white. Not with snow, but with thousands of broken shards of ice that sparkle like diamonds. Everything is frozen in cold, stark beauty.

This must be the Unseelie Court.

I raise my head slightly to look ahead. I see two bald, tattooed heads not far in front of the cage, striding along at a steady pace.

Oh crap, oh crap. How are we going to get out of this? The terrifying reality that we could soon be slaves under Draven's influence crashes down on me. I squeeze Ryn's hand again, but there's still nothing from him. With my other hand, I reach for one of my guardian knives. I feel its comforting warmth form beneath my fingers, then let go before one of the bounty hunters can turn around and see me.

I have weapons. I have magic. And when they open this cage, I'm going to fight like I've never fought be—

Light flashes down from the sky in a crackling zigzag. It strikes somewhere in front of us, sending a shuddering boom through the air. Seconds later our cage crashes to the ground. My head slams into the metal at the top of the cage before I drop to the ground. I hear Ryn moan next to me as I scramble into a sitting position. He has a gash across one side of his face, probably also from slamming into the cage.

Holding a hand to my throbbing head, I look out to see

what's going on. Both bounty hunters are lying motionless on the ground, the ice beside them melted.

"What the freak happened?" I whisper. Did Draven's guards do this? Have they gone back on their deal with the bounty hunters?

Just then, a person slips out of the trees and runs toward the hunters. I can't tell if the person is male or female, faerie or some other kind of fae. So I tug on the bars of the cage to see if anything broke when we fell. When I find it just as intact as before, I turn back to Ryn and start shaking him. He groans again, but he must still be lost in the stunner spell's grogginess because his eyelids don't even flicker.

"Hey, you ready to get out of here?"

I jerk back at the sound of the new voice, a knife already in my raised hand.

"Whoa, hold on there, guardian lady," a girl with short pink-and-blonde hair says. "I'm trying to help you." Without waiting for my reply, she reaches for a lock on one side of the cage and inserts a key. A key she must have just lifted off the bounty hunters. With hands that I notice are unmarked, she swings the side of the cage open and says, "Come on, wake your friend. The Unseelie dudes will be here soon."

When more shaking doesn't wake Ryn, I crawl out of the cage and grab his arms. I drag him halfway out before remembering I can move him with magic. With my arms spread forward, I lift him a few inches into the air. His boots trail across the ice shards as I maneuver him into the trees.

Off to my right, the girl is looking around. She has a large cylinder beneath her arm—a cylinder that looks suspiciously familiar—and is pointing it wherever her gaze falls. "Keep going until you get to the dragon," she says.

"Dragon?"

"Yeah, he's yours. I kind of … borrowed him. Hope you don't mind."

Something whizzes by my ear and lands with a quiet *thwack* in the tree right behind me. I spin around and see a five-pointed star with black, razor-sharp edges embedded in the frost.

"Crap," I mutter. I quickly conjure up a shield of magic and use my mind to pull it over Ryn like an invisible blanket.

"Look out!" the girl shouts. She opens the end of the cylinder and releases another bolt of lightning at whoever's attacking us.

I extend the shield to cover myself, but before I'm finished, pain slices across my left thigh. With my focus broken, Ryn drops onto the icy ground. I scramble for the shield magic, pulling it hastily over both of us, before dropping onto my knees and clutching my leg. The ice shards digging into my skin through my pants slowly turn red as blood spills from the gash.

"Come on!" the girl shouts as she runs past me, dodging flying objects and magic sparks. "I'll get the dragon."

"Dammit, Ryn, wake up!" I grasp my bleeding leg with one hand and shake Ryn with the other.

"Can't … move," he mumbles. I see his eyelids twitch as he tries to open them, but he doesn't seem to be having much success. Maybe they gave him an extra dose of stunner magic this time.

I look behind me and see distant figures hurrying toward us. "Ugh, crapping crap." I grab Ryn's face and do the first thing that comes to mind: I press my lips down on his, hoping to shock him into waking up.

The kiss only lasts a few seconds, but my brain has time to register several things: One, his lips are softer than I expected. Two, the eerie, hypnotic melody clears from my mind, and the sounds around me seem to dim for a moment. And three, the adrenaline spike I wish was running through *him* right now, jolting him awake from his enchanted lethargy, seems to be shooting through my own body.

He moves. I open my eyes—when did I close them?—and pull back. He blinks. "Did you ... just ..."

"Draven's guards are going to catch us if you don't get up NOW." I try to inject as much urgency into my words as possible. He sits up and gets clumsily to his feet. At the sound of crunching ice, we both look around. Arthur is coming toward us, his great, clawed feet crushing the sharpened shards like salt beneath a pestle.

"What ... how ..." Ryn says.

I pull him forward, limping with every step I take. Another throwing star zooms by, nicking my ear. "Dammit." I let go of Ryn and clutch my ear. He seems to have found his strength now, though, because he grabs me around the waist and lifts me up so I can scramble onto Arthur's back. I swing my uninjured leg over the harness and hold onto the shoulders of the girl in front of me.

"Good job, guys," she says as Ryn climbs up behind me. "Oh, I'm Tilly, by the way." She pats Arthur's neck, and he takes off, snapping a few more branches in the process.

I watch Draven's guards and their sparks of magic growing smaller and smaller as Arthur climbs toward the stars. I keep watching, my neck twisted back, as flying creatures arrive and the men climb onto them. But they're so far behind now, I doubt they'll catch up.

I look forward and find Tilly digging inside her jacket for something. The wind bites through my clothes, and I start shaking. I want to create a cocoon of heat around myself, but I also don't want to divert magic away from my leg, which is hopefully beginning to heal. Before I can make a decision, Ryn wraps his arms around me, enveloping me in warmth. My first instinct is to wriggle away; his embrace feels unfamiliar and weird. But it also feels comforting—and, more importantly, *warm*—so I ignore the part of me that feels strange.

"Okay, one of you needs to tell me what's going on," Ryn says, "because I feel like I missed a lot."

"I'll tell you in a sec," Tilly says, "if I can just … find … ah, here it is." She removes a stylus from her jacket. She takes hold of one end and pulls—and the stylus grows longer. Longer and longer until it's at least the length of Arthur's wingspan.

I've never seen anything like it, so I have to ask. "Is that—"

"An extendable stylus? Yeah. Very useful at times." She points it in front of her, so that it reaches past Arthur's snout, and starts making little wiggling motions in the air. "Man," she grumbles. "Writing doorways in the air is always a mission, especially with such a ridiculously long stylus."

"Let me do it," Ryn says. He reaches over my shoulder for the stylus. "I've always been good at air doorways."

"You have to do it quickly," she calls back to him. "Write the words, then drag the stylus across as fast as you can so we can fly straight through the doorway."

Ryn moves the stylus in small motions, then drags it quickly across Arthur's path, pulling open a doorway faster than I thought was possible. We disappear into the darkness. I try not to think of anything, allowing Tilly to direct the paths. Seconds later, light materializes in front of us. Blue sky and a midday sun greet us as we soar above the ocean.

I look behind us, expecting to see manticore riders in the distance, but I can't even see land from here. We must be really far out. Ryn hands the stylus back to Tilly, and she collapses it bit by bit back into itself. Then he wraps his arm around me again—despite the fact that it isn't as cold here—and says, "Tilly, you were going to tell me what happened?"

"Oh, yeah. I saw the bounty hunters capture you guys. I'm not supposed to leave the island, but, you know, I get kind of claustrophobic there sometimes. So I was out on my brother's pegasus that day, and I saw what happened. I followed your dragon—he headed for land, but far away from the bounty hunters' prison—and made friends with him. He's a cool dude." She rubs Arthur's neck and leans forward to give his scaly skin a kiss. "Anyway, then I came back this morning on him, hoping to break into the prison and get you guys out. I stole the lightning cylinder—super cool. I've seen them collecting during storms— and then discovered you were gone. When I found the bounty hunters, they were already going through a doorway with you. So I followed them."

"Wait, you followed them?" I say. "Through the faerie paths? But don't you have to—"

"—be in contact with them to follow them through? Nah. That's what the textbooks say, but my brother taught me a spell that allows you to follow the person in front of you without actually touching them, as long as you enter the paths before the doorway closes. Sometimes it goes wrong. I guess that's why it's not in the textbooks."

"I've heard of that happening," Ryn says. "It happened to you, V."

"Really?" I hate this no-memory thing.

"Yeah, so I'm not sure where we ended up," Tilly says, "but it was super creepy."

"The Unseelie Court," I tell her.

"Seriously?" She twists in the harness to look at me, and I nod. "Oh my hat, my brother is going to be *so* jealous. He and his friends are always trying to outdo each other with daring stuff. Of course, my mom would have a heart attack on the spot if she knew where I'd been. So, uh, please don't tell her."

"Is that where we're going?" Ryn asks. "To your home?"

"Yeah, I thought you might want to get cleaned up and stuff before you're on your way again." She hesitates, then adds, "Oh my word, sorry, do you want to be dropped off somewhere else? I didn't even ask."

"No, no," Ryn says. "We're actually … not sure where we want to be right now. And how would you get home if you left us somewhere with our dragon?"

"Uh, the faerie paths?" she says as if this should be obvious.

"But you're not marked," I say. "Draven's guys monitor the faerie paths for people who aren't marked. They'd come after you."

"Nah." Tilly seems completely unconcerned. "That doesn't happen where I live. We're quite separate from the rest of the world. We even have our own time."

Ryn leans forward, and his breath tickles my ear as he says, "Where exactly do you live, Tilly?"

"Oh, yeah, I didn't say where we were going, did I? Sorry! The Floating Island of Kaleidos."

I'm not sure if this is something I've forgotten or something I've never known, but I have no idea what she's talking about.

"But … no one knows where that is," Ryn says slowly.

"Well, obviously *I* do, silly, because I live there."

"People *live* on the Floating Island of Kaleidos?" he asks.

"Duh. Why else would we be heading there?"

I'm starting to wonder if this girl is really all there upstairs, and I think Ryn might be thinking the same thing. I feel his lips next to my ear. A shiver races down my neck as he whispers, "If I say jump, don't hesitate."

I nod and scoop my flyaway hair behind one ear.

Ryn leans back a little and raises his voice to say, "So, Tilly, I've read that people have gone mad sailing across the ocean searching for the Floating Island of Kaleidos."

I roll my eyes. *Way to be subtle, Ryn.*

"Yeah, well, it isn't the easiest thing to spot," she says. "You have to get really close to see it, otherwise it kind of just looks like a shimmer in the sky. It's like … what are those things you get in the desert?"

"A mirage?"

"Yeah, that. But in reverse, because as you get closer you see that something *is* there instead of not being there."

I'm definitely questioning her sanity now.

"See? Look over there." She points forward, and I'm stunned to find that there *is* actually a shimmer in the sky ahead of us. Of course, there could be nothing on the other side of it.

As we fly toward the shimmer, I feel Ryn's arms tense around me. I guess I'm not the only one worried this might be some new, horrible magic we're flying into. The shimmer changes as we get closer, glistening with colorful smudges like a painting left out in the rain.

"Aaand welcome to my home," Tilly says, spreading her arms out as we shoot through the shimmering layer.

Despite all the magic I've seen in my life, my first reaction when I see the floating island is disbelief. The enormous piece of land is suspended high up in the air as easily as if it were floating on water. The underside looks like a mixture of rock and rich brown earth, and the top is covered in grass, trees, lakes, and mountains. Warm air caresses my skin. The scent of spring reaches my nose.

"No way," I whisper as Arthur soars toward the island. This place is a haven, untouched by the devastation the rest of our world is living through. Part of me wants to land here and never leave.

As we fly closer, I see trees here and there that are larger than the others. Larger, in fact, than any tree I've ever seen or imagined. And along the branches I see shapes that look like … houses. Yes, those are tree houses, but nothing like the tree houses I'm used to, concealed so that no one knows they're there. These are visible for everyone to see, cradled amongst the enormous branches.

Tilly steers Arthur toward one of the lakes. He lands on the bank, his feet sinking into the squishy mud. "Well done, Arthur," Ryn mutters. "The mud is exactly where we want to get off."

"Oh, is your name Arthur, big guy?" Tilly pats his neck and gives him another kiss. "I was wondering."

Arthur climbs up the bank, leaving muddy footprints on the grass beneath the overhanging trees. Tilly slides down, and I follow her. My leg screams at me when I land with a jolt. I guess it hasn't had a chance to do much healing yet.

"What happened?" Ryn asks when he sees me gritting my teeth and clutching my leg.

"A throwing star. It cut pretty deep, but it'll be fine in a few hours, I'm sure."

"You sure? I can give you some healing magic if you—"

"No, no." I wave his concern away. "Don't worry about it."

"Okay, so, I'm not really sure where to leave Arthur," Tilly says. "I hid him here after I first brought him back, but he burned down a tree and tried to eat my brother's pegasus."

Ryn crosses his arms and faces the dragon. "Not cool, Arthur. You don't eat other people's stuff."

Arthur snorts a puff of smoke at Ryn, then starts shrinking. He keeps going until he's no bigger than my hand.

"So. Cool!" Tilly exclaims. "I didn't know dragons could do that."

"Well, not all of them," Ryn says as Arthur flaps his way up to Ryn's shoulder. "You don't have to worry about leaving him somewhere. He'll come with us."

We follow Tilly along a well-worn path toward one of the giant trees. She bounces along as though she's on some energy-inducing spell. The tree has a curving stairway wrapped around the trunk all the way up as far as I can see. Tilly starts jogging up, while Ryn slips an arm around my back.

"Don't argue," he says. "I know you're in pain."

We'll be down here forever if I start arguing with him, so I don't. Besides, it's nice of him to help me up, even though I have a feeling he's only doing it to be closer to me. We're going to have to have a chat about that kiss so I can tell him it didn't mean anything.

Fortunately, Tilly's house is along one of the lowest branches, so we don't have to climb too high. She skips along the wide branch like a tree sprite and opens the door for us when we reach her house.

"Welcome," she says, stepping aside to let us in. The interior is small, but not as cramped as the quarters I've become used to with the reptiscillas and guardians. "My mom would probably say, 'Please excuse the mess,' but I honestly think it looks fine." I hide a smile as I follow Tilly past a living area and into a bedroom with two narrow beds. "This is our spare room. I'm sure my mom won't mind you staying here if you need to."

"Thanks, Tilly," Ryn says. His arm slides away from me. "It's very kind of you to offer."

She beams as us. "Well, I'd better go find my mom. I disappeared before breakfast this morning, and she's probably launched a search party by now. And *you* guys need to have a shower or something because—" she lowers her voice to a mock whisper "—you stink. Bathing room's through there." She gestures over her shoulder with her thumb. "Oh, and your bags are here. I stole them from the bounty hunters' house the day they took you. Nice sword, by the way." She lifts the sword off the top of Ryn's bag and slides it partway out of its sheath. "I love how it glows. Anyway, see you later." She skips away.

CHAPTER 22

I GRAB THE SWORD OFF THE TOP OF RYN'S BAG AND YANK IT out from its sheath, but the glow has already faded. I look at Ryn, who's staring at the sword in open-mouthed shock. "It *glows*?" I say. "Has it done that before?"

He shakes his head.

"Do you think she's the one?" I whisper. "The girl we've been looking for?"

"I don't know. I certainly wasn't picturing someone like … her."

"Yeah, me neither." I turn the sword over in my hands. "Maybe she touched a button or something that we didn't know about. Something that makes the sword glow."

Ryn takes the sword from me and sits on the edge of one of the beds. He begins examining it, pressing here and there with his fingers. Arthur jumps from his shoulder, curls up on the pillow, and promptly goes to sleep.

"Tilly?" A woman's voice rings out. "Tilly!" The frustrated call is followed by stomping footsteps. "Estelle Marie Blakethorn, *where* have you been?"

Ryn straightens. "Did someone just call her *Estelle?*"

"Yeah."

"You know what that means, don't you?"

I have to think for several seconds before I remember the meaning of the word. "Star," I whisper. "Her name means *star*."

"And this floating island is obviously the high land. She's 'the Star of the high land.'"

I slowly lower myself onto the other bed. "We found her. We actually found the Star." Or, more accurately, she found us. I know I should be happier, but Tilly isn't at all what I was expecting. It doesn't seem right that a girl so young should have to be the one to destroy Draven and his power.

Skipping footsteps sound in the passage, and Tilly appears in our doorway. "So, um, my mom said it's cool if you stay here a while. I told her I found you just outside the shimmer and that you're on the run from Draven's dudes. Which ... is ... sort of true. She had to dash out for a meeting, so she'll say hi later."

"Great, thank you, Tilly." Ryn stands. "Do you have a secure amber I can use? Amber with anti-tracking spells on it?"

She tilts her head to the side. "I don't know. But amber messages don't go through the shimmer. No communication does. It's something to do with the time differences."

"Time differences?" Ryn asks.

"Yeah, remember I said we have our own time here?"

I remember her saying that, but that was back when I thought she might be a little bit crazy.

"Time inside the shimmer doesn't match time outside the shimmer," she explains. "Sometimes a day in here is a week out there; sometimes a day in here is only an hour out there. I once went out and arrived at exactly the same moment I'd left almost a month before. You know how I know? Because the same mermaids were sitting on the same rocks by the shore arguing about the same guy they'd both just found out they were dating." She bounces on her feet. "Aw-kward, right? I mean, the dating thing. Not the time thing. Although that's pretty weird too."

I thought Natesa chatted a lot, but she's got *nothing* on this girl. She's so carefree and enthusiastic and ... young. And we're about to lay the fate of our world on her shoulders.

While Ryn rubs his temples and stares at the floor, probably worrying about the time thing, I ask, "How old are you, Tilly?"

"Fifteen. Why?"

"Just ... curious."

"Okay, well, you guys should really visit the bathing room. Check ya later." She bounces away, leaving us in silence.

Ryn paces for a while, then sits on the edge of his bed again. "She's so young," he says. "How can we do this to her?"

"She's only three years younger than us," I point out.

"But she doesn't have the experience we do. She hasn't survived the things we've survived. She's lived a sheltered, carefree life. How can we tell her she's the only one who can put an end to Tharros' power for good?"

I swallow and force the words out. "We have to."

"That part at the end of the prophecy. '*By the strike of the sword, and the death of innocence.*' I've been trying to figure out what the 'innocence' refers to." He gestures to the doorway. "What if it's her? What if we're leading her to her death?"

Would the prophecy really be that cruel? In order for our world to be normal again, this sweet, innocent girl has to die? I grasp for some other meaning. "What if it's ... something else, something bigger—"

"Like what?"

"I don't know! Like ... like *all* our innocence. Like the fact that we'll never be the same after this."

Ryn flops back on his bed, flinching when Arthur's snores burn his ear. "Life is never fair, is it?"

"No," I murmur.

* * *

I lie on the bed, staring into the darkness and listening to the gentle stirring of leaves outside. The floorboards creak occasionally as the giant branches holding the house sway. I breathe in deeply, enjoying the sweet, fresh scent drifting from the purple and white blossoms growing on bushes at the base of the tree. The eerie melody that woke me still plays at the back of my mind.

After getting ourselves cleaned up, we decided to wait until tomorrow to tell Tilly about the prophecy and the sword and her role in the coming fight against Draven. I think we both wanted to give her one more day of ignorant bliss.

We had dinner with her family, and Tilly spent the rest of the evening playing with mini-Arthur. It's strange to be in a place that seems so untouched by Draven. There's no fear here. No loss. People mention The Destruction every now and then, but only as some distant tragedy that has no direct effect on them.

I can't help wondering how long this haven will last, though. Draven will find out about this place eventually, if he hasn't already, and he'll come after the fae living here. He won't stop until he has the entire world under his control—or until we kill him.

I hear Ryn roll over and breathe out a frustrated sigh. "What's wrong?" I ask quietly. "Can't sleep without a wall between us?"

"Yeah, I'm really missing that wall. I now get the loud version of your snoring instead of the muffled version."

"Hey, I do not snore."

"Okay, not *real* snoring. It's more like these cute little half-snores that sound like—"

"I. Do not. Snore."

He sighs. "Okay, if you want the real story, here it is: There's this weird, creepy song playing over and over in my head, and it won't let me sleep."

I turn onto my side so I'm facing him and say, "It's from the Unseelie Court. My brain won't let go of it either. It woke me up, actually. Well, that and my leg."

"Your leg? The cut from the throwing star?"

"Yes. I'm a little worried. It should've healed hours ago."

I hear shuffling and the quiet snap of Ryn's fingers. A flame blazes to life over his hand, and he moves it to the candle beside his bed. He gets up and comes toward me. "Let me see."

I push my blanket back and swing my legs over the edge of the bed. I'm wearing a pair of Tilly's sleeping shorts, so the bandage wrapped around my leg just above my knee is easily visible. I unwind the layers and show Ryn the seeping cut and the angry red skin around it.

He touches my leg and looks closer. His hand is cool against my hot skin. "I had a wound like that," he says. "An Unseelie faerie gave it to me with a black-bladed knife."

I think back to the throwing star and remember the sharp, black edges. "I think it's the same thing. How did you heal it?"

"I didn't. I had to wait till I got to the base. Uri gave me some kind of enchanted salve to put on it. He said the blade leaves magic in the wound that counters the body's healing magic. So your body keeps trying to heal the wound, but the wound keeps fighting back."

"Well, that sucks. I'm guessing you don't have any of that salve with you?"

"No, sorry." His hand slides away from my leg, and I have this insane urge to tell him to put it back. Only because his hand is cool, of course, and my skin is so hot and uncomfortable. No other reason. No reason for my heart to start pumping extra fast. Ugh, I think this wound might be making me delirious.

"So …" he says without getting up, "that was quite a way to be woken up back there at the Unseelie Court."

For a moment I don't know what he's talking about. Then I remember the kiss. "Oh. That. I was just trying to shock the stunner magic out of your system."

"It certainly worked."

"I know. Thank goodness."

He shifts a little, and I feel his shoulder brush mine. I'm suddenly very aware of his hand *right there* and his arm *right there* and his leg *right there*. Does he have to sit so close? Seriously. He obviously has no idea about personal space, because he is definitely invading mine. And I am not cool with it. At all. Which is why I should slide myself away from him. Now. Right now. I'm going to do it—

"Okay, so, we're going to tell Tilly everything tomorrow," he says.

"Yeah."

"I should probably get back to bed."

"Yeah."

"So, I guess, good night?"

"Uh huh."

He chuckles and gives me a knowing smile, although I have no idea what he thinks he *knows*. I wrap the bandage hastily around my leg before lying down. I pull the blanket over me, turn to face the wall, and pretend nothing weird just happened.

The light goes out.

* * *

After breakfast the next morning, Tilly offers to give us a tour of her floating island. Ryn exchanges a look with me, then says, "Actually, we need to talk to you about something. Something really important and … life-changing."

"Oh, okay. Sure." She looks between the two of us, as if trying to figure out what's going on, then says, "Let's go sit on the deck." She leads us out the back of her house and onto a wooden platform with no railing. We sit down and hang our legs over the edge. It's so peaceful here in the shade with birds twittering nearby and sprites with umbrella-shaped wings floating around. I hate to have to ruin it with what we're about to tell her. "So?" She swings her legs back and forth. "What's this big deal stuff you want to tell me about?"

Ryn sighs and launches into his story. He gives her the history first, about Tharros and the fact that even though he was killed, his power was never destroyed. Then he tells her about Zell, the Unseelie Prince who hunted down the chest of power, and Draven, the guy who eventually killed Zell and took the power for himself. Lastly, he tells her about the prophecy, the sword, and the Order of the Guard—and how our journey to find the Star led us to her.

When Ryn finishes, Tilly's legs are no longer swinging back and forth. "Okay," she says, staring at nothing. "Mind. Officially. Blown."

My eyes meet Ryn's over Tilly's head. He gives me a helpless look that says, *Now what?* I touch Tilly's shoulder and say, "What do you think about all that?"

"I think ... I mean ..." She takes a deep breath. "Are you sure it's me? It just seems really unlikely that a fifteen-year-old girl who's never fought anyone before is supposed to save the whole world from the powerful, evil guy who's bent on controlling everything."

I don't tell her that that's exactly what we were thinking.

"Your name means 'star,' doesn't it?" Ryn asks. "And you live on the 'high land.' The sword glows when you touch it. It's never done that before. And when Vi searched for you, we landed up across the world so close to you that you watched us being captured by the bounty hunters. I don't think it can be anyone else but you, Tilly."

She nods slowly, biting her lip and staring through the branches. "Just, uh, give me a minute." She stands, pulls herself up onto a branch leaning over the deck, and climbs onto the roof of her house. She disappears out of view.

I turn back to Ryn. "I'm guessing she's going to need more than a minute."

He pulls his knees up and rests his folded arms atop them. "I don't want to have to force her to do this."

I twirl a piece of hair around my finger and watch umbrella sprites jumping from the tree top. They spin in slow circles as they float to the ground. "I don't think it'll come to that. It's a lot for her to take in, but I don't think she's going to refuse."

We sit quietly, watching the world tick slowly by. I try not to think of how time might be speeding along outside this place.

"Vi? Ryn?" I look up at the sound of Tilly's voice. She hops down from her roof and stands behind us. "We're not safe here, are we? I mean, everyone thinks we are. They think we're hidden from Draven. But he's going to find us eventually, isn't he?"

I nod as I stand. "Draven will find everyone eventually."

She looks at her shoes. "I thought so. It isn't just the world out there I'd be saving. It's the world in here too."

"So, you'll do it?" Ryn stands up beside me.

"Well, duh. I mean, it's to save the whole world, right? I can't say no to that. I didn't even think I had a choice."

"There's always a choice," I say quietly.

She frowns. "You do *want* me to do this, don't you?"

"Yes, of course," I say. "We just … want to make sure you understand what you're getting into. Understand that you might …"

"Die?" She rolls her eyes. "Yeah, I figured that one out. But everyone has to die at some point, right? I may as well do it while saving the world. I mean, not that I *want* to die, but if it has to happen now, then at least it'll be while I'm doing something worthwhile." She smiles, but it doesn't quite reach her eyes this time. I hate that we've done that to her. That we've dimmed the light that seemed to shine perpetually in her eyes.

"We're not going to let you die, Tilly," Ryn says.

Her smile stretches a little wider, and a hint of the light returns to her eyes. "As comforting as that sounds to me, I doubt it'll make my parents feel any better when I tell them where I'm going. I'm pretty sure they're going to freak out."

Her parents. Right. They'll almost certainly tell her she can't do this.

"When do you want to talk to them?" Ryn asks.

"Now." She swivels around and faces the door. "I'm going to talk to them right now. I mean, this is urgent. It can't wait till later. We have no idea what time is doing out there. And if we wait too long, I might get scared and change my mind." She takes a deep breath, then hurries into the house.

I take slow steps toward the doorway. I lean against the frame and listen to the muffled voices behind the closed door of Tilly's parents' bedroom. After several minutes, the voices become raised. Ryn joins me in the doorway.

"Doesn't sound good," he says.

The bedroom door flies open, and Tilly's father storms out. "Where are they? They'd better—ah, there they are." He spins around and heads toward us. "You two need to take your things and leave right now. How dare you come into our home and fill Tilly's head with these ridiculous stories?"

Ryn holds his hands up. "Please, just let me show you the—"

"No! Tilly will have no part in this. She's just a child."

"Dad, I'm—"

"Quiet, Estelle. These people will only get you killed. There is absolutely no way I'm letting you go with them."

I bite my lip. His words could very well be true; we may indeed be leading her to her death.

"Well?" he says. "I asked you to leave!"

I hurry down the passage to the spare bedroom and lift my bag off the bed. Ryn slings the sword strap over his head and places Arthur on his shoulder. "Come on," he mutters. "We're not helping by being here."

We head back to the lake where Arthur first landed. As soon as we reach the overhanging trees and gently lapping water, Arthur leaps off Ryn's shoulder and starts expanding. He flies out over the lake as he grows, and by the time he lands in the middle with a loud splash, he's reached his full size.

"Now what?" I dump my bag on the ground. "We can't leave without her."

Ryn shakes his head. "We have to figure something out. If we go back to the base without her, they'll send a team here to take her by force."

"You think Oliver would do that?"

"He wouldn't want to, but, in the end, I think he would. This is the fate of the *whole world* we're talking about, V. We can't end Draven's rule without her."

I sit down on an oversized tree root and lean my head back against the trunk. "Okay, let's wait a few hours and see if she manages to convince her parents."

Ryn sits down and lies back on the grass. "I don't see that happening."

"Well, there isn't much else we can do right now."

We watch the cotton puffs of cloud through the branches as the sun moves across the sky. After a lot of pacing, sitting, lying down, and playing with Arthur, the sky begins to cycle through the colors of sunset. Night approaches. The stars pop out. After watching their slow trail across the heavens for several hours, I say, "I gather we're spending the night out here."

"Yeah, I guess so." Ryn adds a few more lines to the picture he's drawing in the air with my stylus. "Could be worse, though. It could be Draven's winter instead of a balmy spring on a floating island."

I smile. If we have to be sleeping outside somewhere, this is certainly the place to be.

"How's your leg feeling?"

"Still pretty bad." Like someone is stabbing the throwing star into my leg over and over again, but Ryn doesn't need to know that.

He sits up and leans on one hand. "Want me to try a numbing spell?"

"Thanks, but I tried that already." I push myself up and stretch my painful leg out straight in front of me and bend the other. "I don't enjoy how it makes my leg feel like it's fallen asleep."

"A leg that's fallen asleep probably isn't the easiest thing to walk on."

"No."

He looks down at his hand on the ground, and I realize it's almost touching mine. "I just … hate knowing that you're in pain." His words make me feel warm inside. His gaze catches hold of mine, and I give him a small smile. "When we were about nine years old, not too long before Reed had his accident, you and I were climbing up the gargan tree. Remember I told you about it? The tree we always used to hang out in?"

I nod, still unable to look away. It was one of the many things Ryn told me about when we were in the bounty hunters' prison.

"We hadn't climbed too far when you slipped and fell. You broke your leg. You couldn't walk, so I needed to fetch someone to heal you. We knew some basic magic by then, but we weren't old enough to use the faerie paths. It would have taken me over an hour to run home and try to contact my parents—who were working that night—and explain to them where you were. The sun was setting. Dangerous creatures could have appeared at any moment. I didn't want to leave you alone.

"Being the stubborn girl you've always been, you told me you'd be fine. But I couldn't bring myself to leave you there like that. I could feel ... well, not your pain exactly, because that's a physical feeling, but I could feel your distress. And your fear. And I could see on your face how much pain you were in. I wanted so badly to make it better, so ... I tried. I put my hands around your leg. I didn't have the first clue how to use healing magic, but it just ... kind of ... happened. Maybe I was so desperate to give you my magic that it all just ran out of me. Your pain disappeared, and I was left feeling exhausted. We both stumbled home, and we never told anyone what happened."

"I ... thank you." I don't know what else to say.

He shrugs, looking away. "I'm not sure why I thought of that. Probably because I still feel kind of ... protective when it comes to you. Like if you're hurting, I should make it better."

His eyes find mine once more. It's hard to tell in the moon-light, but I think his cheeks have more color in them than usual. I should really lean away from him or something because he's definitely invading my space again. And I'm not supposed to be cool with that, right? Except ... I know I was lying to myself last night, and I know I'm lying to myself again now. I *like* the fact that his skin is only inches away from mine. I *like* the shiver that zings up my spine and along my arms.

"V ..." he whispers. "I really ... just ..."

Dear Seelie Queen, is he leaning closer to me? Is he about to ... An insane thought enters my mind that he might be about to kiss me—followed by the even more insane thought that I might actually let him.

A *whoosh* in the air beside us makes me jerk away. The picture

Ryn was drawing in the air—which looks like it might be a floating island—bursts into bright orange flames.

"What? How did that—"

"Hey, guys! I thought you'd be here." Running footsteps and the sound of Tilly's voice make me pull even further away from Ryn.

"Tilly?" Ryn swats away the last of the flames and stands. "What happened? Did your parents let you go?"

"Uh, not exactly." Her bag slips off her shoulder, and she pushes the strap back up. "My brother helped me sneak out. I don't know how long it'll be before my parents find out I'm gone, so we should probably leave right away." She heads straight over to Arthur and starts climbing onto his leg.

"Tilly, wait." I stand up and limp after her. "Are you sure this is the way you want to leave? You might ... you might never see your family again."

Her eyes slide away from mine as she nods. "I know. I said goodbye to them in my own way. They just ... didn't know I was saying goodbye."

"Tilly," Ryn says. "Are you sure about this?"

She lets out an exasperated sigh. "Yes, come on! We've got a world to save."

PART IV
VIOLET

CHAPTER 23

"THAT WAS ALMOST TOO EASY," RYN SAYS AS ARTHUR GLIDES
down the landing strip on the transportation level of the Fireglass
Vale base. We decided to risk the faerie paths and exited about an
hour away from the base. I kept watch behind us after we came
through, but if Draven's guards showed up to see who used the
paths, they must have done so on the ground. And, of course,
there are no bounty hunters in this area.

"Yeah, I was expecting someone to chase us," Tilly says,
sounding almost disappointed.

We land, and Ryn jumps down to open Arthur's enclosure.
"We should be just in time for lunch," he says.

"We should probably visit Oliver first and let him know we're
back," I say as I slide down Arthur's leg. I help Ryn with the
enclosure, then usher an already shrinking Arthur inside.

We cross the landing strip and climb the stairs to the floor
with the meeting rooms. "Oliver's probably somewhere here
making plans with people," Ryn says, "if he's not up in the dining
—ah, there he is." We stop by a room with a large table in the
center. Several people are leaning over the table examining pages.

Oliver is off to the side, looking at a book with Amon, the librarian we rescued.

"These are the most recent drawings I can find of the inside," Amon says. "They probably don't show everything, but you can see a number of the rooms, especially the private quarters."

"Thank you, Amon, this is incredibly useful," Oliver says, taking the book. "Now we just need to figure out which of these rooms are Draven's, and then we'll—" His words are cut off as Ryn taps on the door and enters. "You're … you're alive!" Oliver exclaims.

"Of course," Ryn says. "Come on, Oliver. We disappear for a week and you think we've pegged? I'm offended."

"A week?" Oliver pushes the book into Amon's hands and crosses the room. He pulls Ryn into a quick embrace, then says, "Ryn, it's been almost a month since you left. I didn't think we'd ever see you again."

"A month?" Ryn looks over at Tilly, who gives him an apologetic smile.

"I did warn you about the time thing," she says.

"And you found another survivor?" Oliver asks, noticing Tilly.

"No, no, no," Ryn says, ushering Tilly forward. "This, Oliver, is the Star."

Oliver's eyebrows travel up his forehead as he looks between Ryn and Tilly, probably wondering if this is a joke. Before he can say anything, Tilly says, "I know, I know. I'm not the world-saving warrior you were expecting. But … here I am." She spreads her arms wide and grins.

Oliver blinks a few more times, then says, "You're right. You're not quite what I was expecting. But if the prophecy has picked you, then you're obviously the right girl. And your timing couldn't be more perfect, uh …"

"Tilly," she says, sticking her hand out to shake his.

"We've really been gone a month?" Ryn asks, placing his bag and the sword on the ground. "What have we missed?"

Oliver wipes a hand across his brow and sighs. "What *haven't* you missed?"

"That much, huh?"

Oliver nods to the guardians gathered around the table, and they stop their staring and get back to examining the pages I now see are maps. Then he leans against the wall and crosses his arms. "Let's see. A few days after the explosion, which turned out *not* to be an attack, we discovered a group of Draven's faeries hiding several hours from here. So we sent several teams to take care of them, and that turned out to be a trap. Our guardians were completely overwhelmed. Only one survived and made it back here. We've since had attacks on a number of our other teams, until it got to the point where I stopped sending people out unless absolutely necessary. We … lost a lot of people."

"My father?" Ryn asks quickly.

"Your father was injured and almost captured, but he got away. He's fine now."

Ryn nods as relief relaxes his features.

"Anyway, then the elves arrived and then the reptiscillas."

"The reptiscillas?" I repeat. My heart leaps at the thought of seeing my friends again.

"Yes, just those who can fight, though. The rest are still at their hideout. So we then finalized all our alliances and started putting plans in place for our big move against Draven. And who should arrive at that point? None other than the Seelie Queen herself."

"The Seelie Queen?" Tilly's eyes widen.

"Yes. Total prima donna, that one. Thinks she can run the show."

"Well, she is the Queen," I say, looking around to see if anyone else is listening to Oliver's potentially treacherous statements. The only person within earshot is Amon, and he just laughs and shakes his head.

"Sadly, though," Oliver continues, "the Queen doesn't know the first thing about how to plan a successful attack on an evil overlord. Which is why she has us to plan it for her. She needs to accept that and stop being such a control freak."

"Oliver, does that mean my father's here?" I ask. "Ryn said he was working with the Seelie Queen."

"Your father …" Oliver scratches his head. "Uh, yes, he was. But the Queen sent him out about a week ago on some private mission." Oliver clearly doesn't approve of 'private missions.'

"Oh." I try to rein in my disappointment.

"Yes, uh, sorry about that. Right, so, that takes us up to the most important thing you've missed, which is that it's all going down tomorrow night. Our big move. Our last chance. The end of Draven."

"*Tomorrow?*" Tilly squeaks. "So … now probably wouldn't be the best time to mention that I've never had any combat training and haven't the first clue how to fight anyone, would it?"

"Except for shooting people with lightning," I remind her.

"Except for that."

"You have nothing to worry about," Oliver says, pushing away from the wall and placing both his hands on Tilly's shoulders. "You'll be with my team the entire time. It's the largest and most experienced team, since we're the ones who'll be going after Draven himself. We'll make sure you stay safe up until the moment you have to stab him. That's it. No fighting until that moment. Then it's just one move and it'll all be over."

He makes it sound so easy.

"Oliver, if we hadn't come back now, you'd be doing all this without Tilly and the sword," Ryn says. "How exactly were you planning to get rid of Draven?"

"We weren't. We hoped to capture him and keep him imprisoned until we could find the Star ourselves. Not the best plan, I know, but we couldn't wait around for Draven to discover this base and make his move before we could make ours."

"Is that … the weapon?" Amon interrupts. He steps closer to us, looking past Ryn at the sword lying on top of his bag. "The one I've read about?"

"Yes." Oliver reaches for it and passes the strap over his head so that the sword hangs across his back. "Can't leave that lying around."

"Thank goodness it's safe," Amon says. "I was so concerned after the explosion that it had been destroyed. I thought it might have been kept down there with all the other spare weapons."

"No, no, of course not," Oliver says.

"What's it looking like on that level?" Ryn asks. "Still a mess?"

"Oh, no, we couldn't leave it in a state of ruin. The training center is on that level, and our warriors need to keep on training as long as they're not out on missions. And, well, Uri wanted his lab back. With added protective magic, of course. In case of another explosion."

"So, it's all back to normal?" I ask. I remember the extensive damage we passed as we hurried out of here the day we all thought we were being attacked. It must have taken a long time to fix that up.

"Yes, just about." Oliver runs a hand through his messy hair. "Now, uh, I really need to get back to these maps and drawings." He takes the book once more from Amon. "Em will fill you in on what's happening tomorrow night, Ryn. The teams have already been briefed."

"Oh, okay." Ryn looks like he might have wanted to stay longer, but Oliver has already placed the book on the table and is paging through it.

"Oh, wait," he says, turning back to us. "Tilly, I think you should stay here. I don't want to let you out of my sight until this is all over."

Tilly looks at me, then shrugs. "Sure, okay. But only if you tell me exactly what I'm supposed to do tomorrow night because I'm still feeling kind of lost here, and lost is *not* what I want to be when I'm scuttling around the Unseelie Court."

Oliver smiles. "You won't be lost, Tilly. I'll make sure of that."

Ryn lifts his bag off the floor, and the two of us head up toward the dining room. We pass the level that was destroyed by Uri's explosion, and, sure enough, it looks like it's almost back to normal. Cracks line the tiles here and there, and some of the wooden paneling still needs to be replaced, but other than that, you'd never guess it was almost demolished a month ago.

We climb the stairs to the ground level, my aching leg protesting all the way. As we near the dining room, two figures we recognize walk out. Em and Max, arguing about something. Em stops the moment she sees us. "Ryn!" she shouts. "You didn't die a horrible death out there!" She runs over and throws her arms around him. A nasty—and entirely unexpected—monster named Jealousy rears its ugly head in my stomach. I hurriedly beat it back down as Em jumps out of Ryn's arms and pumps her fist in the air. "Woot! Team Troll's Butt is back in action!"

"What happened, man?" Max says. "You've been gone for weeks."

"Time disappeared a little faster than we wanted it to," Ryn says. "But we found the Star."

"Seriously? That's great!" Em gives Ryn a high five, and the Jealousy monster struggles to break free again. And why shouldn't it? I mean, Ryn was mine before I forgot everything, wasn't he? Don't I have some kind of claim over him? He said he had a right to be jealous of my friendship with Jamon, so don't I have a right to be jealous of his friendship with Em? Especially if it was ever more than a friendship?

You're facing the biggest battle of your life tomorrow, and you're worrying about jealousy? *STOP IT!*

Ryn glances at me, then claps Max on the shoulder and says, "What's happening tomorrow night? Oliver said you'd fill me in."

"Yeah, it's all been planned out perfectly. Groups of us are being sent to all the locations where Draven's guardians and warriors are based. So, basically, all the Guilds. And by 'us' I mean every single fae who's allied against Draven. We're going to use the faerie paths, all at the exact same moment. Our enemies won't be able to call for reinforcements because every Guild and base will be attacked at the same time."

"Do we have enough fighters to do that?" Ryn asks.

"Oliver thinks so, and so do the others who are in charge. They know the numbers. We just have to trust them."

"I don't know." Ryn lets his bag slip to the ground. "I feel like we're rushing this. Like we're not ready yet."

"Dude, you've missed out on a month of training and planning. We're way more prepared than when you left."

Em nods. "We can't wait forever. We want our world back, and people are starting to feel like it's now or never."

"And when we come face to face with people we love and care about? Does Oliver expect us to simply kill them?"

"Oh, no, our orders are to capture as many as we can," Em says. "Every faerie will be going in with stunning power already gathered. We're hoping that as soon as Draven has been destroyed, his influence will lift from everyone."

"And if it doesn't?" I ask.

"And what about the fact that up until half an hour ago, Oliver didn't actually have the Star?" Ryn says. "He would have had no way to destroy Draven."

"The merpeople built an underwater prison," Max says. "It's at the bottom of the ocean. We were going to keep every marked person there until the Star could be found and Draven destroyed."

Ryn's mouth drops open. "That was the brilliant plan?"

"Yes, but now we won't have to do that," Em says. "If everything goes according to plan, Draven will be gone tomorrow night."

Ryn takes a deep breath, then starts nodding as he lets it out slowly. "You're right. This needs to end. And we have the Star now, so the prison plan doesn't really matter."

"Exactly," Max says. "But what does matter is that lunch is almost over, and you look like you could do with some food."

"Sounds like a good idea." I take Ryn's arm and pull him in the direction of the dining room.

"See you later," Em says, waving as she walks off with Max.

"Oh, Em," Ryn calls after her. He looks back at me. "You go on without me. I need to talk to Em about something." He squeezes my hand. "I'll see you later." He hurries after her.

Well, that didn't help the Jealousy monster at all.

Feeling somewhat dejected and not exactly hungry, I limp toward the dining room. I look inside, and the moment I see shades of blue-green sitting amongst the black-clad guardians, my spirits lift. Of course. The reptiscillas are here. I squeeze between the tables, searching for Jamon. When I see him, I smile and hurry toward his table, forgetting my sore leg for the moment.

I place my hands on my hips and say, "You left without saying goodbye."

"Violet?" He drops his fork and jumps up. "Well, at least I didn't disappear without a trace leaving everyone to think I'd never be back."

I laugh and give him a hug. "I'm glad to see you noticed I was missing."

"But you're okay?"

"Yeah, we were just out there getting us all one step closer to defeating Draven." I sit beside him and drop my bag onto the floor at my feet. "So how's everyone back at the mountain? Have you told Natesa you're madly in love with her yet?"

"I have, actually."

"Seriously?" I start laughing again. "I'm stunned."

"I told her that if we all get out of this alive, I'm ignoring the rules. I'm not forming a union with some girl I've never met. Life seems too short not to spend it with the people we love, you know? I saw you and Ryn and—" He cuts himself off. "Uh, sorry. I ... never mind."

"What?" I nudge his elbow with my own. "Tell me."

"I just ... I saw his face the moment he realized you didn't know who he was. That moment when he figured out you might never remember, and you might never love him again. And there I was *knowing* that I loved Natesa and *knowing* that she loved me too. How could I throw that away just because some ancient rule says I should be with someone else I don't even know?"

I look down at my hands. Hearing him talk about Ryn like that, about how I've hurt him—intentionally or not—makes my insides squirm. But this isn't about Ryn and me or my guilt that I messed things up for us; this is about Jamon and Natesa. "Yeah," I say, forcing the smile back onto my face. "You did the right thing. I bet your father wasn't too excited about it, though."

Jamon rolls his eyes. "My father ... That's another story. But he'll come around, I'm sure."

We chat for a while as the dining room slowly empties. I tell Jamon about the bounty hunters and the floating island and my glimpse of the Unseelie Court, and he gives me more details on tomorrow night's plan and tells me about the less than friendly welcome the reptiscillas received when they first got here. I try to apologize for my kind, but he waves my words away, assuring me it isn't that bad anymore.

"It was actually quite funny," he says, "the first day we were in the fixed-up training center with guardians, reptiscillas, elves, and all these other fae who stayed here for a few days of boot camp. The guardians were all lined up together, arms crossed and mega frowns on their faces. I swear, their expressions were like, 'Seriously? You're making us fight with *them*? The scum of the fae world?' And by the end of the first day, you could see the surprise on their faces, like, 'Hey, these guys might actually be able to help us.'"

"Good to know they came around in the end," a voice from behind me says. "I was afraid some guardians' prejudices could never be overcome."

Ryn rounds the table and takes a seat opposite me. My stomach does a weird flip-flop kind of thing at the sight of him, as if it's been weeks since I saw him instead of, well, minutes. Ridiculous. Seriously ridiculous.

"There are still a few who refuse to be friendly," Jamon says, "but they're not worth getting upset over."

Ryn nods, and the two of them reach across the table and shake hands. They exchange a few words of greeting. Ryn's smile is open and genuine, not like the guarded looks he gave Jamon when they first met. I guess his own Jealousy monster has vanished.

He leans on the table and says, "V, how's your leg? Have you seen Uri?"

"Oh, no, I haven't left the dining room yet."

"Violet! Violet!" I look across the almost empty dining room and see the scrawny urisk hurrying toward me with one knobbly hand clenched around something.

"Well, speak of the fuzzy little devil, and there he is," Ryn says.

"I've got it!" Uri pants out as he reaches me. "This is the one. The potion that will clear the effects of the other one that made you forget everything."

My heart leaps up into my throat, but I force myself not to get too excited. "Uri, hi." I swing my legs around to the other side of the bench so I can face him. "Um, how did you know I was back?"

"Oh, I have a new friend who's been keeping me company." He pats the front pocket of his lab coat. "He scouts around and keeps me updated on the latest happenings."

A mouse pops its head out of Uri's pocket. "Filigree?" I ask. He lets out a squeak when he sees me, then transforms into a small black bird with purple on the tips of his wings. He flies to my shoulder and chirps a few times before settling down. Does this mean he's forgiven me for not remembering him?

"Anyway, here it is." Uri hands me a small vial with a clear liquid inside.

I stare at it, then notice my fingers shaking ever so slightly. If this works, I'll finally be me again. The real me. And Ryn will get me back the way he wants me. But I won't get my hopes up, because I honestly think the chances of this potion working are slim. And let's not forget about possible negative side effects that Uri knows nothing about.

"Don't worry, Vi, dear," Uri says, "this is definitely the one."

Definitely? For some reason, his certainty doesn't make me feel any better. If anything, I trust the potion even less now. What if something awful happens to me? Like if I forget everything again and wake up on the dining room floor not knowing a thing? Wouldn't it be better to stay the way I am now instead of putting everyone through that?

I look across the table at Ryn. His eyes meet mine, and his gaze is intent. "Take it," he says, his voice barely more than a whisper. And that makes my mind up for me. If things were reversed, Ryn would do this for me. Where I'm cowardly and self-ish, Ryn thinks of the people he loves first. He wouldn't think about the risks to himself; he'd go ahead and swallow this stuff so that I could have him back.

So I'll do this for him.

I pull the tiny cork from the top of the vial and tip the clear liquid back down my throat.

CHAPTER 24

I KEEP MY EYES LOCKED ON RYN, AS IF HIS GAZE IS THE anchor that could pull me back if things go terribly wrong. The potion heats my throat and burns a little on the way down, like alcohol. I imagine it spreading throughout my body, working its magic. I have no idea what actually happens or how it works, but in my imagination it looks like tiny gold sparkles spreading across everything.

I wait for memories to start pouring into my head. Or for darkness to surround me and steal away all the new memories I've accumulated since The Destruction. Or to feel violently ill and start throwing up. Or for some other unforeseen side effect.

Nothing happens.

Nothing. At. All.

"Well?" Uri says eventually. "Do you remember anything?"

I look down at the table before answering. I don't want to see the look in Ryn's eyes when I say the word. "No." I raise my eyes to Uri's. He doesn't look as disappointed as I feared he would.

He nods and says to himself, "The catalyst. It isn't there yet."

I raise an eyebrow. I look over at Ryn, and his expression tells me he's probably thinking the same thing I am: If something wasn't 'there yet,' then why was Uri so sure this one would work?

"Uri," Ryn says, clenching his fist on the table. "You told us this was 'the one.' Why would you give it to Violet if it *wasn't ready?*"

"The potion was ready," Uri tells him, no trace of doubt in his voice. "It's Violet who isn't."

Ryn makes a concerted effort to flatten his clenched fist as he lets out a long breath and says, "Can you help Vi with a cut on her leg that won't heal?" He stares at the table as he speaks, anger simmering beneath his voice. "I think it's the same as the one I had on my cheek from that enchanted black blade."

"Certainly," Uri says, apparently oblivious to the tension he's created around the table. "Come with me, Vi." He squeezes his way between the tables. I pick up my bag and follow him.

* * *

I return to my room with Filigree on my shoulder and a tiny jar of enchanted salve in my hand. I drop my bag next to my bed and sit down. I try to roll up my pants leg, but even though the fabric is stretchy, it's not stretchy enough to roll higher than my knee. That's probably one of the reasons my leg's been in so much pain—too-tight pants. So I remove them. I sit down again and unscrew the jar's lid. After a moment's pause, where I imagine my embarrassment if someone barged into my room without knocking, I wave my hand at the armchair in the corner and send it scraping across the floor and into the door. Perfect. At least I'll have some warning if someone tries to walk in without knocking.

The salve soothes my burning skin. I cover the reddened area completely before lying back on the bed. Filigree turns into a cat —ginger-colored this time—and sits by my left foot, wrapping his tail neatly around his paws. He stares at me, blinking once in a while.

"What?" I ask eventually. "Are you trying to say something?"

He flicks one ear.

"Look, I'm sorry, but I don't know what that means."

He narrows his eyes.

"I really am sorry." I sit up and lean on my elbows. "I mean, you're ... like ... super awesome. Probably the coolest pet ever. So it really does suck that I've forgotten all the fun times we must have had. But you're alive, and I'm alive, and assuming we both make it through tomorrow night, we'll have plenty of years ahead of us to have new fun times. Right?"

He stretches forward and rests his ginger head on my ankle.

"Does that mean you agree with me? You're not angry with me? You ... think my bony ankle makes a good pillow?"

He shifts his head a little and opens his eyes. He starts the staring thing again.

With a sigh, I let myself drop back onto the pillow. My mind is restless. I can't believe everything is happening *tomorrow night*. "What if tomorrow's the end for all of us, Filigree? I mean, this is Draven we're talking about. Most powerful guy our world has ever known. Even if Oliver storms in there with hundreds of guardians, Draven might just swat them into nonexistence as if they're nothing more than pesky sprites."

Filigree moves his head again, and I feel something wet brush my skin. His nose, maybe. Or his tongue.

"I just wish I had more time to spend with Ryn. I know, I know, we've just spent a week in super close proximity, but somehow that makes me want to be around him even more. I know I'm *supposed* to like him, but now I think I actually really do. Like him. A lot. And it's weird, because I haven't exactly known him long—in this lifetime, I mean—but I feel like I kind of ... connect with him. And he's easy to talk to. I mean, we spent *hours and hours* talking when we were locked up in that prison, and it never got boring. Okay, there was that awkwardness in the beginning, but that doesn't count." I raise my head and find Filigree's eyes closed. "And you're not even listening to me." I drop down again with a sigh. I've definitely spent too much time around Tilly because I wouldn't normally say so many words out loud at once.

I stare at the ceiling for a while longer, going over combat moves and running through the list of weapons available to me in my guardian arsenal. I know my favorite is the bow and arrow, and I've used others, like knives, daggers and swords. But Ryn was the one who told me, from the other side of a prison wall, just how many different weapons we guardians have. I'm looking forward to trying out the whip. That should be fun. I should probably practice first, though.

Tomorrow. I'll be doing a lot of practicing tomorrow.

I don't know how long I daydream about weapons before my thoughts go back to Ryn. I close my eyes and let my mind wander to see if I can find him. The image comes to me almost immediately. As if I'm seeing through his eyes, I watch him pull his bedroom door shut, pause for a moment, then head down the corridor. The image vanishes, and the darkness behind my eyelids returns.

I bend my knee and raise my leg so I can take a look at the cut on my thigh. Surprisingly, I see little more than a pink line surrounded by healthy skin. I guess some of Uri's stuff does actually work.

A loud knock at the door makes me jump, and I feel the automatic tingle in my hand that means I was just about to grab a weapon. Good to know my reflexes are still working.

"Um, just hang on," I call as I jump up from the bed, kicking Filigree in the process. He lets out an unhappy yelp.

"Everything okay in there?" It's Ryn. Crap. Must find clothes.

"Yeah, just give me a minute." I rummage through my bag for the pair of loose-fitting pants Natesa gave me. My leg would probably appreciate not being smothered again until it's fully healed. I tug the pants on, give the armchair a magical shove out of the way, and open the door.

Ryn lifts his gaze from the floor and smiles at me. It isn't his cocky, self-assured smile. It's almost a smile that's trying too hard. And from the way he twists his hands together, then pushes them into his pockets, then pulls them out and holds them behind his back, I'd say he's nervous. But my experience of Ryn tells me he doesn't get nervous, so ... I'm a little confused now.

"So, uh, I've been thinking," he starts.

"Is that a good thing?" I try to give him a cute half-smile, to let him know I'm joking. I bet I look like a total idiot.

"Not always," his nervous smile turns into the smile that makes my legs feel like they just did a hundred leg presses. "But I'd like to believe it was the right thing to do this time."

"So these thoughts led you to ... my door?"

"Yup." He hesitates, and the smile slips from his face as he becomes more serious. He looks at the floor again. "From the moment we wake up tomorrow morning, we're going to be preparing for the biggest and most important fight of our lives. And the reality is ... we might not survive it." He reaches for one of my hands, and his voice has just the tiniest shake in it when he says, "So if tonight is the last night we ever have, I want to spend it with you."

For one incredibly stupid moment, I think he means *here*, like, in my bed. Which makes my stomach hit the floor because that is *so* not happening. Then I remind myself that Ryn has been nothing but decent since I arrived here, so he can't possibly mean he wants to spend the night with me like *that*.

He must have picked up on my moment of horror because he drops my hand and adds, "Unless you don't want to, of course."

"No! I mean—yes, I want to … spend the night with you." Are my cheeks as hot as they feel? And why am I so shy all of a sudden? Wasn't I just telling Filigree how easy it is to talk to Ryn?

"Okay." He takes my hand again. "I'd like to show you something then."

I nod, maybe a little too quickly. "Um, just let me get something on my feet."

"Oh, no, you can go barefoot." He shuts my door for me and leads me along the corridor. We descend the main stairway, past the first level of bedrooms, where Ryn stays, and past the ground level where people are heading to the dining room for dinner. Down one more level, and then we're heading left, past Uri's laboratory. Ryn shifts his hand in my grasp and laces his fingers between mine. My heart starts thrumming like a hummingbird's wings, and I seriously hope my hands aren't sweating.

Ryn slows and gestures for me to go through a doorway on my left. I walk inside and take in the sight of a large hall with exercise mats and running rectangles and ropes and poles and weights and a whole lot of other things that make me itch to get my muscles moving and my blood pumping.

"This is the training center," Ryn says. "All Guilds have one. They're pretty similar."

"Okay. The training center is where I spent a gazillion more hours than anyone else who ever set foot in our Guild, right?" I wink at him.

He matches my grin and squeezes my hand. "That would be correct."

"So did you bring me here for some last minute training?"

"As fun as it would be to show you I can still kick your ass—"

"Oh, I highly doubt *that*."

"—no. We're going over there." He points across the hall to an enormous orb shimmering in the corner. "I don't know what its real name is, but at our Guild we always called it the Fish

Bowl. We use it to practice one-on-one combat in all kinds of settings because the inside can be made to look like anything you want it to look like."

"One-on-one combat, huh?" I raise an eyebrow. "So you *did* bring me here so I can kick your ass."

With a smile playing on his lips, he shakes his head. "Just wait and see." We reach the edge of the orb, and he lets go of my hand. The orb's substance is like smoke swirling inside glass, but when I touch it, my hand goes right through, vanishing into the eddying whiteness. "Go in," Ryn says. "I'll be right behind you."

I step forward. Ghostly white tendrils curl around me as I pass through the orb's outer ring. And when I get to the other side … my breath catches in the back of my throat. I'm in a forest scene at night. Not a dead, snow-covered forest like the ones out there in the real world, but a forest alive with magic, color, and light. Glow-bugs dot the trees and leaves, creating their own tiny orbs of gold light, and the river that travels past me seems to be full of floating golden glow-bugs. A small row boat rests in the water, nudging the bank. Sprites with glittering blue wings prance across one of the oars before fluttering into the trees.

"I like to think that special moments should happen in special places," Ryn says quietly, "and since there isn't a place that's special to us anywhere inside this base, I decided to make one."

"It's amazing," I whisper, afraid of speaking too loudly in case I ruin something.

"I happen to know you're a fan of glow-bugs. Or, more specifically, glow-bug butts. That's what made you fall in love with me the first time."

I laugh. "I don't believe you."

He shrugs. "One day you'll remember, and then you'll know if I'm telling the truth or not."

"So it doesn't normally look like this in here?"

"No, it's always different."

"And you made this beautiful scene just for me?"

"Well, I had help. Em did some setting design back at her Guild, but she couldn't get everything the way I wanted it, so I had to go in search of someone more experienced. He wasn't too pleased, what with it being the night before battle and all that, but he added the finishing touches anyway."

I breathe in deeply. "It smells just like those blossoms at the bottom of Tilly's tree on the island."

He nods. "I know you like them."

Of course he does. He probably felt me relax every time I breathed in that fresh, sweet scent.

He gestures to the boat. "Take a ride with me?"

I hesitate. The scene is amazing, and no one's ever made me feel more special—well, not that I can remember—but what does he expect from me? Half the boat is filled with large, squishy cushions that look like they would be extremely comfortable for two people to snuggle on together. Is that what he expects will happen? Do I *want* that to happen?

As if he knows what I'm thinking, which I suppose he sort of does, he says, "No pressure. Just … a boat ride."

I need to get something out of the way before I can get in that boat. I look down at the grass brushing my toes. "Has anything ever happened between you and Em?"

"Violet Fairdale." He brushes my check, leaving a tingling so real I wonder if he trailed actual sparks across my skin. "Since the moment I figured out that you were the one I wanted by my side for the rest of my life, I've never thought of anyone else."

I bite my lip. "So that's a no?"

"A very definite no."

"Okay." I pad across the grass toward the boat. Ryn holds his hand out to help me in, and I take it even though I'm pretty sure

I could navigate a small row boat on my own. He climbs in after me, rocking the boat a lot more than I did when I got in.

"The cushions are for you," he says, gesturing for me to sit down. He sits opposite me on a simple piece of wood that stretches across the boat. He reaches for the oars. "I'm the one doing the hard work."

"Hard work, my butt," I say with a laugh. "There's barely a current for you to pull against."

"We're actually going to be moving with the current. The oars are just for show. You know, to impress you." He gives me his gorgeous grin.

"Right, as if you needed anything else to impress me after this." I wave my hand around to indicate the magical wonderland surrounding us.

Ryn uses an oar to lift a rope looped around a tree stump keeping the boat from drifting away. The gentle current takes us, aided every now and then by a dip and pull of the oars.

I lean against the side of the boat and drape my arm over the edge. I let my fingers trail through the water. "Thank you," I say to him. "I don't deserve this, but thank you."

He frowns at me. "Why not?"

I watch the glow-bugs float past and don't answer. He knows why, even if he pretends he doesn't. I'm responsible for the state our world is in. I'm the selfish girl who couldn't handle the things she'd done so she chose to run away from it all with one gulp of a potion. That girl doesn't deserve a beautiful gift like this.

"Ryn?" I say after a while. "Do you think … do you think you could ever love the new me as much as you loved the old me?"

With a bemused expression, he secures the oars so they won't slip into the water, then leans forward and says, "There's no 'new' you or 'old' you, V. There's just you. And nothing can change the way I feel about you, regardless of what you remember."

I shake my head. "You say I'm just me, but … I feel like a different person. When you tell me about my life and the things I did and the way I was, it sounds like all I cared about was being the best. At everything. I did and said horrible things to you, and it was all just so … petty. I'm not even sure why you loved the old me."

"Don't forget that I was horrible to you too. If you're going to be harsh on yourself, you should be harsh on me too."

I smile at him and shake my head once more. I can't imagine him being a terrible person. He's always worrying about other people, asking me how I am, throwing himself in front of lightning to try and save me.

"You can't compare who you were then with who you are now," he says. "You're looking at the world through the lens of The Destruction now. Everything seems petty in comparison to that, even things that *were* important back then. You're not a different person, V. You're just … maybe a wiser, more mature version of yourself."

"So you think I'm still the same me?"

"Still the same stubborn, intelligent, ass-kicking, beautiful you."

"So …" I lift my hand from the water and start twisting it with my other hand. "When Uri gave me that potion earlier and it didn't work, why were you upset? Wasn't that because you'd rather have the old me back?"

"Of course I want you to get your memories back, but not because it would make me love you any more. I want you to remember everything because it's *your* life and *your* experiences and you deserve to have that in your head, not a black hole of fuzzy confusion. I was upset for you, not for me."

I raise an eyebrow. "Really?"

He rolls his eyes. "Okay, there's obviously *some* part of me that would like you to remember how much you love me. But you know what?" He lifts his shoulders and takes a deep breath. "It's okay if you don't. I've accepted that."

"But what if I ... do. I mean, not *remember*, but ... feel ... what I felt before. But new."

Freak, that made *absolutely* no sense. What the crap am I trying to say? I groan and cover my burning face with my hands. I don't know how to put this into words. All I know is that right here in this boat with Ryn is the only place I want to be. If I had to choose one person to spend my last night with, it would be him. And if I were forced into prison again, I'd gladly endure it if he were the one on the other side of the wall. He makes me feel like I belong somewhere, like I'm not alone anymore. I realize all these things, and a glow far brighter than that of the glow-bugs explodes inside me, sending warmth shooting all over my body.

Is this love? And if it is, am I genuinely feeling it, or am I only feeling it because I know I'm *supposed* to love him? And does it even matter why, or does it only matter that I *am* feeling it?

Oh freaking goodness, I think I might be sick. Is this what love is like? It freaks your insides out so much it makes you want to hurl? Or are these just nerves? Nerves because I want to be wrapped in the arms of the guy sitting across from me who knows more about me than anyone else?

I drop my hands from my face at the sound of liquid splashing. I see spurts of water jumping up from the river and purple sparks zipping around and around the trees' branches. Startled, I pull myself away from the edge of the boat. The sparks and water spurts vanish.

"Wait," Ryn says, holding a hand up and watching me closely with a dazzling smile. "Feel that again."

I start laughing. I can't help it. What he just said is so bizarre, so *him*. No one else would ever say that because no one else would know what I just felt. I cover my face again in an attempt to stop the crazy giggles. I feel a hand gently pulling my own hands away from my face. I find Ryn kneeling in front of me, also laughing. As our mirth subsides, my eyes lock with his. He cups my face with both his hands. I think there's a question in his gaze. Whatever it is, I hope my eyes are saying yes. *Yes, yes, whatever you're asking of me, yes.*

He leans closer to me, his eyes on my lips now. He seems to be taking an awfully long time to get there, and I wonder if he's giving me a chance to back away, if that's what I want.

It isn't.

With only a smidgen of space left between us, he hesitates. "Are you going to stop me?" he murmurs, his voice barely audible.

I give a slight shake of my head. *Stop* him? No. Freaking. Way.

His lips touch mine. Hesitant. Soft. A thrill runs through my body. I slide my hands around his neck and into his hair, pulling him closer to me. My mouth opens against his as our kiss grows in urgency, and I swear I can feel sparks dancing across my tongue. I lean back against the cushions, drawing him down with me. His body moves against mine. His hand slides down over my waist, my hip, my thigh. He grips my leg and wraps it around his waist. As he trails his lips along my jaw, I press myself even closer to him and slip my hands beneath the back of his T-shirt. My fingers tingle as I skim them across his bare skin.

"I've missed you so much," he murmurs before pressing a kiss below my ear. With the leg that's wrapped around his waist, I force him to roll over. I straddle his waist and lean over him to brush my lips against his. I want to tease him, but I end up teasing myself too, because I want the kiss as badly as he does. His tongue sliding over mine is the most delicious sensation ever. Heat grows in my stomach. It spreads until I feel like I'm burning all over.

Something flashes behind my eyes, and I see myself climbing

a tree behind two dark-haired boys. One of them turns back to say something to me, and I see a much younger version of Ryn.

I jerk back, confused.

Flash. I'm sitting on Dad's lap playing with a brand new Filigree.

Flash. Tora wraps her arms around me and holds me as I cry. Tora?

Oh crap oh crap. I can't breathe. I can't see. Dizziness spins my head. I lurch away from Ryn as everything, *everything*, comes rushing back.

Growing up. Creepy Hollow. My home.

Special ability. I can find people. It's a secret.

Ryn. My enemy. My friend. I love him.

Mom. Dead. It happened when I was three.

Dad. Dead—but not really. It's a secret.

Guardians. I'm one of them. It's all I've ever wanted to be.

Graduation. I was top of my class. Tied with Ryn.

Zell. Gathered an army. He wanted me.

Nate. He betrayed me. He destroyed everything I love.

Creepy Hollow. Demolished. My fault.

The Guild. Ruined. My fault.

Tora. Dead. My fault.

I find myself on my hands and knees, my stomach heaving. Tora is dead. She's dead. For four whole years, she was the closest thing I had to family—and now she's gone. And it was all because I chose to trust the wrong person. I wanted to prove myself, and in doing so I ruined everything. I can barely breathe because of the sobs building up in the back of my throat. *She's really gone!*

Darkness crowds the edges of my vision. I smell smoke, hear screams. I feel the world tilt. Falling, falling, falling. I let the darkness and the memories take me.

CHAPTER 25

I COLLAPSE ONTO THE HIGHEST POINT OF MY DESTROYED home and hold my head in my hands as I cry. I can't fix this. I can't make up for it. I don't even know how I can *live* knowing that Tora died because of me.

My hands fall to my sides, one of them coming to rest on a pile of glass. The contents of my emergency kit, scattered and broken. My trembling fingers sift through the items that managed to survive and linger on one of the vials. I pick it up. *Forget*, the label says.

That's what I want. I want to forget everything that's happened. I want to forget that it's my fault.

I unscrew the top.

I lift it to my mouth.

I close my eyes and pour it down my throat.

And nothing happens.

Potions aren't always instant, though, so it's not exactly surprising. And after everything I've done, I don't deserve to forget my misery.

I stumble and slide down the broken pieces of my home. Without looking back, I start walking. I don't know where I'm going; I only know that I want to be as far away from here as possible. *Coward*, my conscience whispers to me. Fresh tears roll down my cheeks, and I bite my lip until I taste blood. I know I'm a coward, but I don't care. I can't stay here. Not after I've brought all this down on us.

My legs carry me haltingly between burned, splintered trees. I don't think I could run if I tried. I rub my aching forehead with the heel of my hand, wondering why I haven't started to forget everything yet. Why haven't I been carried off to a place of blissful ignorance? A vague memory tells me that that's not actually what the *Forget* potion was supposed to do. So I guess I screwed up there too.

I lower my hand and see a figure through the smoke ahead of me. I stop. Normally I'd be hiding by now or have a weapon in at least one of my hands. I'd be tense and alert, waiting to defend myself. But now I'm almost hoping the person coming toward me will kill me quickly and end my agony.

When I see who it is, my legs buckle and I drop to the ground. I might get my wish after all.

Nate.

Draven.

Dressed in black with heavy boots and a coat that reaches his knees. His eyes are hard, and there seems to be a pale green light emanating from them. That isn't right. His eyes are supposed to be brown.

He tilts his head to the side. "Visited your home yet, Vi?"

"You killed Tora," I gasp, suddenly finding my voice. "I hate you. *I hate you!* And the forest? The Guild? The *homes*? What have you done?"

"No, Violet." He takes a step closer. "What have you done? What have *you done*? Didn't you see my message? This is all. Your. Fault. You're the one who handed the comm-glass over to your friend at the Guild. And he took it with him into the Council meeting, as I knew he would. It was so easy to blow everyone up after that."

Bran. The Council members. The explosion. More guilt to pile onto the agony already breaking my heart.

"And that's why I sent you two comm-glasses," Nate says. "I knew you'd hand one over eventually. And I knew I'd need to contact you again." He crouches down in front of me, like adults do when they're talking to small children. "I've been watching you, Vi. You never should have trusted a magical technology you hadn't come across before, but I knew you would. I knew your need to prove that you're always the best would be your downfall. You had no idea I could see you through the comm-glass. No idea I was watching you."

My body starts shaking from the shivers coursing up and down my spine.

"You helped me orchestrate this entire attack, Vi. So don't you dare ask me what *I've* done when none of this—" he gestures to the ruin around him "—could have been achieved without you."

I can't stop shaking. I bite my lip as tears spill from my eyes. "Kill me," I whisper. "Just get it over with."

"Oh no." He stands and shakes his head. "This isn't going to be that easy for you. You're going to watch your world and everyone you care about suffer. And only when I've taken away everything you've ever loved, like you took everything from me, *then* you can die, Violet." He spits my name out as if it tastes disgusting.

"What … what did I take from—"

"Do you know what happened," Nate says, "after I left Zell to find you and you rejected me? I had nowhere else to go. No one else to help me with the growing power inside me. So I returned to Zell, hoping he'd never noticed my absence. But he had. And do you know what he did to punish me? *Do you?*"

"No," I whisper.

"He. Killed. My. Parents. In front of me."

I start shaking. I caused the death of Nate's parents. Two innocent people who should have had nothing to do with this. *No*, I tell myself. Nate didn't have to go back to Zell. He could have taken his parents and run like I told him to.

"So you see, Violet. I have every right to make you suffer like you made me suffer. All of this—everything—is your fault. You started it. You saved my life and brought me into this world when you should have just *let me die*. Instead, the faerie world was revealed to me, and all the power hidden within me was unlocked. And I didn't know what to do with it. I was lost and afraid and you rejected me. All I wanted was your forgiveness, Vi, but you couldn't give me that. I apologized for something I tried my best to stop, and you *threw it back in my face*."

"I ..." I'm starting to feel like I'm going to throw up.

"So when there's nothing left in this world that you care about, that's when we'll be seeing each other again, dear Vi. And that's when your life gets to end."

He turns and strides away, smoke swallowing him up in seconds. I lean forward, planting my hands on the ground and breathing deeply. I feel horribly ill, and I don't think it's only from the smoke and the shock and the agony of losing Tora.

I think it's the potion.

My stomach starts to ache. I lie down on the ground and curl up into a tight ball. The world tilts and spins, even though I know I'm not moving. Things start to darken. A black hole beckons, and I imagine myself crawling toward it. It sucks me in.

This is what I wanted.

* * *

I wake up with Jamon's mother's words in my mind: *You will stop at nothing to rid the world of his evil because you have everything to make up for.* I feel something soft and furry against my cheek. I blink several times before being able to focus on it. A snow leopard. Filigree. Curled up next to me and taking up more than half the bed.

I wrap my arms around his neck and bury my face in his fur. My cheeks are already wet with tears; I must have been crying in my sleep. "I remember it all, Fili," I whisper. "And it's so horrible." He drapes a heavy paw over my back. It feels near enough to someone hugging me that I snuggle even closer to him. Memories I don't want to think about lurk beneath the surface of my thoughts like sea serpents in dark water. They're going to pull me under. I'll never be free. This guilt will follow me forever.

I understand. I finally understand now why I swallowed that potion. I understand why I was so desperate to forget.

And I'm not going to make that mistake again.

I wiggle out from beneath Filigree's enormous paw. I place my hand on his head and murmur, "I love you, Fili."

"Ah, love," a voice from the corner of my room says, startling me. "Cures everything, doesn't it. In the beginning, you wanted to forget love. In the end, it was love that brought everything back."

"Uri?" The candle flickering on my bedside table doesn't reveal much beyond my bed, but I recognize the urisk's shape and his gravelly voice. "What—what are you talking about?"

He climbs off the armchair and comes toward me. "The catalyst. The moment you felt the first whisper of love, the potion kicked in."

"Love? For Ryn?"

"For anyone you loved before you forgot everything. It didn't have to be Ryn. It could have been your father or Raven—or Tora if she were still around. Even Filigree. Your mind had to remember *something* first, even if it was only the feeling. The potion latched onto that and filled in everything else."

"And you knew that was what had to happen? Before you gave me the potion?"

He nods.

"Why didn't you tell us? Ryn was really upset when it didn't work."

"I didn't want to put any pressure on you."

I think about that and realize he was right not to tell me. Knowing I had to reach the point where I loved Ryn in order to get my memories back would have put major pressure on us. And he would have thought I was only trying to love him to make the potion work. I wipe my fingers beneath my eyes, then push my hands through my hair. I take a deep breath. "I'm sorry I doubted you, Uri. I was starting to think you wouldn't be able to fix me."

"No need to apologize." He pats my ankle. "I probably would have doubted me too after the first potion went so horribly wrong. As it is, I had no idea this one would knock you out for so many hours. But I suppose your mind had a lot to process."

I nod. "Was Ryn mad at you when I passed out and didn't wake up?"

"Oh, yes. He was raving about some human faerie story where the prince is supposed to *wake up* his princess with a kiss, not put her to sleep."

"Hmm." I sniff back a few more tears. "Don't know that one."

"Me neither."

"Do you know where Ryn is?" I was expecting him to be the one waiting in the armchair.

"I'm sorry, but he's out."

"Out? Where? What time is it?" I'm suddenly terrified I've slept through the whole day and everyone's gone off to the final battle without me.

"Don't panic, it's still early morning. You've got plenty of time to prepare for tonight."

"So where's Ryn gone then?"

"I'm not sure. Something that needed to be checked."

That doesn't sound right.

I climb over Filigree and jump off the bed. "Thanks, Uri," I say as I yank the door open and rush out. My bare feet slap the tiles as I search for the corridor with the pole. I need to go down five floors to the rooms where the meetings and planning happens. It'll be a lot faster if I don't have to use the stairs.

I can't believe what I put Ryn through. Being terrified I was dead or marked, then finally finding me, and then discovering I didn't have a clue who he was. I have to find him. I have to tell him I love him—before it's too late and we're all marked or dead. Because I do. I love Ryn with every fiber of my being, and I should have said those words to him every single day before I screwed things up. And now he's out there somewhere, and I can't help the terrifying feeling that I've missed my chance. That it's too late. That he'll never get to hear those words from me.

I reach the pole and swing my leg around it. The floor disappears beneath my feet, and I whoosh down, counting the floors I pass. I stop myself in time to jump onto the level just above transportation. I run to the room where Ryn and I found Oliver when we returned with Tilly yesterday, but he isn't there.

"Where's Oliver?" I ask the man looking up at me in surprise.

"Uh, surveillance, I think." When I raise both eyebrows, he points left and adds, "A few doors that way."

I hurry further along the corridor, peeking through half-open doors until I find a ginger-colored head. I push the door open and step inside. "Oliver?" I say. He turns. The moment I see his face, I'm overwhelmed by memories of Tora and how excited she was the first time she told me about him. Fresh tears well up in my eyes. I clamp a hand over my mouth, suddenly unable to speak. When I get control over my voice, I lower my hand and say, "I'm so sorry about Tora."

He stares at me as a sheen gathers over his eyes. "You remember?"

I nod. "Everything."

"How? Was it Uri's—"

"Where's Ryn?" I don't have time to explain Uri's potion to Oliver.

"He's …" Oliver blinks and clears his throat. "Something unexpected had to be investigated. He and Em volunteered, along with two senior guardians. They left about twenty minutes ago."

Anxiety squirms in my stomach. "What do you mean by 'unexpected'?"

"Activity that shouldn't have been there."

"Activity? Like Draven's people? And you sent them out there?"

"We need to know what's going on, Vi. We don't want any nasty surprises tonight."

"Where did you send them?" *Please tell me, please tell me.*

Oliver shakes his head. "You can't go after them, Vi."

"But I need to see Ryn. I need to talk to him."

"You can do that when he comes back."

Which makes sense, except … what if he doesn't come back? I look around, noticing the contents of the room for the first time. Just goes to show how distracted I am; I used to be pretty observant. Against two of the room's four walls runs a counter lined with glass spheres about twice the size of a person's head. Images move within each sphere, and two women with clipboards slide back and forth on chairs with wheels, examining the images and making notes. "What are those?" I ask, nodding toward the glass spheres.

"Surveillance. We've been monitoring Draven's warriors for a while now."

"Even the Unseelie Court?"

"No, but everywhere else groups of marked fae have been gathering."

An elf peers into the room and calls for Oliver. "Look, Vi, I've got to go. And you need to grab a quick breakfast, then come to the training center with everyone else. We're running through the plan for tonight once more."

I bite my lip, nod, and watch Oliver walk out the door.

"Oh, and put your protective gear on before you come to the training center," he adds, poking his head back into the room.

I frown. "My what?"

"You'll find it in your room. The gear should've been delivered while you were sleeping."

He disappears, and I steal another glance at the spheres. Some of them show nothing but landscape or walls. Others show faeries in dark blue walking around. When I see a sphere with a blonde-and-green head crouching behind a rock, my heart thumps faster. I know who that is.

"I'm sorry, Vi, is it?" one of the clipboard women says to me. "I don't think you should be in here. Oliver already told you where you need to be."

I hurry out of the room and take off at a run. I know exactly where Em was crouching. We have to pass that oddly shaped rock every time we fly out of the valley. Which means the unexpected activity Oliver was talking about is happening within the protective dome. And that is definitely disturbing.

Unfortunately, I can't slide up the pole, so I have to use the stairs to return to my room. I run all the way up. I find the protective gear Oliver mentioned at the foot of my bed; I guess Filigree was sleeping on it earlier. He's now a squirrel tucked beneath my pillow. I can see his fluffy tail sticking out.

I strip my clothes off, tug the dark grey gear on—I'm pleased to see it's made of the tight, stretchy stuff I like to fight in—and shove my feet into my boots. My new gear comes with a jacket too, which is thin and close-fitting, but feels unusually warm when I put it on. There's definitely magic in this stuff.

I shove my stylus into my boot as I dash out of the room and head back to the pole. I slide all the way to the bottom this time, then hurry onto the transportation level's landing strip. Yes, I'm aware that my disobeying authority is what got us all into this monumental mess in the first place, but heading out on my own isn't on quite the same level as conspiring with a nameless person from the Unseelie Court. That move got people killed—*don't think about that now*—but this only affects me.

I ignore the doors on either side of the strip. I don't need to go far once I'm outside, so it's not like I need a pegasus or a dragon or anything. I stand in the center of the wide strip, make sure I'm surrounded by a bubble of air, and start running. It takes some concentration to keep the bubble moving with me, but I can handle it. What's a little more difficult is running full-on at a solid wall and reminding myself that I *will* pass through it instead of smashing into it. I add an extra spurt of speed for the last few steps, then dive at the wall. It vanishes around me, and suddenly my bubble and I are floating in the river instead.

I propel the bubble up to the top of the water and out onto the bank. I let it go with a *pop* that sprinkles tiny droplets of water over me. Now, where is that rock? I look around to orient myself. The morning sun is just peeking above the rim of the valley. The waterfall is directly behind me, which means the rock is somewhere up on the left, near the edge of the protective dome.

As quietly as I can, I run between trees, bushes, and rocks. No snow for me to wade through here; I guess Draven's winter couldn't pass through the enchantments. Up, up I climb, using branches to aid me in places that are steep. I imagine Ryn's face when he turns and sees me. I imagine wrapping my arms around him as *me*, the person who remembers every experience we've shared and who knows beyond a doubt that I love him with my whole heart.

I see the rock, but there's no one there anymore. I tell myself there's nothing wrong with that because it's been at least fifteen minutes since I saw Em in the sphere. She and the rest of the group have obviously gone further, beyond the invisible barrier perhaps.

I reach the rock and crouch down behind it. I peer around the side—and my heart stops. Then it kicks into horrifying action, spreading adrenaline and heartbreak throughout my body.

Noooo!

My hand shoots forward, as if I could catch him, as if I could pull him back to safety. But my fist closes around air. I force myself not to run after him, and it's the hardest thing I've ever done. I watch the group of armed men carrying Ryn's motionless form away, along with Em and two others, and there isn't a damn freaking thing I can do about it.

NononoNO!

I clench my other fist and slam it against the rock. Ryn's words from a few days ago come back to me with horrifying clarity. *The last thing I'll do is fight for him. I'd rather be dead.* No, he wouldn't do that, would he? Would he really kill himself before letting them mark him? I find myself hoping Draven casts his spell before Ryn wakes up; at least that way he'll be alive.

Oh, dear Seelie Queen, what if Oliver's team comes across him tonight when they attack the Unseelie Court? If he fights them, and they can't stun him, they'll have no choice but to …

No, stop it!

I lean back against the rock and close my eyes for a moment.

For freak's sake, just CALM DOWN. This isn't the way a guardian acts in a crisis. Figure something out instead of panicking.

Okay, this is not the end of my world. We are, after all, invading the Unseelie Court tonight, so I don't have to wait that long before we can get Ryn back. And the others, of course. But I need to tell Oliver about this right now. Because what the freak are Draven's men doing just on the other side of our protective dome? They're not supposed to know we're here.

I push away from the rock and wipe my shaking hands against my pants. Before I can take a step forward, bright light grows around me, exploding suddenly and vanishing a moment later. I flinch and duck down, even though nothing came near me.

What was that?

It happens again. I spin around in my crouching position as I search the sky for the source of the light. I see it. Bright sparks soar through the air high above me, then explode when they strike the invisible barrier of protection. More sparks shoot into the air, all different colors, all heading straight for the valley.

My gaze drops to the ground, searching for the faeries releasing the sparks, and what I see is terrifying enough to freeze the blood in my veins. Endless lines of faeries are marching toward the valley. Every single one in the front row has his or her arm extended, pointing a stylus at the barrier that I never doubted until this moment could protect us. The flashes of light grow in number and intensity, and still I'm frozen to the spot. And then, with a blast that rings in my ears, a powerful white rush of sparks *whooshes* past me and strikes a tree, igniting it in an instant.

They've broken through.

Oh. Freaking. Hell.

CHAPTER 26

I'VE NEVER RUN SO FAST. I'VE ALSO NEVER TRIPPED SO MUCH in such a short space of time. Damn roots and slippery vines and steep patches with loose sand. I hear shouts behind me and the steady tromp of hundreds of feet. Thousands? I have no idea. The crackle and hiss of flames announces more trees on fire behind me. Smoke fills my nostrils, and all the fear and horror from the night of The Destruction comes rushing back to me.

I don't look back. I jump and slide and run some more. Ryn told me there's an entrance behind the waterfall. Will it be faster to go through there than dive into the river? The ground is flat now as I dash alongside water lit up with orange light. I pump my arms and legs. Faster, faster. I leap onto the rocks below the waterfall, slipping a little, but regaining my balance almost immediately. I dive at the pounding wall of water, hoping desperately that I'm not about to either slam into hard rock or get crushed by the falling river.

I land and stumble a few steps forward on a tiled floor. The foyer. Not far from the dining room. I'm not even wet. "We're under attack!" I scream. Guardians and other fae are already racing up and down the large stairway and along the corridors.

This isn't the bustle of a busy day; a far greater urgency drives them.

They already know what's happening.

I dash out of the way as guardians in protective gear line up in formation across the foyer. Others take their position on the stairs. Elves line up beside them. At a shout from someone, they raise their arms in unison and aim arrows at the waterfall I just jumped through. Light flashes from behind the curtain of water, and sparks skitter across the tiled floor.

Draven's army is almost inside.

And I have to find Oliver.

I race along the corridors without a clue as to what I'm supposed to do now. We didn't prepare for this, did we? Unexpected invasion? Or maybe we did, and Ryn and I missed that part. People run in every direction around me, shouting to each other and pulling on their grey protective jackets. I'm not sure if they have a purpose or if they're as lost as I am.

Tilly. She must be terrified. This isn't what Oliver told her would happen. *Crap, crapping crap.* I slow my footsteps and duck into a doorway to avoid being trampled. Since I have no other orders, I'll make up my own: Protect Tilly. Protect the Star. So where is she? With Oliver, right? Didn't he say he wasn't letting her out of his sight? But she wasn't with him when I spoke to him in the surveillance room ...

Wait a freaking second. Why am I searching the corridors for Oliver when I can search with my head? Surely I've interacted with him enough times for there to be some kind of connection between us? I close my eyes and reach automatically with my mind. *Oliver, Oliver, where are you?*

"Violet!" As if I've conjured him into being with my own thoughts, I open my eyes and find him racing up to me. He grabs my arm and takes a few gasping breaths. "Dammit, I can't find Tilly."

"What?"

"I've searched everywhere! Amon was keeping an eye on her, and now I can't find him either. Can you—"

"Yes, I'll find her. Is Draven here?"

"I don't know. I don't know what the hell's going on. I've only seen guardians and warriors. So many of them are inside already." He tugs at his hair and swears. Then he grabs the sword strap across his chest, lifts it over his head, and thrusts it into my hands. "She'll need this. I ... I have to go." And with that he takes off.

I hold onto the sword tightly, watching Oliver disappear around a corner. Will I ever see him again? *Okay, relax. You'll never find Tilly if you panic.* I turn around and rest my forehead against the door. I grip the hilt of the sword, imagine Tilly's smiling face, and let my mind go. *Relax. She's here somewhere.* My mind brushes past hundreds of others as it searches, reaching further and further as the seconds pass. Searching, searching. Further out. Past the walls of our base ...

Nothing.

Fear grips me with an iron fist. I pull the sword strap over my head and start running. Pushing past people. I can't keep still. Why am I getting *nothing*? This is just like when I searched for Calla and—

I stop. It's because Tilly isn't here, I realize. She's been taken. She must be hidden somewhere protective the same way Calla and all those other prisoners with special abilities were. Either that or she's ... No, I refuse to believe she's no longer alive. If that's the case, we may as well kneel down and let Draven mark us now. But who would take her?

I press the fingers of my left hand to my temple and rub. *Amon was keeping an eye on her.* That's what Oliver said. And Amon wouldn't do anything to her. He's a *librarian*. I remember him being strict, even mean on occasion when unruly trainees needed to be put in line, but he was always willing to help me out with assignments and …

My mind races through the memories I have of Amon and comes to a grinding halt at just one. The night this all started. The night Nate followed me through the faerie paths and set everything in motion. I had to take him back to the Guild with me. I noticed how empty the Guild was because, of course, it was late at night. But I remember seeing Amon there. We passed him on the stairs.

My mind freezes the image of Amon as Zell's words from a night that feels so long ago play over in my ears. *I realized Nathaniel was at the Guild, so I just had my spy inform me when he left, and I waited for him in the forest.* Was Amon watching as Nate and I left the Guild that night? Was he the one who told Zell?

I think of the very first lightning bolt that broke through the Guild's protective enchantments. It happened in the library. Was that because Amon was able to deactivate the spells protecting that area?

And that isn't all. The explosion that supposedly originated in Uri's lab happened the night we rescued Amon and brought him back here. What was it he said about the sword when we returned yesterday? *I was so concerned after the explosion that it had been destroyed. I thought it might have been kept down there with all the other spare weapons.* And the spare weapons are kept on the same level as the lab. My nails dig into my palms. It wasn't Uri who caused the explosion, it was Amon. He was hoping to get rid of the only weapon that could destroy Draven.

And now he's taken Tilly.

"Damn!" I shout as my fists clench tighter.

The floor shudders beneath my feet. I look around, realizing I'm the only one left in this corridor. Everyone else has disappeared while I've been lost in my thoughts. Another tremor rumbles through the floor, stronger this time. The sound of something cracking reaches my ears. I spin around. A faerie is standing at the far end of the corridor. A faerie in dark blue. As he takes a step forward, the floor quakes beneath his foot. *What?* Is this some magic trick I don't know about? He didn't even slam his foot down hard.

I reach into the air and flick my hand. The whip appears, curling around air with a loud *snap*. I pull my arm back, then throw it forward. The faerie jumps. The whip wraps around his ankle. I tug hard before he can land, but it's like the whip is connected to a boulder. I lose my grasp on it. The faerie hits the tiles with the force of a cannon ball. They smash apart, pieces flying everywhere as the ground trembles so violently I lose my footing. *Flipping flip. How heavy is this guy?* I scramble up and run in the opposite direction. I don't know where I'm going or what I'm doing; I just need a moment to *think*.

I leap down a stairway three steps at a time, landing right in the middle of the action on the next level. *Dammit, should have gone* up *the stairs.* A blue-clad figure runs at me. I jump and somersault over his head, then jab a knife into his shoulder before taking off. I dodge and dive between the rest of the fighters until I reach the end of the corridor. I turn into another corridor and run like the wind is chasing me.

Someone steps out a doorway halfway down, blocking my way. He throws his hands out, spreading water across the tiles. *Thanks, dude, that actually helps.* I pump my arms and legs faster, then drop onto my knees and shoot across the water, slashing at the faerie with a knife as I slide past. I slam into the wall at the end of the corridor, jump up, and aim for another stairway.

I run up and up, keeping a shield bubble around me as I go. *Finally, a corridor with no one in it.* I hurry along the corridor, spinning around as I check for people in blue. *Okay, think. Where would Amon take Tilly?* My shield fizzles away as I reach over my shoulder for the sword. If I search once more, maybe I'll find her this time.

Something strikes my back and throws me onto the floor. The sword clatters away from me. I roll over and see sparks ricochet from my arm and vanish into the air. "Nice jacket you've got there," a spikey-haired woman says as she stalks toward me. "It seems to repel magic. I'm betting your skin won't do the same thing, though."

I reach into the air with both hands, grab two knives, and fling them at her. They spin through the air as I jump to my feet. She dodges one but the other catches her shoulder. She clutches it with a grimace, then swivels and kicks at me. I jump back and knock her outstretched leg to the side. Instead of falling, she spins in the air and lands on both feet.

A figure melts away from the wall behind her and throws an arm around her neck. He squeezes tight, but she jabs back with her hand. I catch the glint of a blade before it sinks into his stomach. He stumbles back with a groan, and I realize I recognize him. Jamon's father, Asim.

"No!" I shout.

I push my hands out at her, sending a ripple of power that I hope will knock her down. She laughs and drops to the floor the moment the power leaves my hands. It shoots over her, and she leaps to her feet again. I put up a shield and try to run past her—I can only think of Asim now—but she blocks my way. She dances back and forth, waiting for me to attack. So I do. Blast of magic, punch, jab, spin and duck down, slash with a knife. But every move I make, she's already there, countering me. As if she knows what I'm going to do before I do it.

Crap, maybe she does. Zell collected people who could read minds and hear thoughts. Perhaps she's one of them.

"Trying to get past me, sweetie? You should give up now."

She gives me a triumphant smirk. "I think you know it's not going to happen."

She knows I've figured her out. But that doesn't mean I've lost. If I don't want her to know what I'm about to do, then it's clear that I can't know either.

So I let myself go, kicking, punching, spinning, and ducking purely by instinct. No plan, just fighting by the seat of my pants. This is the Violet who graduated top of her class. The Violet people whispered horrible things about but were too scared to challenge. The Violet who kicked butt at every challenge the Guild ever threw at her. And while I recognize now that that Violet was way too obsessed with being the best, I'm eternally grateful she worked her ass off.

Dodge, kick, spin around, elbow in the face. The spikey-haired woman stumbles backward, grabbing her nose, and I take my chance. I gather up all the power I can access in a single second and throw it at her. It leaves my hands as a giant purple flame—and strikes her at the same moment someone whacks her over the head with a broken piece of banister.

She collapses to the ground, clothes burned and eyebrows singed. Jamon is standing behind her. "You messed with the wrong people, *sweetie*," I growl as I jump over her. I hurry to Asim's side along with Jamon.

"Dad!" He crouches down, his eyes on the blade protruding from his father's stomach. "What do I ... Tell me what to—"

"Go," Asim gasps, waving toward the noise of battle. "Fight for ... us. I'll ... be fine."

Ignoring Asim's words, Jamon wraps both arms around his father and holds him tight. "We're never going to win this, Vi," he whispers. "There are way too many of them. And they're not ... normal. They can do things other faeries can't. They're ripping through us."

I hear screams, the clash of weapons, the zing of sparks, and running footsteps squeaking on tiles. The air is hazy with smoke. But I refuse to let this be the end. "We are going to win this," I tell him fiercely. "This is *not* the end for us."

I get to my feet, fetch the sword, and head away from the noise and chaos. I know how this has to go now. I have no other choice. In fact, I think some part of me has known what has to happen since I woke up with the memory of my last meeting with Nate fresh in my mind.

I find another quiet corridor—making certain it's empty this time—and stop in front of the wall. I sling the sword over my back, reach into my boot, and pull out my stylus. I rest my hand against the wood paneled wall for a moment, then write the familiar words to open a doorway.

I'm leaving. And this isn't me being a coward. This isn't me being selfish. This is me facing what I've done and trying to make it better. Because even though Ryn said I shouldn't blame myself, that all of this would have happened somehow anyway—even if I hadn't saved Nate's life or broken his heart—the simple fact is that it *did* happen this way. And I *am* responsible. And if anyone stands a chance of fixing this, it's me.

I press my lips together, take a deep breath, and step into the darkness. I don't know how this is going to go. I don't exactly have a plan. All I know is that this started with Nate and me, and it has to end with Nate and me.

I picture the cold beauty of the Unseelie Court. The frozen fountains and the shards of ice. When the darkness of the paths clears, I'm surprised for a moment that it's still night here. But, of course, I have no idea where the Unseelie Court really is. Clearly it's far away from Fireglass Vale, where the rising sun is witnessing pointless bloodshed.

I walk forward, my eyes trained on the dark shape of a palace rising above the trees ahead. Light flickers from the tallest tower, but other than that, the Unseelie Palace is shrouded in darkness.

Ice crunches beneath my boots as I continue forward, my footsteps far more confident than my thoughts.

After about a minute, I hear a noise behind me. I stop walking and raise my hands. I don't want to get myself shot before making it through the front doors. Rapid footsteps move across the ice before a figure comes into view in front of me. He holds a sword in one hand and a throwing star in the other. From his glance over my shoulder, I know there's at least one more person behind me.

"What do we have here?" he says. "Another guardian, huh?" I guess my sleeves aren't quite long enough to cover my guardian markings. The Unseelie guard smirks at me. "You here to hand yourself over?"

"Yes, actually. Draven's expecting me."

"You—What?"

"And he'll be *very* disappointed if you don't take me to him right now."

The twisted smile returns to his face. "Well, if that's what the lady wants, that's what the lady will get." He nods his head. A figure appears on either side of me, gripping my arms before I have a chance to move. Something cold snaps around my right wrist, and I suppress the almost overwhelming urge to shriek out loud in frustration. I'm now magic-less. *Again.* Stupid metal bands.

The guards jerk me forward. The one I spoke to moves behind me. I feel the point of his sword between my shoulders as I walk. The path widens as we reach the circular space in front of the Unseelie Palace's entrance. A round pond sits in the middle, frozen and glittering. At its center is a formation of silver fish, icicles spurting from their mouths. They seem to be suspended in midair with nothing to hold them up.

I'm dragged past the silent fish fountain and around to the side of the palace. I guess they don't take trespassers through the front door. Branches lean over us like crooked fingers as we walk between the trees. I don't know if it's my imagination or if some of them lean down to touch me as I pass by. Either way, it's exceptionally creepy.

We come to a side door, and the first thing I notice is the strip of metal running around the doorway. The same metal that's wrapped around my wrist. Has Draven put it on every door? What about the windows? Is he really that desperate to keep interfering magic like mine from getting into his palace?

The faerie behind me steps forward and raps the hilt of his sword against the door. Moments later, the door opens to reveal another guard. I'm shoved into his arms. "Take her to Draven. Apparently he's expecting her."

CHAPTER 27

He drags me up to a tower. I know because the winding staircase seems to go on forever and ever. At the top of the stairs, before I can get a good look at what's up here, he tries to take the sword from me.

"Sorry, but that's not happening," I tell him.

"Excuse me? Do you really think I'm going to let you into Lord Draven's presence with—"

"Leave it," a familiar voice commands. "She can't use it on me."

With a final glare in my direction, the guard heads back down the stairs. I take a deep breath before turning. The round, stone room is bare except for an ice-white glow-bug sitting in each narrow window and several elaborate tapestries hanging on the wall. I can't imagine them being Nate's style; they must have been here before he arrived. A shadow moves in the rafters above, but I can't see enough to figure out what creature is lurking up there. Across the room from me is a wide stairway leading out onto a balcony. That's where I see him standing, facing me, his hands behind his back.

Nate. Lord Draven.

Light flickers behind him, casting his front in shadow. He takes a few lazy steps down. When he reaches the bottom step, I can finally see him properly. His hair is longer, brushing his shoulders now, and his skin is paler than before. The disturbing green light I saw in his eyes last time we met is still there, but it's brighter now. No trace of the soft brown that once captivated me.

"Violet," he says. "You're just in time to watch the real fun this evening."

I can't figure out if I'm shaking because I'm cold or scared or just plain shocked that I'm standing in front of the guy who ruined our world. "And what would that be?" I manage to ask.

He gestures behind him. "Why don't you come and see?"

No thank you. But I find myself walking forward anyway. Not because he's forcing me to, but because the reason I'm here is to talk to him, and I need to do it face to face.

"So," I say as I slowly place one foot in front of the other. "How's the Unseelie Court working out for you? I bet the Queen wasn't too pleased about sharing."

"No. Which is why she received the same fate as her son."

My stomach twists as I remember Zell's headless body hanging inside the Rose Hall at Creepy Hollow.

"It was for the best," Nate continues. "After all, there is no Seelie and Unseelie anymore. There is only the fae realm and the human realm. And even then, I plan for those two realms not to be so separate one day."

Seriously? That sounds a lot like what Tharros wanted to do …

I stop a few paces away from Nate. My eyes flick over his shoulder. I see a great white cloud hanging in front of the balcony. And … are those moving images in the cloud?

"Take a look," Nate says, stepping aside and holding his arm out toward the balcony. I look, but I don't move another inch. "I miss television," he tells me. "Being entertained by moving images on a screen. So I created my own screen. Now I can watch the battle without having to be there."

That's what the moving images are? I look closer and see Fireglass Vale filled with fighting fae of all types. All across the valley, bright colors dart and spin, and sparkling weapons slash and fly. Fires erupt, only to be quenched moments later by a patch of rain or a miniature blizzard. Screaming, running, fighting, falling. It's a silent nightmare.

"I've been watching your valley for a while," Nate continues. He laughs quietly. "They thought they were watching me, but everything they've seen is exactly what I wanted them to see."

Of course it was. Nate always likes to be at least one step ahead, doesn't he? "I'm sure it helped having someone on the inside," I say, unable to keep the bitterness from my voice.

"Yes." Nate turns away from his 'screen' and focuses on me once more. "I was lucky Amon transferred his loyalty to me after I killed his former master."

"Hmm." I tilt my head to the side. "Makes you wonder how easily he'd turn on you if someone else offered him a better deal."

"No, it doesn't. There is no better deal than what I offered him, and he knows it."

Right. Sadly, that's true, so I don't argue. I place my shaking hands on my hips and start chewing the inside of my lip. I came here to say something, and I need to say it.

"Nice sword you've got there," Nate says before I can get my words out.

I reach back and touch the hilt. "I assume Amon told you about this too."

"He did."

I watch him. He watches me. I break first. "What did you do with Tilly?"

"Contrary to what you're probably thinking, I didn't kill her.

I'm actually not the killing machine everyone seems to think I am. Sure, if someone insists on fighting me, I have no choice but to kill him or her, but otherwise, I value life. Magical life, especially. So, no. Tilly isn't dead. But I've made sure she's on my side now."

"You marked her."

"Of course. I marked someone else for you too. Someone you once told me you'd never love, not even if the continuation of your kind depended on it. Someone I'll let you say goodbye to before the night is over."

Ryn. Leaden fear attaches itself to my heart and drags it down. "What are you going to do to him?"

Nate watches me closely. "Is that why you came here, Violet? Did you think you could rescue him?"

I shake my head. Tears form behind my eyes. "I came for an entirely different reason."

Nate crosses his arms. "Well, get on with it then. Our time is almost up."

This is it. The moment that should have happened so many months ago. The moment that could have prevented everything. But the words are stuck in my throat; I want to make sure I mean them before I say them.

I look past the glowing eyes that hate me and remember the guy who kissed me and made me laugh. The guy who asked the most ridiculous questions about my magic. The guy who got caught up in a world he wasn't prepared for and never should have entered. The guy who had no idea how to save both his family and the girl he loved, so he ended up betraying them both. For the first time, I think I can imagine his pain. I imagine him risking his life to get away from Zell to come and find me, only to hear me say I never wanted to see him again. I imagine his broken heart, his loneliness, his despair. I imagine him having to watch his parents die.

My eyes ache as tears drip down my cheeks. "I forgive you, Nate," I whisper.

His face twists into an ugly expression. "I don't want your forgiveness."

More tears. A deeper ache. "Nate does. The real Nate. The one buried beneath this evil exterior. He's the one who came to apologize for betraying me. He's the one I turned my back on, and I want to tell him I'm sorry."

"That Nate doesn't exist anymore. You made sure of that, Violet. I barely remember him."

I step closer to him, staring into the green glow of his eyes and hoping desperately that I can somehow reach him. "Nate. I'm sorry. With all my heart, I'm sorry."

He stares at me for so long I begin to wonder if I'm getting through to him. Then he says, "Is that it? That's all you've got to say?" He shakes his head. "Did you really think that would be enough to save everyone? To make me stop all this? You show up here with your pathetic offering of forgiveness and hope that everything can go back to the way it was? I'm disappointed, Vi. I expected you to put up a good fight."

I close my eyes, forcing more tears to spill down my cheeks. "Then you've missed the whole point," I whisper. I didn't come here to fight him. I knew that would never work. I came here to right a wrong I never should have done. I knew there was only a slim chance that forgiveness and an apology would work, but since that's what was at the heart of all this, I had to try.

"Well, it was probably a pointless point," Draven says. I can't think of him as Nate anymore. He's right. That person is no longer here.

Draven climbs the stairs. "Now that we've got that out the way, let's get on with tonight's show. We're going to say goodbye to a few people who are no longer necessary. Then we'll enjoy the rest of the battle. And then—" he looks back down at me with a smile "—you can decide if your life is still worth living."

With a great effort, I manage to blink my tears away. I follow him up the stairs, and this time, I'm not the one in control of my feet. He forces me out onto the balcony where I can't help looking at the horrifying scene in the valley. So much fighting. So much smoke. Too many bodies lying still.

"Can I trust you not to try anything stupid, Vi?" Draven asks. When I don't answer, he says, "Hmm, no, I didn't think so." Something snakes around my wrists, pulling them tight behind my back. I'm not sure what he thinks I might do with my hands. It's not like I can use any magic. "Now, let's say hello to tonight's guests of honor." He looks over my shoulder, and I swivel around.

Ryn. Tilly.

My chest burns as if someone stabbed a blade into it. My heart thrashes fiercely, trying to tear itself free from the pain. I watch them, standing against the outer wall of the tower, staring blankly ahead as if the situation doesn't interest them in the slightest. A crack cleaves my heart in two. They're lost now. Taken. Enslaved within their own minds. I can hardly stand to look at them, at the blankness on their faces.

"Do you remember what I told you, Vi?" Draven asks. "That you would have to watch your world and everyone you care about suffer? That only once I'd taken away everything you cared about would you have my permission to die?"

I remember all too well. I remember his words and the burning forest and my broken home and Tora crushed beneath a tree. I can almost taste the scorching smoke in my throat.

He leans closer and whispers into my ear, "That time is almost here."

No. Draven steps back. I stare at Ryn through a haze of tears. His gaze points straight ahead. His face is still too blank for me to tell whether he's thinking or feeling anything. I watch as his hand moves slowly, carefully toward Tilly's. He grips her fingers and squeezes, then lets go.

Strange, a voice in my mind whispers to me. *Why would he do that?*

Maybe he's just as scared as I am. His loyalty now lies with Draven, but he can probably still feel fear. He must know as well as I do that Draven won't let any of us come out of this alive.

"Ryn, you'll be leaving this world in a minute," Draven says, "so if you'd like to say goodbye to your darling Violet, now's the time."

A sob escapes my throat, but I can't seem to get my body to move. It can't end like this. It's not supposed to end like this.

Ryn nods and steps forward. His eyes finally meet mine, and he smiles. "It's over, V."

No no no it can't be over!

"Draven has finally given me a cause worth dying for. Don't try to save me." He comes closer and places a kiss on my cheek. His lips brush my ear as he whispers, "I've already been saved." His fingers slip behind my back, away from Draven's gaze, and something sharp cuts the bonds around my wrists. Over his shoulder, Tilly winks at me. Ryn steps back, his meaningless smile morphing into the one I love so much. "Goodbye, V." He raises his hand and gives me a little wave, and I notice the tiniest smudge on one side of the black ring that marks his palm.

Is it possible … ?

"Now," Draven says, "if you'd just climb up onto the railing so it's easy for Vi to push you off, that would be great."

My stomach drops.

Ryn turns to him. "I don't think so, halfling boy." He lunges at Draven, striking him hard in the chin with the heel of his hand and following it up with a guardian dagger straight to the stomach. With a shout of fury, Draven stumbles back.

I can't move. My brain struggles to catch up. Small hands push my shoulders down, and Tilly yanks the sword from its sheath on my back. "Out the way!" she yells at Ryn. She runs. He ducks. And the glowing sword plunges into Draven's chest.

Everything seems to stop. Nothing moves except for blurred images in the smoke. Draven takes a shuddering gasp as he stares in horror at the sword protruding from his chest. Then he wraps his hand around the hilt and slowly pulls it out. He drops the sword onto the stones where it lands with a loud clatter.

His simmering gaze rests on each of us before his hand whips out and strikes Tilly with such force that she flies back and tumbles down the stairs. He kicks the sword after her.

I take a shaky step backward as Draven's eyes lock onto me. Why is he alive? Why didn't it work? With a wordless shout, he slams his elbow into Ryn's chest, knocking him backward off the balcony.

"Ryn!" I scream, running forward. Draven catches me and wraps a hand around my neck as my panicked brain screams words at me. *He's a faerie. He can stop his fall. He won't die. You have to fight back.*

"Well, isn't that interesting?" Draven snarls. "Looks like somebody found a way around my mark. Drew their own pretty circles on their palms. I'll have to investigate that once I've got rid of all the traitors in this tower." His hands squeeze tighter around my neck.

Fight back, dammit! I squirm and kick. I claw at Draven's arms, his face, his neck. There's a chain there, disappearing beneath his shirt, and for a crazy second all I can think is, *Why is he wearing a necklace?*

The next thing I know I'm being thrown across the balcony and back into the tower room. I land on my side, the way I've been taught, and roll several times before coming to a stop. The shadowy shape I saw earlier moves across the rafters above, then drops down toward me. I scream and swing my body out of the way, but I recognize the figure the moment I jump to my feet.

"Dad?"

Before Dad can answer, Draven comes storming down the stairs. Literally storming. Wind swirls around the room and rain begins to fall. Dad throws a shield up in front of us just as lightning crackles and hundreds of miniature manticores swarm toward us. Darkness descends in the form of heavy grey-black clouds. They grow thicker, filling the tower room like stuffing inside a cushion. The manticores vanish into the darkness. Rain falls so heavily on the other side of Dad's shield that I can't see a thing except when the lightning flashes.

"I can't … last," Dad shouts. I snap myself out of my shock and try to add my own strength to the shield. When it doesn't work, I remember the metal band on my wrist. My magic wouldn't do much good anyway. There's so much power behind Draven's storm, it's like trying to hold a dam back with a handful of twigs. "You have to … separate him … from his power," Dad gasps. "You have to—"

The storm shatters our shield.

We're thrown backward onto the slippery stones.

"Violet!" Dad throws his arm out toward me, but lightning hits him, tossing him aside like a leaf.

"Dad!" I try to scramble across the stones, but an invisible force holds me back. I swing around and scream into the drenching rain. One wordless scream packed with every emotion splitting my heart into thousands of pieces.

The rain slows and stops. The wind spins itself into a gentle breeze. The clouds lift, pull apart, drift away. Through the dim light, I see Draven. He takes his time stalking toward me. "It's just you and me now, Vi. No one left to hide behind."

The invisible chains disappear from my body. I climb onto shaky legs as I look around. Ryn's gone. Dad's down. Tilly's down. Her motionless fingers lie inches from the sword that didn't work—and I just figured out why. *You have to separate him from his power*, Dad said. And what were those words in the prophecy? *She is hidden, but the finder will find her. She will break the whole in half.* 'She will break the whole in half,' I murmur, my words leaving my lips as little more than shaky breaths. I thought the 'she' was Tilly, but maybe it isn't. Maybe it's the finder.

Maybe it's me.

"Aren't you going to come and get me?" Draven taunts. "I've always wanted to fight the great guardian Violet."

My wet boots slap the stones as I run at him. I know what has to happen, I just don't know *how*. I grab the tops of his arms and shake him. "Nate!" My shout comes out as half a sob. "Please come back. Please!"

He laughs and pushes me away as easily as if I were made of paper. I trip over Tilly's arm—she groans in pain—and fall backward. Draven crouches down beside me and holds a hand over my chest. "Do you know I can boil you from the inside out?"

I grasp the sleeves of his jacket and tug weakly at them. "I know you're in there, Nate," I sob. I reach out with my mind, searching desperately for the guy with the laughing eyes and the beautiful smile. If he's still there, I'll find him. I remember the connection we once had, and I hold onto it as tightly as I can. "Nate, come back." My chest starts to burn. The breeze around us whips itself into a rising wind. "I'm sorry." The wind swirls into a hurricane gale. "Come back, *please!*" Burning, burning, unbearable heat. *"I loved you and you broke my heart and I'm SORRY!"*

The heat and wind vanish. Draven's gaze falters. He shudders. The glow in his eyes intensifies, then seems to lift away into the air. Wisps of green drift out of him until he's completely surrounded by a green haze. I see him through it. Startled. Confused.

"Vi?" he whispers.

A hand brushes against my hip. Tilly. I look over at her. Our eyes meet. I grasp her hand, wrap it around the sword, and lift it. "I'm sorry," I gasp out. "I'm so sorry, Nate." I bring her hand down, along with the glowing sword, straight through the green haze and straight through Nate.

We let go. Tilly's hand flops to the ground. Nate's eyes bulge in shock. He falls away from me, onto his side, as the green haze seems to tighten around him. Then it rushes outward, filling the room for an instant before vanishing.

"Nate?"

A brilliant flash of silver light bursts forth from his chest. I throw my arm across my eyes to shield my face. A rushing sound fills the tower, and a gust of wind swirls and twists and spins like it's trying to suck the life out of the room. Just as I'm about to rise off the ground, the wind scatters. My wildly blowing hair falls onto my shoulders. The light fades.

I slowly lower my arm.

Nate is gone.

I twist around, but he's nowhere to be seen. The sword is gone too. A groan at my feet makes me scramble to Tilly's side. I push her wet hair off her face. "Tilly, can you hear me? Are you okay?"

"Mm hmm." I help her to sit up. "Crud, my head is *seriously* throbbing." She looks around. "What happened? Did we do it? Is he ... really gone?"

"I think so." I feel a shuddering in my chest, like I want to collapse in on myself. The relief that crashes into me is exhausting. I want to cry for days. It was all just ... so ... much.

"V? V, honey?"

My hands shake as I push myself to my feet and look around for Dad. Holding his wounded arm close to his body, he comes toward me. With his good arm, he pulls me to his side. Careful not to hurt him, I wrap my arms around his waist and start crying. I cry myself empty as the same thoughts play over in my head. *It's over it's over and I don't know how many people died and I don't know where Ryn is and I don't know what's going to happen now and I wish the real Nate hadn't had to die but it's over. It's over.*

When the tears are gone, I pull away from Dad and hurry across the tower room to the stairs. The cloud-screen shows Fireglass Vale and the people who survived the battle. They're helping each other up, checking the fallen for those still alive, hugging, crying. I walk across the balcony, slowing as I near the railing. If I see Ryn down there, on the ground, the pieces of my heart will never become whole again. I grip the railing and look down, but I can't see enough past the wisps of cloud and tree branches to know if he's there or not.

"V?"

I turn around, and the air rushes out of my lungs at the sight of him. I don't seem to be able to move, but joy bubbles up inside me and escapes in a half-cry, half-laugh.

"Is it you?" he says, and I know what he's asking.

My fingers go to my neck and lift the tiny key hanging from the chain. "Guessing Game Number Twenty-Four," I say. "This is the answer. The gold key from my mother. You threw it down the singing well in Creepy Hollow, and I didn't see it again for years. But you found it. You gave it to me the night of our graduation. The night I finally realized how much you mean to me."

He crosses the balcony in a few quick strides. He takes my face in his hands and rests his forehead against mine. "I missed you so much, my Sexy Pixie." He presses a soft kiss to my lips.

Bright colors explode in the cloud beside us. Firework sparks rise high above the valley and shower down on the victorious fae below. Blue, green, red, gold.

I smile against Ryn's mouth and whisper, "I love you. With all my heart."

CHAPTER 28

FAE DRESSED IN EVERY COLOR OF THE RAINBOW LINE THE banks of the Neverending River. A little higher upstream, the Infinity Falls thunder down, creating a cloud of spray that reaches high into the air. I watch the spray and imagine all the places in our world where fae are gathering to say goodbye to their fallen loved ones.

This is my fourth celebration-of-life ceremony—the first three were for my mother, my father, and Reed—and it's by far the largest. There are many who lost their lives in the past months. I've only been here with faeries before, but the mingling of races on the banks of this river is a testament to the way we came together to fight for our world.

Ryn lays a kiss on top of my head, and I lean against him for a while. Filigree wriggles in my pocket, then settles. His tiny presence comforts me as much as Ryn's does. I look down at the garlands of fresh flowers in my hands. Normally there'd be a canoe to place the flowers in, alongside the fallen body, but some of the lives we're celebrating today were lost months ago. Like Tora's.

"You ready?" Ryn asks. I nod and squeeze his hand. I look

over at Flint to let him know. He comes forward to take my hand, and we walk down the bank to the river. We hold the garland together, whisper our final goodbyes, and toss it into the water. He's saying goodbye to his sister; I'm saying goodbye to a friend, sister, mother, mentor ... I'm not sure I'm even aware of all the roles Tora filled for me. I squeeze my eyes closed and feel the tears dripping down my cheeks. For someone who spent so many years determined not to cry or feel any kind of distressing emotion, I've certainly made up for it in recent months.

I open my eyes. Flint turns and heads back up the bank. I'm not finished yet, though. I have another garland in my hand. Not many people know who it's for because not many people would understand. They didn't know him before everything turned bad. They didn't know the real Nate. *By the strike of the sword, and the death of innocence, evil will be laid to rest.* Nate was the 'innocence.' I figured that out the moment Tharros' power lifted from him and the real Nate looked down at me. Lost. Confused. Alone.

I always told myself I never loved him. I told myself I didn't know him long enough. But I realized, in that last moment before it was all over, that in some way I did. Not like I love Ryn, but a different kind of love. The kind that arrives swiftly like a gust of wind, turns everything topsy-turvy, and is gone moments later.

I whisper once more to him the words that can never make up for everything. "I'm sorry." Then I lean down and place the garland carefully on the water. I watch as it travels magically, inexplicably, against the current. I keep watching until both his and Tora's garlands disappear into the thundering falls.

I straighten and look across to the other side of the river. Among the many fae there, I see Em and Max laying flowers in a canoe beside Fin. I didn't know him all that well, but I get the feeling he's far more at peace now than he would have been if he'd survived this. Jamon is there too, standing in water up to his waist as he gets ready to slide the canoe carrying his father away. Asim fought hard, but reptiscillan magic isn't as strong as faerie magic. He couldn't survive being stabbed. His wife, Jamon's mother, stands on the bank just behind her son. She looks across the water at me. She gives me a sad smile and inclines her head ever so slightly.

I return the nod. "We did it," I whisper.

I turn and shift my gaze up the bank. My father is there, standing beside Ryn and his mother. I thought she'd be happy to find out Dad's still alive—after all, they were friends for many years—but it turned out she was rather angry. I kind of feel like there's something I missed there, but I'm not letting it bother me. I know she'll forgive him. She's already softening.

I want to give her another hug and thank her again. I could probably thank her every day for the rest of my life and it wouldn't be enough. She endured so much to make sure we didn't lose this fight. When we gave her the cure and it worked, she could have easily come back with us. Instead, she hid her bare palm, stole Em's bag of cures, and walked back into the heart of it all. She lived a lie right under Draven's nose, with a faked mark on her palm and thoughts of treason in her heart.

It terrifies me to think what would have happened if she hadn't been there to cure Ryn and Tilly. I usually stop my thoughts at this point because the world becomes a dark and bleak place when I consider the future that might have been.

I climb the bank, and Ryn pulls me against his chest as I turn back to face the river. He wraps his arms around me and rests his chin on my shoulder. I lean back and stare up at the sky. Draven's winter is gone, but real winter is almost on its way. Within hours of his death, the enchanted winter melted away, and Creepy Hollow forest began to heal itself. Shoots grew up and green leaves popped out. Then, as if suddenly remembering it was supposed to be autumn, they turned orange, red, and gold overnight. I expect they'll fall in another few days, but for now everything feels rich and warm.

Someone on the other side of the bank starts singing. After a few words, I recognize Farah's voice. I close my eyes, feel the sun's warmth brush my skin, and let the sound of her song fill my heart.

* * *

The sun moves toward the horizon as I climb across the giant ruins of the old Guild. Afternoon light peeks through tree branches, and a cool breeze curls around my neck. Ahead of me, pixies skip and spring across the ruins before leaping off and dancing away. This place has already become part of the forest playground.

Air ripples beside me and melts into a doorway. At the sight of Ryn, my heart dances just like the pixies. It always seems to be ridiculously joyful whenever he appears. I know he can feel my happiness, and from the kisses I usually receive soon after he arrives, I'm pretty sure he feels the same way.

Today is no different. He steps in front of me, pushes both hands gently into my hair, and brings my face close to his. His lips linger on mine as his fingers brush the back of my neck and send shivers across my arms. I lean into him, running my hands down his back. Warmth curls around my stomach.

"I got your message," he says against my lips. He moves his mouth across my cheek, kisses each of my closed eyelids, and pulls away slightly. "Why did you want to come here?"

I reach down and take his hand. I look around. "I'm not sure exactly. Maybe I just feel like I need to say one last goodbye. To this place, where so many important things in my life happened."

Ryn nods. His thumb brushes over my skin as we walk. "Have you been back to the new Guild since we visited it?"

I shake my head. The day after the celebration-of-life ceremony, I went with Ryn and my father to see the new Guild. The one the guardians built during Draven's time. "It's just ... it's similar enough to make it feel like a familiar place, but every time I saw something different, it felt so wrong and out of place. And I don't know if it will ever feel right without ..."

"Without Tora being there," Ryn says.

"Yeah." I lean down and pick up an ornately carved piece of wood. I think it was part of a door once. I run my finger over the patterns. "I don't know. I suppose I'll get used to it in time. But then I think ... maybe I *shouldn't* get used to it. Maybe I don't belong there anymore."

"Are you thinking about Jamon's idea?"

"I am. It sounds crazy, and I imagine it would be almost impossible to get the Guild to agree to it, but I think I want to be part of it."

"Well, you know I'm one hundred percent in favor of his idea. I don't know if it's actually possible—I mean, throughout history, the Guild has only ever been open to faeries—but if it is possible, you should go for it. Things have changed drastically since The Destruction. We just might have non-faerie guardians one day."

Non-faerie guardians. Jamon's idea is certainly a revolutionary one. "And what about you?" We come to a low wall, and I push myself up onto it. I swing my legs. "Do you want to work at the new Guild?"

"I don't know. Still thinking about that." He stands between my legs and leans his hands on the wall on either side of me. He kisses my nose, then says, "I have a feeling we're all going to be living and working out of the Fireglass Vale base for some time."

"Yes, with only so many architect faeries around, and a world full of faerie homes to rebuild, I have a feeling you're right," I say with a laugh.

"I don't think I mind, though." Ryn leans closer and brushes his lips along my neck. "I like knowing that your room is just up the stairs and along the corridor."

A smile stretches across my lips. I wrap my legs around Ryn's waist and pull him closer. "Pretty sure I don't mind either," I say, my voice coming out a little breathless. His lips graze a trail over my jaw toward my mouth. I close my eyes, losing myself in the tingling on my skin. As my legs slip down, my boot snags on something in Ryn's back pocket. My eyes flicker open. "What's that?"

"Hmm?" His kisses move across the other side of my neck. I slip my hand down his back and into his pocket. "You just want to feel my butt," he says between kisses.

I roll my eyes and try not to laugh. "I'm actually trying to find out what's in your pocket."

"Oh." He pulls back abruptly and clamps his hand over the pocket I'm trying to search. "Right. I forgot about that. I have something for you."

"Ooh, a present?" I slide my hand away and clasp it together with my other hand.

"I'm not sure if it really counts as a present if I've already given it to you." He removes his closed fist from his pocket and holds it in front of me. When he opens it, I see a ribbon bracelet and a ring with a gold-flecked purple stone.

I sit up straight in surprise. "I thought I lost those in The Destruction." The bracelet is made from ribbons that belonged to my grandmother, and the ring is something my father left for me when he 'died.'

"I saved them from the wreckage of your house. I meant to give them to you after we found each other, but I forgot."

"Thank you," I whisper, tears prickling behind my eyes.

Stupid tears. I'm like a leaking tap these days. With everything behind us now, I'm hoping the tap will stop running soon.

Ryn fastens the bracelet around my wrist, then pushes the ring onto one of my fingers. My heart squeezes and tumbles over itself as my crazy mind conjures up an image of a future Ryn and me and a ring that means something entirely different.

Oookay. Not ready to go there just yet!

Ryn tips my chin up so he can look into my eyes. With a puzzled smile, he asks, "What was that about?"

"Nothing. Never mind. You don't need to know." I wrap my hands around his neck and pull him close for another kiss. I forget about the world around me. It's only the two of us. My fingers in his hair, his hands trailing down my back, the sparks on my tongue, my heart pounding in my ears. I only pull away because I need air.

Ryn rests his forehead against mine. "Want to go for a walk?" he asks, sounding as breathless as I feel.

"Yeah." I need to calm my racing heart and the fire in my veins.

I lace my fingers through his and slide off the wall. We climb down the side of the ruins and wander through the trees. Color, life, sounds, scents. Everything is back to the way it should be.

"I have a suspicion," Ryn says eventually.

"Oh yeah?" I lift my hand, and a sprite with shimmering purple wings lands on my palm. She waves shyly at me, then flits away. "A suspicion about what?"

"My mother. Your father."

I stare up at Ryn, puzzled. "Your mother? My father?" Then it clicks. I stop walking. "What? No. Why? Have you seen something?"

Ryn shakes his head.

"But you *felt* something?"

"Maybe. I'm not sure. But she was far more upset than

necessary when she discovered your father was actually alive all these years. And now that I think about it, after Reed died and my dad left, your dad started visiting us a lot more than he used to."

"He did? I didn't know that."

"Well, you and I weren't exactly on speaking terms back then."

We start walking again. "So … you think they …"

"I don't know."

"That's just weird."

"Yeah."

"We should talk about something else now," I say.

"Deal." Ryn laughs. "Um … did you know the Unseelie Court has a king now?"

"Oh yeah, I heard about that. King Savyon. Zell's older brother."

"It'll be strange having a king in one of the courts," Ryn says. "So much of fae history has been ruled over by queens."

We reach a fallen tree. "Well, like you said, things have changed since The Destruction."

"Yeah." We climb onto the tree trunk and jump down the other side. "Hey," Ryn says, "look where we are."

I raise my eyes. We're standing near the old obstacle course. The one our mentors used to bring us out to during training. It's scorched in places, but the ropes, nets, pool, wooden bars, and other obstacles are still here.

"You know, we never did race this obstacle course against each other," Ryn says.

I wander over to the starting line. "You were always too scared to take me on. I am, after all, the supreme record holder of all time."

"By, like, a fraction of a second."

"Still counts."

Ryn stands on the starting line beside me. "I think we should see if that record still holds."

I tilt my head to the side. "Is that a challenge, Mr. Larkenwood?"

"You bet your Sexy Pixie ass it is, Miss Fairdale."

With a grin I can't suppress, I crouch down and get ready to jump. "Fifty silvers says I kick your ass."

I hear the smile in his voice. "You're on."

Thank you for reading *The Faerie War*!

Turn the page for bonus scenes from this book.

RYN

Hanging out for a few hours in Titan's Tavern had been exceptionally risky, but Ryn considered it an evening well spent. After he and his team had drawn fake marks onto their palms and sauntered into the Underground tavern as if they owned it, they'd discovered the place packed with marked guardians relaxing after a hard day's work serving Lord Draven. The perfect opportunity to collect information.

Ryn and Em managed to gather details on the current protection level of the new Creepy Hollow Guild from a guy who was part of the protective charm casting team, and Fin and Max had overheard a discussion about an upcoming attack on a group of elves still hiding out in one of the Underground tunnels. When discussions turned to their new leader, and everyone began saying how magnificent Lord Draven was and how grateful they all were that he'd given them a true purpose, Ryn decided it was time to leave.

Now, as they slipped through the snow-dusted trees, magic concealing their footprints, they quietly discussed what they'd learned. Em sent a message to Oliver about the impending attack on the elves, and Ryn made the chirping noise that would call their ride. As the shadow of the magic carpet slid over them, Ryn heard another voice nearby.

He halted his steps and held his hand up. The other three stopped and looked around, listening intently. The voice was gone now, but Ryn could feel someone nearby. He sensed a wariness that didn't belong to his team; they generally felt confident while wearing blue uniforms and sporting marks on their palms.

A flicker of movement caught his eye, and he swung in its direction, a bow and arrow already tingling beneath his fingers. "Stop where you are!" he commanded. That's what Draven's guards would do. They didn't hide in the shadows. They demanded to know who was traveling across their master's land. Ryn took a step forward and noticed something strange a few paces ahead: the outline of a man who appeared to be made of the same substance as his surroundings.

Clever, Ryn thought with a chuckle. That was reptiscillan magic, wasn't it? "I can see you," he called out. "Well, I can see your outline. It's a good disguise, but not good enough."

The man made no move to reveal himself, probably because of the four sets of sparkling weapons pointed directly at him. Which wasn't necessary, Ryn decided. If the man was out here alone, using camouflage magic to hide himself, he wasn't likely to be one of Draven's marked followers. "Look, we're not interested in hurting anyone," Ryn said, "so why don't we put away our weapons, you drop the transparency act, and we all have a civilized conversation."

Apparently that didn't sound convincing enough, because the man remained hidden.

"Okay, look," Ryn continued. "I'll put my weapon away first." He allowed his bow and arrow to disappear and indicated to the rest of his team to do the same. He raised his hands. "Please," he said, hoping that might put the man slightly more at ease. "Show yourself."

"We've all put our weapons away," Em added.

Nothing. Ryn lowered his hands and began walking slowly toward the outline.

"Stop right there!"

The voice came from behind. In less than a second, Ryn and his three companions had spun around to face the owner, weapons blazing in their grips. Ryn had one knife pointed forward and another pointed back as he tried to keep track of both the camouflaged man and the woman who had snuck up on them. She was a guardian—evident from the glittering bow and arrow in her hands—but the shadow of her hood kept Ryn from being able to see if he recognized her.

"I know you're lying," she said fiercely, "and there's no way you're taking either of us without a fight."

That voice.

Ryn's weapons vanished in an instant. *It's her. It has to be her.* He pushed between Max and Fin, desperate to get close enough to see if he was right. As if in a dream, his feet carried him slowly toward her. He stared intently, struggling to make out the details of her face behind the bright light of the arrow still trained on him.

"I said *stop!*" she shouted.

Violet.

It was her. She wasn't dead. She was *here* right in front of him, and his stunned mind could barely take it in. "Violet," he whispered.

Her hand twitched, the arrow flew, and he jerked to the side as it sailed past his ear.

"*Flipping* … You just shot at me!" He struggled to comprehend what was happening. His mind was still stuck on, *It's her. It's actually her!* "Violet," he repeated. "It's you, isn't it?"

She hesitated, but then her grip tightened around her bow.

Another arrow appeared as she said, "Stay back or I'll shoot you again."

What?

"Shoot him and we'll shoot you," Em said.

"And then *I* will shoot *you*," her reptiscillan accomplice said, melting from the shadows and moving to stand beside Violet. "Or stab you," he added, raising his knife.

"No!" Ryn raised his arms to hold his team back. "There won't be any shooting or stabbing." His eyes never left Violet. What the hell was going on here? What he wanted most in the world was to pull her close and wrap his arms around her, and instead he was trying to convince her not to shoot him. "V, do you honestly not recognize me?" he asked slowly. An icy finger of fear ran down his spine. "Are … are you marked?"

"No. But you are."

Of course. She thought he worked for Draven now. He just needed to explain the truth, and then everything would be fine. "I'm not—"

"Show me your palms," she snapped.

He did, watching her eyes narrow at the sight of the black circle. "It isn't real," he said. "It's our disguise so we can go unnoticed among Draven's followers."

"Oh really? Well, isn't that convenient?"

Clearly she didn't believe him, and he could hardly blame her. Well, he would just have to show her then. He brought his left hand up to his mouth and blew gently into his cupped palm.

"What are you doing?" she demanded. "Stop that!"

He lowered his hand to show her the water that had formed there. He let it trickle onto his right palm, then rubbed over the mark with his thumb. Black ink smudged across his skin. "See?" he said. "It isn't real." He expected her to run into his arms now that she knew the mark was fake, but she still eyed him with wariness. Almost as if … as if she didn't know him. "Come on, it's me," he said, desperation tugging at his heart. "Ryn. Please tell me you remember me." *Please, please, PLEASE.*

She frowned. "What ... what did you say your name is?"

Yes. Remember. Please remember. "Ryn," he repeated. "Oryn."

Her frown deepened as her eyes traveled over him. When they returned to his face, she lowered her arms and let her bow disappear. "I ... I'm sorry," she said. "I don't know who you are."

No. NO!

Hope crumbled into dust and settled around the broken pieces of his heart. How could she not remember him? *How?* They had an entire lifetime of shared memories, yet she remembered *none of it?*

"Ryn?" Max said, breaking the silence. "You okay, man?"

Ryn blinked. "Yeah." He wasn't okay. He was so far from okay. But his team didn't need to know that. "Lose the weapons, okay? V, you're coming with us. You're welcome to bring your friend."

She blinked. "Excuse me? I'm not going anywhere with you."

Stubborn as ever. The familiarity of the situation stabbed like a knife in his chest. He swallowed his pain down. "Where exactly do you plan to go?"

"With my friend. There are a whole lot of us in hiding, and I don't plan to abandon them. Why don't *you* come with *us?*"

Her words managed to pierce through his heartache and reach the calculating warrior part of his brain. His gaze moved to the reptiscilla. "There are more of you? I mean, more *free* reptiscillas?"

"Yes," he answered. "Are there more of you?"

Em laughed as she walked forward. "There are a *lot* of us. And we have a massive hidden base where everyone who's willing to fight Draven is gathering."

The reptiscilla turned to Violet and spoke to her in low tones. She started nodding. Ryn watched the two of them and wanted to yell, tear his hair out, pummel the nearest tree, *something* to express just how utterly, horribly, painfully cruel life was. He finally had her back, the girl he loved more than anything else, and all she saw in his place was a stranger.

He couldn't look at her anymore. It hurt too much. He crossed his arms tightly over his chest and turned away. He made a weak attempt to feel the emotions of those around him, hoping to dilute his pain. He couldn't. He was drowning in his own despair. *She doesn't remember you*, a voice kept taunting at the back of his mind. *She doesn't remember you.*

She doesn't remember you.

AMON

AMON WAS THE HEAD LIBRARIAN AT THE CREEPY HOLLOW Guild for ninety-one years before it fell. For sixty-eight of those years, he was a spy. As someone who was neither physically fit nor particularly brave, he'd never felt appreciated by guardians. They lived for the thrill of the fight, caring little for the vast storehouse of knowledge Amon watched over in the Guild's great library.

But knowledge was exactly what Prince Zell wanted, and he was happy to pay for it. Knowledge of Tharros. Knowledge of his power that was never destroyed. Knowledge of the discs used to lock away that power. Knowledge of what those discs did to children born under its influence. And, of course, knowledge of any goings on at the Guild that might prove useful to a prince of the Unseelie Court.

Amon felt no loyalty to the Guild and its members, so agreeing to be Zell's spy was easy. He didn't particularly care for Zell either, but the arrangement he had with the prince was purely a business one. Which is why it was with no great difficulty that Amon transferred his allegiance to Draven after the halfling took it upon himself to behead Zell.

Amon was centuries older than the young 'lord' he now

served, but he didn't find that to be too much of a problem. Age was of little importance next to power, and Draven was the one with all the power. And he was offering a whole lot more of it to Amon than Zell ever had. Where Amon had been a tiny spider in the giant web Zell was weaving, he was now a key player in the game Draven had set up.

"Would you like to be part of the game?" he had asked Amon. "Would you like to move the pieces into position yourself? Would you like to watch first-hand as our enemy scrambles to stay one step ahead, when in reality they've always been miles behind?"

Yes. He wanted all of that. Guardians had always thought themselves better than everyone else, and he would greatly enjoy watching them fall.

So that's how he found himself clinging to a tree trunk late one night, waiting for a magic carpet to rescue him. Draven had sent him out days before and told him to wait somewhere in Creepy Hollow. Unmarked fae still snuck around there at times, and Amon needed to get someone to rescue him. Someone, hopefully, who would take him back to the heart of the rebellion against Draven. From there, he could begin moving pieces across the game board.

When he'd heard the commotion of a fight somewhere near the ruins of the old Guild, he'd run a little further before using magic to assist him up a tree. He'd meant to get a better view of what was happening and where the best spot would be to reveal himself to his potential 'rescuers,' but he'd been luckier than that: They'd flown right past him and seen him. They slowed down, and he knew they were coming back for him. As he waited, he reminded himself of his role. He was scared. Exhausted. Fleeing from danger and unable to save himself. That would feed those guardian egos.

As the carpet neared him, he looked up and acted startled

enough to almost fall from the tree. In all honesty, though, it was only half an act. He hadn't expected to see the girl who'd unwittingly assisted in Draven's first spectacular move against the Guilds. But there she was, giving him an encouraging smile, holding her hand out to him.

Play the game, he reminded himself. As he grasped her hand and launched himself clumsily from the tree onto the carpet, he heard the last words Draven had spoken to him:

It's your move now.

RYN

Ryn woke on the floor of an opulently decorated sitting room. As he blinked and stared up at a tapestry hanging on the wall, he thought back to his last conscious moments, trying to figure out how he ended up here—wherever 'here' was.

He'd been in the boat with Violet, and she'd finally felt all the things he'd been longing for her to feel. He'd kissed her, but then something happened and she'd grown feverish and passed out. He'd sat beside her bed for hours. Then he'd gone in search of Oliver, desperate to do something other than wait. Movement had been reported just outside the protective dome. Ryn, Em, and two other guardians had gone out to investigate. They'd passed through the protective dome, and then … He wasn't sure after that.

He sat up and looked around the room. On the rug beside him lay Tilly. He touched her arm, but she didn't move. Strange. Where was Em? And the other two guardians?

He couldn't quite bring himself to be concerned, though. None of the things he should be concerned about—Violet passing out, Em being gone, Tilly lying on the floor beside him

—seemed as important as the one thought that now eclipsed everything else: He was finally free to serve Draven.

He looked down at his right hand and felt a great relief when he saw the black snake circling his palm. He rubbed his thumb across it. It didn't smudge.

The mark was real.

"Finally," he breathed. Someone had opened his eyes to the truth. He was free to fulfill his true purpose by serving Draven.

He stood up and looked around the large sitting room. No one else was there aside from Tilly. He checked her hand and found her palm marked as well. Thank goodness. She wouldn't be able to hurt Draven now. He crossed the room and looked out one of the windows. The glacial beauty of the Unseelie Court lay before him.

A door opened, and he swung around. A woman with dark curly hair slipped inside and shut the door behind her. "Mom!" Ryn strode across the room and wrapped his arms around his mother. "I'm so sorry I fought you by the old Guild," he said when he stepped back. "I know you were only trying to do what was right for me. I understand now."

She nodded, smiled, and patted his cheek. "And now I'm trying to do what's right for you again."

Her stunner magic hit him square in the chest, throwing him backwards against the curtain and onto the floor. She hadn't put much power behind the strike, though, because instead of being knocked out, Ryn found himself blinking through a sluggish haze, trying to move limbs that felt like dead weights. Through half-open eyelids, he saw the murky image of his mother coming toward him. He was vaguely aware of her holding something cold to his lips. Liquid hit the back of his mouth, and he swallowed instinctively. It burned all the way down his throat. He rolled onto his hands and knees, coughing and gasping. A shudder passed through him, and he stilled.

He thought of Lord Draven. He thought of serving him, bowing before him. He thought of how that single thought had filled his mind, bringing him joy. He thought of killing people in Draven's name.

And he almost threw up.

"Mom," he gasped. Still feeling weak from the stunner spell, he grabbed onto the curtain with a hand now free of the mark and pulled himself to his feet. "How did you do that? How did you save me?"

"Ryn." She grasped his arms and looked into his eyes. "It worked. The cure you gave me that night worked."

"But …"

"The mark disappeared. My mind cleared. I knew I'd never wanted to serve Draven. But in that moment, I saw how I could make a difference. If I could just get back here and put a fake mark on my palm, no one would ever know the difference. I'd be on the inside. A spy."

"So … you tricked us."

"I'm sorry I couldn't say anything." Her eyes pleaded for him to understand. "I knew there were other guardians just seconds away from joining us, and there was no time to explain. I had to make it look like it hadn't worked so I could get back in here."

Ryn nodded. "I get it. It was really dangerous, but I get it."

"And when I chased you, it was so I could get the bag of cures your friend had."

"Of course," Ryn said, remembering. "Thank goodness you managed that, or I'd be in a great deal of trouble right now."

"I don't even want to think about it," his mother said, shaking her head.

"So where exactly are we?" Ryn asked. "And how do we get out?"

"This sitting room is part of Draven's quarters. He told his guards to dump you here once you'd been marked. But there's no point in leaving, Ryn. It's too late."

"What?"

"Fireglass Vale is already under attack. But Draven isn't there, he's still here. He's waiting for Violet. I don't know why. I don't know the story. But for some reason he expects her to show up and try to fight him. And that's why you and this other girl are here." She gestured toward Tilly. "He's going to use you both against Vi. Or make her hurt you. Or something. I don't know, but you're both part of his plan."

Ryn shook his head, his eyes closed for a moment as he tried to follow his mother's hurried words. The last time he'd seen Violet, she'd been unconscious. But he didn't know how long ago that was. She could be awake by now. "Okay," he said eventually. "Okay. So how do we stop this?"

"We don't," a voice behind him said.

Ryn spun around and found Violet's father entering through a door opposite the one his mother had come through. "Kale? How did—" He looked back at his mother. "Wait, so you know now. About his death being faked and the undercover—"

"Yes," she said, her eyes on the floor and her voice terse. "I know about it now. Apparently the death of one of my closest friends was nothing more than an elaborate stunt. A trick meant to fool us all. But that isn't something we need to discuss right now. We need to cure the girl and wake her." She crouched down beside Tilly and produced one of Uri's vials from her pocket.

Ignoring the hostility directed toward him, Kale crossed the room and stood before Ryn. "We don't stop this. We let Draven believe everything is going according to his plan. And, for some reason, his plan includes the belief that Vi will show up here tonight. I don't have time to ask you why. Just tell me if it's true. Will she come?"

Ryn thought about Violet's history with Nate and her guilt

over everything he'd ended up doing because of her. If everyone was under attack and she thought confronting Nate might make a difference, would she come? "Yes," he said. "She'll be here."

"And will she bring the sword with her?"

"Of course." Unless, for some reason, it was impossible for her to get to it.

"She has to, Ryn. That's the only way we can end this."

And Violet knew that. She knew there was no end to any of this without that sword. "She'll bring it," Ryn said, no longer doubting his words.

"Then we need to wake the girl, explain what's going on, and get a fake mark onto both of you. When Draven's guards return to fetch you, you will both be the most loyal and compliant followers Draven could ever ask for."

"Yes, sir."

"And once the sword is here, the girl *must* use it on Draven before he has a chance to either destroy it or kill her."

"I'll make sure it happens."

"Ryn, if you don't—"

"I *will* make sure it happens," Ryn said fiercely.

Kale nodded. "I'll be with you, hidden in the shadows."

"Good."

Kale grasped Ryn's hand. "Let's end this."

Ten years later, the story continues!
Join beloved characters and new heroes in *A Faerie's Secret*!

*Calla Larkenwood wants nothing more than to be a guardian, but
her overprotective mother has never allowed it. Battling fae creatures
is too dangerous a job for a young girl, and there's that pesky Griffin
Ability she needs to keep hidden from the Guild. How can she do
that if she's working right under their nose?*

*When circumstances change and Calla finally gets to follow her
dream, she discovers guardian trainee life isn't all she hoped it would
be. Her classmates are distant, her mentor hates her, and keeping her
ability a secret is harder than she thought.*

*Then an Underground initiation game goes wrong, landing Calla
with a new magical ability she can't control. She needs help—and the
only way to get it is by bargaining with the guy who just discovered
her biggest secret.*

ACKNOWLEDGMENTS

I am forever grateful to God for the imagination he's given me, the abundant blessings he's poured over me, and for being there every step of the way.

My heartfelt thanks go to Kittie Howard for her superior editing skills. She can turn any clumsy sentence into eloquent prose! Kittie, you've been with me since the moment Vi first stepped onto the page. Thank you for sharing her journey with me.

Thank you to Nicola Vermaak for once again waiting patiently for the very last version of the book. Your proofreading eyes are always a great help when I've read my work a gazillion times and all the words start to blur together! Thank you also to my beta readers for taking the time to read *The Faerie War* and provide valuable feedback.

To everyone who's followed Vi's story since the beginning, to everyone who's written reviews, to everyone who's spread the word about my books, to everyone who's left comments that give me warm, fuzzy feelings—THANK YOU, THANK YOU. You encourage and inspire me. And if you were one of the readers who finished *The Faerie Prince* with WHAT THE FREAK JUST HAPPENED written across your face, I hope you were satisfied with the ending Vi got!

And to Kyle—thank you for putting up with all my early mornings, late nights, and never-ending "I'll just be a few more minutes!" I love you. With all my heart.

Rachel Morgan spent a good deal of her childhood living in a fantasy land of her own making, crafting endless stories of make-believe and occasionally writing some of them down.

After completing a degree in genetics and discovering she still wasn't grown-up enough for a 'real' job, she decided to return to those story worlds still spinning around her imagination.

These days she spends much of her time immersed in fantasy land once more, writing fiction for young adults and those young at heart.

Made in the USA
Middletown, DE
15 March 2023

26765274R00194

The str[...] *than anyone had a right to be.*

Serenity sighed. Though he was inches away, his warmth enveloped her. His distinctive male scent filled her senses. She thrummed with delightful, forbidden longings. The memory of his recent kiss haunted her, branding her soul forever.

A fantasy of making love with him sneaked into her brain. She nearly groaned aloud, passion overtaking her.

Could she?

Would he?

What would be the harm?

Once his memory returned, he'd be leaving, wouldn't he?

And didn't they deserve some happiness until they learned who he was...and why he was here?

Dear Reader,

Brr... February's below-freezing temperatures call for a mug of hot chocolate, a fuzzy afghan and a heartwarming book from Silhouette Romance. Our books will heat you to the tips of your toes with the sizzling sexual tension that courses between our stubborn heroes and the determined heroines who ultimately melt their hardened hearts.

In Judy Christenberry's *Least Likely To Wed,* her sinfully sexy cowboy hero has his plans for lifelong bachelorhood foiled by the searing kisses of a spirited single mom. While in Sue Swift's *The Ranger & the Rescue,* an amnesiac cowboy stakes a claim on the heart of a flame-haired heroine—but will the fires of passion still burn when he regains his memory?

Tensions reach the boiling point in Raye Morgan's *She's Having My Baby!*—the final installment of the miniseries HAVING THE BOSS'S BABY—when our heroine discovers just who fathered her baby-to-be.... And tempers flare in Rebecca Russell's *Right Where He Belongs,* in which our handsome hero must choose between his cold plan for revenge and a woman's warm and tender love.

Then simmer down with the incredibly romantic heroes in Teresa Southwick's *What If We Fall In Love?* and Colleen Faulkner's *A Shocking Request.* You'll laugh, you'll cry, you'll fall in love all over again with these deeply touching stories about widowers who get a second chance at love.

So this February, come in from the cold and warm your heart and spirit with one of these temperature-raising books from Silhouette Romance. Don't forget the marshmallows!

Happy reading!

Mary-Theresa Hussey

Mary-Theresa Hussey
Senior Editor

Please address questions and book requests to:
Silhouette Reader Service
U.S.: 3010 Walden Ave., P.O. Box 1325, Buffalo, NY 14269
Canadian: P.O. Box 609, Fort Erie, Ont. L2A 5X3

The Ranger &
the Rescue

SUE SWIFT

SILHOUETTE *Romance*®

Published by Silhouette Books

America's Publisher of Contemporary Romance

If you purchased this book without a cover you should be aware
that this book is stolen property. It was reported as "unsold and
destroyed" to the publisher, and neither the author nor the
publisher has received any payment for this "stripped book."

The various details of the Texas Rangers
and their operations were the sole creation of the author.
This book is dedicated to my critique partners, Cheryl Vincent Clark
and Janet Shirah, who continued to believe when I didn't.
I'd like to thank my critique partners and others who helped me with this book:
Judy Dedek, Jackie Hamilton, Celia Zweig and Colin Swift.
My editors, Darlene Winter, Diane Grecco, Kim Nadelson
and Mary-Theresa Hussey, have been enormously helpful.
As always, I depend upon the love and support of my husband.

 SILHOUETTE BOOKS

ISBN 0-373-19574-5

THE RANGER & THE RESCUE

Copyright © 2002 by Susan Freya Swift

All rights reserved. Except for use in any review, the reproduction
or utilization of this work in whole or in part in any form by any
electronic, mechanical or other means, now known or hereafter
invented, including xerography, photocopying and recording, or in
any information storage or retrieval system, is forbidden without
the written permission of the editorial office, Silhouette Books,
300 East 42nd Street, New York, NY 10017 U.S.A.

All characters in this book have no existence outside the imagination of
the author and have no relation whatsoever to anyone bearing the same
name or names. They are not even distantly inspired by any individual
known or unknown to the author, and all incidents are pure invention.

This edition published by arrangement with Harlequin Books S.A.

® and TM are trademarks of Harlequin Books S.A., used under license.
Trademarks indicated with ® are registered in the United States Patent
and Trademark Office, the Canadian Trade Marks Office and in other
countries.

Visit Silhouette at www.eHarlequin.com

Printed in U.S.A.

Books by Sue Swift

Silhouette Romance

His Baby, Her Heart #1539
The Ranger & the Rescue #1574

SUE SWIFT

A criminal defense attorney for twenty years, Sue Swift always sensed a creative wellspring bubbling inside her, but didn't find her niche until attending a writing class with master teacher Bud Gardner. Within a short time, Sue realized her creative outlet was romance fiction. Since she began writing her first novel in November 1996, she's sold three books and two short stories.

The 2001 president of the Sacramento Chapter of the Romance Writers of America, Sue credits the RWA, its many wonderful programs and the help of its experienced writers for her new career as a romance novelist. She also lectures to women's and writers' groups on various topics relating to the craft of writing.

Her hobbies are hiking, bodysurfing and kenpo karate, in which she's earned a second-degree black belt. Sue and her real-live hero of a husband maintain homes in northern California and Maui, Hawaii. You may write Sue via e-mail at sue@sue-swift.com or at P.O. Box 241, Citrus Heights, CA 95611-0241. And please visit Sue's Web site at www.sue-swift.com. An interview with Sue is featured at the author area of the Harlequin/Silhouette Web site at www.eHarlequin.com.

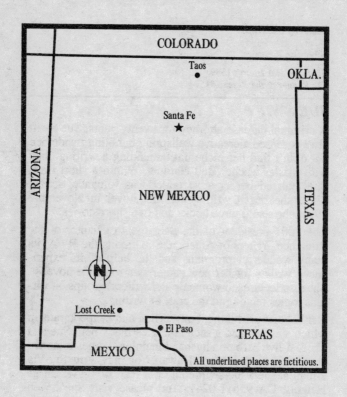

Chapter One

The most beautiful man Serenity Clare had ever seen stood at her door. Tall, lean, and utterly virile, his appearance was as unexpected as the proverbial snowball in you-know-where.

A slender ribbon of desire unfurled deep in Serenity's body, tingly and warm.

She blinked, surprised. She'd thought Hank had destroyed her passion for any man. What was different about this guy?

He removed his Stetson, revealing short, sable hair. The pressure of his hat in the searing heat of the New Mexico summer afternoon had stuck his hair to his skull.

Rubbing his scalp, he asked, "Lori Perkins?"

Serenity took the question like a punch to the gut. Pleasure fled, blown away like dust in the desert wind. She shrank back, craving the solidity of the doorpost behind her.

She hadn't used that name in close to a year and didn't want to hear it now. She gazed at him while breathing deeply to recapture a calm state of mind. "I'm afraid you've made a mistake. Excuse me."

She tried to close the door, but he stuck his booted toe in the way. "You're Lori Perkins. I've seen a picture of you."

Resignation filled her chest, a frightful, leaden weight. "Who are you?" she managed to whisper.

He hesitated. His Adam's apple bobbed. Bambi-brown eyes looked too gentle for his craggy face. He shifted from side to side; his heels crunched on the gravelly stoop.

"I don't rightly know, ma'am." His twang reminded her of home.

A tremor ran through her body. Texas was the past, something she wanted to forget. This was getting worse and worse. "You don't know what?"

"My name. I was hoping you could help me." He swayed slightly. "I...I woke up in the desert, and I remembered your name and address."

The icy fingers of fear clawed at her wits. Serenity sucked in a deep breath, commanding her body to quit trembling and her mind to begin functioning. She had to discover who this man was and how he had found her. "Do you have an ID?"

"Huh?" He stared, glassy-eyed.

"Turn around."

He did. *Hmm,* she thought. The left back quarter of his jeans showed a lean, shapely buttock. A faded square marked the place in the back pocket where ninety-five out of one hundred men kept their wallets.

Vanished, it would provide no answers, reveal no secrets.

"Why do you know my name, but not your own?"

Turning to face her, he opened his hands in a helpless gesture.

"Bend down. Maybe you took a whack to the head."

"I do have a headache."

He obliged, leaning over from the waist.

Serenity gingerly ran her fingers through his thick, dark hair, catching his male, musky scent while she parted the locks. He jerked as she contacted sticky wetness.

"Oh, my." At his temple, a lump the size of a half-dollar oozed blood. It looked bad.

She released him, then regarded him thoughtfully as he swayed, obviously ill, on her doorstep. If she sent him away, he could die. In his current weakened condition, without remembering the reason he'd been sent to find her, she was sure she could keep him under control.

"Hmm. You know me, but I don't know you...and *you* don't know you. Well, you've come to the right place." Serenity opened the door wider, inviting him inside.

"How's that? Do you know me?"

Her mind raced. What could she tell him? "Um, no, but I'm a psychic. Don't worry about a thing—the cards see all, know all, and have all the answers. And if the cards don't tell us what we want to know, we can always try the crystal ball or the Ouija board. Don't worry—something will work."

He gulped. That Adam's apple again. He was positively edible, this amnesiac cowboy who'd turned up on her doorstep like a tumbleweed.

Serenity reminded herself that he couldn't be the only person who knew the location of Lori Perkins. Feeling exposed while standing outside, she retreated into her home.

Her stomach clenched and twisted. How had this stranger found her? She bet he'd been sent to check her out and to report back to—back to—

Her mind flinched away from the thought of Hank.

Until she figured out what to do, she'd keep this stranger close. In his befuddled condition, she was sure she'd remain safe…at least for a while.

He remembered to duck as he entered Lori Perkins's house, but that was about all he remembered. That, and the woman. But the black-and-white photo he recalled bore only a slight resemblance to this flame-haired sprite. Maybe the snapshot was old; in any event, he remembered it only through a haze of pain and confusion.

"Give me your hat." She hung the battered Stetson, dirty with grime and a splotch or two of blood, on a wooden coatrack near the door.

"Come." Lori led the way through a whitewashed living room sparsely furnished with a futon-style couch and a couple of cushions in turquoise and coral. A braided rag rug in the same tones covered part of the wooden floor. A row of shiny, multicolored crystals sat on a narrow mantel above the curved adobe fireplace.

"Sit." In the kitchen, she indicated one of four ladder-back chairs drawn up to a farmhouse table. After wringing out a worn-looking towel in steamy water, she applied it to his head. She seemed nice, wincing in empathy as she dabbed at the bump on his scalp, first with hot soapy water, then with ice.

While she brewed tea, he had a chance to look at his hostess and her home. Lori's graceful movements reflected her simple speech. The white cotton dress she wore, brightly embroidered, harmonized with the Mexican-influenced decor. She lived modestly, but had a feminine knack for making this plain place a home. The small stuccoed, whitewashed house was typical of that part of New Mexico—and from where did that strange bit of information come? he silently asked himself.

The lack of appliances struck him. No television or radio, no dishwasher. He could hear wind chimes faintly tinkling in the quiet. He had a vision of pretty Lori Perkins washing her clothes on rocks in a stream. Was there even a phone?

She stood at the kitchen counter, dripping honey into a glass of iced tea. Her back was turned.

Pressing the ice pack to his temple with one hand, he poked at a pile of papers on the table with the other. Was he ordinarily a snoop? Maybe his rudeness was the result of the bump on his head. He hoped so, but in the meantime the bills he examined showed that his Ms. Perkins used a different name. A *very* different name. Serenity Clare. What kind of a wacky name was Serenity Clare?

He caught himself frowning, then consciously smoothed out his expression. Who was he to judge anyone else? He could be a Stetson-wearing version of Ted Bundy for all he knew.

Aha. A cellular phone bill in the name of Serenity Clare. Civilization did extend into the New Mexican desert wilderness.

A hand with short, buffed nails plucked the papers from his grasp. "Well, we know something about you," she said. "You're nosy."

He actually became hot with embarrassment. Then, when she smiled, his temperature rose even more. She had a gorgeous smile, one that could coax the sun out from behind a cloud.

"What's your name?" he asked.

She didn't answer for a moment, then spread out her hands. "You know my name. Lori Perkins." Placing the glass nearby, she sat across from him at the farmhouse table. Her fingers fiddled with the yellow gingham cloth. Between them, in the center of the table, stood a blue earthenware pitcher filled with a tangle of wild grasses. Their subtle fragrance perfumed the air.

"Who's Serenity Clare?" He put down the ice pack.

"I'm Serenity. I'm a psychic, remember? Lori Perkins is, well, just a little too mundane for your friendly neighborhood fortune-teller. So please, call me Serenity."

"Serenity." He tasted the name on his tongue, deciding he liked it. It matched the small, friendly woman who sat before him, matched her open face, guileless smile, and calm green eyes. He noticed a small scar, pale and almost invisible, cutting through one brow. "You're a psychic? I thought all that stuff was a scam."

Her eyes widened.

Damn, he'd probably blown it. The woman had rescued him, taken him into her home, and he'd insulted her. "I'm sorry."

She held up a hand. "It's okay. I'm used to skeptics. We all are."

"'We'?"

"Are you familiar with Lost Creek? This town is a vortex site."

"A vor—what?"

"A vortex site." Lori—no, Serenity, he reminded himself—grew animated, waving her hands in the air. "See, the Native Americans used to gather here. You can see their ancient trails in the arroyos. This place is *full* of mystical energy." She leaned toward him over the table, her gaze intense. "Can't you feel it?"

Only to humor her, he closed his eyes and tried. His headache throbbed as though a road repair crew with twenty jackhammers had moved into his skull.

He sensed the dampness of condensation on the sides of the cool glass of iced tea in his hand. He opened his eyes and took a swallow. Cold and tasty, the tea had a flavor he couldn't define. "Hey, this is great. What's in it?"

"It's a blend of my own. Sage is a general tonic. I also put in chamomile, to ease your pain, and valerian to promote healing and rest. It's very healthful, much better for you than that nasty caffeinated stuff."

"Well, thanks, Serenity." He sipped some more, then set the glass on the table. "I'd love to stay here and shoot the breeze, but I s'pose I should be on my way. Do you know where the police department or the sheriff's office is in this town?"

"Oh, uh, er, it's the weekend." Serenity ran a hand

through her short red hair, tousling it into untidy spikes. ''Nobody's there right now.''

''No one? No one's in authority here?''

''Lost Creek is a very small town. There are fewer than three hundred permanent residents. We don't have full-time law enforcement,'' she explained. ''There's no crime.''

''It sounds as though I've landed in Paradise.'' With effort, he stood, managing to smile at her. ''But I can't take advantage of your hospitality any longer, ma'am.''

''Of course you can.''

''What?'' Already he'd discovered that Serenity made the most surprising statements. Heck, he wanted to stay just to hear her talk about the vortex thing. He'd bet that every crystal in the living room had its own story.

''I mean, I'm the only link you have with your past, huh? I'd feel bad if you were to leave with no money, nowhere to go and no idea of who you are, with that bump on your head and—and all.''

He sat, relieved. Dog-tired, hungry, and dirty, he really hadn't wanted to go anywhere. Despite the healing tea, his head hurt so much that he couldn't move or speak without waves of pain reverberating through his brain.

She'd offered, and he found that he wouldn't mind imposing on pretty Serenity Clare for a while longer. ''Maybe you're right.''

''If you left, where would you go?'' Serenity asked.

''I don't know.'' He touched the bump on his head.

It seemed to have gone down a tad, but not much. Still hurt like the dickens.

"You'd better stay here." She sounded definite. "I'll call a friend of mine. Mairen is an expert at psycho-spiritual integration. And that's got to be the solution."

"What?" This woman said the damnedest things. Maybe he was a reporter, or a scout for one of them TV talk shows, and he'd been sent to interview Serenity Clare.

"The blow to your head caused a psycho-spiritual rift. That's why you can't remember anything. Heal the rift and your memory returns." She patted his hand.

The slight touch of Serenity's delicate fingers made his flesh ripple and heat. He squelched his desire along with his growing interest in her, hoping her talents of tarot reading and crystal ball gazing didn't extend to clairvoyance. Otherwise, she'd throw him out of her house.

He wanted to stay. This sexy, screwball little sorceress was the only link to his identity.

"How long has it been since you ate?" Standing, she went to the refrigerator.

"I don't know."

"I have some nice tofu lasagna from last night, if you don't mind leftovers." She took a rectangular pan from the fridge and put it on the tiled counter.

"I'll eat whatever you put in front of me." He realized he wasn't merely hungry, but famished. He'd never heard of tofu lasagna, but he wasn't in a position to be picky. The clock above her microwave indicated four-thirty. He guessed he hadn't eaten since the day before, possibly longer.

Serenity cut two chunks of food from the pan, her knife scraping on the metal bottom. She placed each portion on a plate. After covering them with waxed paper, she put them in the microwave and punched some buttons.

The machine hummed. "So you have some modern conveniences," he said.

She smiled. "Did you suppose I used kerosene lamps and cooked food over an open fire?"

"I can't see a TV or a radio."

"I live simply, not stupidly. With electricity, I have the modern conveniences I choose. I don't want mass media." She refilled his glass with tea. "The outside world is...disturbing to my meditations."

"What do you mean?"

Serenity shrugged. "The news seems to consist of foreign wars and local crime. TV and movies are full of car crashes and shootings. Why distress myself with such violence?" Forks and napkins in hand, Serenity set the table.

"Do you get a newspaper?" The enticing aromas of oregano and garlic began to fill the kitchen. His mouth watered.

Amnesia sure was crazy. He remembered that he liked lasagna but didn't know his own name. Crazy.

"Not a daily. There's a weekly paper that covers local matters. That's enough for me." The microwave buzzed. She took out the food. "Lost Creek is my little world." She removed the wrap from the plates, releasing a fragrant, steamy cloud.

He sniffed appreciatively. "Most people have broader interests, don't they?"

Serenity handed him his meal, then sat opposite him. "Do they?" Her eyes held a quizzical gleam.

He dug into the tofu lasagna. The piping-hot square of pasta, oozing spicy-smelling red sauce, didn't look unusual. But how would he know? He blew on his bite before hesitantly placing it on his tongue. It tasted as good as it smelled, maybe better. He chewed and swallowed, then said, "Lordy, but this is good. Whatever else you might be, you're one heck of a good cook."

"Thank you."

Why did Serenity go all red? "You act as though nobody ever complimented your cooking."

Her gaze dropped to her plate. "I'm surprised you appreciate natural food. Few men do." Serenity toyed with her fork before eating a bite.

"What's so natural about it?"

"The pasta is whole wheat and the sauce is made from organic tomatoes and herbs. Instead of meat, I used crumbled tofu."

"Tastes like normal lasagna, maybe a little better than most." He took another hearty, yummy mouthful.

"That's what's great about tofu." Serenity's eyes sparkled. She waved her fork in the air for emphasis as she warmed to her subject. "It's practically flavorless. If you put it in salsa it tastes Mexican and makes a great taco filling. With tomatoes, garlic and oregano, it's Italian. And no fat whatsoever. Tofu's the best protein around."

Was she the kind of woman he usually dated? He

hoped so. He'd hate to regain his memory only to discover he detested this charming, likable person. But was that how amnesia worked? He frowned.

"What's wrong?" she asked.

"Nothing. I'm...thinking." He ate another bite of lasagna while considering the situation.

Who was Serenity? She must be the key to his identity, he realized. Why else could he remember only her?

She must know who I am. But why won't she tell me? What's her game?

He glanced up from his plate. Serenity sat, calmly eating her supper. She didn't look like a person with secrets. But why would she welcome a stranger into her home?

Maybe she was just friendly. "Are you sure you don't know me?"

She looked up. "Never seen you before in my life." After finishing her portion, Serenity carried her plate to the sink and poured him more iced tea. She filled another glass with water.

"You don't want tea?" He gestured with the glass. "It's delicious."

"No. It's a healing tea, remember? I don't need it. You do."

Replete, he leaned back into his chair with a satisfied sigh. "That was great. Thanks, Serenity. I think you saved my life."

Her answering smile was ready, yet nervous. "You're very welcome."

"Now, I think I should go to town and maybe try to contact the authorities."

Reaching across the table for his empty plate, her

nose crinkled. "Uh, um, do you want to clean up a little before we go? You might cause some comment if you don't."

"Do I really look so bad?"

Her eyebrows lifted. "Come with me."

He followed Serenity through the living room, then down a narrow hallway to a bathroom. Upon seeing his strange image in the mirror, he couldn't restrain a shocked gasp.

Short, black hair stuck up in filthy spikes on top of his head. The gash on his temple needed rinsing. Bloodshot brown eyes. A two-day beard. "Oh, man. I could scare a prison gang right out of their tattoos." No wonder she didn't tell him anything. He looked like a pretty tough customer. "Why'd you let me in your house, lady?"

"Your aura is pure." Serenity smiled at his reflection. "Do you recognize yourself?"

"I'm not sure." He watched the mirror as the unfamiliar mouth, narrow and a little mean-looking, scowled. "I don't know if I like my appearance."

"The soul is what matters, and yours is a sweet one if your energy is any indication."

"Uh, well, thank you kindly." *I guess.*

"Why don't you shower? Cleanse the outer body to match the inner spirit. Meanwhile, I'll wash your clothes."

"Yes, ma'am." He grinned, figuring that he'd now learn if she used the rocks-in-the-stream method of laundry.

The bathroom door opened a slit and the stranger's sinewy arm, dusted with dark hair, thrust out a bundle of dirty clothes.

"You can use my razor. It's in the shower." Serenity grinned, wondering what he'd make of her pink-flowered shaver. "And there's a new toothbrush and some antiseptic under the sink."

She took the clothes to the laundry room. Located off the kitchen, it contained an old-fashioned washer and a broken dryer that Serenity's cheap landlord refused to fix. Anyway, Serenity preferred the scent of clothes dried on the line in the desert sun and wind.

Fingering the heavy jeans, she chuckled to herself as she tugged his leather belt free. The pants would take all night and part of the next day to dry, at least. Another day keeping the stranger in her home away from the authorities—such as they were—in Lost Creek. The next day, Sunday, would find the Lost Creek Police Department deserted. Two days of security gained. Two more precious days during which she'd decide what to do about the threat posed by the amnesiac cowboy.

Lucky for her, she'd decided to major in psychology when she'd attended college. She didn't know much about amnesia, but recalled that no certain cure existed. The likelihood of the stranger recovering his memory soon was slight.

She pulled a flimsy scrap of leopard-print cloth out of the jeans, then tossed the pants into the washer with detergent and set the water to the hottest setting. After vainly checking for a label in the shirt, she added it to the washer with the socks.

Coming to the underwear, she stopped. Leopard-print thongs seemed out of character for her cowboy. Were they silk? She poked at the fabric. Searching for the label, she thought they were the kind of sexy underclothing that a man might receive as a gift from a lover.

Her teeth ground together. She took a deep breath, seeking calmness, before putting the underwear into the wash with his other clothes. She told herself that she cared if he had a girlfriend only because a lover would miss him and, perhaps, search for him. Otherwise, Serenity decided, she wasn't concerned at all. Letting a man into her life wasn't an option for her.

She dropped the lid over the churning, bubbly wash and went to the kitchen to clean up the remains of their supper. Nice of him to flatter her cooking. Hank never had. She washed the plates and stacked them in the drainer to drip dry.

She sniffed at the dregs of his iced tea before rinsing his glass. The tea should promote sleepiness, if her *Healing Herbs* book was to be believed. She doubted its efficacy. She doubted everything.

He'd drunk close to three glasses. If the stuff worked, he should be so woozy that he'd fall asleep in the shower.

Walking down the hall, she listened as the sound of the water stopped. The glass door creaked, then slammed. She guessed that he'd stepped out and was drying off.

She imagined a taut, muscular body gleaming with wetness as he rubbed one of her towels across his chest. Her feminine, peach-colored linens would be a spine-tingling contrast with his developed pecs and furry, masculine chest.

Leaning against the doorpost of the guest room, she

mopped her damp brow with the sleeve of her dress before squelching those wild thoughts. She hadn't dared to dream about any man since shortly after she'd married.

She couldn't be attracted to him. That was just plain stupid, and she hadn't survived by being stupid. Chances were that Hank had sent him. She'd been lucky that this stranger had lost his memory.

The usual treatment for amnesia was to place the sufferer back into his normal environment. There, surrounded by the familiar, each reminder of who he was would trigger a flood of memories. But that remedy wasn't an option for the stranger. In her home, she could keep him comfortable but ignorant.

Who had said *keep your friends close but your enemies closer?* That was her plan, though deep down, big men still frightened her.

She'd have to get over it.

Serenity opened the door to the guest bedroom. She generally used the room for craft projects—stringing crystal necklaces and the like. Since she was a naturally tidy person, no evidence of her work littered the desk. Her unexpected visitor would dwarf the narrow, single bed, but she couldn't change either the size of the bed or the stature of the stranger.

Besides, she wouldn't want to change him. She liked his stature just fine.

Serenity parted the beige drapes, then slid open the screened window to let the warm, sage-scented desert breeze into the room. She adjusted the black-and-white Mexican serape covering the bed, then fluffed the pillow. A rustle warned her of his presence. She turned.

He filled the doorway, tall and lean and powerful, with only a small peach towel covering his narrow hips. Droplets of water sparkled in his hair. A curly, dark masculine fluff dusted solid-looking pecs.

Blood roared in her ears as a long-dormant need awakened. Seminude, he looked better than she'd imagined. Where undecorated by hair, his amber skin looked satiny, touchable. She'd love to give him a massage, have a legitimate excuse to explore that body without fear. He wasn't so big as to be intimidating, she realized. Not a giant. Just a man, though a very good-looking one.

She remembered to breathe. "Excuse me." She had to get out of there fast, before she hyperventilated.

"Uh, Serenity, where are my clothes?"

"In the washer. They were filthy."

He grinned, eyes twinkling at some unknown joke.

"What's so funny?" she asked.

"Nothin'. Hey, what am I supposed to do, run around nekkid?"

Not a bad idea. She swallowed. "Aren't you sleepy?" Given the amount of tea he'd drunk, he ought to collapse.

Blinking, he stretched his arms over his head. His triceps bulged. The towel slid.

Sweating, she averted her eyes. A regular at the local clothing-optional swimming hole, she wasn't body-shy. But this unknown stranger aroused a feminine passion she hadn't felt for a long time, and one she didn't want to feel now.

She peeked. His stretch made him look like a lean, powerful cougar, golden and sleek. He rolled back his shoulders, then cracked his knuckles. "I do believe you're right, ma'am. After that delicious supper and nice, relaxing shower, bed would feel fine." He winked at her.

On fire, she fled for the door. She didn't want to think about, much less see, his entire body as he dropped the towel and slid between the sheets. "I'll...I'll get you another cold compress." But she was the one who needed to chill out, though a little bitty compress wouldn't cool the sudden fire he'd ignited.

She probably needed the entire North Pole.

Chapter Two

He ran through the darkness, fleeing a nameless, shapeless foe. Clinging sand conspired with the sharp desert wind in his face to slow him down.

He rolled over the side of an arroyo, hoping to find cover to wait out the threat. Easier to run on the firm-packed bottomland, but dangerous. The fitful moonlight concealed as much as it revealed, distorting the path. Any shadow could be a leg-breaking, ankle-wrenching pothole. With his pursuers gaining, a fall would be disastrous.

Rising, he sprinted down one twisting, turning cleft, then risked a look over his shoulder. His eyes confirmed what his ears already knew: they were closer.

Subterfuge, then. He dodged behind a boulder and crawled, wishing that the slight concealment would shadow his movements as he turned ninety degrees into a branch of the arroyo.

Bad move into a dead end. *Dead end*. He'd always hated that turn of phrase.

He checked for a cave at the back of the cleft, hope warring with his knowledge of the desert.

Nothing. Unless he could climb out fast, he was a goner.

His nose twitched, scenting an aroma different than the ordinary smells of sage and sand that perfumed the desert at midnight.

It was warm, with good associations, yet burning. Not wood smoke.

Coffee?

He opened his eyes. Early dawn light, pearly and pink, snuck through beige curtains at the window. Skin sweaty and muscles tense, he shifted his legs in a too short, too narrow bed, untangling himself from the twisted sheets.

Where was he? Who was he? Had his dream been a memory? Who had been chasing him? Why?

He remembered where he was. *Safe*. Relief flowed through his body like a cooling tide. He was safe in the guest room of the mysterious Lori Perkins, aka Serenity Clare, fortune-teller and organic cook.

His heartbeat tripped, then slowed. He stretched his body as much as he could in the tiny bed, taking inventory. His head hurt, but only at the site of the injury. The headache had gone, he realized with a sigh of relief.

Rising, he didn't see his clothing. He chuckled. He didn't mind going au naturel if nakedness got the reaction he wanted from pretty Serenity. He bet she had a trim little body underneath her loose, hippie-style clothes.

Guilt gnawed at the edges of his conscience. Serenity had generously welcomed him into her home and showed him nothing but kindness. She didn't deserve a needy male getting fresh with her.

Besides, she might have a lover. Though he hadn't seen a ring on her left hand, a woman as cute and nice as sweet little Serenity probably attracted men the way water drew horses after a long day's ride.

He sniffed again. Coffee. How natural was coffee? Knowing Serenity, the coffee had probably been organically grown, roasted over an open fire, then ground by holy-spirited Tibetan monks. She'd brew it with Evian or some other kind of fancy, pure water, in a hand-blown, glass coffeepot that was free from hazardous chemicals.

He laughed out loud. He was doggone cynical, wasn't he? Wrapping the now-dry towel around his midsection, he went in search of Serenity Clare and her magic coffee.

After striding into the living room, he stopped, arrested by the spectacle that met his surprised eyes.

The curtain on a wide picture window was open, giving a view of dawn over the desert. In front of the glass, an enormous, curved chunk of amethyst stood on a wooden holder. Ambient light caught and refracted through the lavender crystals studding the rock.

Before this display, Serenity sat, cross-legged, on a mat. Clothed in a gauzy robe that clung to her lithe body, her arrow-straight back was silhouetted by the first pale rays of dawn.

His pulse thundered in his ears. He sucked in a breath.

She emitted a hum. "Ommmmmm..." Her chant grew in volume as the sun rose.

A sunbeam, pure and sharp as a blade, knifed over the horizon and struck the amethyst. Split by the crystal into a thousand disparate rays, rainbows bounced around the room.

Serenity leaped to her feet, hands flung above her head, stretching her slender body as though she wanted to touch the sky. She arched back, her body bowing, then forward, slapping both palms on the ground.

He was confronted by her upturned bottom, outlined by her enveloping robe. Lust whipped through him, elemental and violent as lightning.

Shame immediately followed. How could he even think of repaying Serenity's kindness with a pass during her morning meditation?

He crashed down the hall to the bathroom, scrabbling for control. Turning the shower on full-blast, he jumped in, punishing himself in the stinging, icy spray.

He hated not knowing who he was, but did he really want to find out? What kind of jerk was he? He hoped he didn't react like a caveman every time he laid eyes on a woman. Sure, Serenity was pretty and nice, but he'd better learn to control himself around her. Or he'd have to leave, and he had no idea where to go or how to seek his past.

When he emerged from the bathroom, he heard her singing. Not "om," but something lively and charming about a hard-knock life. Tentatively touching the healing bump on his head, he found that the song struck a chord with him.

He walked through the living room, now blessedly vacant of the resident dawn worshiper. At the kitchen door, he spied Serenity, dressed and seated at the table, earthenware mug nearby.

She looked up, her smile sunny as the newborn day. "Good morning. Did you sleep well?"

"Uh, I guess," he answered, remembering his nightmare.

"What's wrong?" She rose, approaching to press a palm to his forehead.

"I'm okay. I had some odd dreams, that's all."

Her smile faded. A concerned little pleat appeared between her eyebrows.

Before she could say anything, he asked, "Are my clothes dry?"

"I'll check." She left the kitchen through a door he hadn't yet investigated. The yellow skirt of her loose, summery dress swished around her calves.

When he followed, he found a room full of ancient appliances. One was a washer, so his question was answered.

Serenity walked through a door that opened onto a small patio. The broken concrete adjoined an expanse of scrubby grass lined with desperate-looking succulents. A vine, leaves limp from neglect, hesitantly twined halfway up the back fence. The ground beneath it looked parched and cracked.

Next to the door stood two chairs, similar to those in the kitchen. One had a broken rung. A clothesline, hung with his apparel, dominated the tiny yard.

Holding on to his towel, he rubbed his heavy denim jeans between two fingers. Still damp and unwearable. His blue chambray shirt could also use more time in the sun. Only a minuscule scrap of leopard-print silk had dried.

He didn't remember taking off underwear. He must have pulled down the thongs when removing the jeans. Fingering the silk, he stared at Serenity. She wore a small, ironic smile, the mate of the cynical grin he'd already seen on his own face when he'd looked in the mirror.

"These are mine?" he asked, breaking the silence.

"None other." Her smile broadened. "Leopard-print thongs just aren't my style."

He couldn't resist. "So what is your style?"

She went pink, a good color with her yellow dress and lightly suntanned skin.

He discovered that he loved to flirt, at least with Serenity Clare. He dangled the thong in her face by one thin strap. "Not natural enough?" he asked with a wink.

She chuckled. "Not unless spun by organic silk-worms on a communally owned farm."

He guffawed. Serenity, the New Age priestess, had kept her sense of humor.

"Coffee?" She stepped back into the house.

After she'd gone, he draped the towel over the line and donned the skimpy underwear, feeling like an idiot. Once again he wondered what kind of a man he could be. He didn't much like the thong. Was he a Chippendale dancer or something?

Seated at the farmhouse table, Serenity watched as the stranger entered the kitchen, clothed only in the scantiest scrap of silk she'd ever seen. She envied the fabric clinging to his body. How would his warm, satiny skin feel, caressed by her hand?

Tearing her mind away from that forbidden thought, she poured herself more coffee. "Paper?" She offered him the sports section of the Lost Creek weekly. Hank had always read the sports first.

What am I doing? Serenity angrily asked herself. *I don't have to please him. I don't have to please any man. I have to please myself!*

She dropped the paper onto the table and stood to fill his coffee mug.

He sat, sipped, and nodded. "Ma'am, I don't know about organic java, but this sure is good."

Serenity found herself beaming at his cheerful approval. She wanted to please him, but in a different way than she'd groveled to Hank. This stranger made her feel good and worthy, like the rest of her friends in Lost Creek, who also praised her cooking and enjoyed her company. She relaxed as much as she could in the presence of six feet of potent, sexy male, a man who might be threat…or seductive promise.

"When are we going into town?" He picked up the sports section and began reading it. A puzzled look stole over his face.

"When your clothes are dry."

"When do you s'pose?"

She shrugged. "Maybe this afternoon." Ignoring his frown, she asked, "Granola?"

"Uh, I guess. You know, I don't recognize any of the names here." He waved the paper. "Who are the Dallas Cowboys, and why would anyone care about their player trades?"

Serenity grinned. Here was the perfect man: a stud

with no memories and no love of football. If it weren't for his mysterious origins, she'd keep him forever. "While we're waiting, why don't we try a traditional path to knowledge. How about a tarot reading?"

After breakfast, Serenity sat on the floor of the living room and spread out the cards with assurance. Though a dyed-in-the-wool skeptic, she knew she had a gift with the tarots. Time and again, customers returned to tell her that her readings had come true with uncanny accuracy.

Her life had delivered so many knocks that she didn't believe in much. Not in the love of a husband or in the support of parents, and absolutely not in the kindness of fortune. Odd, but the tarots had never let her down.

Too bad she couldn't use them to foretell her own fate, but the cards didn't work that way. Otherwise, there'd be tarot readers winning the lottery and betting on the horses in every town. A pity.

Clearing her throat, Serenity flipped cards over onto the polished surface of her wooden coffee table. "The Hermit." She raised her gaze to meet the stranger's brown eyes.

He sat on the couch opposite her. His gaze still held a befuddled mistiness. Good.

"You seek higher knowledge," she said.

His eyebrows pulled together. "Huh?"

"You are opposed by forces symbolized by the Seven of Cups. This is typical. We often become sidetracked by the things of the outer world—gold, riches, and so forth." She looked up. The stranger had donned his blue chambray shirt. Half open, it exposed a set of sinewy pecs furred enticingly by a mat of dark, masculine hair.

She wanted to run her fingers through that sexy, virile pelt. Would it feel silky or rough against her hand? Shoving away the fantasy, Serenity shifted her attention to his face.

The stranger quirked his narrow, well-shaped lips. "Does that mean I have a lot of money?"

"Not necessarily. It means you *want* a lot of money, power, whatever." She turned another card. "This symbolizes you. Hmm. Justice. That's interesting."

"Why?"

Serenity couldn't tell him what she thought, but she guessed now that he was one of her ex-husband's employees who'd gotten cold feet. She'd bet he'd tried to cross Hank. When Hank had found out about the stranger's treachery, he'd been whacked on the head and left in the desert for dead.

After drawing in a breath, she let it out slowly. *Stay calm.* "Well, Mr. Justice, this card has an obvious meaning. You are a fair person, trustworthy and just."

"That's good, isn't it?" His eyes took on a hopeful, puppy-dog look.

She couldn't help smiling, even though his arrival at her home meant complete disaster for her. "Of course." She flipped over another card, then another. "These next cards predict the future." Her gut clenching, she gulped.

"What's wrong?"

"The Knight of Swords portends danger and violence. But it's followed by The Lovers.'' She stared at him.

His craggy, handsome face revealed nothing.

"Well, Mr. Justice, you're in for a bad time.'' Serenity swallowed hard. As she divined the meaning of the cards, her armpits grew damp and sweaty with tension. "But it looks as though everything is going to turn out all right for you.'' Though not for her.

Sure as the sun rose in the east, Hank was going to come and get her. The reading favored the stranger, but the mere presence of The Lovers said nothing about *her* fate. The card could refer to his joyful reunion with his wife. Serenity loathed the notion.

Surprised by her jealousy, she stood, then shuffled the tarots together, even shakier than before.

The stranger grabbed her hand. "Wait. There has to be more than that.''

Serenity jerked away. The cards flew out of her chilled, stiff fingers. "There isn't. I predict that you will recover your memories, but it will be a difficult process.''

"What are you so scared of?''

"I'm n-not scared.'' She knelt to gather the cards, cursing them, the stranger, and Hank. Why couldn't the world let her alone? Hadn't she suffered enough?

"You're terrified. Your hands are trembling and ice-cold. When I touched you, you pulled away as though I'd slapped you. What's going on, Serenity?''

"Nothing's going on. I just don't like being touched, that's all.'' Standing, she put the cards on the table.

"You let me into your home. You saved my life.

You obviously trust me. I'm…I'm Mr. Justice, right? Why can't I touch you?''

Serenity fought back sobs. This was something that Hank, that beast, had done to her. Her throat threatened to close with unshed tears. "I can touch you. You can't touch me. That's just the way it is." She ran to her room, overwhelmed.

Flinging herself onto her bed, Serenity rolled into a tiny ball, wanting to shut out the world. She'd cry herself to sleep even though it was only nine in the morning.

She wanted him, but she could never have him. What good would it do? She'd freeze up, just like the other times.

He stared after her. What the hell had just happened? Generally, Serenity Clare resembled the name she'd picked for herself. She reflected a clear, calm joy in living that he found very compelling, even attractive.

Now, a crack appeared in her tranquil facade. Walking down the hall, he contemplated the door she'd slammed then locked behind her, as though she were hurt or afraid.

Fear he could understand. Without a memory, he was scared himself. He couldn't intrude, not even to comfort her. Nor could he probe further about her strange behavior.

What did her extreme reaction to the card reading mean? She obviously believed in the message of the tarots. Dumb to think that pieces of paper could predict anything, but Serenity wasn't a dumb woman.

She'd been truly distressed by the Knight of

Swords and The Lovers, and hadn't wanted him to touch her.

Skittish. Was she on the run?

Returning to the living room, he picked up the cards and studied the Knight of Swords. A fearsome figure clad in full armor, his lips were skinned back from his teeth in a feral grin. This warrior relished the battle. Sword upraised as if to strike, he rode a racing warhorse through a barren landscape topped by a wind-whipped, stormy sky.

He shuddered. If the tarots told the truth, he was a killer.

Was Serenity his prey? Had unknown masters sent him to murder her?

Unacceptable.

He dropped the card, then found The Lovers. Adam and Eve, naked, stood in a grassy garden planted with a flaming bush and a fruit tree entwined with a snake. Surmounted by a glorious angel, the card's symbolism was clear.

He didn't wear a wedding band and couldn't see a dent or a tan line to reveal that one had ever circled his left ring finger. But that meant nothing. Many married men didn't wear a ring. *All the better to cheat.* He grimaced. He hoped he wouldn't discover that he was the kind of man who'd two-time his wife.

His wife. Did she exist? Who was she? If he'd had such a powerful love in his life, why couldn't he remember her, or any children they had?

What kind of monster was he?

He picked up Justice, the last of the cards. "Mr. Justice," she'd called him. He hoped the silly moniker wouldn't stick. But if he were a hired killer, the name had an intriguing irony.

Later that day, Serenity exited the shower and rubbed her wet hair with a towel. Examining her blond roots in the mirror, she decided to tint them the next time she shampooed. Combing her short "do," she smiled at the scant five seconds it took to complete the task.

After wrapping the towel around her body, she opened the window to let out the steam. She'd better get a move on. The Labor Day festival, which the Lost Creek New Age community had planned to jump-start the fall tourist season, was only a few days away. She needed to string more crystal necklaces and meditate to put herself in the right frame of mind.

Her new and returning customers would demand scores of tarot fortunes. Sometimes they'd bring their friends or tape record their sessions until she became hoarse and exhausted by the strain. But she couldn't say no. Her fortune-telling income was crucial to her survival since she'd fled from Hank.

She leaned her elbows on the frame of the window, which faced east. *Hank.* The merest thought of her abusive ex-husband made her innards cramp. She breathed deeply of the crisp, clean wind, seeking inner peace.

Perhaps she'd jumped to conclusions. If the stranger came from Hank, Hank knew her address. But he would have come for her himself. Her darling ex-husband wouldn't have deprived himself of the pleasure of beating her to a pulp.

Again.

On the other hand, maybe Hank was nearby, watching, torturing her with uncertainty and suspense. Her flesh shivered and chilled at the thought.

No. One of the hallmarks of her beloved ex-husband's character was his complete lack of patience.

Sucking in another deep breath, she ruthlessly forced Hank out of her consciousness, then left the bathroom. On the way to her bedroom, she encountered the stranger in the hall. Her pulse jumped. Conscious of his semi-nude state, and hers, she wrapped her towel more closely around her body.

"Afternoon, Serenity."

He was so courtly, so polite. Her heart melted. By his tone of voice, she knew that if it were proper to wear a hat inside the house, he would have tipped his Stetson for her. "H-hello, Justus."

His eyebrows arched. "Feelin' better?" Full of concern, his rich, brown eyes scanned her face.

"Yes. I'm...I'm sorry I blew up at you like that. You didn't deserve it."

He reached out, though not for her towel. One finger stroked her cheek. She tried to not flinch, but failed when he gently touched the scar on her forehead Hank had inflicted.

She remembered the occasion: their first fight. Six months into their marriage, he'd made mai tais and shoved pineapple rinds down their cheap garbage disposal. When she'd tried to stop him, he'd backhanded her across the face into a kitchen cabinet, and the sharp handle had cut her forehead.

Happy memories indeed.

"I can tell something's troubling you." Her cowboy's Texas twang brought her back to the present.

Serenity flinched again.

"You don't have to talk about it until you're ready."

"I know that." She hated the defensiveness edging her voice. Serenity had worked hard to become someone other than Hank's victim. She wanted to destroy the protective shell she'd developed, but couldn't seem to grow beyond it.

"But I do want to talk." His scrutiny shifted to the peach-colored towel cloaking her body.

Uh-huh. Talk. "Perhaps later." Serenity retreated to her bedroom, clutching the towel around her.

Chapter Three

By late afternoon his jeans had dried, so Justus explored the streets of Lost Creek with Serenity at his side. Her wild grass fragrance mingled with the chaparral scent of the desert town. The sun slanted through dust motes, turning the wooden planks of the walkways to white-hot gold. Some of the buildings had hitching rails and false fronts that he remembered from Wild West shows. Part of the tourist attraction of the place, he supposed.

Strange that he recalled scenes from old movies but not his own name or life.

"Late in August, it's pretty quiet here." Serenity's wide-brimmed straw hat shielded her face from the sun's fury. "Too hot for tourists. We hope some will come back for the Labor Day weekend festival, but it isn't until Samhain that the place really starts to rock and roll."

"'Samhain'?"

"What most people call Halloween."

He blinked, taking that in.

"There's the police station." She pointed across Main Street.

He started across the dusty avenue without going to the corner or checking stoplights. He halted in the middle of the asphalt. Jaywalking felt...funny to him, as though he normally obeyed traffic signals without question. What had he been, a crossing guard?

He looked left, then right. Of course there was no traffic. Serenity was right. The August heat had turned Lost Creek into a ghost town.

The deserted police station reflected the general sleepiness of the place. Peering in a window, he tried to peek through battered Venetian blinds. He saw only a wooden counter behind which sat a couple of tired-looking chairs near a beat-up metal desk.

The scene looked...*wrong* to him. He didn't know where the images came from, but he knew he should see a bunch of busy people inside, working on computers and answering phone calls. Maps with pushpins should paper the walls, with the acrid smell of burned coffee tainting the air.

Perhaps he'd watched a lot of cop shows on TV.

He heard the soft slap of Serenity's sandals on the plank sidewalk behind him. "There's funding from the State of New Mexico for a full-time lawman, but no one wants the job." She shrugged. "I guess cops want to be in a big city capturing crooks and making a name for themselves."

"Maybe if you become a policeman, you go for excitement." He turned away from the window. No answers there. "Is there a doctor in town?"

"Um, we're pretty small. No. Won't you try my friends? They're talented holistic healers. They've helped a lot of people." Sweet of Serenity to look so anxious about his welfare.

"Okay." What did he have to lose? "I s'pose I can go see a regular doctor if these, er, healers can't help me."

"What can a doctor do except give you drugs?" She frowned. Serenity clearly didn't approve of drugs.

He didn't, either. "No drugs. I won't take any pills." He wondered about the immediacy and firmness of his reaction. Maybe he'd had a bad experience with drugs in the past.

She looked relieved. "Good. Let's go see Mairen." Taking his arm, she led him down the street.

"Who's Mairen?"

"I told you. Mairen can fix you up." Serenity strolled down the planking, towing him along. "I'm sure that the division within your spirit can be healed with the application of the right crystals and breathing methods."

Was she nuts? "No."

She stopped, looking a tad upset. "Why not?"

His mind went blank. Why not, indeed? Besides, he liked Serenity and didn't want to offend her. "Um, will it hurt?"

"No, of course not. Mairen is the gentlest of souls. You'll see."

At the intersection of First and Main, Serenity paused in front of a bookshop at the corner. Its sign, painted on wood with colorful rainbows, read Great Bear's Book Nook. As she pushed open the door, a bell tinkled, heralding their arrival. He followed her when she entered.

Inside, he smelled sage and incense. Crystals winked from shelves, reflecting the afternoon sunlight. Racks of esoteric books lined the store while an oval counter in the center displayed Native American jewelry and artifacts. Soft flute music played, interspersed pleasantly with the murmur of several table fountains.

A door in the back of the shop opened to reveal the largest man he'd ever seen. Broad and tall, the copper-skinned fellow wore a tie-dyed T-shirt and shorts. His gray-streaked hair, braided with feathers and beads, reached his shoulders. He beamed at Serenity.

"Great Bear, this is the stranger I told Mairen about." Serenity gestured. "Justus, this is Great Bear, Mairen's soul mate. Great Bear discovered my true name and totem animals in a naming ceremony."

Sounded pretty strange, but he couldn't be picky. And Great Bear seemed friendly enough.

"Welcome, Justus," Great Bear boomed. "Enter our home."

A perky woman with white hair bobbed up behind Great Bear. "Want some fresh carrot juice?" she asked in a high, sweet voice. Clad in a flowing, robe-like dashiki, her bracelets clattered as she waved a glassful of orange liquid.

"Mairen." Serenity kissed the woman's cheek.

Great Bear remained in the shop, presumably to welcome any customers. Mairen led them into the kitchen in the back of the store and served large glasses of chilled carrot-orange juice.

He discovered he enjoyed the sweet blend. Serenity and her friends sure were unusual, but they ate and drank well.

"Mairen, this is yummy." Serenity set down her glass after draining it.

"Even better, the electrolytes will promote the return of your memories." Mairen directed her cheery smile at him.

"Thank you, ma'am." He drank more electrolytes. Lucky for him they tasted so good.

"Come with me, stranger." Her colorful skirts flowing, Mairen led the way into an adjoining room, which contained sofas, chairs, and a television set with a VCR. Evidently Mairen and Great Bear didn't share Serenity's disdain for mass media.

A brown-and-rust Native American-style rug decorated with a tree of life design lay in front of a brick fireplace. After closing the curtains, Mairen went to a cupboard and retrieved a long, misshapen swatch of umber-colored leather. She spread the hide over the rug.

"I usually let Great Bear do the smudge purifications," she confided to him, "but I have had more success with issues involving mind-spirit integration."

"Uh, what exactly will this, um, purification do, ma'am?"

"It'll clear your mind and spirit of unwanted energies that could interfere with your memory."

He tentatively fingered the leather. Its softness rivaled a woman's cheek, and he bet it had been handtooled. "What is this, ma'am?"

"It's a doeskin. Great Bear killed the animal himself and tanned her skin after asking her permission to use her hide for healing work.''

He didn't recall asking permission from anything he'd killed. The certainty that he'd taken life hit him with the force and power of a wrecking ball. Shattered, he went cold. He couldn't speak. He couldn't tell these good, innocent people he was a killer. He didn't know if he wanted to conquer his amnesia. What if he found out he was a criminal?

Mairen reached into the cupboard again and removed a bundle of dried, leafy branches, about eight inches in length, tied with colorful strands of silk.

Recovering his voice, he asked, ''And this is?''

''A sage smudge stick. It'll purge the atmosphere of any negative energy or harmful spirits which might interfere with your healing.''

Yeah, right. ''Oh, okay, I guess.''

Serenity smiled at him. ''Your skepticism is acceptable, though you have no reason to disbelieve anything you see or hear today, do you?'' She lit a candle that sat on a nearby shelf.

He blinked. ''You're right. I haven't any experience with any of this that I can remember. Who knows, it could be the best thing since sliced bread.'' He looked at Mairen. ''Go for it, witchy woman.''

She giggled like a kid. ''Lie down on the hide.''

He did, resting his head against the soft doeskin. His reclined position gave him a good view of the cracked stucco and a water stain or two on the ceiling. *They oughtta reroof this place.*

Serenity sat at his feet, cross-legged. She beamed at him. One high, elegant cheekbone reflected the candle's mellow light.

He'd go through a thousand purification rituals just to see her smile.

Mairen, at his head, gently rubbed his temples. Her silver-and-turquoise bracelets softly clinked. "Tell us about your dreams."

He tensed.

"It's all right." Serenity stroked his calves above his boots. "You're safe here."

Her hesitant caress calmed him. "Okay." He told them about his nightmare, trying to avoid reliving the intense fear he'd felt during the chase through the arroyo.

Serenity took a deep breath. Tilting down his chin, he watched her small, shapely bosom rise and fall several times. Her breasts would fit his hands perfectly.

He closed his eyes. He had no business thinking about touching her, loving her. He didn't know who he was. Heck, he could have a wife and a dozen kids!

"What are you running from?" she asked, tenderness in her voice.

He told himself to focus. "I don't know. I just know that I'll die if they catch me."

"'They'?"

He nodded slowly. "Yeah, I'm sure there's at least three men, maybe more, after me."

"Running usually symbolizes the joy of physical activity." Mairen continued to rub his temples with a gentle, relaxing rhythm. "Canyons, like your arroyo, mean that there's a passageway in the flow of consciousness."

"What does that mean?" He wanted to know.

"Maybe physical activity will lead you to your reality."

"What about the cave?" he asked.

Serenity went bright red. "I think that's obvious." She stopped massaging his legs through his jeans.

"Oh." Face heating, he was glad the closed curtains darkened the room, and that no candles illuminated him. He didn't want Serenity to see his reaction. "Does that mean that, um, sexual activity will cure my amnesia?"

Avoiding his gaze, Serenity cleared her throat. "Uh, maybe. The Hindus believe that Tantric sex is a path to enlightenment." She became redder. "I've never tried it."

"Me, either." *But it sounds fun.*

"Let's try a purification ritual," Mairen said.

Overcome by the smoke from the purification ritual, which involved a smudge stick and a lot of chanting, Justus had closed his eyes. When he opened them again, the dark, empty room held only a faint scent of the sage smoke.

His limp muscles wouldn't allow him to rise immediately. Instead, he sat for a few minutes, rubbing his head. He didn't have a headache and wondered why. He'd fallen asleep in a smoky room, so he ought to feel dizzy and ill. But his body had an unexpected lightness, and his mind seemed clear.

He walked into the kitchen. Serenity and Mairen sat at the table, talking.

"You're back! How went your journey?" Mairen asked.

"Uh, fine, I guess. How long was I out?"

Mairen glanced at a wall clock. "About an hour."

"Whoa."

"Can you make it home?" Serenity stood and walked to the door.

"I s'pose so." He turned to Mairen. "Thank you for your hospitality, ma'am, the smudge and the electrolytes and…and all."

"We have some clothes for you, also." Mairen handed him a paper bag.

He opened the bag and took out the item that lay on top: a tan robe made of linen with arrows printed on the front.

"The arrows symbolize protection," Mairen explained.

"Why, thank you. That's mighty kind." He tucked the robe back into the bag.

"I'll talk to you tomorrow about the Labor Day festival," Mairen said to Serenity. "We mailed out the flyers to bookstores in Albuquerque, Taos, Santa Fe, and Roswell last week."

Roswell, he thought. Justus dimly remembered something important about Roswell, but what was it? An image of a triangular green face with a pointy chin and slanted, almond-shaped eyes flashed through his mind. *Aliens.* Yes, that was it.

After they left, he said to Serenity, "You have very nice friends." *Aliens. Lordy.*

She swung her hat by its ribbon as she ambled down the wooden sidewalk. "You think we're strange."

He remembered that she claimed psychic powers. If she was for real, lying was out. "Well, yes."

"That's okay. You don't have to believe, just accept. Tonight, I'd advise guided dreaming."

"'Guided dreaming'?"

"Yes. If you find yourself in an uncomfortable dream, try to make it come out all right, so to speak."

"Like, if I'm in the arroyo, find a cave and hide?"

"Right." Serenity sounded enthusiastic. "Or find a tunnel and escape through it to my house."

And lead the bad guys to you. He didn't voice the uncomfortable notion.

They turned the corner onto Serenity's now-dark street. The hair on the back of his neck stiffened with awareness as he scanned the shadows.

Near her doorstep, he peered warily at her black windows. They hadn't left a light on inside before leaving for Mairen's. He didn't like returning to a dark house. Dangerous.

Serenity reached into a pocket of her dress to retrieve her key. "Just remember to enjoy the journey."

Far from enjoying the journey, he entered the house ahead of her and immediately flicked on the lights. Funny how he'd remembered the switchplate's exact location by the front door. He flung his Stetson onto the coat rack while he darted a quick, suspicious glance around the living room. Then he stalked through the kitchen and laundry room to look outside. He couldn't see anything much in Serenity's pitiful backyard, dimly illuminated by the rays of the rising moon.

When he returned, Serenity asked, "What on earth are you doing?" Still near the front door, she stared at him with open astonishment on her face.

He stopped short. "I—I'm not sure." Letting in-

stinct take over, he walked down the hallway to peek
into the bathroom and each bedroom. In Serenity's
room, he caught a glimpse of a Native American print
bedspread and a nightstand stacked with books.

One of them jolted his memory. *When Bad Things
Happen to Good People.* He'd seen it before, maybe
even read it. Where? Why?

"Hey!" Serenity had followed him to her room.
"Get outta here!" Shoving him out, she closed the
door behind her, then turned to face him.

"I don't know what just came over you," she told
him firmly, "but don't enter my room under any circumstances. Understand?"

He felt his face flame. "I was just checking." Boy,
that sounded lame.

"'Checking'? Checking for what?"

For the millionth time, his mind went frustratingly
blank. He waved his hands around, as though he
could pluck a rational explanation out of the air. "I
don't know. I don't know!" He stumbled to his room
and leaned on the doorjamb, rubbing his healing temple. He hated feeling like a lost, confused soul.

Some primitive, male urge to protect her had
leaped forth when he'd entered the darkened house.
He'd had to search it to make sure no threat lurked.
What kind of freak was he?

Cursing his Neanderthal character, he looked up.
Serenity stood inches away in the hall, scrutinizing
him. He couldn't read her expression.

"I'm sorry," he said hoarsely. "I won't intrude
upon you again."

"It's okay." She patted his shoulder. His mood
transformed with blazing speed. Her very touch held
magic, igniting his libido like a torch.

Chapter Four

Serenity went out front to her doorstep and leaned against one of the porch railings. She watched the pale moonlight touch the lines of her house, turning the cacti and chaparral silver, painting the desert with lunar magic.

The discussion of Tantric sex and the meaning of the cave in the mysterious cowboy's dream had set off erotic firecrackers in Serenity's body. Suddenly, she'd yearned for a lover's touch, his tender caress.

Though stunned and delighted, she couldn't act on those long-submerged, oh-so-sweet desires. She certainly couldn't make a move for the compelling stranger who had inspired her passion after its hibernation.

Serenity knew what Justus's dream meant. He was one of Hank's henchmen. Either he'd been chased by law enforcement or he'd crossed Hank, and Hank was out to get him. She needed to maintain her distance. A romance was out of the question.

She'd landed in trouble—again. Someone, probably Hank, was going to follow the stranger, and she had to be ready.

Or she had to leave Lost Creek. The thought made Serenity's heart go hollow and achy in her chest.

The infinite stars of a New Mexico summer night emerged from the indigo sky.

The way Justus had searched the house when they'd returned from Mairen's rang Code Three alarms in Serenity's head. Sure as shootin', some inner survival instinct had asserted itself. The stranger hadn't yet remembered the nature of the threat, but Serenity knew damn well that Hank was coming to get both of them.

Serenity pressed trembling hands to her face to stop their shakiness, then looked again at the familiar, beloved desert stars. Forcing back tears, she bit her lip. She loved her home and her life in Lost Creek. Protected by the obscurity of the town and the closeness of its New Age community, she'd been safe here.

She didn't want to leave. But how much time did she have?

Maybe none. Edgy, Serenity fiddled with her hair. Perhaps he didn't have amnesia at all, but was toying with her, lulling her into a false sense of security until Hank came along to deliver the coup de grâce.

Serenity sighed. "Soon," she said to the stars. Soon she'd have to take a stand and face Hank. Was she ready?

Reentering her home, she found it redolent with the aromas of chili and spice. In the kitchen, Justus stood near the stove, stirring a dark, rich-looking liquid in a saucepan.

"What are you doing?" She leaned over the pan and sniffed. "*Mole* sauce?"

He smiled at her. The spicy chocolate sauce matched his eye color. "Yep. Found a recipe in this here book."

A cookbook lay on a nearby counter. Her mouth dropped open. Hank would have shaved with broken glass rather than prepare a meal. He called cooking "woman's work." Astounded, she realized no man had ever made dinner for her before.

"Do you remember that you like *mole* sauce?" she asked. Composed mostly of chocolate and chilis, the arcane Mexican delicacy didn't tempt the taste buds of many whites. Serenity, who wanted to keep an open mind, couldn't decide whether she liked the stuff even though she'd tried it several times.

Using a spoon, he dipped a portion and sampled it. "Yes, ma'am, it tastes right fine. Wanna try some?" He offered her the spoon.

She took it, then hesitated. If she shared his spoon, they would draw closer in some subtle way. Did she want that?

Serenity sniffed the dark-brown liquid. Spicy and sweet. She looked up, meeting the stranger's chocolate-brown gaze.

Spicy and sweet. Need, almost painful in its intensity, arrowed through her body in a direct line southward from her heart, pooling deep inside her.

She couldn't deny her want, but she could hide it. She had to.

Serenity breathed in. Then out. Then in again, seeking a calmer state of being. Her rational mind clicked on. *It's just mole sauce, Serenity!*

She licked the spoon. An explosion of warmth and flavor, complex with chocolate and serranos, danced inside Serenity's mouth. "Nice," she said, hoping her mild tone of voice hid her inner turmoil. She took another breath. "You've added something different. What is it?"

"I didn't put in any salt. Seemed wrong, somehow."

She leaned past Justus to dip the spoon in the pan again. His nearness shook her to the core. Why did he have to be so damn appealing? And why did she get so close? Wrong move, but she could fake a New Age attitude of inner tranquility. "Whatever you did, it's right. How are you going to serve it?"

"I thought we could add tofu and lettuce, and eat it in tacos."

"Sounds great." She couldn't get over the fact that he'd fixed supper for her.

After their meal, they took their drinks outside to the back patio to enjoy the evening. This time, Serenity sensed something different. She inspected the few shriveled plants that managed to survive the unforgiving New Mexican summer. The scent of damp earth filled her nostrils. "Justus, did you water out here?"

"Yep."

"Thanks." She could see that the vine at the back fence had perked up. She'd thought that one was a goner for sure.

Justus sat in the broken chair, to Serenity's dismay. "Don't! You'll hurt yourself." She feared the chair, with its split rung, would collapse beneath his weight.

"It's okay, Serenity. I repaired it this morning after

you, um, went back to bed. See?'' Standing, he picked up the chair to exhibit his handiwork.

She squinted at it in the dimming light. Several squiggly pieces of metal joined the shattered rung. ''What are those? How did you do that?''

He frowned. ''I don't remember what they're called. I found some with a hammer in the laundry room cupboard. They're sharp and pointed on one side, and I just hammered a bunch of them in. I'll paint it tomorrow.''

''Wow.'' He cooked, watered the plants, *and* fixed things. She envied the lucky woman who'd claim this man.

''What else can I do to help you out?''

''You don't have to do anything. Just…be you. That's enough.'' *And don't remember who you are.*

''No, it's not. I can't live here rent-free, Serenity. A man has his pride, you know. Put me to work.''

''Okay, I will.'' She chuckled. ''Next weekend will be busy.''

''That festival?''

''Yeah.''

''What are you going to be doing?''

''Telling about a million tarot fortunes.'' She tipped her head back and looked at the stars. As the night darkened, they seemed to shine with more clarity. ''Maybe selling some crystal jewelry.''

''How can I help?''

''Tomorrow, you can start by making necklaces. The materials are in your room. During the festival, you can control the flow of customers, get me water, stuff like that.'' She wondered if she could trust him to hold the money. "Oh, and help me set up and break down the tent."

"A tent, like a Gypsy?"

"Yep. Thank you, Justus. It's very nice of you to offer."

"Hey, how long are you gonna keep up this 'Justus' stuff?"

"I have to call you something." She sneaked a peek at him. She didn't like his frown. "'Hey, you' just doesn't cut it, in my opinion."

"I guess so." He still looked grim.

"Is there another name you'd prefer?"

He sat down, every line of his whipcord-lean body reflecting dejection. "No, ma'am. I guess I'd better find out who I am right quick. Justus. Lordy."

She reached over to pat his hand, seeking to comfort him. "I'm sorry." The warmth of his skin tempted her to boldness, and she didn't remove her fingers. "You've...you've been very kind. Thank you for the meal and the chair."

He shifted. "It's not much, considering what you've done for me."

Somehow, Serenity managed to keep touching him, ignoring her fear. The skin on the back of his hand felt curiously smooth and inviting. She wanted more.

He turned his head. Their eyes met. In the dusk, she couldn't distinguish his expression.

Could this mysterious stranger unlock the chains Hank had bound around her heart?

Did she want him to?

Leaning back, he cleared his throat. "Um, I borrowed your cell phone to call a doctor."

Serenity's muscles went limp with dread. She

dropped her hand. This was bad. If he recovered his memories, and proved to be one of Hank's lackeys, she was roadkill. "Oh, uh, who did you talk to?" She struggled to keep her voice even.

"Well, it took me a few calls to find one who'll come to Lost Creek. Thought I'd have to get to El Paso or Las Cruces, but we don't have a car."

She noticed he'd said "we." *We* don't have a car. Her heart pattered. What did that mean?

Probably nothing. She cleared her throat. "That would have been okay. I could have arranged a ride."

"But I found Dr. David Feeger, a neurologist. He says he'll be out here in a few days for that festival."

"Dr. Feelgood?" Serenity couldn't help grinning.

"No, Dr. Feeger. Uh, do you know him?"

"Oh, yeah. He'll be one of the doctors who staffs the medical tent."

"What medical tent? What's that?"

"We have some straight docs and nurses around in case someone drinks too much or goes on a bad trip."

"There are drugs at this festival?" Disapproval darkened his tone.

She shrugged. "Not officially, but we can't stop what folks bring in. So, you'll talk with Dr. Feelgood about your amnesia. Good." Serenity stood and went inside to the kitchen. She sat, her knees suddenly weak and quivery with fear.

She had no great faith in Dr. Feelgood's medical talents. He had a reputation as a partier. However, he'd made it through medical school. He'd practiced for years as a board-qualified neurologist.

Serenity saw fate closing in on her. But what could she do?

* * *

The next morning Justus donned his underwear and the robe that Great Bear had lent him. Nice thought, but Great Bear's clothes tended toward the outrageous: tie-dyed T-shirts and dashikis. Justus's discomfort with the neo-hippie, New Age clothing emphasized his innate conservatism. However, he wasn't in a position to be picky.

The tan-colored robe bore black Native American signs. The back featured a giant thunderbird, while the front had the arrows he'd noticed yesterday.

He went to the front room where Serenity quietly meditated, joining her on the mat. Today she wore a flowered, silky robe with a matching nightgown. The pastel, feminine lingerie, though it covered her almost completely from neck to ankles, disturbed him as much as yesterday's gauzy outfit. It flowed over her gentle curves, revealing shapely calves.

Averting his gaze, he looked through the window and let his breathing slow, matching hers.

Strangely, his mind did begin to calm. *Maybe there's something to this meditation stuff.* Then, since he knew what to expect, he also jumped to his feet when the sun's first bright ray leaped over the horizon. He copied Serenity's morning exercises as best he could.

Aware of Justus nearby, Serenity could hear telltale snaps and pops from his joints as he struggled to copy her. She grinned. He might look good, but she could tell that he didn't normally maintain a regimen of hatha yoga. Most people ignored stretching, which was as essential to fitness as exercise.

Legs spread wide, she flung her arms out, then bent

to the right. She grabbed her ankle with her right hand to stretch her side.

A squawk sounded from Justus. "Oh, hell!"

"What's wrong?" She straightened.

Justus collapsed onto the couch. "Pulled something in my back, or my shoulder, or…somewhere."

"Let me see." Though untrained in massage, she had an inborn skill—or so her friends said. Her women friends, that is. She didn't like to touch men. She chewed on her lower lip.

But he'd been so sweet and helpful, and now he'd hurt himself trying to keep up with her. She ought to help him, if she could.

Turning his back to her, Justus dropped the robe to his waist. She poked his lats with an uncertain fingertip, aware of the smoothness of his skin, his rich male scent. She prodded a tight muscle. Wincing, he yanked away.

"Sorry," she said. "I guess you don't do yoga very much."

"I guess not."

"I can't see. The light's bad. Lie down on the couch and I'll turn on a lamp." She reached for the reading light that stood on a side table. "I'll get some tiger balm for that muscle."

After scurrying to the bathroom, she rummaged in the medicine cabinet, her breath coming in short, heated pants. She consciously calmed herself by slowing her respiration, letting her pulse return to its normal, even state.

She didn't know if she could touch Justus's nude flesh, but something told her that doing so was a necessary stage of her healing. If she could give ease to a man, perhaps one day she'd mend enough to accept pleasure from one.

Would that man be this stranger? Probably not, considering the situation. Maybe he was one of Hank's cohorts, maybe not. Regardless, nothing said he'd be her buddy once he recovered his memories.

Questions about Justus still plagued her. Who was he? Why had he sought her out?

Shoving aside her concerns, Serenity reminded herself that he was here and he was hurt.

When she returned to the living room, he'd stretched out on the sofa, face down, head pillowed on crossed arms. The sight of his naked back made her gasp. Her oh-so-sweet guest had two puckered, roundish scars in his upper right shoulder. She didn't have medical training, but what else could they be but healed bullet wounds?

Serenity put a hand to her chest and gulped air. However, no breathing exercise could help her achieve inner peace after seeing *this*.

"What's wrong?" He raised his head to look at her. "You're pale."

"N-nothing," she squeaked. She cleared her throat. Perhaps he hadn't seen them. With no memory of any gunshot wounds, why would he inspect his back? She'd never encountered a male vain enough to check his back in the mirror. Hank would suck in his gut and expand his chest—something Justus didn't have to do—but she had a feeling that the stranger didn't know about his telltale scars.

With shaky fingers, she picked up the tin of salve and dug out some of the pungent, orange balm with a nail. She rubbed her hands together, letting friction warm it before spreading it over his right shoulder and side.

She hesitantly caressed the healed wounds. "Does this hurt?"

"Oh, no. It's great. That spot feels a little numb, though."

Nerve damage, maybe. She continued to rub while more worries haunted her. What kind of man would have gunshot scars on his back?

A gangster. Oh, God, Hank had gotten on the wrong side of some mafiosos or the Mexican mafia or something, and they'd sent an operative to Lost Creek to take her hostage.

"Ow!" Justus's body jerked, and she realized she'd accidentally dug her nails into his flesh.

"Sorry." Serenity pulled back, using only fingertips to stroke his neck.

She made an effort to soothe herself. This was a stupid line of thinking. How competent could the gangsters be if they thought they could punish Hank through her? She choked back a rueful chuckle at the thought and ran the flat of her palm down Justus's back. Hank would very happily join in whatever painful destiny any gangster planned for her.

This is all speculation, she thought. *Stop torturing yourself!*

She focused on the pulled muscle in his side. Again, she almost giggled. She'd been nervous about touching this attractive man. Well, here she was, having rubbed him for five minutes without a trace of the kind of anxiety she'd expected.

Her other troubles had been a distraction, but awareness of the stranger as a male animal rose to the surface, though she hadn't forgotten his gender from the moment they'd met. His olive skin looked silky-smooth, satiny, and now her fingers discovered that her eyes hadn't lied. Except for the bullet holes in his shoulder, his muscular body was sleek and perfect, tempting her as nothing else ever had. The spicy scent of the tiger balm mingled with his own distinctive aroma, creating a sensual haze that clouded her thinking.

She didn't want to dream of what loving this man could be like. Regardless of the warning posed by the bullet scars, he'd treated her with kindness. He was fast becoming her friend.

This man would be both a skilled and considerate bedmate.

Friends and lovers. The enticing combination could lure her into recklessness.

She'd better keep a tight rein on her emotions around this stranger. Serenity reminded herself of the peculiar way he'd inspected her house last night.

She couldn't trust him.

"Oohh, baby. I could get used to this. Will you marry me?"

He had to be joking. Her fantasies fled, and in their place, regrets gnawed at her aching heart. *Not a chance.* "Thanks for asking, but no thanks."

He cradled his chin on his hands, resting his elbows on the table. "Aren't I good enough?"

"You're...very nice, but I can't see marriage in my future."

"Why not?"

She didn't want to talk about her marriage, which

had soured her on the institution for life. "What if you're already married?"

Turning his head, he gave her a sharp glance that told her he'd noticed she'd avoided discussing herself. He flopped back down. "I don't think I'm married. Wouldn't I remember someone as important as my wife?"

"Some men don't consider their wives important." She kept her tone light. She didn't want him to know how much the subject rankled.

"You think I'm that kind of guy?"

"No, but maybe the blow to your head caused a personality change as well as a memory loss." Again, Serenity glanced at the bullet scars. This rough-and-tumble man acted like a teddy bear...at least, for right now. How would he behave when the amnesia faded?

The tight muscle finally loosened, becoming tender and pliant beneath her fingers.

He emitted a pleased hum from deep in his throat. "Lady, I'm your slave for life."

"Flatterer." Pleased, she found herself purring with delight.

He roped a sinewy arm around her neck and kissed her. His kiss was exciting and exhilarating and very, very scary. The rub of his hard mouth against hers, the gentle scratch of his stubble, and his heady, masculine scent combined to create a terrifying, overpowering neediness.

She yearned to touch him, to mold her body to his.

She wanted to hide in the darkest tunnel of Carlsbad Caverns.

She yanked away as soon as he let her, huddling into the furthest corner of the couch.

''Oh, damn! I forgot. Serenity, I'm sorry.''

Stiffening her spine, she straightened to glare at him, jaw clenching.

He sat up on the sofa, now under control—or so she hoped. ''We have to talk about this.''

Serenity stifled a laugh at the New Age line. Lost Creek had him under its countercultural spell. ''No, we don't,'' she said.

''Yes, we do. I'm interested in you, Serenity, in the way a man gets interested in a woman. And I can see that you're attracted to me, too.''

She closed her eyes. Was she so obvious? Embarrassment swept her in hot waves.

''Look at me.'' Justus's tone was insistent.

Though trembling with anxiety, she obeyed.

Leaning toward her, he took her chin in one hand.

Serenity recoiled. Her eyes filled with searing tears of shame and disappointment, disappointment in herself. She'd never be a normal woman, able to enjoy the touch of a handsome man without fear.

''I won't hurt you.'' He reached for her again.

This time she let him, though she didn't know how. Perhaps it was the way his gentle brown eyes entrapped her gaze, enchanted her healing heart.

His fingers delicately stroked her face, caressing her with an overwhelming tenderness that penetrated to her soul. Warm tears slid down her cheeks. He dragged one finger, rough with a callus, across them.

''You're a beautiful, sensual, loving woman.'' His voice rumbled, low and soft. ''I don't know who did this to you, but if I ever find him, he's a dead man.''

Serenity sucked in a tremulous breath, sure he meant it. With his craggy face rough with last night's stubble, he looked dangerous. The scars on his body told her he'd taken potentially killing strikes. Could he give violence as well as take it? Did she harbor a murderer in her home?

"I don't know what I am, Serenity, but I know what you are. You're a good and worthy human being and an astoundingly lovely lady. I don't know what claims any other woman has on me, so I can't make love to you."

Looking into his gaze, she read pain and need. For her?

He went on, "But as long as I'm here, I'm here for you. To care for you and protect you."

"Thank you," she whispered. She closed her eyes, certain he meant what he said…for now.

"Now, how about some coffee and breakfast?" His voice had turned casual.

She opened her lids. Justus had covered his torso with the robe and retied the belt. He smiled at her, his heated glance belying his easygoing tone.

Did he want her? The possibilities both turned her on and scared her through and through. She knew he wouldn't wait forever, that one day, he'd take what he decided was his…or he'd leave.

Which would it be?

And what did she want?

Justus winked at her, then walked toward the kitchen.

Serenity rubbed her upper chest, where a strange flutter seemed to have taken permanent residence beneath her sternum. She was way out there. She'd jumped to conclusions. He probably said he was interested in her because he enjoyed the back rub and figured she'd be fun in bed. If they made love, the act probably wouldn't mean anything to him.

Why was she plagued by these awful attractions to dangerous men? Her heart had fluttered for Hank, and look at how he'd turned out.

Serenity followed Justus to the kitchen, finding him at the fridge taking out the coffee.

"Not for you, Mr. J.," she said. "I don't want all my work spoiled by muscles tensed by caffeine. I'll make you some of my special tea."

"I like your tea, but no coffee?" His brown eyes pleaded, wistful as a pup's at dinnertime.

She shook her head firmly. "You'll live. And only a light breakfast."

He shot her a resentful look from beneath lowered brows. Darn him, his curly lashes had to be an inch long. "What are you eating?"

"Melon, and so are you." Serenity went to the fridge and took out a melon. "Heads up!" She tossed the fruit across the kitchen.

It hit him in the stomach. "Oof!" He managed to grab it before it fell to the linoleum and split into a thousand messy pieces. He leaned against the counter and roared with mirth.

After a scared moment, she did, also. Limp with laughter and relief, she leaned against the refrigerator. Hank had never joked around about anything. They'd never laughed together after that first fight.

She didn't know what had just come over her, but she was glad she'd given in to the insane impulse that led her to play catch with a melon. If she'd done that to Hank, she'd have gotten a split lip. But Justus took her playfulness the right way...a good sign.

She'd never let herself fall in love with him, but she liked knowing she was safe in his presence.

After breakfast, Justus went to his room to string crystal bead necklaces while Serenity meditated. He welcomed the mindless task and the isolation, because he had a lot to ponder.

Her kiss. How she'd tasted. How she'd smelled. How she'd melted against him for an instant before she pulled out of his arms. Her small, trim body had nestled into his with unmistakable passion and need. Strange how petite Serenity's slender form had perfectly fit against his lankiness, as though they'd been created for each other by the hand of a gracious God.

After picking up a bowl of tumbled amethysts, he began stringing the softly rounded stones on a length of filament fishing line.

Serenity Clare, that little, redheaded sorceress, had bewitched him. He couldn't think of much else. She filled his heart, every minute of every day. He supposed that was natural, since he lived with her and couldn't recollect anyone else in his life.

How did he end up in the same house with a woman he couldn't have? The very question told him something about himself, but it was information that didn't fit in. If he was a killer, why did he retain such an upright moral stance? A man who didn't hesitate to take life shouldn't balk at making love with a beautiful, willing woman.

He tied off the first necklace, then started another.

Except she wasn't willing, though Serenity didn't reflect simple reluctance. Something in her heart held her back from giving herself. What could it be?

He remembered the book on her nightstand. *When Bad Things Happen to Good People*. He dimly recalled the book was frequently read by the bereaved.

Perhaps Serenity had lost her husband, and had loved him so much that she'd decided that she could never give herself to another man. That made sense. She'd retreated to tiny Lost Creek to heal from her pain. She'd rejected mass media, contemptuously describing television news as "all car crashes." He guessed that she and her late husband had been in a traffic collision, and he'd died. Maybe that was how she'd gotten the scar on her forehead.

Poor Serenity. She'd loved her husband so much that she'd never remarry or take a lover.

Damn.

What had he been like, the mysterious Mr. Perkins? A regular guy or a New Age psychic fitness buff like his wife?

Justus wondered when the accident had occurred, and if she'd ever recover from her grief. He sure hoped so. He wanted to have a chance with her.

His male intuition told him that they'd be good together. And she projected an air of fragility that made him want to put on armor, mount a white horse, and ride to her defense. A vulnerable woman struggling for strength, she aroused protective instincts he didn't know he had.

He sighed. There was a lot he didn't know about himself. When would the clouds obscuring his mind lift?

Taking a break, he went to the bathroom. After he washed his hands, he stripped off his T-shirt instead of tucking it into his jeans. He twisted his body in an effort to see what had so startled Serenity during the back rub.

Lordy. No wonder she'd blanched. Those pock-marks had to be bullet wounds. The scars confirmed what he already knew: he was a killer who'd lived an exceptionally rough life. He scowled at himself in the mirror.

He didn't deserve a woman like Serenity. He just oughtta stop thinking about her in *that* way.

Yeah, sure. And pigs would sprout wings and fly to Mars. There'd be bacon and eggs served on the Red Planet.

After returning to his room, he started to string ambers.

But who was he? What about his life, his commitments? Would it be fair to offer himself to Serenity?

No. He'd meant it when he'd told her that he wouldn't take her until he knew that loving her was right for both of them.

That settled it. For any hope of a romance with Serenity, he'd have to recover from the amnesia and regain a normal life.

If a hitman had a normal life.

Chapter Five

On Friday morning at ten, Justus and Serenity were ready for festival early birds. They'd already pitched her red-and-white tent at one end of Main Street, near Great Bear's Book Nook.

"Won't they be mad?" he asked Serenity, who stood at the door flap of the tent.

"Who, Great Bear and Mairen? Mad? Of course not. Why?" Serenity, dressed in a calf-length, crinkly cotton skirt of green and yellow, stared at him quizzically.

"Don't they sell crystal necklaces, too?" He gestured at the jewelry displayed on black velvet.

"Nah, they tend to stick to the Native American stuff. By the way, we can use their apartment behind the store to take breaks." Serenity tied the tails of her leaf-green blouse around her midriff. The shirt sweetly cradled her breasts.

"That's nice of them." He tried not to gawk, without success. "Um, Serenity, when will the medical tent be set up?" He really needed that doctor.

"Later in the afternoon."

If he didn't get away from her, he'd try to steal another kiss. "Is it all right if I take a look around?"

"Sure." She gestured. "You might be able to pick up a few dollars helping others set up their tents. Or you can trade for a pair of shorts or something."

"That's a good idea." He hadn't wanted to wear one of Great Bear's dashikis, and he'd grown tired of his jeans. More clothes would come in handy.

Setting his Stetson on his head, he wandered down Main Street, passing other colorful tents and rickety stands. Their Gypsy-like denizens advertised their wares: everything from potted plants and embroidered shawls to crystal healing sessions. The festival logo, a yellow sun on a blue field with a peace sign, appeared everywhere, on the sides of tents, on T-shirts, on flyers and programs.

Somehow, he felt drawn to the police department, which, as usual, was closed. A sign on the door read At Festival On Patrol. He perked up right away. Maybe today he'd find someone who'd help him. He started to look for festival security.

Justus introduced himself to one woman who advertised herself as an "aura photographer and interpreter extraordinaire." She didn't appear to be extraordinary in any way, despite a long brown braid streaked with gray and a striped, robelike costume.

After he'd helped pitch her tent, she took a Kirlian photograph of him that showed a reddish mist surrounding his head, shot through with green-and-yellow streamers.

"You have much sexual energy, intelligence, and courage." The older woman gave him a salacious grin, handing him the Polaroid snapshot.

He winked. "I had already figured out the sexual part for myself."

"Come back after the evening ritual if you feel the need to be de-energized."

"Uh, thank you, but I'm kinda with someone right now. I need a pair of shorts, not a...de-energization."

"Perhaps some other time." She shrugged. "If you're looking for more work, try Owen. He might need a husky male to keep the peace." Tossing her long braid over one shoulder, she pointed.

He turned to see a tall, reedy fellow in shorts and sandals talking to Serenity at the door of her tent. His blue T-shirt read Festival Security. Justus noticed that Serenity stood at least a foot away from Owen, and when Owen moved in, she retreated, maintaining her personal space.

He didn't like the way Owen kept crowding Serenity. Couldn't the fool see he bothered her?

Justus's concern spiked. He returned to her side.

Serenity immediately relaxed. She'd dated Owen when she'd first arrived in Lost Creek, but nothing came of his awkward attempts at intimacy. Owen hadn't taken her rejection well.

"Oh, Justus. This is Owen." She sidled closer to bask in Justus's comforting aura. Strange how she felt so good near him, unlike most other men.

He smiled at her, raising a heat more intense than the desert sunshine. "I hear you're the law around here," he told Owen.

Owen had thinning, sandy hair and a frail physique,

while Justus resembled a sleek golden puma, muscular and powerful. Serenity was struck by the contrast between the two men. Maybe she hadn't wanted Owen because she...just didn't. She turned that thought over in her mind while the males interacted.

Owen tilted his nose into the air. "I am a musician. But by common agreement of the people, what law enforcement we need in Lost Creek, I supply."

"Owen plays the lute and the guitar," she said. "As I mentioned, we don't need much law enforcement."

Justus frowned. "At an event like this one, aren't there thefts or fights?"

"Occasionally," Owen said. "I'm playing on the stage at the other end of Main Street at two and four. You can help out at that time."

"Sure. Do I have to be some kind of deputy or something?"

Owen laughed and tapped Justus on the head, then the shoulder. "I dub thee deputy."

If Justus were indeed one of Hank's toughs, the irony was over the top. Serenity couldn't restrain a chuckle.

Justus seemed unaware of any incongruity. "Thanks. By the way, have you seen any missing persons reports recently?"

Serenity tensed. Though spacy, Owen wasn't stupid.

"What?" Owen looked clueless. She relaxed.

"I don't know what Serenity's told you about me, but I have amnesia. I'd like to think that someone, somewhere, is looking for me and knows who I am."

"I'm afraid I haven't checked the telefax in the

police department for a while.'' Owen's snotty tone revealed that such a menial task wasn't worthy of his time. ''After the festival, I'll find the key and unlock the building, and you can check to see what's come in.''

Serenity winced. No wonder she hadn't stayed with Owen. Compared to Justus's courtliness, Owen's attitude rankled.

On the other hand, if Owen pursued his part-time role as top cop of Lost Creek with any diligence, Serenity could be in trouble. Given that Owen's major interest in life was fourteenth-century lute music, she could stay calm.

Justus kept his smooth manner. ''Thanks.''

''Any time.'' Owen strolled down Main Street.

''Find the key. Lordy,'' Justus said to Serenity.

She smiled. ''I know what you mean. Hey, did you get shorts?''

''No, but look at this.'' He showed her the Kirlian photograph.

''Oh, my.'' Serenity took the snapshot, her cheeks growing pink.

''The lady said that I have a lot of sexual energy.''

''Randi tells everyone that, but in your case, it's true.'' She handed him the photo. ''That's the red in the picture.''

Was Serenity jealous? ''She invited me over to de-energize.''

She rolled her eyes. ''She tells everyone *that,* too.''

''Oh, and here I thought I was special.''

They both laughed.

''Are you going to the festival invocation tonight?'' she asked.

"Are you?"

"Probably. It's fun. There'll be food and dancing."

"An invocation. I don't think I've ever been to one of those. I think I'd remember it if I had. But, Serenity, I don't want you to buy me supper there. I feel bad about taking your money."

She raised her eyebrows. "You'll be earning your keep. I told one of my friends you'd set up and break down her kitchen every day of the festival. I hope you don't mind."

"No, not at all. I'm eager to work. Who is it and what will we make?"

"Her name is Yazmin and she should arrive soon, so she can set up before lunchtime. She sells vegetarian organic falafels and lemonade, and we get all the food we can eat during the festival." She grinned at him. "It's good, too."

"Great idea, Serenity. Now I need to find someone selling shorts."

"Someone will probably be selling used jeans, so you can cut down a pair. And maybe you can find more of those leopard print panties." She gave him a saucy wink.

Suddenly hotter, he plucked his T-shirt away from his chest. "They're not panties, they're…they're…"

"What?"

"Uh, something. I don't know. I don't know where they came from, either. I can't figure myself out. I'm a mass of contradictions. I saw those scars on my back, same as you did."

Again, she paled.

"And I'm mystified. I don't think I'm a bad person. Do you?"

"I, uh, no, n-not at all." Stuttering, she seemed unable to force her words through her lips.

"Then, why would anyone want to shoot me? What was I doing out in the desert? Why do I remember you and no one else?" Questions tumbled out of him like a spring waterfall. "Wasn't anyone else important to me? And if you're the only important person in my life, how come you don't know me?"

She didn't meet his eyes. Pure guilt shot across her face, quickly replaced by a phony sympathy.

Temper flaring, he grabbed her by the shoulders, shaking her. "Do you know me, Serenity? Have you been holding out on me, keeping some vital piece of information to yourself?"

Again lifting her eyebrows, she placed trembling hands on his where they gripped her shoulders. He released her.

She recovered her color. "Justus, I promise you that I never met you in my life until I opened the door and saw you. I have never seen your picture or heard of you. Ever." She leaned toward him, so they were eye-to-eye, nose-to-nose.

Lip-to-lip.

"And you can take it to the bank." Her green eyes glinted with challenge.

If he leaned forward just a tad, they'd kiss. Again. A wave of pure carnality roared through him, elemental and powerful as an tsunami.

But she didn't want him…yet. He backed off, smiling at her, forcing his libido down to neutral. "Is there a bank in Lost Creek?"

She grinned back. "Take it to the bank in Las Cruces or Lordsburg."

"Okay, I believe you. But I still don't understand myself."

She shook her head. "Justus, why should you be special? Do you understand yourself any more or less than the rest of us?"

"What do you mean? You know who you are. No one whacked you on the head and left you for dead."

"Am I Lori Perkins or Serenity Clare? The two halves of my life intersect and clash constantly. As we grow, we develop out of our old selves and leave them behind, like discarded cocoons."

"That was a choice you made. No one made it for you."

"Oh, no, my friend. I *had* to leave my old life. None of us has a choice." She shook a finger in his face for emphasis. "We all have to grow. The difference between you and me is that I'm stuck remembering my old self while I mature into the new one. You, you can be whoever you want without the past dragging you down."

"You sound bitter." Now he was sure she still grieved for her late husband.

"I am bitter. But please, don't ask why. I don't want to have to taste the bitterness again by speaking the words. It's more than enough to be stuck with the memories." Turning, she swished inside the tent and closed the flap, leaving him outside.

Setting up Yazmin's food stand proceeded without incident, except for testing the lines from the gas tank to the generator. He didn't recall how to set up the

machinery and almost caused a small explosion. Fortunately, another vendor came to the rescue.

He looked down the street to Serenity's tent. She
emerged to tie back the flaps. Soon, a steady stream
of customers visited her.

Yazmin, a pleasant, North African woman in her
forties, and her assistant started making falafels at
noon. Justus took two lunches to Serenity's tent. Between customers, they ate the delicious falafels,
drippy with tahini dressing and crunchy with vegetables and fried chickpeas.

When he wasn't selling jewelry, he kept her cup of
ice and lemonade replenished as the hot, dusty afternoon wore on.

The neurologist showed up at the medical tent in
midafternoon. Between dealing with splinters,
scrapes, and heat exhaustion, Dr. Feeger looked into
Justus's eyes with a brightly lit instrument, checked
his chest with a stethoscope, and took his blood pressure.

"No concussion." The graying, fiftyish doctor adjusted his tie-dyed headband. Its faintly rakish look
contrasted with the dull green scrubs he wore.
"That's the good news. The bad news is that there's
no definitive cure for what you have."

"What?" Justus felt as though his world collapsed
anew. He'd pinned his hopes on the doctor.

"This ailment isn't traumatic amnesia. A lengthy
loss of consciousness or coma is the main symptom
there. This appears to be a case of hysterical amnesia."

"What? I'm not hysterical."

The doctor smiled, looking tolerant. "That's just a

clinical phrase referring to a condition caused by an emotionally stressful event.''

''So the blow to the head didn't mean anything?''

''Oh, it meant something.'' Dr. Feeger stood, beginning to pace the short length of the medical tent. ''Amnesia is caused by trauma to the brain that slows the rate of accessing your memory. In short, your memories haven't disappeared, but the links between them and the parts of your brain that allow you to get to them have been, shall we say, short circuited.''

''How do I...rewire my brain?''

''Well, there's not much anyone can do about your condition. Hypnosis can be helpful. Returning the patient to his usual environment is the best treatment—''

''But I don't know where that is!''

The doctor beetled his bushy eyebrows. ''I know that doesn't appear to be an option. There are cases where the patient is reunited with his family through publicity. In nineteen ninety-eight, an amnesia victim was identified via the Internet. Newspaper articles often lead to these mysteries being solved. Do you have a picture of yourself?''

Justus hesitated. If he were a criminal, he'd go back into the clink for sure if his photo were distributed. But what choice did he have? He had to find out, or he'd go crazy. Reaching into his pocket, he removed his aura photograph.

''Hmm.'' The doctor examined it, smiling. ''Dear Randi's work is always so predictable. But this will do. I'll put it on my website and also fax copies to newspapers and law enforcement. Don't worry, son.''

He clapped Justus on the shoulder. "We'll help you find your way home."

By 6:00 p.m., Serenity had dealt the cards and predicted the future for fourteen impressed clients, an average of one every half hour. "I'm done in," she told Justus.

"Say no more. I am, too." He closed the flaps, plunging them into a sweltering, candlelit darkness. "Can we leave this up overnight?"

His male presence and scent dominated the darkened tent. Ignoring the unsettling trip and stumble of her pulse, she stirred, stretching her tight muscles. "I think so. I always bring home the jewelry for the night. Let's count the take."

She emptied her pockets onto the shawl-covered table she used for fortunes. After a few moments, Justus whistled. "Lady, I never dreamed this was such a good business. There's close to a grand here."

"Yes, we should clear three or four thousand for the festival. But remember, this has to last. I may tell a fortune or two on weekends in the next few months, but this is most of what I'll earn until the Samhain gathering at the end of October."

"I have to find a way to contribute to the household finances while I'm here."

While I'm here. She heard the words as though they were a dreaded harbinger. "You planning to go somewhere?" She strove to keep her tone nonchalant.

"No, but Dr. Feelgood might track down my past. He's distributing my picture. And I figure that at some point, you'll kick me out." He smiled at her. The cute crow's feet in the corners of his eyes bunched together, making his eyes twinkle.

Her heart twisted with fear and dread. She'd heard that doctors now used computers to communicate with each other. If that were true, her brief time with Justus by her side would soon come to an end.

She didn't want to see him go. The realization struck her with the intensity of a fierce desert rain flooding an arroyo. Even if the truth proved that Justus was one of Hank's toughs, she knew deep in her heart that he wasn't an evil person. He wasn't cruel and mean like Hank. The stranger had lost his temper and become frustrated once or twice, but he wasn't abusive.

And he'd filled a lonely space in her heart with his kindness and companionship. How could she go back to her empty house after he'd filled it with memories of his tenderness and friendship?

Serenity managed to say, "You're welcome as long as you care to stay." She gathered the cash and tied it into the shawl.

"Even after our fight today?"

"You call that a fight?" She laughed ruefully. "Honey, where I've been that wasn't even a ripple in the water."

"I grabbed you." His eyes had turned dark and serious.

"So you did, but you didn't hurt me. I guess I learned today that I won't break." She touched his arm, aware of the tight muscles underneath his satiny skin, his scent, his nearness. She suppressed the sharp need slashing through her body, stepping away before she did anything she might regret. If they became closer now, she'd miss him all the more when he moved on. "I can't blame you for being unhappy."

He started to pack the remaining jewelry. "Yeah, but I shouldn't get mad at you. Are you sure you don't know anything about me?"

"Positive." She hoped her calm tone hid her fears. Craving cooler air, she untied the tent flap and blew out the candles. "Let's drop this stuff off at home, then go to the invocation."

"I have to go help Yazmin break down her kitchen."

"Oh, that's right. Doesn't she want to sell food tonight?"

"Maybe. Let's go check."

Yazmin did want to sell falafels at the party, so Justus and Serenity helped her move the stand to the empty field on the outskirts of town. By the time they were done, Serenity hungered for the quiet and peace of her home. She needed to rest.

Justus walked beside her in the gathering dusk, carrying the cash, his boot heels clattering over the wood planks of Lost Creek's sidewalks. Around them, her colleagues played guitars, shared their suppers, and passed bottles of cheap wine and beer. The aromas of incense and food perfumed the air.

When they left Main Street, the sounds and scents of the festival receded. The familiar bouquet of the desert night—sage and sand—tingled in her nostrils. The harsh barks of coyotes punctuated the evening.

He stopped suddenly and, with an outstretched arm, halted her. She heard footsteps behind them. Her skin crawled.

The stealthy sounds ended. Had she imagined them?

She looked at Justus. His rugged features seemed set and tense. "We're being followed," he said.

"The money." Serenity clutched his arm. *Or maybe it's Hank.*

"Yeah. Take it and walk in front of me. If I, uh, get involved, run home as fast as you can." He shoved the shawl into her arms.

"'Involved'? What do you mean, involved?"

"I think you know what I mean. Get going." He gave her a little shove.

"Let's both get going, okay?" She couldn't help the thready, hysterical note edging her voice.

"You won't get any arguments from me." He lengthened his stride, dragging her along with him.

When they turned the corner onto her street, he gave her a firm push. "Now run!" he snapped.

Serenity ran for about a half block, then turned to look back. She couldn't see Justus.

A dark form rounded the corner into her view, too thin and lanky to be Hank. One of his employees? Her heart raced, threatening to pound right out of her chest. A shadow detached from the side of a nearby house, seeming to spring from nowhere.

Justus. Oh, God, they're gonna fight. After her violent marriage, she hated confrontations. Bile rose in her throat. Her pulse beat hard and heavy in her ears.

She swallowed hard and took a deep breath, wondering what to do. She'd be safe if she ran home, but what about Justus? Serenity swayed from one foot to the other, indecisive. She had to check. What if he got hurt, and she could have helped? She blundered back onto the street.

Serenity found Justus sauntering along the sidewalk as though nothing was amiss. Her adrenaline rush heated into fury.

"What happened?" she cried.

"You look like death warmed over." He seized her arm. "How come you aren't home?"

She wrenched free. "Don't grab me like that."

"I'm sorry, but if you'd been around, that could have been a bad situation." His cold, dark eyes regarded her in the light of a street lamp. "Serenity, when I tell you to go, do me a favor and git, okay?" Taking the shawl, he stalked toward the house.

She glowered at his retreating back. "Hey, what makes you the authority on what I should do?"

He stopped, turned, and sighed. "Serenity. That man was going to rob us and do God-knows-what to you. Because you were out of the picture, there wasn't a fight. I just told him very peaceably that he'd better get a move on."

"How do you know he was going to rob us?"

"I guessed." He started walking again. "Then when we talked, I found he's from El Paso and is camping on the other side of Lost Creek. He has no reason to be in this part of town except to mess with us."

El Paso. The name made her heart freeze, then thump as if she'd run twenty miles. "What did he look like?"

Justus gave her a startled glance. "Why do you want to know that?"

"Humor me." They'd reached her little cottage. She fitted the key into her front door.

"He was a young guy, sixteen or so. He looked…he looked like your average scumbag. Pretty nondescript." Entering her house, he tossed his Stetson onto the coat rack near the front door.

She relaxed fractionally. That definitely wasn't Hank. Hank was spectacularly blond and handsome, a husky, Nick Nolte look-alike. The creep could have been one of Hank's pals, but she doubted it. The more she thought about her predicament, the more certain she became that if he knew where she was, Hank would come himself.

Besides, Hank wouldn't hire a kid. Too unreliable. His hired hands tended toward oil-field roughnecks.

She frowned at Justus. *Average scumbag.* Where would a man come to know an "average scumbag?" Probably from his friends and associates, that's where. She shivered and wrapped her arms around her torso. She hoped Justus would never change, would remain the same sweet man who shared her life.

But she was going to lose him, wasn't she? A pang stung her heart. Resolutely, she ignored it, telling herself she couldn't care about Justus.

"Where do you keep this?" Justus held out the shawl.

"In my room. Here—" She untied the shawl and handed him fifty dollars.

"What's this for?"

"You worked hard today…and tonight. Go on out and have some fun."

"Wouldn't have much fun without you."

She laughed lightly, aware of her skin heating with

embarrassment. She'd forgotten how to respond to a man's compliments. "That's...that's very kind of you."

"Just the truth." He left, presumably to do his restless, haunting survey of her home, which had become his habit every time they returned from an outing.

She showered and, dressed in a nightgown and her long silk robe, stretched out on the sofa. Enough time had passed so that she trusted Justus and could kick back around him. A gentleman, he hadn't taken advantage of her, and she was sure he wouldn't.

"Want some supper?" He appeared in the doorway to the kitchen.

Serenity hesitated, remembering her earlier feeling of nausea. "Maybe some soup. There's a can of minestrone in the cupboard, I think."

She leaned back her head to close her eyes for just a minute.

After heating the soup, Justus came back to the living room. Serenity, sprawled on the couch, twitched in her sleep.

Her robe gaped open in the front, exposing a softly mounded cleavage beneath a silky gown that matched the pastel-printed robe. His heartbeat tripled. He told himself to calm down.

But he better not let her sleep the whole night through on that sofa. Her shoulder was twisted against the couch arm at a crazy angle. She might get a crick in her neck. Stepping into the forbidden environs of her bedroom, he turned back the spread and the sheet, then plumped the pillow for her. She'd worked hard that day and deserved her rest.

Returning to the living room, he slid one arm beneath her knees and the other under her shoulders. He clasped her to his chest, supporting her head and neck.

Nestled in his arms, she felt as light as the desert breeze. Mumbling drowsily, she lifted her arms and draped them around his neck, tucking her head into the hollow of his shoulder. Her hair, dark red and damp, tickled his chin. Her skin held the fragrance of wild grasses.

With a soft tread, he carried Serenity to her room and laid her on the bed. Her arms clung.

Her pink lips parted. She sighed in her sleep.

He couldn't resist.

Leaning over, he fluttered the lightest possible kiss on her pretty mouth. "Good night."

"Goo-nite." She pressed her lips on his, then fell back onto the pillow with a sigh.

Justus covered her with a sheet, draping it over her shoulders and tucking it around her chin. He didn't want her to take a chill from her damp hair.

His protective instincts had kicked in full-force when he'd heard someone stalking them. Some primitive, atavistic impulse drove him to confront the man who'd been following them. Though glad he hadn't had to fight, he knew he'd been willing to risk injury to defend Serenity.

He'd never felt the same way about any other woman...or had he? The doubts continued to gnaw at him, making every day—and especially the nights—a torment.

Chapter Six

"Did you go out last night?" Serenity asked Justus the next morning over coffee. She'd come to enjoy their mornings together. She avoided thinking about how she'd feel when he left.

"No, too tired. You don't remember what we did?"

"Not really. I guess I went to bed." She didn't want to discuss her dream. Too embarrassing to tell her guest that she'd fantasized he'd tenderly put her to bed with the sweetest of good-night kisses.

He smiled at her, brown eyes twinkling.

She tingled with an aliveness she hadn't experienced for years, a frisson of sensual awareness that zinged through her body. She didn't want Justus to know how deeply he affected her, so she chuckled to cover the weird, disconcerting emotion.

Serenity tried to rid herself of her stupid, useless yearning for someone who couldn't become a permanent part of her life. She reminded herself yet again that falling for Justus would be crazy, then returned to their conversation. "We must be getting old. When I was a kid, I used to work all day and party all night long."

He looked troubled. "I wish I could remember."

"I'm sorry." She put a hand to her face. "There I go, shoving my foot in my mouth. I didn't mean to remind you—"

"It's okay. About the only thing I remember is that I don't remember anything."

She inwardly damned her tactlessness. To change the subject, she said, "Listen, let's stick around until the full moon ritual tonight."

"'Full moon ritual'? Lordy."

"Hey, it's fun. Have you ever danced in the moonlight?" Serenity didn't mention that some danced naked. A brief fantasy of Justus nude at midnight flashed through her mind. She blanked it out, along with the erotic sizzle torching her body.

"I'll dance with you anytime, in the moonlight or out of it. As for the siesta, I'll skip that to find extra work."

"Or spend some of your earnings. There's lots of opportunities here, ones that could help you. Why don't you try Reiki, or a crystal healing?"

"Uh, maybe." His expression said, *Maybe never.*

With Justus by her side, Serenity had another busy day. They again helped Yazmin move the falafel stand from Main Street to the site that had become known as the ritual field. The teens attending the festival called it the Party Hearty Place.

After stuffing themselves with falafels at supper, Serenity and Justus lay next to each other on a serape, watching the sky darken.

As the evening deepened, the air cooled and stars emerged from the blue-velvet dusk. More folks joined them to await moonrise and the ritual. Colorful blankets dotted the field. To her right, Justus sprawled, his lids half-closed. The sooty fringe of his lashes curled over chiseled, tanned cheekbones. Why couldn't she have been born with those lashes? Serenity sighed. The man was better-looking than anyone had a right to be.

Though inches away, his warmth enveloped her. His distinctive male aroma filled her senses. She thrummed with delightful, forbidden longings. The memory of his kiss haunted her, branding her soul forever.

A fantasy of making love with Justus sneaked into her brain. She imagined how he'd feel and nearly groaned out loud, passion overtaking her.

Could she?

Would he?

And what would be the harm? He'd be leaving, wouldn't he? Didn't she deserve to find some happiness while he was still hers?

She watched him, remembering the flare of desire that had shot through her when they kissed. His lips, cleanly carved, had a definition and firmness she liked.

A lot.

That wonderful mouth, replete with the promise of pleasure, parted. He emitted a gentle snore. She jabbed Justus with her elbow.

He grunted. "What was that for?"

"You snored."

"Did not. That was the sound of my body turning into a falafel."

She chuckled. "Bored with Yazmin's food?"

"I don't mean to seem ungrateful, but I wish she sold something else."

"Maybe you can trade."

"I already did. I traded my falafel lunch for these shorts and sandals."

She glanced at him. Like Owen, Justus wore a festival security T-shirt. The cotton knit hugged his developed chest like a lover. Sandals and khaki shorts exposed brawny, tanned legs.

His bare limbs, fleeced with a inviting dark fuzz, lay close to hers, unbearably exciting. She wondered how his roughness would feel against her calves if she dragged one leg against his, stroked it up and down, up and down.

She swallowed. "You look cooler and more comfortable than you did in those heavy jeans and boots."

He ran his hand through his hair. "I feel good. That bump's gone away. I'm not achy all over anymore. I'm almost...restless."

"You movin' on?" Her throat tightened.

"Where would I move to?" Darkness had fallen, so she couldn't see his face, but she heard hopelessness in his voice.

"I'm sorry," she lied.

"Don't be. I want to stay with you, Serenity, but every day's so hard." He rolled toward her, leaning up on one elbow. His dark shape blotted out the stars. "The nights are worse."

She sucked in a breath.

"Not being with you is killing me," he said.

"I'm...I'm...I don't think I'm ready."

"I know. Neither am I. I won't be until I know who I am."

A shiver ran up her spine. "I don't know if I want that, Justus. Can't you wait?" She wanted him, but the downside terrified her. She'd given herself before and been hurt in the most brutal possible way.

"I have to wait." Justus rolled away from her, every line of his body vibrating with tension. "Look, I can't stay here and pretend. I'm exhausted. You ready to go home?"

Tired from the day, Serenity decided to go straight to bed after they'd walked to her cottage. But her thoughts roiled, a whirling chaos of uncertainty compounded with lust and fear. So after her shower, she stepped into her small backyard to commune with the night, seeking tranquility.

She blinked, noticing that pale buds had emerged on the vine interlacing the back fence. The stars glimmered, sharp, bright flames crowding the lapis vault of the sky. They seemed close enough to touch. Could she reach heaven so easily?

The first ember of attraction that had glowed for the stranger had blazed into a bonfire. And why not? During the past few days, they'd worked together like two perfectly meshed gears. He'd fixed her chair, made her pathetic yard bloom. Protected her, helped her, cared for her.

Her desire had grown into passion. Even better, she found she respected him. Would her need and admiration mature into love? She didn't know if she wanted a romance with anyone, least of all someone as compelling and mysterious as Justus.

Intelligent. Kind. Caring. Thoughtful. Strong. He deserved her love, but did she have any love to give? Could she fulfill his masculine demands?

Her feminine instincts told her that his restraint hid a healthy male animal. He'd demand more than she had. She slumped into a chair, the same one Justus had fixed.

She remembered the stroke of his fingertips. A wanton quiver rippled her flesh.

But he'd decided that a relationship wasn't possible until he recovered his memories. Then she'd have to defeat her past to join him as a whole, free woman.

She sighed, facing the inescapable truth. Justus had sought her out. Therefore, he'd been entangled with Hank. Serenity no longer believed that Justus was Hank's hired tough. The courteous way he handled himself shot holes in that idea. Hank hired roughnecks for his dirty work.

But the stranger's involvement continued to haunt her.

Perhaps he was one of Hank's slimeball attorneys. Maybe at some time in his past, an angry client had shot at him, leaving wounds.

Then later, during his involvement with Hank, perhaps Justus's conscience had forced him to threaten to blow the whistle on the whole scheme. That would explain everything.

Justus would have found her after one of Hank's toughs whacked him on the head, then dumped him in the desert. Memory gone except for her name and address, he'd wandered to her doorstep.

But why hadn't Hank shown up? She leaned back in her chair, passing a hand over her achy forehead.

Justus checked the property with a new, proprietary air. In the past two days he'd earned his right to live in it. Now at Serenity's bedroom door, he gazed at her back as she stood at the white-painted wooden dresser brushing her hair.

She wore her flowered silk robe. The fabric flowed over her small, shapely body like water, clinging to her gentle curves. With a delicate nightgown beneath, it accentuated her dainty femininity. He'd never liked a garment so much, but wanted to get rid of it so badly.

He wanted her, and by now, he knew he'd treat her well.

He deserved her, dammit.

He needed to know. He needed to know how long it would take, if ever, for her to be able to open herself up to him.

She met his gaze in the mirror. "Can't sleep?"

"Nope. Serenity, we have to talk."

"About what?"

"About us. I know you miss your husband, but—"

"Miss my husband?" Serenity dropped her brush. It clattered onto her dresser. Ignoring it, she whirled. "What are you talking about?"

"Well, uh, it's obvious you're grieving. I figured he'd died and—"

She staggered past him to her bed and collapsed on it, shoulders trembling. "Miss my husband?" She buried her face in her hands.

Oh, hell. He'd gone and upset her again. Inching

into her off-limits room, he gingerly sat next to her on her bed. "I'm sorry I brought it up, but the situation—"

Giggling, hysterical, she lifted her face, streaked with tears. "You don't understand at all. Miss my husband?" She laughed, a tortured, broken sound. "Oh, that's rich. Miss him because he died? Don't I wish."

"Serenity, what's going on? I'm tired of trying to guess about you. I'm struggling to find my past, while you're ignoring yours. Now quit talking in riddles and tell me what's goin' on!"

She rolled against her pillows and laughed harder. Then cried.

Astounded, he offered her a tissue from the box on her nightstand. "Please."

She calmed herself. "Okay. It's just so ironic—" Her thoughts seemed to send her into another spurt of mingled laughter and weeping.

She blew her nose, straightened, and looked him in the eyes. "Listen to me. My ex-husband is not dead, nor do I miss the rat who turned me into his punching bag throughout our marriage."

His mouth fell open. "You—you were—" Springing to his feet, he stalked across her room, fists balled. He was gonna kill him. He didn't know when or how, but he was gonna track down the snake who'd hurt Serenity. With difficulty, he controlled his temper, and said, "You were a battered wife."

"Yes. I'm ashamed to admit it, but yes. And I stuck around way too long."

"Oh, baby." He wanted to comfort her, but couldn't grab for her. If she'd been abused, she had to come to him. So he opened his arms wide, hoping she'd take the invitation.

She went to him, cuddling into his hug as though she'd been born to nestle there.

He kissed the top of her head. "I'm so sorry." She aroused every one of his protective instincts.

"Sorry? Why? *You* didn't hit me."

"Sorry you went through that. Sorry I was such an idiot." *But I'm not sorry you're free.*

"You're not an idiot. You're the best man I've ever known."

"Yeah?" He slipped one hand around to her nape to hold her steady for his kiss before she had a chance to protest. But she was willing, judging by her slack, languid muscles. No fight-or-flight response here, just a slow, easy mingling of their lips, teeth, tongues, mouths that made his body harden and sent his soul into heaven.

She tasted of herbal toothpaste and woman and he couldn't get enough of her, especially since he now knew she was free, unfettered by the sorrow of widowhood. Wanting to feel her softness molded to him, he tightened his embrace. She settled into his body as though they were parts carved from the same whole, destined to fit together forever.

He stroked down her silken robe to find one erect, pointed nipple. Her arousal incited him, so he eased his hand inside her nightgown.

She recoiled, startled.

"I'm sorry. That was too rough, wasn't it? I didn't mean to rush you."

Tousled from their kiss, her red hair stood on end. "I, I, uh, I'm okay." Visibly agitated and confused,

FREE GIFTS!

NO COST! NO OBLIGATION TO BUY!
NO PURCHASE NECESSARY!

DETACH AND MAIL CARD TODAY!

© 2001 HARLEQUIN ENTERPRISES LTD. ® and TM are trademarks owned by Harlequin Books S.A. used under license.

PLAY THE
Lucky Key Game

Scratch gold area with a coin.
Then check below to see the books and gift you get!

315 SDL DH24
215 SDL DH2Y

YES! I have scratched off the gold area. Please send me the 2 Free books and gift for which I qualify. I understand I am under no obligation to purchase any books, as explained on the back and on the opposite page.

NAME   (PLEASE PRINT CLEARLY)

ADDRESS

APT.#   CITY

STATE/PROV.   ZIP/POSTAL CODE

2 free books plus a gift

2 free books

1 free book

Try Again!

(S-R-OS-02/02)

Offer limited to one per household and not valid to current Silhouette Romance® subscribers. All orders subject to approval.

The Silhouette Reader Service™ — Here's how it works:

Accepting your 2 free books and gift places you under no obligation to buy anything. You may keep the books and gift and return the shipping statement marked "cancel." If you do not cancel, about a month later we'll send you 6 additional books and bill you just $3.15 each in the U.S., or $3.50 each in Canada, plus 25¢ shipping & handling per book and applicable taxes if any.* That's the complete price and — compared to cover prices of $3.99 each in the U.S. and $4.50 each in Canada — it's quite a bargain! You may cancel at any time, but if you choose to continue, every month we'll send you 6 more books, which you may either purchase at the discount price or return to us and cancel your subscription.

*Terms and prices subject to change without notice. Sales tax applicable in N.Y. Canadian residents will be charged applicable provincial taxes and GST.

If offer card is missing write to: Silhouette Reader Service, 3010 Walden Ave., P.O. Box 1867, Buffalo, NY 14240-1867

BUSINESS REPLY MAIL
FIRST-CLASS MAIL   PERMIT NO. 717-003   BUFFALO, NY

POSTAGE WILL BE PAID BY ADDRESSEE

SILHOUETTE READER SERVICE
3010 WALDEN AVE
PO BOX 1867
BUFFALO NY 14240-9952

NO POSTAGE
NECESSARY
IF MAILED
IN THE
UNITED STATES

Serenity wrapped her robe more closely around her small frame, covering her breasts. "I'm just uh, not, whatever." A frown wrinkled her forehead.

He ached for her and what she'd suffered. He'd never make her endure a moment's doubt or pain. He cared for her too much for that.

He hated his crudeness. How could he have pushed someone so frail?

Serenity watched him leave. Maybe she shouldn't have exposed so much about herself. She hated talking about her past; somehow, verbalizing what had happened to her gave it more energy, more power over her reality.

On the other hand, forgetting the lessons she'd learned from Hank was out of the question. And here was another forceful male moving in on her.

She shuddered, resolving once more to never fall into the snare of a relationship with a man who'd try to control her. But she already had a relationship with Justus, didn't she? Stupid to pretend that there weren't any feelings between them.

She wanted him.

He wanted her.

They liked and respected each other.

They worked well together. Heck, they *lived* together with a sense of comfort and joy she'd never before experienced.

The situation was a surefire recipe for disaster, especially since the truth had changed Justus's attitude toward her. Before, he'd apparently believed she was a grieving widow. Now, he seemed to have concluded she was fair game for romance.

Sexier than ever, the long, lean lines of the stranger's body exuded a sensual intensity he'd previously lacked. And his kiss...he'd swept her to nirvana and back again. He could seduce a nun right out of her vows.

Only fear had prevented her from continuing what Justus had begun. Fear, and the suspicion that the stranger would soon regain his memory.

Would he be friend or enemy?

She bit her lip. Intuition told her that Dr. Feelgood's efforts would soon bear fruit. When the stranger's amnesia cleared, she figured she'd be back in the same mess she'd escaped nearly a year ago. She didn't know if she was ready for her past to overwhelm the present she'd so carefully crafted.

This time, she'd have to do the right thing. But was she ready to face the consequences?

Justus tossed and turned in the narrow bed, seeking rest. Sleep eluded him, the darkness instead bringing nightmare landscapes punctuated by brief swatches of disjointed memory.

Entering the limo, he studied the husky, blond man sitting inside. Without fear, just a tight, tense watchfulness, he waited for the trap to snap shut.

But something had gone wrong, horribly wrong. He'd awakened in the desert with a headache that defied description, stripped of his wallet and his gun. After walking for hours in the night, he finally reached a dirt road. The dawn light showed a battered metal sign reading Lost Creek, New Mexico.

He'd remembered that the tiny, obscure hamlet con-

tained what could be the biggest clue of all. The woman, Lori Perkins. He'd maintained that she was the key. He'd wanted to interview her before the sting went down, but he'd been overruled.

Everyone else in the unit had been sure that the dumb blond ex-wife of the ringleader had the brains of a box of rocks and knew nothing about anything. "Forget about her, Gutierrez," Carson had said. "Perkins'll go down without wifey's help."

But Perkins hadn't gone down. Like a fox, he'd smelled the trap and had bitten the hand that set it. Justus's hand.

When he reached Lost Creek, he discovered that Lori wasn't Lori. Instead, Serenity Clare had snared him with her web of enchantment.

He awakened early, desperate to retrieve the shreds of his dream. Shaking with excitement and frustration, he sensed he was close, so close. The information that Serenity had revealed—that her ex-husband was alive, and was violent—had been the catalyst.

Though he recalled he'd been hit on the head and dumped in the desert, he couldn't quite remember why. He almost knew who he was, but the information, which had floated in with his nightmare, had drifted away with the ebbing tides of sleep.

Did Serenity know? Maybe, but he didn't want to push her. He understood her frailty. Though she hid the truth well, any mention of her ex-husband deeply distressed her.

She still hadn't healed from the battering. He remembered that she'd spent most of a day in bed last week, a sure sign of depression.

He could seduce or break her, but wanted his woman to come to him whole and intact.

His woman.

He never wanted to let her go, and if Perkins came around, well, Perkins had just better watch his back, his front...every angle.

Entering the living room, he joined Serenity at her morning meditation. Today, the calmness that had formerly attended this ritual eluded him.

Serenity seemed to sense his distraction, shooting him a quizzical glance when she started to exercise.

Perhaps the yoga will help, he thought. He bent, twisted and stretched with Serenity, noticing that his body had loosened. He hadn't developed her suppleness, but would with time.

He wondered how her limber body would twine around his when they made love. *Soon.*

To Serenity's relief, the rest of the festival proceeded peacefully, with no stalkers trailing them to their home. By Monday night, all the tourists and vendors had left, and Lost Creek again assumed its guise of a sleepy, dusty ghost town.

"What's on the agenda?" Justus asked her over coffee on Tuesday morning.

She sat opposite him at the farmhouse table. "We've both worked hard lately. How 'bout a day off?"

"To do what?"

"I want to go to Lost Springs for a picnic."

"Where's that?"

"A few miles out of town." She waved a hand in

the air. "It's a great spot for picnics. Not many people know about it."

"I didn't think there was anything except desert around here."

She beamed at him. "That's the joke. Lost Creek isn't really lost. It goes underground and emerges as Lost Springs. It's the local swimming hole."

"I don't have a bathing suit."

"Neither do I." She'd discovered in the past few days that she enjoyed flirting with him, and he seemed to feel the same way. They'd continued to live and work together like lock and key. With each passing moment, Serenity felt the barriers around her heart dropping. Her love had blossomed like a flower opening to the sun.

Leaning in his chair, he threw his head back and laughed. "Oh, baby. You are this fella's dream come true."

"I don't know what you expect to happen," she said demurely. "We're going to swim, then eat too much. I predict you won't feel like, um, that."

He laughed harder. "Right."

A loud knock interrupted Justus's guffaw. He stared at Serenity. "Who could that be?"

"I don't know. I don't get many unexpected visitors. You were the first and last one." She winked at him before going to the door, with Justus tagging along.

The biggest man Serenity had ever seen stood on her doorstep. Had he been dressed in red with a white beard, she'd have expected to see him at Neiman Marcus in December with a child on his knee.

"Lori Perkins!" Then his glance shifted to Justus,

standing behind her. "Matt!" The big man shoul-
dered her aside and engulfed Justus in a bear hug.

Dread froze Serenity. Reality had just walked
through the door.

Chapter Seven

The stunned expression on the stranger's face mirrored Serenity's feelings. Quiet with shock, they sat in her stiff, ladder-backed chairs around the kitchen table, trying to absorb the truth, but it sounded like a bad movie.

Name: Matt Gutierrez.

Age: thirty-four.

Status: single.

Occupation: Texas Ranger.

Matt's boss, Carson, leaned toward him, his rotund body dwarfing the kitchen chair. "We found you on the Internet, see. Some doctor had posted your photo and this address."

"But what's all this about? How did M-Matt get here?" Serenity tried to piece together the story while she prayed these new revelations wouldn't change anything between them.

"I don't rightly know, ma'am, except he was part of a unit investigating Hank Perkins."

Her stomach sank right down to her toes. "My ex-husband."

Matt reached out and covered her hand with his. She turned her palm over to clutch his fingers. Through all these surprises, Matt still remembered that any mention of Hank distressed her. Perhaps her cowboy was still the same kind, gentle man who'd filled her life with happiness. Her mood lifted a little.

"Perkins had a pyramid scheme goin'," Carson said. "He'd sell shares to the first group of investors and use the money to wildcat wells. He'd sell stock in the same well to group two, and on and on. He hoped to make a big strike, pay everyone off, and no one would be the wiser."

"How'd you figure him out?" Matt asked. "You've told me a lot, but I still don't have much recollection of this at all."

"We'd received complaints. Perkins was making enough money to keep afloat, but not enough to pay off the investors."

Matt's eyes narrowed. "What do we need to do to trap Perkins?"

Carson turned to Serenity. "Ma'am, we need your help. We can't send Matt back in. They know his pretty face. It'll take too long to plant someone else into Perkins's operation. We need you to smoke him out."

"She's not a law enforcement officer." Matt's voice rose. His hand protectively squeezed hers. "You can't use her as bait!"

"We'll protect her every step of the way." Carson glanced at Serenity. His shrewd blue eyes glinted.

"Heard he treated you pretty bad, ma'am. Wouldn't you like to get your own back?"

Serenity clenched her jaw. "The desire for revenge is incompatible with an enlightened state of being. Hurting Hank won't make me whole."

"Yeah, but it will prevent him from stealing the money of other innocent people. And what about the next young lady he entraps?"

Darn it, he was right. Serenity envisioned another kid, fresh out of college, falling for Hank hard and fast, just as she had. Another sweet little punching bag to satisfy his ego. She gritted her teeth. "What do you propose?"

"It's very simple. Write a letter to Perkins demanding money. We'll tell you exactly what to say, but basically, it'll be a blackmail demand."

She sucked in her breath. "He'll come to kill me."

Carson gave her a feral grin. "Ma'am, we're countin' on it."

Afraid she'd crack like an egg if she actually had to confront her ex, she asked, "Will I have to see Hank?" Writing a letter to the beast would be bad enough, but a meeting might destroy the healing she'd accomplished.

"Yes, sirree. You'll be wired for sound and you'll have to get him talking about the scheme. If he drops the money and leaves, it's all over."

Her chest tightened. "That won't happen. Believe me, if Hank thinks I'm alone and unprotected, he won't be able to resist the opportunity."

"Opportunity?" Carson asked.

"He'll attack me. I assume that's when the cavalry will come riding over the hill to rescue the damsel in distress?'' Though the idea of seeing Hank again made her want to puke, she managed to keep her tone casual.

Carson grinned at her. ''You betcha. It would be great if he went for you. We could get him for attempted murder.''

''Jolly.'' Sweating, she could smell the acrid scent of her own fear. ''Maybe we should move.''

''When this is all over?'' Matt asked.

''No, now. When it's over, I'll want to continue living in Lost Creek. I like it here. But for right now—don't they have special places called safe houses?''

''Yeah, we do,'' Carson said. ''You can stay at one in El Paso. As for the drop site, we'll pick a hotel.'' He turned to Matt. ''When ya comin' back to work, boy?''

''I hadn't thought about it.''

''They'll all be happy to see your sweet, shinin' face.'' He winked at Matt. ''They've all been missin' ya. Keri and Sandi and Carole and Kitty—''

Serenity's heart twisted. She dropped his hand.

Matt reddened beneath his tan. ''I don't recall who those people are.''

''Well, they sure remember you.'' Carson smirked.

''This is my case, and if we're using Serenity as bait, I'm staying with her.''

''Your cover's blown. No reason not to give you another assignment after we get the staff doc to clear ya.''

Serenity decided that if Matt wanted to leave, she'd let him go. Carson's comments meant that Matt was quite a player. After hearing the list of women he'd left, she figured she didn't want him around. *Nice try, Serenity,* she told herself. *Keep repeating it to yourself and one day you might even believe it.* Losing him would hurt worse than any of Hank's blows, but a clean break would be best.

"Better go, Matt." She gave him a big, saccharine smile. "Wouldn't want to leave Carole and Kitty all alone too long."

After arguing all day, they'd decided nothing. With tension thickening the air, the three of them ate Szechuan tofu with vegetables over brown rice that evening. Matt tucked away dinner with his usual gusto. "I worked pretty darn hard in the last few days." He smiled at Serenity.

Remembering Sandi, Carole, Kitty and her friends, Serenity hardened her heart. She gave Matt only the merest twitch of her lips in response.

"Didn't know you liked this hippie food, boy." Carson grinned at Matt while dumping more dried chili flakes into his already spicy dish.

"Really?" she asked. "What did Matt normally eat?"

He winked at her. "Ol' Matt here's a meat-and-potatoes man. Didn't he tell ya? His daddy and his grandpappy before him raise prime beef out there near Abilene. Been herdin' steers for generations."

Serenity nibbled a strip of red pepper. What other surprises did Matt Gutierrez hide?

"Never saw him cook, either." Carson swigged his beer.

"Hmm." Serenity filed that bit of data away. *Will the real Matt Gutierrez please stand up?*

Matt coughed. "'Scuse me, but I would appreciate it if the two of you wouldn't talk about me as though I'm not here." He carried the empty plates to the counter, turned on the hot water, and squirted detergent into the sink.

"Washin' dishes? You got Matt washin' dishes?" Carson fixed Serenity with a surprised glance. "Good goin', girl. I guess you done tamed the golden boy."

She poured herself another glass of chilled lemon water. "Who?"

"Golden Boy Gutierrez. That's what his women call him."

She closed her gaping mouth, then said, "'His women'?"

Carson winked at her again. "You got a hot one there, young lady."

Professing fatigue, Carson retired to the guest room, so Matt and Serenity could speak freely. They went to the back garden for more privacy. Behind Matt, Serenity could see the vine blooming against the back fence, its white flowers glowing pale in the dusk.

"I don't like it," Matt said.

"Me, either. How on earth did you put up with it?" she asked. "All the stress—"

"Now that you mention it, I'm not sure." He began to pace. "I recall taking a lot of pride in the badge. The Rangers are an elite corps, you know."

"Yeah, I know."

"Besides, I liked the people I worked with."

She noticed he used past tense, but didn't call his attention to it. "Why'd they send *him?*"

"He's heading the investigation into your ex's activities."

Serenity found herself twitching with agitation. "I don't mean to be temperamental, but I'm not sure I like him."

"But you're willing to go along with his plan." He stopped.

"He says it's the only way to trap Hank. I guess I have to, Matt." Serenity wrung her hands together. "I have to end this…this control Hank still has over my life. I'm tired of the fear. I'm tired of hiding and running."

"I don't know." Matt worried his lower lip with his teeth. "I feel—I feel like I have conflicting loyalties. I'm a Ranger, so I should encourage you to help, but…"

"What do you mean?"

"This could be dangerous, Serenity. If you were hurt…I'd never forgive myself if something went wrong." Matt rubbed his face.

"Like what?"

His features went taut with tension. "I'm not sure. I can't help wondering who set me up."

"I don't understand."

Releasing her, he stalked back and forth across the cracked concrete, his shadow faint in the moonlight. "It's all coming back to me, you see. In bits and pieces. I remember I spent months infiltrating Perkins's operation. My cover was perfect. Yet I ended up in the desert half dead. Someone set me up. That's the only explanation."

She sucked in a fearful breath. "You think it was a Ranger? Carson?"

Matt hesitated. "No. Maybe. I don't know! All's I know is that if you're gonna go along with this, we have to be very, very careful."

"'We'?"

"Yeah, we. Hey, is there something wrong?" He came closer and slipped his arm around her, raw pulling her near his heat.

"I—I feel like I don't know you anymore."

"Me, too. All that weird stuff about women I'd never heard of—"

"Yes, and the meat-and potatoes thing and taming Golden Boy Gutierrez—"

Even in the faint light, Serenity could see a muscle in Matt's jaw spasm. "I don't know how Carson can be a lawman. He just can't control his flapping lips."

"Hey, I thought I knew you." Pulling away, she faced him. "I thought you ate organic food, helped with the dishes, and were a one-woman man. Now I find out that you're—you're—Mr. Golden Boy Meat-Eating Player."

Matt burst out laughing. "Mr. Golden Boy Meat-Eating Player? That's a good one. I oughtta write that down and make sure I remember it." He leaned toward her. "I'll make sure you remember it, too."

"What do you mean?"

"Look, Carson's trying to throw me off this case." Matt's lips had gone thin and tight. "I won't let anyone separate us. I want to be in for the kill."

Serenity gasped.

"Honey, I didn't mean that the way it came out. But you want me there, don't you?"

"Of course I do. But—"

"Let's get married."

"What?"

"Look, you're the bait. They need your coopera-tion. I've seen operations before where husbands in-sisted upon staying with their wives, and law enforce-ment let them."

"Matt, I can't marry you. I can't marry anyone! I don't know if I can..." Sinking down onto a chair, she hid her face in her hands. How could she tell him?

"Don't know what?"

She raised her head, blinking away tears. "I'm not sure if I want to remarry at all, but if I do, I want to marry for love. This is all so sudden. I c-care about you, but I don't know if I can be a, um, proper wife."

"A proper wife?" He grinned, his teeth flashing. "What if I prefer an improper wife?"

"What? Why would you?"

Standing, he lifted her into his arms. Amazingly, he felt great, not threatening at all. "I want a very improper wife," he purred into her ear.

She giggled, then sobered as she remembered their somber situation. "I don't know if I can do, um, *that* yet." Shame overwhelmed her. When would she be healed?

Perhaps confronting Hank was the only way. And she knew she didn't want to face down Hank without Matt by her side.

"*Yet* is the operative word. Don't worry, Serenity. Everything will turn out okay. You'll be safe if we stick together. Now let's go to bed."

She shifted in his arms, uncomfortable with the idea of sleeping with him so soon and so unexpect-edly. "Uh, where? Carson's in the guest room—"

Matt set her on her feet. "I'll take the couch...for tonight." He stalked inside.

The next morning, seated at the farmhouse table, they worked on the letter. Carson dictated and Serenity wrote.

I know about the fraudulent shares in the oil wells. I photocopied numerous incriminating papers during our marriage. They're in a safe-deposit box. If you want them back, personally deliver one hundred thousand dollars to me at the Grand Hyatt in El Paso. I'll be registered there—

"When?" she asked Carson.

"Tell him in two days' time."

"No!" Matt and Serenity said together.

"Why not?" Carson sounded impatient. "Let's wrap this one up and go on to something else. Time's a-wastin'."

"I, uh, want to teach Serenity some self-defense skills. I don't want her facing Perkins without them." Matt was insistent. Serenity guessed he wanted time to persuade her to agree to his crazy marriage scheme. She bit her lip.

Carson expelled an impatient breath. "Son, someone will be in the next room. She'll be protected at all times."

"I'm not ready. If you want my help, you'll have to slow down. I have to prepare myself to see him again." Serenity couldn't control the tremble in her voice. She wondered if she was truly ready to confront Hank, even with the help of Matt and the Rangers. And she needed time to accustom herself to the idea of marriage.

She'd sworn that she'd never again wed. Marriage was a trap. But to set the trap the Rangers wanted to set for Hank, she had to let herself be trapped.... Her head spun. Too many plans and schemes. Too many traps. She wanted a simple life. She wanted all of it to be over.

"All right." Carson sounded reluctant. "In a week or so. Say September fifteenth. Tell him to meet you at the Grand Hyatt September fifteenth at 9:00 p.m. You'll be registered there. He can come to your room."

"Oh, great."

"We'll rent you a suite. You'll meet him in the living room, and we'll be in one of the bedrooms."

"He's gonna wonder how I can afford such an expensive room."

"With the cash he's bringin', of course." Matt gave her a long, slow smile that hinted of masculine possessiveness and protection, of lovers' secrets and intimacy. The expression in his eyes wrapped around her heart, enclosing it in a warm, safe embrace. Chains Hank had bound around her soul loosened and began to fall away.

She'd fight a thousand Hanks for the promises in Matt's smile.

In a burst of faith, she decided she'd go through with all of it—the marriage, the trap, everything. *You'll never know unless you try,* she told herself. She returned Matt's smile and gave him a thumbs-up.

Serenity completed the letter, and hesitated when

it came time to sign. She bet Hank didn't know the name Serenity Clare, and she hoped he never would. But she'd sworn to never again use his name. She thought of Perkins as her slave name. She tapped the pen against the table, trying to decide.

"What's holdin' ya up? Sign the thing."

Serenity found Carson's impatience irritating. She had become used to the slow pace of Lost Creek. Her friends spoke, moved, and acted deliberately, savoring every moment. She couldn't fathom someone who wanted to rush through life.

She wrote "Lori Waddell" with a shaky hand. She tried to grin when she added a smiley face over the "i" in Lori. That signature would push Hank's explosive temper over the edge.

"What did you write there, girl?" Serenity noticed that Carson hadn't once used her true name. "Why didn't you write Lori Perkins?"

"Waddell is my maiden name. He'll know it's me and, besides, he'll flip his lid."

Matt peered over her shoulder. "Especially with the smiley face."

After Carson left for El Paso to do advance work for the operation, Matt walked with Serenity to the Book Nook to tell Serenity's friends the good news. He kept his arm securely around her waist in a possessive clasp. She was his woman, and he'd protect her at all cost.

Neither Mairen nor Great Bear seemed surprised at their decision to marry, though Matt's line of work appeared to startle them.

Great Bear slapped Matt on the shoulder, nearly

knocking him into next week. "Should'a known you were law enforcement, buddy. You were pretty good with crowd control at the festival."

"A lot better than Owen," Mairen said.

Matt snorted. "An elementary school crossing guard would be better than Owen."

Serenity asked, "Great Bear, will you marry us?"

Mairen clapped her hands together. "Yes! Yes! Oh, that will be such fun."

"Will it be legal?" Matt asked.

"Sure it will," Great Bear rumbled. "I'm an ordained minister of the Universal Spirit Church. I conduct a ceremony, take the license to the county seat, and it's official."

"Let's do it as soon as possible," Matt said. He didn't want Carson returning early and wrecking their plans. He intended to stick to Serenity like a foxtail on a dog.

Chapter Eight

Serenity wanted to have the ceremony at Lost Springs, and Matt didn't object. Anyplace would have worked for him, but the trio of Great Bear, Serenity and Mairen seemed concerned about the auras, vibrations, and spiritual aspects of the wedding.

The four of them left on foot at dawn on the morning of the ceremony, carrying packs loaded with water and food. They hiked past a field of red and yellow pepper plants, with the scent of chilis in the sun hanging heavy in the air. Matt saw irrigation ditches, shining silver in the harsh light, watering the crops. A few yards away from the verdant land, the desert shimmered in the heat.

Serenity led the way along a track in the dry, flat plain toward an outcropping of reddish stone. A big white hat, festooned with lace and gauze, shaded her head and shoulders. Matt wore an embroidered white shirt, which Mairen called a Mexican wedding shirt. That suited him fine.

Their destination didn't seem far away, but Matt knew that the clear, pure air made estimating distances tricky. Removing his Stetson, he rubbed his head. He figured that their destination lay another a mile or two away.

"What's this?" He pointed at the track.

"A Native American trail. Leads from one vortex site to another." Serenity pulled her white gauze gown away from her body, letting it float in the soft breeze.

"Is Lost Springs a vortex site?"

"Yes," Mairen answered. "The Native Americans believe that the water heals."

"It does," Great Bear said. "After the ceremony, you'll find out." He winked at Serenity, who blushed.

When they reached the outcropping, they climbed into a disorganized tumble of giant rocks. As they ascended a winding trail through it, Matt smelled greenery and heard a creek before they came to the site of the ceremony: a pool sunk into the harsh desert, surrounded by gray-green sage and a few shrubby trees.

The surface of the pond bubbled. The underground spring, he guessed. Water poured over the far lip of the natural cauldron, forming a thin waterfall.

Great Bear removed a ceremonial robe from his leather knapsack and draped it over his shoulders. After sipping some water, Matt shoved their packs under the shadow of a bush. Mairen lit a smudge stick.

Serenity took Matt's hand and smiled at him. "Are you sure you want to do this?"

"A thousand percent. I thought you were the one who had doubts."

"I do, but...but something in me wants to make this work. I can't let Hank destroy me."

Great Bear rumbled, "Are we ready?"

Mairen waved the smudge stick around and over them while Great Bear conducted the simple ceremony. Matt was surprised to find that the brief service was fairly traditional.

When it came to the ring, he remembered that he didn't have one. He stood there like a fool until Great Bear pulled out two of the silver rings he sold at the Book Nook. He said, "We are honored to give you these rings, which are inscribed with symbols for constancy and happiness."

"Thank you, Great Bear." Serenity extended her left hand to Matt.

His heart pounded as he slipped the ring on her finger. Thoughts tumbled through his mind. His amnesia wasn't cured, but he knew he'd never expected to marry a psychic neo-hippie in a New Age ceremony conducted by a Native American shaman at a swimming hole in the New Mexico desert.

He fastened on the only important fact. He'd sworn to himself he'd protect Serenity with his life, and he'd meant that promise. "With this ring, I thee wed." His voice was husky.

"With this ring, I thee wed." Serenity whispered. She looked as affected by the ceremony as he.

"You may now kiss the bride," Great Bear concluded.

Matt restrained himself, giving her only a brief brush of his lips on her cheek, though he wanted more...much more. "I'm saving up for later," he murmured in Serenity's ear.

She smiled nervously before she turned to thank Great Bear and Mairen, who already were preparing to leave.

"You don't want to stick around, have a bite to eat?" Matt asked.

Mairen shook her head, smiling. "We would not intrude on this most private of moments. Enjoy your honeymoon." She kissed Serenity before they left.

"Well, what now?" Matt asked Serenity.

"I don't know about you, but I'm sweltering. I want to swim." Tossing her hat aside, she pulled her gown over her head.

He didn't want to stare at his wife, but he couldn't help watching her shed her clothing. She had a perky little body he longed to caress.

Matt could only guess at what she'd been through with Perkins, and now he wanted to show her that loving could be tender, not brutal.

His poor, abused sweetheart. He'd make sure no one ever hurt her again.

He took off his clothes. "Please." He held out his hand. Serenity had to come to him willingly.

"What?" She eyed him, her face pinkening as her gaze roamed his body.

Flattered by her admiring scrutiny, he felt his heartbeat quicken, his muscles tighten with desire.

She took his hand. *Yes!* A burst of relief ran through his system.

He picked his way over the uneven, stony ground toward the pool while Serenity strolled with familiar ease. Tugging on his fingers, she led him to a spot where the rocks formed a natural set of steps into the swimming hole.

Putting an arm around her, he said, "Um, shouldn't we talk about this?"

Splashing into the water, she said, "Maybe later. Let's relax now." She rolled onto her back and floated. The tips of her nipples pointed, pink, hard, and high, at the cobalt sky.

Matt slipped into the pond and tried to shove the idea of lovemaking out of his mind. His wedding day could be a very long, frustrating experience, given his physically reluctant bride. Thank heaven for the coolness of the water, which went a long way to calming his eagerness.

He closed his eyes as he drifted on the pond's gentle currents. The top layer of the pool was warmed by the sun, while the chillier, deeper water kept his body in check.

He bumped against Serenity, who passed a soft hand over his torso.

He moaned. "Oh, baby, please." A warm weight settled on his chest. His feet sought the rough bottom of the pond.

Matt opened his eyes. She'd draped herself over him, wet red hair plastered to her skull, moisture dripping off her nose.

"Tell me what you want," he said.

Serenity stared into Matt's brown eyes. His expression had changed from gentle to fiercely intent.

"Please. You have to tell me what you want. Although I'm your husband, I...I won't force myself on you, ever."

Her breath caught in her throat. Her heart stopped for a moment, then started thumping in her chest fast as a desert hare.

Was she ready? Had Matt's kindness unlocked her emotional chastity belt?

She wouldn't know if she didn't try.

Matt's flesh was warm against hers, the texture of his smooth skin irresistible. She closed her eyes to better savor the tingling, carnal passion that pervaded her body. She passed one palm over his chest, delighting in the prickliness of his masculine fur and the solidity of his muscles, so different from her, yet so enticing and beautiful.

She opened her eyes. "I want...I want...I want you." She slid her arms around him, pulling him close.

He smiled. The crow's feet radiating from the corners of his eyes tightened. His brown gaze held loving promise. "I'm yours, Serenity."

She sucked in a breath. Her nipples, grazing his chest, grew hard and taut with need.

"But you have to tell me exactly what to do, every step of the way."

"Uh, I do?" She didn't know what to say. Hank had always taken what he wanted. Her desires had never entered into sex.

Matt nodded.

"I don't know if I can do that." Would she have to use words she hated, those ugly words that Hank had used to shame her?

"I don't want to go faster than you can handle. If it were up to me, I'd have been in your bed that first night." He touched the tip of her nose, then kissed it. "So you have to take the lead."

Serenity closed her eyes, banishing Hank to the

past where he belonged. Lifting her lids, she again met Matt's warm, brown gaze. "I'm ready, Matt."

"Are you sure?"

"As sure as the sky's blue." She blinked the moisture away. "You're a good, gentle man. You fix my chairs and water my yard and take c-care of me."

"Seems to me you're the one who does most of the caretaking." His encircling arms supported her. She let her feet lift from the pond's bottom.

She caressed his face. "Let's say we take care of each other."

"Then let's take care of each other now." He kissed her palm. "I want you, Serenity. I want you so bad I'm about to die from it. So tell me what you want."

"Oh. Well, uh, how about this?"

She touched her mouth to his sweet lips. His embrace tightened. She ran one hand through his hair, then rubbed her body against his, again relishing the firmness of his hard chest against her aroused breasts.

His body crowded, hard and warm, against her. She didn't know what made her tremble, anxiety, excitement or nerves. The thought of him taking her tightened every muscle to an unbearable tension.

She released him, then drifted to the side of the pool.

He followed. "Serenity?"

"I—I need a break." She climbed out and pawed through their packs for towels.

"That's fine, honey." Matt took a towel from her.

Abruptly, her eyes filled with tears. "You're not angry?"

"What's to be angry about?" He dried his hair, then hers.

"I don't mean to be a tease."

"You're not. We're married. We have all the time in the world. What's the point in hurrying? It's just over that much faster."

Serenity peeked at him.

His calm eyes smiled.

He meant it.

She sighed a relieved breath. "You're so good to me."

"That's something that goes both ways." Spreading his towel, he sat on it, tugging her down beside him.

She leaned against him, letting him pull her close. The terrifying anxiety dissipated, routed by the affection in his embrace. She tipped her head back to kiss along the line of his jaw. Then she rubbed her lips across it, enjoying the slight raspiness of his stubble on her mouth.

He turned his head and gently nibbled on her lower lip.

She slid her tongue between the ridge of his teeth.

For a moment he didn't respond. Then his entire body seemed to hum and vibrate with intense currents of passion. His arms surrounded her, bringing her close to his heat. His tongue met hers halfway, flicking at the tip.

An erotic shock, stunning in its potency, flashed through her. Reaching out, she explored him, running her fingers through his hair, sculpting his face, rubbing down his neck to his torso. The sunshine sparkled on his damp skin, glowing on his flesh and hers.

"Yeah, that's right, baby. I'm yours. Touch me all you want. I'm here for you." His open mouth sucked and licked every part of her he could reach.

Matt pulled her high onto his lap. She moaned as he veiled the sensitive skin at her throat with kisses. He leaned back onto his towel, still holding her.

She straddled his hips.

"I don't know if I'm ready for this."

"Take your time. I'm not going anywhere." Matt stroked her bottom. "Show me how you like to be touched."

She gasped. "I—I've never—" Her face heated with embarrassment.

"It's okay, sweetheart. Show me." His tone was gentle, but insistent. "I want to please you. Show me what to do. Please."

The raw want in his voice undid her completely. She'd do anything to satisfy this man. She wanted to return everything he'd given her, multiplied by ten. The kindness. The pleasure. The love.

Chapter Nine

Matt thought he'd explode from needing Serenity
so much. Hovering above him, she took him slowly,
hesitantly, edging down with exquisite finesse. She
breathed in sexy little pants, urging him higher and
higher, demanding his response.

He worried that he'd finish too fast, but managed
to hold back until she'd taken her pleasure. Then he
let go everything he felt for her, burning from head
to heels with joyous rapture. She collapsed onto his
chest and he held her hips as they went over the edge
to forever.

Matt didn't know how long they lay together, their
naked, damp bodies melded into one ardent soul. Images and memories clashed in his mind, glittering,
shimmering just out of reach. Clarity followed, the
clouds in his brain swept away by their loving.

He knew. He knew everything he needed to know,
including how much Serenity had changed him.

He wanted to jump and dance and laugh out loud, but didn't want to disturb her.

Serenity still lay across his chest, muscles relaxed and limp.

Finally she stirred, easing off him and rolling to his side. He lifted up onto one elbow and leaned over her to kiss her.

"You okay, sweetheart?"

"Yeah. Wow. It was…it was better than I'd imagined."

He couldn't stop his cockiness. "'Course it was."

"Listen to you." She lightly smacked his arm.

Grinning at her, he stood. "Let's take another dip. And Serenity, we need to talk." He offered his hand.

She took it, but looked tense. "What do we have to talk about?" Serenity slipped into the pool.

Matt followed, enjoying the water's caress. "Well, from everything that's happened, the amnesia's finally gone. I remember everything."

"What a great wedding present!"

Matt laughed, joy welling up from his heart. Except for that rascal Perkins, everything was perfect. "Yeah, it sure is."

"So what's the story?"

"Everything Carson said is true. I'm in a unit assigned to investigate fraud in oil leases. That snake Perkins had me hit me on the head and dumped in the desert. He tried to kill me!"

"That makes two of us. And, you know, everything fits in. Heck, you weren't in Lost Creek more than a week before you'd become the local deputy. How did you get the scars on your back?" Fear shadowed Serenity's lovely face. "Hank?"

"No." After his swim, Matt sat in the shade of a bush, avoiding the intense midday sun while he toweled himself off. "I was shot by drug dealers while on patrol in Dallas. See, to get into the Rangers, an applicant has to have seven years of law enforcement experience. I was with the Dallas P.D. for a decade before I joined." He rubbed his hair with the towel.

Serenity stepped out of the pool, then reached into the pack for water. She opened the bottle and sipped before handing it to him. "Matt Gutierrez, Texas Ranger." She crowded into the same shady spot by his side.

"Yep. My family has lived in Texas for generations." He drank the deliciously cool water.

She cleared her throat. "Speaking of family..."

"Oh, yeah. Well, you already knew that I'm thirty-four years old and single." He grinned at her. "And free of romantic entanglements except for a certain redheaded sorceress."

She giggled.

"Who is actually a blonde." He stared pointedly at her.

She looked down. "Oops."

"Why the dye job, Serenity?"

She took in a deep breath, then slowly released it. "Hank, of course. The root of all evil."

"That scumbag." His poor, sweet darling. "Tell me everything."

She raised her eyebrows. "There's not much to tell."

"Did you know about Hank's scams?"

Serenity sighed again. "Not when we got married. At first, everything was fine. He went off to work each day just like every other husband. Then things started to disintegrate.''

''What happened?''

''He pressured me into quitting my job. He said that we didn't need the money. He didn't like me to associate with the neighbors. He called them lowlifes and said we didn't need them, that we'd be mingling with a much richer crowd when this big deal came through.''

Matt opened the food pack and took out a carton of strawberries. He handed her one. ''Isolating the victim is a classic behavior of a batterer.''

''Now, I know. Then, I didn't.'' She bit into the lush fruit.

''We don't have to talk about Hank if it upsets you.''

She chewed and swallowed. ''It's okay. If it weren't fine, I couldn't eat.'' She grimaced. ''I got real skinny after he started hitting me.''

''When was that?'' He nibbled on a berry. Serenity had sprinkled them with chocolate shavings.

''About six months into our marriage.''

''Why didn't you leave, honey?'' he asked around his mouthful.

''Hank knows a lot of El Paso judges and cops. The local family court judge is one of his poker buddies. I figured that my odds of getting a restraining order or police protection were slim to none. I had to wait until I could get away.''

''That's interesting. No wonder we had so much trouble getting search warrants,'' Matt mused out loud. ''He has the judges in his pocket. Hey, what about your family?''

She blew out her breath in a huff. "My daddy died when I was fifteen, and my mother—" She grimaced again. "No love lost there. She had me when she was in her forties. I don't think I was planned," Serenity said in a low voice. "She's old-fashioned, told me that I'd made my bed and I could lie in it."

"Lordy." He whistled through his front teeth. "That's cold. So you had no support."

"Nope. I'd met Hank shortly after I moved to El Paso after college. Everyone I knew in El Paso was Hank's friend. They thought he was the greatest guy in the world."

"How'd you escape?"

"I got lucky. On a ski vacation in the California Sierras, Hank and his brother left me alone with the car keys and a vehicle. I lit outta there and drove to Mexico after I went to a store and bought scissors and hair dye. Lori the long-haired blonde became Serenity with a red pixie cut."

"Good thinking."

A silence fell. Matt gazed at Serenity, who'd turned her face away. Something in the tense lines of her body grabbed his attention. "What is it, Serenity?"

"There's something I have to tell you." She faltered, then appeared to gather her strength. "He hit me in the belly real hard...more than once." Her eyes welled with tears. "And...and...it doesn't matter that we didn't use protection just now. I probably can't have kids."

Serenity looked at Matt. At age thirty-four, he could be a great father. He deserved more than she could give. "Do you still want me?"

Matt leaned closer and took her in his arms. "I

want *you,* not some imaginary baby I've never met.
Now, tell me what you did in Mexico.''

Serenity sighed with relief. She might be selfish,
but she didn't want to give him up. ''I stayed long
enough to establish residency and get a divorce. I
didn't want to do that in the United States. Hank
could mess with me, even in, say, Las Vegas, but I
knew his reach didn't extend into a foreign country.''

He hugged her tighter. ''And in the border towns,
it's easy to find outfits that'll forge new ID papers.''

''Yeah. And I rented a room from a really nice
family. Eventually, I told them everything. They were
wonderful about it.'' She fell silent for a moment,
remembering Eduardo and Stefano. The Perez males,
who'd adopted her as their own, had wanted to go to
El Paso and hunt Hank down.

''How'd you end up here?''

''The Perezes helped me. Believe it or not,
Mairen's true name is actually Marina Perez. She's a
cousin.''

''So that's why you didn't settle farther away from
El Paso.''

She nodded, still pleased by her cleverness. ''I bet
that Hank would never look for me so close. Plus, I
sold the Jeep in Baja, near Ensenada, to get cash and
throw him off the track.''

''That's about five hundred miles away. A lot of
cruise ships go through there, too.''

''Yep. Say, how did your unit find me?''

''I don't remember that.'' He shrugged. ''You
probably left a paper trail, honey. It's hard to disappear in this technological society.''

Serenity frowned. She'd been so careful. ''Maybe

it was Owen. When we…well, he asked me out, and I went once, and things didn't work out between us. I told him about Hank, and Owen was really angry.''

''Angry enough to try to do something about it?''

''Maybe.''

''I recall that we suspected Hank Perkins of committing widespread fraud, so he was investigated thoroughly.'' Matt shifted his weight. ''Someone tracked you down. I remember studying your file closely. I thought we ought to talk with you. No one else agreed.'' Lifting her chin, he looked into her eyes. ''I assumed you left because you knew that Hank was in pretty deep and you didn't want to be a part of it.''

His brown eyes looked questioning. Did he suspect her?

Anxiety returned, an icy shard of dread piercing her chest. Though no better than a criminal, she'd married a lawman. Though they hadn't wed for love, they'd just been intimate. Serenity never had casual sex, and surely lovemaking on his wedding day meant something to her husband.

So their new closeness implied commitment and obligation—the obligation of honesty.

Her stomach writhed. Should she tell Matt her secret?

Could she?

That night, Serenity headed outside for her usual evening meditation. Events had sped by too fast for her to absorb. She'd accustomed herself to the tranquility of Lost Creek and didn't like her routine hurried.

Matt's arrival had changed everything, but he'd

quickly adjusted to her lingering pace. Carson, who was expected soon, would never slow down; he didn't want to, couldn't see the necessity. He wanted to trap Hank, close the file, and move on.

The days since Matt had knocked at her door had been the most stressful in her life since she'd left Hank. Exciting—she wouldn't trade her Ranger for anything—but stressful.

At last, the thought of her ex-husband didn't make her shudder. When she'd told Matt her story, she'd been surprised at her calmness. In the past, she'd never been able to discuss any aspect of her first marriage without nausea. *Maybe I've changed.* She hoped that her growth was permanent, enabling her to go through with Carson's plan. The Rangers didn't need her to fall apart when she confronted Hank.

Matt had reacted matter-of-factly to her tale, which pleased her. She didn't want his pity. Rejection as damaged goods would have been even worse.

She'd discovered wonders and marvels she'd never imagined. Matt was a tender and generous lover. His skill quickly erased all the bad memories of her marriage bed with Hank Perkins, who'd been a clumsy, insensitive oaf.

She was glad she'd mentioned she probably couldn't have children. She didn't want to keep any secrets from Matt.

But she'd kept one last secret, hadn't she? Serenity heated with guilt. No doubt she'd trashed her karma so badly she'd be reborn a roach. She slumped into the chair he'd fixed. How could she tell Matt what she'd done?

* * *

Matt showered and, back in Serenity's room, prepared for bed. He wondered which of her many moods he'd encounter that night.

He couldn't blame her if she developed cold feet about their relationship. Though she'd given her heart and her hand in marriage, she'd opened up to the soulful stranger, not a lawman. Tomorrow, when they traveled to El Paso for the operation against Hank Perkins, she'd meet the real Matt Gutierrez, Texas Ranger.

He winced at much of what he remembered about his past. With despair, he realized that he couldn't think of anyone less compatible with Serenity Clare than Golden Boy Gutierrez. He hadn't thought of himself as a meat-eating, skirt-chasing jerk. But if he was, he'd never be the right man for her.

He'd desperately wanted to reclaim his past, but now he feared it. What if renewing his old life destroyed his fragile marriage?

Hardening his resolve, he decided he'd do whatever he must to keep her. If he had to eat tofu and drink organic carrot juice until his dying day to prove himself to her, he would.

He heard the shower switch on. Probably Serenity cleaning up for bed. He decided that he wouldn't push her. It had been a very long week for them both, full of too many revelations.

Matt sat on the bed, wondering which side she preferred. His mind shifted to Carson, Perkins, and the task that lay ahead. He'd meant what he'd told Serenity. She needed to stay alert and watchful. Maybe

the next day he'd teach her some self-defense tricks
so she wouldn't be entirely helpless.

Serenity entered, wrapped in one of her cushy
peach towels. She smelled like soap and wild grasses.

He wanted to take her in his arms and protect her
forever. "Which side?" he asked, patting the bed.

She hesitated before giving him a teasing grin. "I
usually take the middle." She opened the window.
The soft desert breeze flapped through the thin lace
curtains, cooling the room.

"That's not an option, unless you're gonna kick
me out to the sofa." Matt tried to make his eyes wide
and soulful.

"No, but I can't promise bedroom fireworks tonight." She tossed the towel over the half-open closet
door.

"Are ya mad, or sore?" He gazed at her breasts.
Were they still a little flushed from his loving? He'd
never forgive himself if he'd hurt her.

"No, just…uncertain." She took an oversize T-shirt
from a drawer and slipped it over her head. The shirt
reached her knees, covering her as effectively as a
darn overcoat.

"Well, me too." He opened his arms to her.
"Don't worry. My mom always said that things have
a way of working themselves out."

Serenity curled up in his embrace. "It must be nice
for you to have your memory back."

"It is. It's a big relief." He nuzzled her hair. "But
if it causes me to lose you, well…I'd rather have you."

"Really? Not have your family, friends and job,
just me?"

Matt nodded. A little bit of exaggeration wouldn't

hurt, especially since he figured he could have it all...if that was what he chose.

Shivering, she pulled out of the circle of his arms. "That's a lot of responsibility."

Matt couldn't help grinning. Any other woman would preen at the compliment. Trust Serenity to have a different, quirky take on the situation. "I'm sure you can handle it. I've been very happy here for the past ten days. Now—" He shrugged. "The future seems so unpredictable."

"Why? You have your life back."

"I don't know if I want that life anymore." He yawned. "Honey, I can't think about this right now. Too much has happened today."

"I know." Serenity pulled back the print bedspread and slipped between the sheets.

"The right side, huh?"

"I like to be close to the window."

He joined her, spooning her so they lay comfortably together on their sides, his front to her back.

Later, Serenity came to awareness, feeling Matt's hand on her breast.

"You awake, sweetheart?" His voice was low, soft, dangerously seductive.

"You know I am." She stretched against him, reaching one hand behind her to stroke his hip.

He jerked. "Careful. You might get more than you wish for."

"Who says I don't wish for it?"

"You said no bedroom fireworks." He caressed her breast.

She sucked in a trembling breath as the tender flesh tingled, the glow spreading throughout her body. She squinted at her clock: 5:00 a.m. "That was last night. It's a new day."

He pushed against her. "May I?"

Serenity faltered. She decided to trust her body's knowledge and Matt's tenderness. "Okay," she whispered.

Together they created a slow, subtle, erotic dance that took them to heaven and back. Bliss engulfed Serenity, with an unexpected but marvelous sense of completion. She lay sated.

After a few moments, she rolled over toward Matt, wanting to hold him. "Hey, love," she said. She'd never before felt so cherished.

"Hey to you, too, love." He kissed her on the mouth.

She hesitated. *It's now or never.* "I don't want any secrets between us," she whispered. She knew honesty was the best way, so why did she feel so scared?

"What's up?"

"I, um, there's something you need to know."

He shifted. The sheets rustled softly. "What is it?"

"I, uh, it's about Hank."

"Yeah?" His tone sounded more alert.

"I kinda helped him, I guess."

"You what?" His voice rose.

Oh, God. If honesty was the best policy, why did confession feel so painful? She couldn't bear this shame. "He, uh, used to throw these parties. For prospective investors." Her voice dropped; hard as she tried, she couldn't raise her voice above a whisper.

He sat up in bed.

"I was there. Like…arm candy. Or an advertisement. You know, like, buy into this oil well, get the girl, the cars, the house." Serenity could barely force the words out. "I know it was wrong."

Matt looked down at her, his face stark and set. "You're a criminal."

"No, no, no!" She jerked upright. "I didn't know it was fraud! Hank never told me anything!"

He jumped out of bed. "You deliberately kept this from me. Then I married you! Married a damn conspirator!"

"*What?* But I didn't know! How could I?"

"For God's sake, Serenity! Why didn't you tell me this before?" He paced back and forth.

"I'm telling you the truth now. Don't I get some credit for that?" She hated to beg, but she was close.

"What are you looking for, extra credit toward an 'A'? Life isn't a classroom." He grabbed his jeans. "I'm leaving."

She sat up in bed, her eyes streaming. He looked away. If he saw her tears, he'd bend, and then he'd break.

"Why? What was I supposed to do? Argue with Hank and get beat up some more?"

Matt tugged on his jeans with jerky fingers. "Serenity, I can't trust you. How can we stay married if there's no trust?"

"Of course you can trust me! I love you!"

He huffed. "Is that right?"

"Don't you believe me?" Her voice cracked.

"Why should I?" Someone had betrayed him to Perkins. Matt was sure someone in his unit, someone he trusted, had blown his cover. And now, this! He would have cheerfully given his life for Serenity's, believing she was the one person in the world he could love and trust unconditionally.

But that was before her confession. She'd helped to defraud countless innocent victims. And she'd tricked him, tricked him into a marriage he couldn't abide.

He pulled on his boots, ready to leave. "We'll divorce after the operation's over."

Chapter Ten

As soon as she stopped crying, Serenity went to the bathroom to wash away the sticky traces of their love-making. More tears poured down her cheeks, mingling with the water from the shower.

She'd badly mistaken Matt. Deluding herself, she'd believed he'd started to care for her, even love her. She thought she could trust his devotion. She now knew what she'd done was wrong, but she hoped he would forgive her. Why not? Why couldn't he understand?

At the time, she hadn't known that there weren't oil wells. She'd have done anything to avoid another beating.

She remembered all Matt's loving words. *We have all the time in the world... I'm not goin' anywhere...*

Ha. At the first stumbling block, he'd hit the road, never to look back. He was probably halfway to El Paso by now.

I'm here for you. I'm yours. The cruelest words of all. And she'd believed him. "Fool," she muttered.

She stepped out of the shower and grabbed a fresh towel. After dressing, she sat on her rug in front of the burgeoning day.

But neither the pale dawn nor the first flash of daylight brought her the peace she sought.

Her mind still ran around the same endless, useless track. Matt was a cop. Hadn't he ever worked with battered women? Didn't he know *anything?*

Did she need someone so rigid, so unforgiving? Maybe she was better off without him.

The thought tore her in two. She dropped her head into her lap and choked back the keening wail that burst from the very heart of her. Rocking back and forth, she slapped a hand over her mouth to stop the scream before it left her lips.

Nothing had changed. She pounded a fist into the floor with frustration. She was still the same pathetic emotional cripple that Hank had made.

She wouldn't let Hank win. She couldn't.

Serenity crashed out of the house, desperate for solace.

After walking in the desert for hours, Matt returned to find Serenity gone. Carson had arrived, so together they searched the town. The sun was high when they walked into Great Bear's Book Nook.

"Get out," Mairen said.

"We need to talk to Serenity." If necessary, Matt would get on his knees and plead. His heart had been ripped apart by Serenity's deception, but he was determined to resurrect something from the shambles. He'd take down Perkins, whatever the cost.

Great Bear loomed, filling the apartment doorway. "Brother, come back another day. She can't help you now. She has to help herself."

"Look, big fella. We'll come back with a warrant if we have to." Carson's jaw thrust forward, a belligerent signal.

Great Bear's dark eyebrows lifted. "I'll be sure to tell Serenity. By the time you return, she'll be long gone."

Matt hesitated. He needed Serenity's cooperation.

"The desert is a very large place." Mairen gestured. "These hills are pocked with caves. Perfect for a vision quest, which Serenity badly needs." She paused, eyeing Matt. "Mexico is but a stone's throw away. We understand you need her help."

Matt tried not to grind his teeth.

"We agree with your goals," Great Bear rumbled. "I would personally like to tear her ex-husband apart. We will not stand in your way, but we will protect our friend. We will not allow her to be abused in any way. Otherwise, we are no better than *him*."

Matt knew Great Bear referred to Perkins.

"Serenity's a fighter. Give her a day or two. She'll be ready." Mairen closed the door in Matt's face.

Three days later Matt awakened. Scenting coffee, he went into the living room to see Serenity quietly meditating on her mat as though nothing had happened. Dawn broke; she rose and exercised, then drank coffee and ate breakfast.

But a great deal had changed. Wariness shuttered

her gaze. She didn't look him in the eyes. She didn't smile.

She'd bleached her hair blond, and Matt had the uncomfortable feeling that Serenity Clare had disappeared, replaced by Hank Perkins's battered wife, Lori.

Guilt clawed at him. Had he caused her to backslide?

But she couldn't be trusted.

He couldn't love her. He didn't dare.

Matt decided he'd just have to tough it out until he got out of the habit of caring about her. That's all this need was: a habit, born of his misconceptions and his amnesia. When he returned to his home in Midland, he'd be back to normal in no time at all. Then he'd file for divorce and forget about all of it.

The rented gray sedan screamed ''cop'' but Serenity got in anyway. At this point she just wanted the whole mess over as soon as possible so she could return to her life. Matt sat in the front passenger seat while Serenity occupied the back. Neither spoke much. Carson, who drove, mailed the letter at an El Paso post office before delivering her to a safe house in a middle-class section of the city.

The rambling two-story comfortably housed her and several revolving sets of bodyguards. Every morning and afternoon, she saw a different pair of faces. She hated that. She had structured her life to avoid the unexpected. She disliked change.

She didn't see Matt, for which she was grateful. Maybe he'd been reassigned, as Carson had threatened. Good. Matt had caused her a lot of pain. As hard as she tried, she couldn't become accustomed to the notion that she'd never see him again. Life without Matt had become a barren wasteland.

But as much as it hurt, she had no choice. She'd divorce him, then concentrate on getting over their short, disastrous romance. Hank had taught her she could survive anything.

But would she ever find happiness?

By Tuesday afternoon, Serenity had become so bored with the house that she wanted to take a jackhammer to the walls and escape. Her guards refused to let her leave, citing safety.

Annoyed, Serenity put on a dress, sandals, and a hat. While her guards were distracted by their shift change, she went to the front door and opened it. A male presence loomed on the step, hand upraised.

She shrank back, lifting her arm to ward off a punch. Then she realized that it was Matt, not Hank, who reached for the door knocker.

She shoved on his rock-solid chest, pushing him aside, and headed off down the El Paso street. She didn't know where she was going and, at that moment, she didn't much care.

The searing weather could blister the hooves off a horse. Serenity jammed her hat further down onto her forehead and sprinted down the sidewalk, ignoring Matt's call.

"Where're ya goin'? Did Carson say you could leave? Wait!"

She heard his heavy footfalls behind her. She hadn't looked, but it sounded as though he had on those boots again. Not very sensible.

Her own soft sandals didn't impede her flight, but he quickly caught up to her and grabbed her arm.

Turning, she yanked free. Something in her expression forced him back. *Smart move, Matt.* She hadn't learned how to control this unaccustomed anger, an anger that clenched her fists, straightened her back, made her want to hurt and hit and kill. She didn't know from where the boiling, fierce rage had come. Hank? Carson? Matt?

All of them.

"What do you want?"

He stepped back. "You don't have to snarl at me."

"I can do whatever I want." She pivoted and continued down the street, jaw tight with fury.

"You don't even know where you're going!"

"How do you know?" she asked, without slowing. "I used to live in El Paso. Don't insult me."

His boot heels clattered on the pavement as he hurried to keep up with her. "Serenity, you can't go haring off. The deal's supposed to go down tomorrow night. Any slip-up could destroy months of planning."

"The operation seems pretty off-the-cuff to me." She flung the words over her shoulder.

"This phase, yeah, but we've been investigating your husband for a year or two."

"My *ex*-husband, please. You're my husband, remember?"

"I've never seen you act this way."

"You don't know me."

"I know everything I need to know about you."

She gritted her teeth. "Yes, you do, don't you?" He knew every inch of her body, inside and out. She wanted to slap him for that zinger, but she'd have to stop to whack him one. Besides, violence was unenlightened.

"If this is about our fight, take it out on me. Don't risk the operation!"

"Don't tell me what to do. I'm tired of being treated like a prisoner. You're as bad as Hank!"

"Don't say that to me, ever!" He seized her arm again, jerking her around to face him. He tore the hat off her head. Without its protective cover, he could see her cheeks were blotched and streaked with tears.

"How dare you touch me!" She ripped her arm out of his grasp, then turned to escape again.

Matt couldn't bear to let her go, despite what she'd done. These past few days without her had taught him that he had to have her in his life. He loved her, dammit. Why had he fallen for her? His weakness was wrong. Shouldn't love and trust go hand in hand?

He could forgive her, but didn't know how to win her back. He'd known of her deep insecurities, but had messed up big time when he'd let his temper speak for him.

Since their fight, he and Serenity hadn't exchanged a private word. Carson had run him ragged setting up the site where, hopefully, they'd trap Hank Perkins. Matt had also phoned his family, who'd been delighted and relieved to hear from him.

The more he learned and remembered about himself, the more he realized that the nickname "Golden Boy" fitted him to a "T". He'd been a fortunate man, but now it appeared as though his luck had run out.

The woman he loved couldn't be trusted. Did he truly want her back? Right now, it appeared as though he didn't have a choice. The situation had a certain irony. In his desk, he'd found a little black book full of women's names and numbers, but the only number he wanted had bleached hair and a nasty temper hidden beneath her tranquil, New-Age facade.

Now that same bleached blonde stomped on his foot, squirmed free of his grasp, and zipped down the street.

Matt followed, forcing his thoughts onto their normal, security-oriented paths. He looked around, realizing that the two of them stuck out like a ballerina on a baseball team. In this brutal weather, few pedestrians walked the avenue.

Serenity started to cross the street when a souped-up, lowered Chevy roared around the corner and headed straight for them.

Fear grabbed his gut. Swearing, Matt hauled her out of the Chevy's way and into his arms. Staggering over the sidewalk, they collapsed in a tangled heap on a nearby lawn.

Her hair, smelling of wild grass and herbal shampoo, tickled his nose. With the danger over, her slight, small body pressed against his made his libido stand up and cheer.

She jerked away from him as though someone had laid a whip on her back.

"That's flattering," he muttered.

She rubbed ineffectively at grass stains on her yellow summer dress, glaring at him before she stood.

He grabbed her ankle. "Don't even think about leaving."

"Why am I a prisoner? By what right do you hold me?"

"Now, don't get all legalistic on me, Serenity. Do you want to give Perkins the chance to take you out before the sting goes down?"

"El Paso's a big town. He doesn't know I'm here."

"Maybe. Maybe not. Did you recognize anyone driving the Chevy?" He stood, watching her with wariness. He didn't trust her. She could make a break for freedom anytime.

"No. They were teenagers. Hank never employed kids. Said they were unreliable."

"I'm still worried about the possibility of a leak."

"If there's a leak, then Hank knows where I am."

"But he can't take you out at the house. The leak would become obvious. If someone in the unit has turned, you can bet he doesn't want anyone to know."

An uncertain expression crossed Serenity's face. "One of the people guarding me could be...could be..."

"That's right. A traitor, someone on your ex-husband's payroll."

"But why?" she whispered. "Don't they know how perfectly evil he is?" A quiver shook her slender frame.

She looked so frail and alone. Matt ached to hold her tight, to soothe her fears with his body. He bit his tongue and made himself pull back, but boy, it was tough. He loved her despite what she'd done.

Instead, he shrugged. "Guess some people always want more. I'm happy with my salary, but maybe others aren't."

Turning, she slowly walked back to the house, her shoulders slumped in an attitude of resignation.

Before she went in, he glanced at his watch and said, "They've had you cooped up here for days, right? Come with me. There's some people I want you to meet." Matt led her to the rental car he used while in El Paso and opened the passenger door for her.

Serenity got in, but without saying a word. Her face remained closed. She turned her head to look out the window as he drove, and he wondered what she could be thinking.

As they pulled up to a fast-food joint, complete with golden arches and a play place, Serenity winced. "Matt, you know I can't eat the food here."

He exited the car and opened her door. "So you're a vegetarian. You can have fries or ice cream. Besides, we're not here for the food. It's the company."

"Another cop?" Serenity asked, cranky. She'd met more than enough cops in the past three days.

"Heck, no. Remember those thong panties? Well, you're gonna meet the person who gave them to me." Matt gave her a slightly crooked grin. "Another mystery solved."

She rolled her eyes but allowed him to take her arm. She couldn't stop her heart from softening at the courtly, courteous gesture. He opened the door to the restaurant and she walked in.

Since it was midafternoon, only a few customers dotted the room. She went to the counter to scrutinize the menu, sure there'd be nothing she'd want to eat.

But Matt didn't follow her. Serenity turned to see a tall, lovely brunette dressed in jeans leave a table to fling her arms around him. Serenity's heart hardened anew, then solidified into granite when a little girl hugged Matt's legs. After he picked her up into his arms, Serenity could see that the doe-eyed child bore an unmistakable resemblance to him.

The bottom dropped out of Serenity's stomach. "And he has the nerve to think *I'm* dishonest," she muttered. He'd concealed his lover and child! Their romance was truly hopeless.

"Hey, Serenity." Matt beckoned her over.

With feet made of the heaviest lead, Serenity advanced. Swallowing against the giant lump in her throat, she vowed she wouldn't cry. *I can survive this. I can survive anything!*

"Marianne, this is Serenity Clare, the woman who saved my life."

Marianne gazed at Serenity with enormous, hazel eyes that filled with tears. She grasped Serenity's hands. "Thank you," she murmured. "You have no idea how we suffered when he was missing. I thought our mom and dad would go out of their minds."

"Mom and Dad?" Serenity's mind went blank.

"Our parents. Serenity, Marianne is my younger sister. This is Rachel, my niece."

"Oh!" A weight the size of Lubbock lifted from Serenity's heart. He hadn't lied. "I, uh, hi."

"Sit down and get to know each other. I'll order some food." Matt left Serenity alone with Marianne. Rachel still rode in his arms.

Matt's sister withdrew a tissue from her purse and dabbed at her eyes, smiling mistily at Serenity. An awkward silence fell.

"We've always been close." Marianne pushed her hair out of her face. Loosened from her mane, a bobby pin tumbled down her white T-shirt to her lap.

She groped for it. "Oh, Matt and Raymond used to give me a hard time when we were young, but I always looked up to my big brothers."

Serenity didn't know why she was curious. With no interest in Matt anymore, she told herself that she was just going to make polite conversation. "Matt has an older brother?"

"Yes, Matt is the middle child. Ray got the ranch, and Matt became a cop. He shocked all of us." Marianne stuck the bobby pin back into her hair.

"Matt can be...startling." Serenity didn't want to talk about him. "What do you do?"

"I also live in Midland. My husband's a contractor and I do bookkeeping. I've worked out of my home since I had Rachel."

"Oh."

"We came in for a few hours to see Matt. I wanted to see for myself that he's all right." She smiled at Serenity.

Matt returned with the food—burgers, fries, ice cream, and drinks piled onto a tray. Behind him, Rachel carried napkins and forks. He distributed the food, giving Serenity a large order of fries and ice cream.

"This is full of fat and salt." Serenity picked up a French fry and glared at it.

"C'mon, Serenity, one meal of fried food won't hurt you. It's not animal fat."

"True." She licked the salt from the fry.

"Wish I were that fry," he whispered in her ear.

She blushed, completely tongue-tied. If he kept flirting with her, her resolve would crumble like a sandcastle at high tide.

Matt sat across the table from her beside Marianne and chowed down on a double hamburger with cheese. Serenity tried to not stare in disgust. His perfect table manners didn't bother her, but the meal confirmed that he was indeed a meat-and-potatoes man. What were a burger and fries but meat and potatoes? Their differences made her painfully aware yet again of the rift between them, a chasm wide as the desert.

She nibbled a fry and met his eyes. He winked at her. His denim-clad leg rubbed against her bare calf. A sudden, unwelcome warmth curled through her body, heating her all the way up to her cheeks. She didn't understand why he flirted with her. The situation had become worse and worse.

Rachel ate about two bites before she appeared to lose interest in the food. Leaving her chair, she tugged on Matt's sleeve. "Unka Matt, take me to the play place. I wanna climb up the ladder and go down the slide."

"Sure, honey. I'll help you up the ladder." He picked up the rest of his sandwich. With Rachel hauling his free hand, he accompanied her through the glass door that led to the kids' play area.

"Matt has told me so much about you." Marianne leaned across the table, her attitude one of a woman who wanted to gossip and trade secrets.

Serenity didn't want this warm, fuzzy feeling that had invaded her chest. But she couldn't help it. She liked Marianne's openness and obvious loving nature. However, she didn't want to care about either Marianne or Matt.

But it was too late. Marianne said, "I've never seen

him so crazy about a woman since he brought home Katie Rosen after the senior prom.''

Serenity's heart stuttered. ''Crazy about a woman?''

''Oh, yeah. It's all over him. Even before he disappeared, he obsessed over your picture.''

''Me?'' Serenity suppressed the warm pleasure that pervaded each cell. But Matt had made her feel special since the moment they'd met. That she'd been the only one he'd remembered from his past was enormously flattering.

''Yeah, you. So where are you and Matt gonna live? He only has a little apartment.''

Serenity didn't know what to say. Clearly, Marianne didn't know the details of their marriage. Serenity didn't want to upset this openhearted, kind woman, but couldn't be dishonest, either. ''We've never discussed the future.''

''He will. He's in love, all right.''

Her heart leapt. Could Marianne be right? Could Matt love her despite everything? Serenity hesitated. How much should she confide in Matt's sister? She decided to take the plunge. ''Well, we've had some problems. I, uh, didn't tell him about some stuff when we met. Important stuff. When I finally told him, he flew off the handle.''

''Matt has a temper, Serenity. I won't hide that from you.'' Marianne sighed. ''We all do. But he's really not a mean guy.''

''Well, that's a relief.'' Matt's quick temper had reminded Serenity of Hank, who also had a tendency to explode. Difference was, Matt walked. Hank had stayed around to hit her.

"He never holds on to grudges," Marianne said. "He's probably over it by now."

"No, he's not. He said he can't trust me."

Marianne frowned. "Trust is crucial. Gotta have it."

"Yeah. Love without trust is no good."

Marianne's eyes narrowed. Except for the lack of crow's feet, her expression was remarkably similar to Matt's. "Girl, you gotta hold out for what you want."

Matt took Serenity back to the safe house after a satisfying visit with his sister and niece. He liked the bond he'd seen growing between the two women while Rachel played. Maybe there was hope for their marriage.

He pulled into the driveway. The only thing that bothered him about the afternoon was the food. He used to love burgers, but today the meal had tasted so salty. It sat heavy in his belly, unlike the light, healthy dinners he'd eaten in Lost Creek.

As they passed the front door, Matt picked up the duffel bag he'd dropped when Serenity had pushed him aside in her headlong rush to escape. Following her up the stairs, he deposited the bag on the queen-size bed in her room.

"What are you doing?" she asked.

"Unpacking." He gave her a lazy smile, hoping it would have the same effect it'd had on her before they'd fought.

"Why?"

Matt tested the bed with a palm. His heart tripped and thudded like a badly tuned engine. What if she said no? "That should be obvious."

She raised a brow. "What's obvious is that you're deluded." Serenity picked up the bag and left the room with it, walking down the hall.

He trailed. "It's for your own protection."

She entered the next bedroom. "Yeah, sure." With a thump, she dumped his bag on the polished wood floor. "We've made a lot of mistakes, and I'm not gonna make things worse by sleeping with you again."

"I don't see making love as a mistake."

"Don't you? Then what were you thinking the other morning, when you walked out?" She stared into his eyes, fearless, with an implacable look in her green gaze.

He hesitated. "So we had a little fight. What's the big deal? I love you, Serenity, and I know you love me...unless you were lying."

Matt reached for Serenity's hands, but she flinched away. "I'm not a liar or a crook, no matter what you think."

He sat on the bed, wishing she'd join him. "What we think doesn't matter as much as what we feel for each other."

Serenity's hands fluttered indecisively. Then her jaw firmed. "Both matter. You made your position very clear. Tell me something. Do you trust me?"

He couldn't look into those glittering, angry eyes.

"That's all the answer I need." Her shoulders rose and squared. "Matt, I deserve it all. Love *and* trust. If you can't understand and forgive what I did, then...then that's it. It's over."

Chapter Eleven

Serenity left the room, closing the door on Matt's blank gaze, his open, shocked mouth. Leaning against the wall, she gasped, then sucked in one long, cleansing breath. It should have calmed her, but instead, a searing agony rose from her soul, as if she'd cut off a vital part of herself.

Wobbly legs unable to hold her upright, she slid down the wall, curling into a tiny ball on the floor. Tears drenched her eyes, slipped down her cheeks. Though Matt had finally admitted he loved her, love was nothing without trust. She knew she'd done the right thing. So why did she feel so shattered, so destroyed?

She tried to pull energy from the core of her being, but she found...nothing. Instead, she shuddered with the pain knifing her heart. Could she survive without Matt's love?

Serenity wondered if, one day, she'd be able to

smile at the irony. She'd wanted to complete her healing, to feel whole again as a woman. She hadn't anticipated that falling in love would include this devastation.

Somehow, she'd find her strength, she promised herself. There'd be ups and downs, but as heaven was her witness, she'd make it through.

But would she ever be happy?

The next morning Matt hesitated in front of Serenity's closed door. He'd adopted the habit of meditating before dawn. He guessed she continued her spiritual practice, but where?

His reluctance to intrude upon her privacy stopped him from knocking, especially after their fight the previous afternoon. She'd actually tossed him out of her room. Serenity was the only woman who'd ever denied him her bed. Her protective walls had been re-erected and he was shut away, on the other side.

He fumbled his way downstairs in the early morning darkness.

Today, Wednesday, the sting would go down. In less than eighteen hours, Hank Perkins would occupy a jail cell. Serenity would finally be free of the fear that haunted her.

And Matt would have to figure out a way to let her go. She'd been as clear as one of her crystals. She demanded love and trust, despite what she'd done. He loved her, but trust?

No. Maybe he was wrong, but he couldn't.

The bottom of the stairs opened onto the entry hall. From the left, he could smell the beckoning aroma of coffee brewing in the kitchen. On the right, a soft golden glow came from the corner of the living room. It illuminated Serenity's still, elfin face as she meditated upon a candle flame. Matt could see light flashing on the facets of the crystals she'd arranged around her.

It was stupid to think that these objects could bring the inner peace she sought. But she'd been happy before he came, hadn't she?

He sat beside her on the rug. Not a flicker of an eyelid betrayed any awareness of his presence. When the eastern sun pierced the morning, she stood, stretched, and completed her yoga. She moved with power and assurance.

"Good morning." His calm voice didn't reveal his jangled nerves. Or so he hoped.

Serenity nodded before blowing out the candle. Fragrant smoke trailed from the burned-out wick. She walked into the kitchen, where the coffeemaker dripped and steamed. She poured for herself, then drank her brew, but didn't give him anything.

Serving himself, he sniffed his coffee for the aroma of mysterious herbs. "I thought we'd work on some self-defense techniques while we're warmed up."

She eyed him coldly. "Can't someone else take care of this?"

These were the first words she'd spoken all morning. Though she normally wasn't rude, she hadn't greeted him. *So maybe there's hope,* he thought. If she were indifferent, why the hostility?

"Serenity, please. I have a job and so do you. Let's try to make this as pleasant as possible, shall we?"

She shrugged. "Where and when?"

"Now. We can clear a pretty big space in the living room."

"In this?" She swished the long dashiki flowing around her ankles.

"What are you wearing tonight?"

"I don't know. Something that covers the equipment, I suppose."

He sipped his coffee. "We've decided not to wire you, but the room itself."

"Won't that take time to set up?"

"That's what we've been doing. The suite we rented has two bedrooms and a sitting room. That's where you'll meet Perkins. We've already planted cameras and mikes, and put the reception equipment in one of the bedrooms."

"What if he checks that room?" She topped off her mug.

"The doors will be locked from the inside, and if he asks, you'll tell him that you locked them so he couldn't intrude on your privacy."

Serenity nodded, appearing mollified. "That's something I'd do and say."

He smiled at her. "I know."

"Will there be people there in case he gets...aggressive?" Her hand shook, very slightly.

"You betcha." Matt hoped he sounded comforting and capable. "Yours truly, among others. Now, let's begin." He gestured toward the door.

"We'll wake everyone else up."

He hadn't noticed her stubbornness before. Maybe he was losing his infatuation for her. *Yeah, sure.* "So what? They're working, not sleeping in. Come on. We have a lot to do today."

Clutching her coffee mug, Serenity unwillingly followed Matt back into the living room. Self-defense techniques. She'd renounced violence. What was she doing?

Until he turned and grabbed her by the arms, she hadn't realized that these exercises would entail physical contact with Matt.

His touch zapped her, electric and powerful. She hated to discover he still could affect her as no other man ever had.

Raising her arms and twisting, she ripped out of his hold without really thinking about it. The coffee slopped. She brought the mug around fast, missing his head only because he ducked.

"Good!" Matt's praise startled her. "Good, but you can make it better. After you break the hold, turn to the side and jab me with your elbow, really hard."

"You *want* me to hurt you?" She put the mug on a table, then plucked tissues from a nearby holder to dry her fingers.

"Yeah. I'll live, and you need the practice. When you elbow me, use your body weight. If you do it hard enough, you can crack or break an assailant's ribs."

Serenity dropped the tissues and stepped back, shaking her head. "I don't want to learn how to hurt people."

He looked her in the eyes. She couldn't read anything there except an impartial concern. She told herself that was all she needed from Golden Boy Gutierrez.

"You're facing your ex-husband tonight, in a room, alone."

Her body twitched involuntarily.

"Don't you want to have a few moves under your belt?"

"But...but you'll be close by." She hated the pitiful whine in her voice.

"Yeah, but I bet you'll feel better if I teach you a few tricks. You don't have to use them, you know."

"That's true." But she didn't want to be corrupted by violence, believing that she'd be as low as Hank if she resorted to his methods.

"Did you know that the Asian martial arts were invented by Buddhist monks?"

"Really?"

Matt nodded. "The monks of the Shaolin monastery created kung fu."

"You're kidding. Like on the TV show?"

"No lie. They'd all taken vows of nonviolence. So how could it be wrong just to know the moves?"

"I guess it's not."

Matt grasped her by the throat, wrapping two big hands around her neck.

"Hey!" she squeaked. Serenity tried to bend back one of his fingers.

"Break the hold," he said. "Or hit me, kick me, anything you can think of."

She grabbed his shirt and tugged him closer before she raised a knee into his crotch. He jerked away just before she nailed him, releasing his grip on her neck.

Rubbing her throat, she glared. "You don't have to be quite so realistic."

"Hank will be," he said, without a trace of apology in his tone. "Let's try some ground fighting."

Serenity sensed only a slight kick at her ankle before she tumbled ignominiously to the carpet, landing with a thud. Matt dropped on top of her, resting most of his weight on his elbows.

He gave her his heart-stopping smile, the one that could induce cardiac arrest at twenty paces. Serenity pressed her lips together, ready to grace him with a piece of her mind. Then he shifted his weight, rubbing her hips with his.

She glowered at him, hoping she looked as mean as she wanted to feel.

What she actually felt couldn't be described in anything but an X-rated movie. Every nerve ending sparked and hummed with life, pleasure radiating right out to her fingertips.

He brought his face, his magic lips, closer. His mouth grazed hers, feathering with exquisite expertise. "Now I've got you right where I want you. What are you gonna do about it?"

Who says I want to do anything? Desire and fury warred in her heart. She knew she shouldn't accept second-best. She had to hold out for what she wanted—no, what she *needed*—in her marriage.

But Matt was so close, so alluring and available. The aromas of coffee and man filled her nostrils. Before he'd come to her door, she'd been starved for the sensual contact that made her feel like a woman. He'd awakened the desires Hank had beaten out of her. She had a right to her passions, she argued to herself.

He bent his head again. The press of his hard mouth on hers lit carnal fires all over her body. A whimper sneaked out of her lips.

Loathing that show of weakness, she yanked away.

She couldn't, wouldn't, take anything less than what she knew she deserved.

She bucked her hips, hard, while she shoved on his shoulders, throwing him off.

Matt landed on his rump, looking bewildered. "Hey!"

"You asked me what I was gonna do about you. I just did something." Serenity scrambled to her feet. "Any questions?"

"No. Nice job. Have you ever studied wrestling or judo?"

"Uh, no. Am I supposed to?"

"Wouldn't hurt, but you just employed basic wrestling principles to throw me." He stood.

"How'd you get me down?"

"That's called a sweep. You were close enough to me so that I could just hook a foot around your ankle." He demonstrated. "The lesson is...don't get close to Hank. Keep him at least one of his arm's lengths away."

"No problem. Frankly, I'd rather not be in the same room!"

Matt's face turned serious. "I still have my doubts about this operation." His voice lowered. "I don't want to use you as bait, but Carson's right. It seems to be the only way we'll trap Perkins within a reasonable time. After he discovered me—or my presence was leaked—you can be sure that he's been doubly on his guard. It could take years to nail him again."

Serenity nodded. "I want him to go away for a long, long time. Then I can go home and forget about the last five years of my life."

He fixed her with a soulful gaze. "All of it?"

She looked into his big brown eyes, telling herself she didn't care if he'd get hurt. Heck, he'd ripped her heart right out of her chest.

"Yes," she said. "All of it."

Though a bundle of nerves, Serenity meditated and napped that afternoon. She wanted to be fresh for the night's events.

After showering, she surveyed her meager wardrobe. She hadn't worried about clothes for months, but now she couldn't decide what to wear. Besides, what constituted proper civilian attire for a law enforcement operation? What did one wear to a successful blackmailing?

She hadn't brought much from Lost Creek, so her choices were limited. Her yellow summer dress had grass stains. The striped dashiki seemed too lively for the occasion, which called for something more on the order of a slinky black outfit, à la Ida Lupino in *The Maltese Falcon*.

"I'm just fresh out of film noir slink," she muttered. She'd have to settle for a T-shirt and jeans. Remembering one of Great Bear's maxims—walk softly and wear a loud shirt—she picked a vivid, rainbow-hued number. The tie-dyed shirt was sure to raise Hank's blood to a nice simmer. He'd always wanted her to dress the part of a demure, upper-class matron.

She giggled as she skipped down the stairs at five o'clock. Matt looked at her as though she were certifiable. Well, maybe she was.

In the car, he explained, "We have the cooperation of hotel management. The computer system will reflect that one Lori Waddell checked in at 6:00 p.m. and left directions that Hank Perkins was to pick up a room key and proceed to the suite.''

Serenity squirmed. ''I don't want him walking in unexpectedly.''

''He won't. The front desk will phone the room when he picks up the key.''

She nodded, taking a deep breath. As the minutes crawled by, her chest became tighter and tighter. Her innards knotted. Her throat dried.

By confronting Hank, she was taking the greatest personal risk of her life. Facing Hank while controlling her terror meant that she'd banished all the demons he'd planted in her soul.

Serenity refused to consider the possibility of failure. Everything she'd done—the meditation, the yoga, the pure diet, the vision quests—had led to this night.

She glanced at Matt, who was driving the same dull little rental car. While he focused on the road, she could examine his chiseled profile without shame or embarrassment.

Even the lovemaking with Matt had helped. She'd reclaimed a part of herself that she'd thought lost forever. Determined to resist the distraction Matt posed, she couldn't ponder the hope that their marriage had meant more.

Despite everything that had happened between them, she could depend upon him to protect her physical safety. She'd look out for her own spiritual progress and emotional wholeness.

Her heart...well, that was another issue entirely. When Matt left her and returned to his old life, he'd take her love, whether he wanted it or not.

His lack of trust rankled, but she'd put that aside for this operation. Too bad it would separate them forever. She had imagined a forever with Matt. She bit one fingertip and forced those useless dreams out of her head.

Matt passed the wide, well-lit driveway of the Grand Hyatt, turning instead into a dark alley at the side of the hotel.

"What are we doing here?" Serenity asked.

"In case he's watching the front entrance, we're going to slip in the back. We don't want him to recognize me or to snatch you before you're in the suite." He parked the car.

After she got out, he hustled her through a side door and up a back elevator to the penthouse.

Serenity looked around the sitting room, which boasted a cream-and-gold brocade couch, a coffee table, and a small dinette in one corner. A French country style cherrywood desk held a phone, a printer, and a fax. The doors on either side of the room concealed the bedrooms and the bathroom, she supposed.

She'd stayed in many such places in her past life as Lori Perkins. Hank always treated himself to the best hotels, Dom Pérignon, and caviar. He'd boast to his friends about his high-living ways.

Doubts crept in. Serenity Clare had no place here. She took a deep breath, reclaiming her determination.

"Show me the location of the cameras and bugs," she said to Matt.

He grinned. "There isn't a spot in this room that isn't wired. But do your business with Perkins at the desk. There's mikes in the drawer—keep it open a little—and three cameras trained on the area. We'll get a nice view of your ex-hubby giving you lots of money to conceal his crimes.''

Tightening her jaw, she sat at the desk. She wanted to familiarize herself with the feel of the padded chair under her bottom. The carved cherrywood backrest jabbed into her spine.

''Who else is here?'' she asked.

''Let's find out.'' Matt went to the left-hand door and knocked.

It swung open to reveal a luxurious bedroom festooned with sound boards, video monitors, and other machinery Serenity didn't recognize.

''Dude.'' A skinny fellow with long blond hair disentangled himself from a wealth of thick black cables to approach Matt.

''Jeff.'' Matt greeted the technician by pounding him on the back.

The whack would have sent Serenity sprawling. *Must be a guy thing.*

''Serenity, this is Jeff Townsend, one of our best techies. We spent the last few days in here putting this all together.''

''Thanks, Jeff.''

Jeff stared at the floor. A blond forelock covered his eyes. He seemed unable to speak.

''Jeff here doesn't talk much. He prefers to express himself through his work.''

Jeff peered at Serenity through his hair. A computer geek. She recognized the type. She smiled at him, which sent his gaze back to the floor.

She cleared her throat. ''Uh, are the two of you the only ones who'll be here?''

''No.'' Matt glanced at his watch. ''It's barely six

now. Everyone else will be trickling in after seven. By eight-thirty we'll have a small battalion here ready to take on Hank Perkins." He rubbed his palms together, looking expectant.

"We've got a lot of time, then." Serenity reached for the phone and called room service.

"I'm not sure we're allowed to do that," a high, anxious voice said.

Serenity smiled. "Jeff, what would you like to eat for dinner?"

"Uh, pizza and Coke. But Carson'll have a cow."

"The least the state of Texas can do for me is to pay for my dinner and that of my...friends." "Friends" might not be the right word, but it would do well enough. Serenity ordered vegetarian pizza for the three of them.

She had a mouth full of pesto pizza with zucchini and sun-dried tomatoes when someone pounded on the door.

"Open up, Lori, I know you're in there!"

She glanced at Matt. "I think Hank's arrived," she said.

Chapter Twelve

Matt's mouth went dry. Lordy. *He's more than an hour early!* He choked down the bite of pizza in his mouth. He gulped Coke to help the food on its way as he skedaddled to the back bedroom on Jeff's heels.

"How the hell did this happen?" he snarled, teeth gritted.

"I don't know." Jeff flicked switches to turn on monitors and speakers.

"Hurry up!" Perkins sounded drunk and dangerous.

Matt returned to Serenity's side to give her a quick, hard kiss. Squeezing her slender shoulders, he was struck anew by her frailty. "I don't know why we're going through with this. He's a killer!" he muttered. "He beat you up regularly in the past—"

She patted his cheek, the touch of her fingers cool and reassuring. "Don't worry," she murmured.

"I'll never forgive myself if you get hurt."

"I can handle him. Now scoot!" She pushed him toward the bedroom.

"Move it, Lori!"

"I don't use that name anymore." Now in the bedroom, Matt could hear Serenity's cool, calm voice through the speakers. Concern for her warred with pride. Even though they'd fought, he admired the way she faced Hank, surely her greatest fear.

"What am I supposed to call you?" Perkins's growl was low, menacing.

Jeff clicked on another monitor, the one receiving the signal from the video camera in the hall. Matt could see the top of Perkins's head. His thinning blond hair exposed pink scalp.

Serenity tipped her head to one side, appearing to consider the question. "You can call me...ma'am."

Matt nearly groaned out loud. She was baiting him. Deliberately. How could she be so crazy?

Perkins pounded on the door. "Open up!"

On another monitor, Matt watched Serenity pick up one of the two pizza boxes and walk toward the second bedroom. She tugged on the door, which was locked.

As she turned, he could see her frown. At last, he realized what she was doing. She could eat one pizza, but the presence of two boxes was a sure sign that someone else was around. "Smart girl," he breathed. Serenity didn't want to tip off Hank, who continued to hammer impatiently on the suite's outer door.

Pulse pounding, Matt opened the door. Serenity strode across the room, thrusting the pizza box at him. She closed the door quietly before picking up the extra Coke and putting it into a trash can.

"Use your card key, Hank," Serenity called. She stationed herself behind the desk, opening the top drawer a slit.

"I don'—don' have a damn card key. Came right up. Didn't stop in the lobby."

That explained why they hadn't heard from the front desk.

Serenity's eyes narrowed. "How did you know which suite's mine?"

"Only one big suite in this here hotel, pretty baby. I knew where you'd be. Now open the damn door!"

Serenity's jaw clenching, she sat on the chair behind the desk and crossed her legs. "Ask nicely."

Perkins laughed, sounding derisive. He leaned against the doorjamb.

"I have some paperwork that I understand the Texas Rangers would love." The smile on Serenity's face shocked Matt. Lordy. The woman enjoyed wielding power over her abusive ex.

Perkins straightened. "Baloney. You never knew nothin'."

Matt's brain began to race like a rat chasing cheese through a maze. If Serenity hadn't known—

"And if you got so much, why don't you give it to them?" Perkins taunted.

"They don't pay the way you will, sweetiekins." Serenity's smile broadened.

"If you don't let me in, I can't give you any of the nice wad of cash I have for you."

"It better be more than a crummy wad." Her voice toughened. She sat erect in the chair. "Get me the hundred grand I want or I pick up the phone right now. And when you come back, come back sober, with the card key and the cash. Got it?''

Perkins began to wheedle. "You never used to be this way, all hard and cold. You used to be such a sweet li'l woman. The very sweetest. We had some good times, didn't we, babe?''

Matt watched Serenity roll her eyes. "Yeah, sure.''

"And we'll have good times again, won't we, honey? But you have to open the door.''

"Get with the program. Money, card key...and sober as a judge. Or else you'll be talking to one while you're in custody.''

"Which one they gonna send me to? Cartwright or Sanders? They're both in my pocket, Lori, baby. You know the judges are my golf buddies. You won't win this.''

Matt alerted. Serenity lost her cocky grin. Her eyes hardened. "What do you mean, they're in your pocket?''

"Moolah, baby girl. Cash up front for what I want done. I want it, I pay for it, I got it. See?''

Serenity turned her head and smiled at the doorway behind which Matt sat. She gave him a thumbs-up signal. He opened the door and gave her an A-OK sign, with his index finger curved to touch his thumb. This evidence of bribery would help them convict Perkins and possibly nail the corrupt judges, too.

She turned away, visibly focusing her attention on the door behind which Hank Perkins leaned. "So that's how you got away with the oil well scam for so long?''

"Nah. I got away with selling phony shares because people are stupid. They want to buy dreams.

They want to pretend that they're J.R. Ewing and own oil wells.''

''Even though the shares are worthless?''

''Even though. Honey, open up.'' He pounded again.

Racing out of the bedroom, Matt sprinted to the door of the suite and jerked it open. Perkins faced him, hand upraised.

Matt grabbed the fist and used it to twist Perkins into a control hold. ''You are under arrest. You have the right to remain silent—''

''You!'' Perkins spat, struggling for release.

Matt yanked Perkins's wrist higher up his back. With his free hand, Matt reached for his cuffs. ''Yep, it's me.''

''You're supposed to be dead!''

''Funny how things go wrong.'' He clipped one wrist into a handcuff. ''Your ex-wife rescued me.''

''Lori!'' Perkins jerked away from Matt, breaking the hold. He bolted into the sitting room. Diving over the desk with his hands outstretched, he grabbed for Serenity's throat.

Something in her hand flashed, burying into Perkins's side.

He howled.

She stepped back. ''It's just a letter opener, Hank. I think you'll live.''

Straightening, he looked down at his side, as did Matt. No blood, and Perkins's shirt was intact. ''I'll have one hell of a bruise,'' he grumbled.

''Poetic justice.'' She smiled. ''Matt, can you take this garbage out, please?''

* * *

The chilly interrogation room was too brightly lit, smelling of burned coffee and human desperation. The hard chairs didn't invite relaxation. The discomforts were designed to encourage prisoner revelations without stepping over the bounds of constitutional law.

Perkins was a tough nut to crack but Matt knew they'd get him, if only because of the man's massive arrogance. He'd refused an attorney, telling Carson and Matt that he "knew as much as any ol' ambulance-chasin' crook." He then laughed heartily at his own joke.

"How'd you make me?" Matt asked Perkins.

"Ain't a cop on this planet I can't sniff out." Perkins smirked. "Y'all smell, you know. Like freshly killed skunk."

"That's not a satisfactory answer." Matt picked up a pen to take notes. "You'll have to come up with something better."

"I don't have to come up with anything a'tall." Perkins leaned back in his chair. "Y'all have to come up with probable cause to arrest."

"Oh, we have that," Carson said. "Your conversation with your ex-wife was recorded and videotaped. You admitted selling phony shares in oil wells and bribing judges."

"Hearsay."

"You tried to kill your ex-wife, Perkins." Matt tried to stay calm, but he wanted to break the slimeball, fast and hard. "I saw you reach for her throat like you were gonna choke her. Attempted murder in the State of Texas will earn you two to twenty."

Perkins opened his eyes, trying to fake a look of boyish innocence. "Can't a man try to kiss his wife?"

"She's not your wife," Matt snapped. The thought of Serenity sleeping with this toad sickened him.

Perkins arched a brow at Matt. "So you're her latest? Yeah, Lori was a sweet little piece. She was especially fun when she said no."

A brilliant, red rage overpowered Matt. He lunged across the table, seized Perkins by the throat, and squeezed.

Carson grabbed Matt's shoulders, tugging him off the prisoner. "Stop it! Don't you see he's baiting you?"

Matt shrugged free of Carson's grip. He straightened his shirt and his dignity, glaring at Perkins.

"You'd better leave, son. This scum's not worth a minute of your time in jail for assault."

Matt didn't take his gaze from Perkins. "Buddy, you better pray for a long prison sentence. If I'm not in my grave, I'm gonna come and get you."

When Matt left, several Rangers from his unit entered the interrogation room. He wasn't a sadist, but his mood lifted. Perkins faced a very tough night.

Matt stationed himself behind the one-way glass to watch. "Think he'll break?" he asked Joe Lancaster, another Ranger.

He shrugged. "Carson's good. And so are you, Gutierrez, when you keep a rein on that temper of yours."

I have a temper? Matt wondered. His mind flashed to his fight with Serenity. He grimaced. Had that been his hasty temper talking? Shame swamped his conscience in punishing waves. Maybe she deserved better.

Serenity had been through hell and back with this monster. Perkins himself had said she hadn't known about the scam. Matt knew his wife well enough to realize that she'd told him the truth. If she'd cooperated with her ex, it was to avoid a beating.

Then, when she'd recovered and started a new life, she'd generously cooperated with law enforcement. She helped bring Perkins down, even though she could have remained safe and happy, hidden in Lost Creek.

Matt knew he'd been wrong, absolutely wrong. And he'd chopped a hole in his own heart when he'd fought with Serenity. He needed to find her to ask for her forgiveness. If necessary, he'd get down on his knees and beg for her to take him back.

She was the only woman who had ever meant a damn to him. How could he have turned his back on her?

But when he returned to the hotel room, he couldn't find her. Serenity was gone.

Chapter Thirteen

The first storm of autumn damped down Lost Creek's dust, filled its arroyos, and ripped apart the vine in Serenity Clare's backyard. Lonely, she drifted from room to room in her little cottage, vainly trying to recapture a sense of tranquility and calm.

Weeks had passed since she'd walked away from the Grand Hyatt's luxury. On foot, she realized she didn't have the address of the safe house and wouldn't return even if she did. She didn't need anything there. She left behind her old dashiki, a few T-shirts, and a grass-stained summer dress.

If she'd touched that yellow dress, she would have let tears overwhelm her. The memory of Matt protectively wrapping his arms around her and tumbling with her onto the lawn would have been too much. The thin shell cradling her fragile emotions would have cracked like mishandled china.

Staring out her front window, she pondered the gray sheets of rain.

After he'd hustled Hank out of the hotel room, neither Matt nor any of the Rangers had contacted her. She hadn't heard a single word from any of them. She phoned the local jail in El Paso and discovered that Hank had been released on half-million dollars bail. She'd shrugged her shoulders, wondering when he'd show up. But he didn't have power over her anymore.

She knew she could face down Hank. She'd done it before, and she'd do it again, if necessary.

But the calm and joy she'd hoped to achieve remained elusive.

Matt.

She missed him every moment of every day. The house held so many memories of him. "I oughtta move," she said out loud. But she didn't want to leave Lost Creek, and rentals were few in the small town.

And a tiny part of her wanted to remain accessible so Matt could find her, even though she bet he was filling out divorce papers that very moment.

She rubbed her stomach. "Hey, shrimp," she murmured. Should she disappear once more, if only to safeguard the tiny, delicate life growing within her? She shuddered to think of the consequences if Hank attacked her again. If he caused her to miscarry, she'd go mad.

Besides, Lost Creek wasn't exactly a medical mecca. On the other hand, Mairen knew a local midwife, and most births were routine.

But what if Hank came?

Abandoning her tangled, pointless thoughts, she examined her front room with a critical eye. If she painted the walls pale yellow, recovered the couch in a nice flower print and moved it against the side wall, would that help exorcise the ghosts?

Maybe. But then again, maybe not. She sighed.

Stepping into her bedroom, she donned an oversize purple sweater and thick socks for warmth. She could easily change this room. Getting another bed might help. The nights were the worst. Sleeping on the same sheets, the same bed where she and Matt probably had conceived their child, tore her apart.

She'd taken to sleeping on the sofa in the front room, which didn't do much to console her. There, she suffered through memories of the back massage and the first kiss he'd seized.

She couldn't blame Matt for dumping her. He was Mr. Justice, a lawman who honored truth and abhorred deception. Too bad understanding and compassion weren't part of his makeup, as well. "Too bad for me," she muttered.

Weeks before, she'd decided she wouldn't contact him, not to tell him about the baby or for any other reason. He had to see his way to loving and accepting her fully, with all her faults. He had to come to her.

Serenity went into the guest room. She hadn't invaded his privacy while he lived with her, so few images of him infested this room. Perhaps she'd redecorate and move into it, leaving her bedroom for the baby.

Their baby. She rubbed her stomach again, letting bliss sweep her soul. That emotional roller coaster again. She couldn't help grinning at herself and her wild hormones.

Though she missed Matt, she'd never regret anything that had happened, and certainly not their love-making. He'd made her feel better than she had in her life. A home pregnancy test confirmed what she'd suspected from her bizarre cravings for chocolate shakes and potato chips. She was going to have a baby. She'd danced down the dusty Lost Creek streets.

All her dreams had come true. Except one.

A knock at her door raised the hair at her nape. Who would be abroad in such lousy weather? *Hank.* Sprinting to the kitchen, Serenity grabbed a kitchen knife. She went to the door, holding the weapon behind her back.

The handsomest man she'd ever seen stood on her doorstep.

She dropped the knife with a clatter.

His Bambi-brown eyes twinkled when he smiled at her, despite the rain streaming off his Stetson. Water dripped down the key he held up for her inspection.

She gawked at Matt for a long time. Had she conjured him? Was her imagination working overtime? Had she finally gone nuts and created a hallucination?

"Aren't you gonna let me in?"

He was real. Her cowboy had come home.

"Uh, uh, yeah." She stood aside. "Uh, what's that?" she asked, nodding at the key.

He strode in and took off his wet hat, tossing it onto the hall rack as though he'd never left. A battered leather jacket, drenched with rain, followed.

There he stood, larger than life, it seemed, dressed in his usual garb: a chambray shirt, worn jeans, and boots. His silver wedding ring still adorned his finger, as did hers. Her spirits lifted.

She wondered if he wore his leopard-print thongs, and if she'd find out. A hot shiver, contrasting with the chilly autumn weather, zipped up and down her spine. It set off a sensual tingle that leaped through her body.

Matt was back.

"Uh, uh, what are you doing here? And what's the key?" Taking it from him, she examined it. It wasn't the key to her door, so what was the big deal?

He smiled at her, looking smug and insufferable and charming and oh, so handsome. "That, ma'am, is the key to the Lost Creek Police Department."

Surprise lifted her eyebrows. "The one Owen never found?"

"The very same."

"And?" She could hardly shove the word out, she was so excited.

"And you are looking at the new police chief of Lost Creek."

She squeaked and rushed to hug him. "You're back? You're really back?"

He enfolded her in his warm, loving arms. "I'm back. And I'll never, ever leave."

"Promise?"

"I promise." He kissed her hair.

Serenity pulled back so she could look him in the eyes. "So you forgive me? You understand?"

"Aw, honey. I forgave you weeks ago." Matt hugged her again, rubbing his palms up and down her back. The warm, sexy sizzle he caused was incredibly distracting.

But she wouldn't be distracted. "Why didn't you tell me?"

His hands fell away. He went to sit on the couch. "A bunch of reasons. I was scared and didn't know if you'd forgive me, 'cause I'd been so mean to you. Besides, I didn't want to come to you and then leave, because I knew how you'd react. So I had to get the job here first."

"What did you think I'd do?" Serenity sat next to him, nestling into his warmth.

"If I came and then went away again, you'd wonder if I was telling the truth. You need me by your side." He slid an arm around her shoulders. "And I need to stay."

Gazing into Matt's rich, brown eyes, Serenity knew he was right. He was her happiness and her security, and she needed him always. Since she'd left El Paso, she hadn't drawn a breath without loving him and missing him.

Oh, she'd discovered she could get along without him, but her life had resembled the gray, drizzly day, dull without end. "But you've never lied to me, not about anything."

"But I was hard and cold and completely without understanding. Can you possibly forgive me for being such a jerk?"

"Maybe." She chuckled. "How were you a jerk?"

He looked shamefaced. "I made such a big deal over what you said. I never let you explain. When I learned what he'd done to you... You had good reasons, Serenity. I heard Hank's interrogation."

She shivered and huddled closer.

Matt continued. "It was very revealing. You were totally justified in what you did."

"But I helped him. And then I didn't tell you about it."

"You did what you had to do. If you thought Hank had sent me, I'm surprised you didn't throw me out to die in the desert."

"I couldn't do that. That would have been wrong."

"See what I mean?" He kissed her forehead. "You're a good person, Serenity Clare, and I love you. So can I stay?"

"Of course you can stay." She smiled at him, thrumming with anticipation at the news she had to share. She framed his face with her hands. "How could I turn away my husband, the father of my child?"

Matt's mouth dropped open. "B-bu—but—"

"But what?" She chuckled, leaning back into the sofa.

He grabbed her, squeezing her tight. "I—I—I—I thought you couldn't get pregnant."

"I was wrong. My cycle was irregular from stress. I thought it was because Hank had hit me and hurt me. But I was wrong. It was stress, and when I relaxed, everything was fine."

Matt grinned. "Yeah, I did get you pretty relaxed, didn't I?"

She laughed at his male smugness. "But I didn't plan this and neither did you. Are you sure you're okay with having a baby?"

"Oh, honey!" He hugged her tight. Serenity read joy in his delighted eyes. "I feel like dancing down the street, but—" He glanced out the window at the rain.

"That's what I did when I found out. Skipped and danced down the street to tell all my friends."

"But you should have told me." His tone had turned serious.

Serenity shrugged. "I thought about it. Believe me, Matt, I did. Every day. But I felt it was important that you come back for me. Remember what you said? You wanted me for me, not for an imaginary child you'd never met. So I decided it was important for you to forgive me. I didn't want you to return because of the baby."

He considered. "Yeah, I guess I understand. Would you have ever told me about the baby?"

"Hmm. Yes, but not for a while." Matt started to speak, and she held up her hand to stop him. "I know it's unfair, but it had to be. I didn't feel I could tell you until I got over you. I wouldn't have the strength."

A frown wrinkled his forehead. "What do you mean?"

"I know you. You're an honorable man. You'd insist upon doing the right thing by the mother of your baby. And I wouldn't be able to resist. If I saw you, even once, I'd want to be with you, but we'd be together for the wrong reason. So I decided to wait until I was...over you."

Matt smiled. "So you're not over me yet?"

"Not by a long shot."

"You gonna let me do the right thing by the mother of my child?" He moved closer. His heat threatened to burn through her fragile composure.

Serenity wanted to twine up him the way the vine embraced the back fence. Instead, she gazed at her lap, fluttering her eyelashes and trying to look demure. "Maybe, if you ask nicely." She was delighted to find she still enjoyed flirting with him.

"Maybe?"

"Well, are you asking or not?" She narrowed her eyes at him.

Matt knelt on the floor beside her, his face serious. He took her hand. "Let me stay. Let's renew our vows. Stay by my side forever as my partner and my mate and the mother of my children."

Tears prickled Serenity's eyes. She slipped her arms around Matt and pulled him close, reveling in the comfort of his embrace. "By your side, forever and always?"

"Yes." He kissed the palm of her hand. "Forever and always."

She ignored the wetness sliding down her cheeks in favor of her husband's beloved touch, as necessary to her as light and breath. With all her fears and hurts healed by the power of their love, she never doubted her answer. "I'm yours, forever and always."

Matt sat beside his wife and wrapped her in his arms, finally achieving the completion he'd craved all his life. His quest for Serenity's love and forgiveness had ended, but their life together was just beginning.

He squeezed her tight. "A baby. We're having a baby."

She beamed at him, her green eyes shimmering like a springtime stream. "Yep, sure are. Unless every pregnancy test known to medical science is wrong."

"You tried more than one?"

She laughed. "I was so surprised that, yeah, I used several, then went to a doctor."

"Mom and Dad will turn cartwheels. They've been bugging Marianne for another grandkid since Rachel turned two."

A pensive frown twitched Serenity's brow. "What will they think of me? I'm not exactly a conventional bride."

He chuckled. "Honey, they already love you. You know how Marianne loves to talk. Heck, that girl should start a P.R. agency. With what she told them, my parents can hardly wait to meet you. Give them another grandkid to spoil and they'll start calling you Princess Serenity."

More laughter rippled from Serenity's throat, warming his heart. Lordy, but he loved to hear her laugh. "Should I wear a tiara at the wedding?"

"Whatever you want, your highness."

"Wow. A family." She sat back, nestling into the circle of Matt's arms. "I can't believe it. I have an entire new family."

"You're marrying into two parents, a sister, an older brother...and having a kid."

She gazed at him. "No more lonely little Serenity, wanting what she could never have."

Matt kissed the tip of her nose. "No more loneliness. Forever and always."

* * * * *

Don't miss the reprisal of
Silhouette Romance's popular miniseries

When King Michael of Edenbourg goes missing,

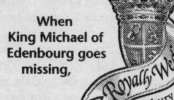

his devoted family and loyal subjects make it their mission to bring him home safely!

Their search begins March 2001 and continues through June 2001.

On sale March 2001: **THE EXPECTANT PRINCESS**
by bestselling author **Stella Bagwell** (SR #1504)

On sale April 2001: **THE BLACKSHEEP PRINCE'S BRIDE**
by rising star **Martha Shields** (SR #1510)

On sale May 2001: **CODE NAME: PRINCE**
by popular author **Valerie Parv** (SR #1516)

On sale June 2001: **AN OFFICER AND A PRINCESS**
by award-winning author **Carla Cassidy** (SR #1522)

Available at your favorite retail outlet.

Where love comes alive™

Visit Silhouette at www.eHarlequin.com

SRRW3

Award-winning author
SHARON DE VITA
brings her special brand of romance to

Silhouette

SPECIAL EDITION™
and

SILHOUETTE *Romance*™

in her new cross-line miniseries

SADDLE

FALLS

This small Western town was rocked by scandal when the youngest son of the prominent Ryan family was kidnapped. Watch as clues about the mysterious disappearance are unveiled—and meet the sexy Ryan brothers...along with the women destined to lasso their hearts.

Don't miss:

WITH FAMILY IN MIND
February 2002, Silhouette Special Edition #1450

ANYTHING FOR HER FAMILY
March 2002, Silhouette Romance #1580

A FAMILY TO BE
April 2002, Silhouette Romance #1586

A FAMILY TO COME HOME TO
May 2002, Silhouette Special Edition #1468

Available at your favorite retail outlet.

Silhouette®

Where love comes alive™

Visit Silhouette at www.eHarlequin.com   SSERSFR

Silhouette Books invites you to cherish
a captivating keepsake collection by

DIANA PALMER

They're rugged and lean...and the best-looking, sweetest-talking men in the Lone Star State! CALHOUN, JUSTIN and TYLER—the three mesmerizing cowboys who started the legend. Now they're back by popular demand in one classic volume—ready to lasso your heart!

You won't want to miss this treasured collection from international bestselling author Diana Palmer!

LONG, TALL
Texans

CALHOUN, JUSTIN & TYLER
(On sale March 2002)

Available at your favorite retail outlet.

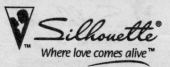

Silhouette®
Where love comes alive™

Visit Silhouette at www.eHarlequin.com

PSLTT

If you enjoyed what you just read,
then we've got an offer you can't resist!

Take 2 bestselling
love stories FREE!
Plus get a FREE surprise gift!

Clip this page and mail it to Silhouette Reader Service™

IN U.S.A.	IN CANADA
3010 Walden Ave.	P.O. Box 609
P.O. Box 1867	Fort Erie, Ontario
Buffalo, N.Y. 14240-1867	L2A 5X3

YES! Please send me 2 free Silhouette Romance® novels and my free surprise gift. After receiving them, if I don't wish to receive anymore, I can return the shipping statement marked cancel. If I don't cancel, I will receive 6 brand-new novels every month, before they're available in stores! In the U.S.A., bill me at the bargain price of $3.15 plus 25¢ shipping and handling per book and applicable sales tax, if any*. In Canada, bill me at the bargain price of $3.50 plus 25¢ shipping and handling per book and applicable taxes**. That's the complete price and a savings of at least 10% off the cover prices—what a great deal! I understand that accepting the 2 free books and gift places me under no obligation ever to buy any books. I can always return a shipment and cancel at any time. Even if I never buy another book from Silhouette, the 2 free books and gift are mine to keep forever.

215 SEN DFNQ
315 SEN DFNR

Name	(PLEASE PRINT)	
Address	Apt.#	
City	State/Prov.	Zip/Postal Code

* Terms and prices subject to change without notice. Sales tax applicable in N.Y.
** Canadian residents will be charged applicable provincial taxes and GST.
   All orders subject to approval. Offer limited to one per household and not valid to current Silhouette Romance® subscribers.
   ® are registered trademarks of Harlequin Enterprises Limited.

SROM01   ©1998 Harlequin Enterprises Limited

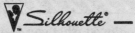

Silhouette® —

where love comes alive—online...

buy books

♥ Find all the new Silhouette releases at
everyday great discounts.

♥ Try before you buy! Read an excerpt from
the latest Silhouette novels.

♥ Write an online review and share your
thoughts with others.

online reads

♥ Read our Internet exclusive daily and weekly
online serials, or vote in our interactive novel.

♥ Talk to other readers about your favorite
novels in our Reading Groups.

♥ Take our Choose-a-Book quiz to find the
series that matches you!

authors

♥ Find out interesting tidbits and details about
your favorite authors' lives, interests and
writing habits.

♥ Ever dreamed of being an author? Enter our
Writing Round Robin. The Winning Chapter
will be published online! Or review our
writing guidelines for submitting your novel.

All this and more available at
www.eHarlequin.com

SINTB1R2